The mind ⟨...⟩ judge
worked his controls. The room lighting went
out, and stars began to form in the space
between the couches.

Then, nightmare . . . A ship swept out of
nowhere, so close overhead that Keira ducked
to avoid it. He swore at it, and his words
foamed from his mouth in long streams of
blue and purple ribbons, broken only by the
brighter pink flash of a hard consonant. He
groped for the nonexistent console. He knew
it was there, but his hands moved through
hot glue that smelled of roses.

He shook his head to get rid of the blurring
ache.

"What the hell is going on?" he said, directly into the headpiece's microphone. There
was no answer from the fog-shrouded judge's
box.

A malfunction, he thought. But the status
boards showed green: the machinery was
functioning, but neither tape nor human operator controlled it.

The fog drew back slowly, the judge's box
emerging first. Keira caught his breath. The
judge was slumped over his console, arms
outstretched, forehead resting on the atmosphere controls.

Then something flashed from the wall of
fog. He thought it was another illusion, but
then it cut through one of the drifting phantoms:
reality—a real knife—spinning end over end.

MELISSA SCOTT
THE GAME
BEYOND

A BAEN BOOK

THE GAME BEYOND

This is a work of fiction. All the characters and events portrayed in this book are fictional, and any resemblance to real people or incidents is purely coincidental.

A Baen Book

Baen Enterprises
8-10 W. 36th Street
New York, N.Y. 10018

First Baen printing, November 1984

ISBN: 0-671-55918-4

Cover art by Alan Gutierrez

Printed in the United States of America

Distributed by
SIMON & SCHUSTER
MASS MERCHANDISE SALES COMPANY
1230 Avenue of the Americas
New York, N.Y. 10020

For L. A. B., for everything.

THE DOMI AUREAE

The Imperial Domus: Rules Avalon, the Tor, Citadel, Sander's World, Jerra.
  Oriana III Silvertree, Empress

The Old Domi

Domus de Terranin: Rules Verii Mir, Altus.
  Grand Duke Matto de Terranin, Chancellor, Speaker for the Eger Edouard de Terranin, Overlord of Verii Mir, Grand Duke's Heir
Domus de la Mar: Rules Oceanus.
  Grand Duke Satinka de la Mar
    Nuriel de la Mar, Overlord of Oceanus, Grand Duke's Heir
Domus Ojeda: Rules Castille, Aragon, Jant', Far Haven.
  Grand Duke Balint Ojeda
    Kypria Ojeda, Overlord of Castille, Grand Duke's Heir
Domus Hamm'tt: Rules El Nath, Sahara, Simba, Cape Fear.
  Grand Duke Desolin Hamm'tt

The New Domi

Domus Channis (formerly Renault): Hellmouth, Hell.
  Grand Duke Brede Channis
Domus Santarem (formerly A'asta): Babylon, Ninevah, Tyre.
  Grand Duke Raman Santarem

Domus Xio-Sebastina (formerly Fabian): Mist.
    Grand Duke Azili Xio-Sebastina

The Lesser Systems

Electorate of Somewhere: Somewhere, Somewhere Else.
    Royd Lovell-Andriës, Elector
The MarchWorlds:
    Vasili Andros, Lord of the Barbaries

Prologue

The ambassador's shuttle swung high over the Palace compound, waiting for permission to land. Ioan Denisov-Graham, formerly of the Mars Highlanders and now the Terran Federation's representative to the Court at Avalon, senior Terran representative within the Imperium, stared out the window, brooding. Night had fallen some hours before, but the Palace complex was brightly lit, the multi-colored glass roofs of the Palace corridors glowing warmly. He could trace the invisible buildings by the colors: the criss-crossing lines of amber and paler gold that marked the roughly rectangular perimeter of the Palace also marked the public areas of the buildings. The ambassadorial suites were there, as well as the public meeting rooms. A cluster of blue lines led away from the main compounds, one set toward the darkened, shadowy hall where the assembly of the nobles—the Eger—met, the other toward the cluster of towers where the off-world nobles were housed while at court. Green lines and squares marked semi-secure areas, usually reserved for the bureaucracy. The center of the Palace was dark, topped with armored steel and surrounded by a broad band of red-roofed corridors: the empress's personal quarters.

The shuttle tilted sharply, and the Palace slid away beneath its wing. The massive Cathedral, glass walled and as brilliantly lit from within as

9

the Palace, passed below him, and then the landing field slipped past. The long lanes of fused earth were utterly empty. He leaned forward to touch the pilot's shoulder.

"What's going on, Martine?"

"I don't know," the woman answered without turning. "We were told to hold, and then—nothing." She nodded to her own tiny viewscreen. "That's the Council's ambassador over there."

Denisov-Graham leaned across the aisle. He could just make out the oddly mismatched wing lights of the other shuttle. Despite the fact that the Federation and the non-human conglomerate, whose title was roughly translated as the Council of Planets, had been at peace for generations, despite the fact that the Council had more or less withdrawn its attention from the human volume of space after its last devastating set of raids a hundred years before, he could not help feeling a slight shudder every time he had to deal with the Lors Vedn who represented the Council. He could only be grateful that the Council had very little to do with the Imperium.

"Have you heard anything, boss?" the pilot asked. This time, she did risk a quick glance back at her passenger. Denisov-Graham tried to meet her eyes impassively.

"The empress has been ill for a few weeks, and isn't reported to be getting any better," he said slowly.

The pilot's eyes widened slightly. "If she dies. . . ." She did not complete the sentence.

Denisov-Graham nodded. Oriana III Silvertree, empress and absolute ruler of the Imperium, had neglected to provide herself with an heir. No, he corrected himself automatically, that was hardly fair. There had been attempts, first to bear a child and then to produce a viable clone, all of which had failed miserably. But she had still failed to name any of the eligible nobles—and there weren't many of those, the ambassador thought grimly—and the message summoning him to the Palace had been cryptic enough to set the embassy speculating about her condition. If she were to die without an heir, the Imperium would be in chaos, with every major noble able to make a claim to the throne, and none of them able to hold it.

He leaned forward again. "What odds do the bookmakers give for a successor?"

The pilot looked around nervously, her wide mouth pulling down at the corners. "The commoners don't bet on that question, boss."

"They bet on everything," Denisov-Graham said.

"Not on this," Martine insisted. "That would be petty treason. Maybe not so petty—" She broke off and reached for her comunit as lights flashed on the communications panel. "Federal shuttle 572."

Denisov-Graham looked out the window again, as the shuttle swung back toward the Palace on the other leg of the interminable holding pattern. The lights in the Cathedral had gone out.

"Boss, she's dead," Martine said. She adjusted the comunit. "Listen to this."

She flipped a switch, and the rich voice of an imperial Herald boomed from the cabin speakers.

"—Majesty, Oriana, third of that name, died one hour ago, in the hospital wing of the Palace. Her passing is greatly mourned by all loyal subjects."

That sentiment had a rote quality, Denisov-Graham thought. Get on to the important things.

"Her late Majesty's will has been opened by the priests of the Order to whom it was entrusted," the Herald went on. "In it, her Majesty named Keira Renault, hereby declared a majore, as her heir."

There was more, but Denisov-Graham had stopped listening. Who? he thought stupidly, and then knew.

Keira—never mind the Renault, that family had supposedly been wiped out by Oriana's grand-father—had been the empress's favorite for the past ten years.

"Boss?" Martine said. "Even I know the Re-naults don't exist any more."

"It sounds as though they do," Denisov-Graham said grimly. "Get us landing clearance as quickly as you can."

Chapter 1

Keira sat on the end of the bed in which the empress had died, no longer aware of that fact as more than mere fact, and waited. There was a muted buzzing from the spybox at the head of the bed, and an exchange of voices: the nobility, or at least those majores and land-minores who had been present to hear the will, were at the red circle, and would soon reach the Quarters. He would be ready; he was ready now. His Talent, that freakish combination of inbred almost-telepathy and the knack for reading patterns, tugged capriciously at his mind, dazzling him with glimpses of the fifty possible futures radiating from this present. He forced it down, trying to ignore the temptation. He had to remain as he was, at the first level of awareness, where he could watch and Read the patterns of response in the nobles' faces, and fit them into the pattern of his own desires. His blood was up, singing with the excitement of handling more variables than he'd ever faced before, and it took a physical effort to keep himself from smiling, from laughing aloud for sheer pleasure. In ten years, he had not been able to indulge himself so fully.

He frowned, bringing himself back to earth. Slowly, concentrating his entire mind on each separate movement, he brought his hands together and folded them neatly in his lap. He sat very straight, both feet flat on the floor, his head perfectly balanced on top of his spine. The position was supposed to bring calm, a tranquility that helped one remain in the state in which one Read faces and futures, but it did little to still his own Talent. He thought, I would bet the Order never intended the exercise for times like this.

Bet. The word touched off mental fireworks, ricocheting from one memory to another, from the games that were the pastime of the entire Imperium to the half-memory that was his own particular nightmare. He struggled for control, but he might as well have reached for Avalon's moon. His Talent swept him away, carried him to his homeworld, Hellmouth, to the terrace of the Government House at Satansburg. He sat with his back to the cave mouth, and the sunrise framed in it—and was not himself. In the dream-vision, he could see his own face, and knew it was not himself but some ancestor who sat there, facing the Terran. And the Terran was not Denisov-Graham, as he should be; the faces were similar, kinship plain, but it was not the Denisov-Graham he knew.

"We could do it," the dream-self said, "and we will do it. We will be emperors one day."

"We?" Denisov-Graham's ancestor asked, laughing.

"One of my kin," the Renault said, and he, too, laughed. "But one of us will."

"A Domus whose proudest boast is that they are descended from Old Federal transportees?" The Denisov-Graham shook his head. "Your nobility will never stand for it."

"What would you care to wager that they will?"

"What stakes are you offering?" the Denisov-Graham asked.

"My life and family."

"What good is that to me?" the Denisov-Graham countered.

The Renault smiled. "Very well, privileges for the Federation. And you?"

And it was at that point that even Talent failed

him. The scene faded, melting away in a wash of
pale grey and sand. He bit his lips in frustration,
but knew it would do no good to try and force his
Talent further. He had never been able to dredge
up the stakes, no matter how often he had seen
this vision, and there was no time to try to do so
now. But I want it, he thought. I want whatever it
is this Denisov-Graham owes me.

He forced himself to relax, to return to the posture of controlled Talent—back straight, head up,
hands loose. You are not yet emperor, he told
himself and his Talent. The bet is not yet won.
Concentrate on winning it, on winning the Imperium to your side, and when that's done, claim
your prize.

The spybox buzzed again, and the red warning
light went on: the nobles had reached the Quarters.
He rose hastily and went out into the receiving
room, seating himself in the high-backed chair
Oriana had used for informal audiences. He touched
the concealed button that activated the wall speaker,
and listened while the Chancellor, who was no
longer Chancellor and had not been since Oriana's
death, argued with the sergeant on duty at the
inner door. His Talent felt more cooperative now,
reduced by the vision to a manageable level, and
he permitted himself one last smile. Then he
touched the switch that activated his own microphone.

"Admit them."

The slender man was dwarfed by the flaring
back of the chair, but he still managed to convey
the sense that these others, babbling through and
across each other's conversations, were the intrud-
ers in the Imperial Quarters, not he. General Doran,
watching from behind the ranked nobles of the
Domi Aureae, the nine great families that dominated the Imperium, could not understand how

they had all been so deluded. For the past week, as Oriana, third of her name, had fought for her life, they had all pressed her to name her heir. The empress had refused, saying only that she had left her empire in competent hands. And then, when the Order had shown the will. . . . Doran shook his head, still not believing. Oriana had admitted she had not ruled, except perhaps in the first unsteady months of her reign. Then she had seen a copper-haired sailworker in a MarchWorld schooner station and bought out his contract. No one had thought much of it then: the empress had had many favorites, noble and common alike, and tired of them quickly. But for ten years, this Guildsman, this Keira—and Doran wondered if that were his proper name, since Oriana had also called him majore and a Renault—had remained first in the empress's favor. He had gotten minore status, too, but only the Order, in its non-religious function as judge of Talent and Convention, could certify the truth of that, and of Oriana's more extravagant claims.

"My Lords." Keira's voice crackled with Talent, and Doran, though only a minore, could feel it sparking the multiple Talents of the majores. Eyes widened or went empty, bodies tensed, then slowly relaxed. Nervous hands stilled, and conversation died, until only a few minores exchanged furtive whispers. Doran glanced quickly from face to face, seeking the reactions of the Domus nobles. Most showed only shock: despite the empress's statement, no one had really expected to find a major Talent. It made it more than possible that Keira really was a Renault, and the general could see that awareness on a few faces. There was a new piece on the board; or, rather, it was like yrriban, where the pieces themselves shifted value, and you suddenly found yourself facing a Power where you had been sure there was only a pawn.

Beside Doran, the Federation's ambassador stirred uneasily. At first, Doran thought he was checking the reaction of the Council representative, standing either bemused or aloof in the background, but then the Terran muttered something. Doran edged closer, caught the last words.

"—face is right."

Doran frowned, and shifted to see past Santarem's massive shoulder. Keira's face was different, all right, but it was only from Talent. The underlying structure was the same—prominent cheekbones and aristocratic nose—but the eyes seemed paler, and there was something— For a moment, Doran, too, felt as though he had seen it before, in a portrait somewhere, but the memory slipped away.

"I take it you have seen her late Majesty's will?" Keira asked.

There was an exchange of glances among the majores, and then Desolin Hamm'tt, Grand Duke of the most junior of the nine Domi Aureae, said, "The Councils have seen it." She gave him no title, not the "lord" of a minore or the "dan" to which he was entitled as the empress's favorite and a guildmaster. Matto de Terranin, as head of the most senior Domus both Chancellor and Speaker for the nobles' assembly, the Eger, kept carefully silent.

"Then you know her Majesty named me her heir, in the absence of an heir of her own bloodline," Keira said.

"Forgive me," Hamm'tt interrupted, and the lack of a title was very noticeable, "but you can hardly expect the nobility to accept you as emperor on that word alone."

Some expression—amusement? anger?—flickered momentarily across Keira's face. "Come, you can See I'm majore. And surely one of you can certify my bloodline." His eyes swept the room, paused on Denisov-Graham, then fixed on Owen Castellar, majore lord of Hell. "You, Hell-Lord. You know what I am."

Castellar said, reluctantly, "You have the Renault face."

Keira nodded. "Yes, Hell-Lord, and the genes. You can trace my pedigree—as the empress did, as the Order did—but surely you don't need to. You can see that I am a Renault, senior of my Domus, by birth and blood Grand Duke, and by book—by the terms of the will—emperor."

"The Renaults are minores only," a new voice said. Doran turned his head, found the speaker: Hetiya Ayakawa, one of the Tyrian land-minores who were richer than many majores, prevented only by lack of a major Talent from taking a more active role in government. Keira's pale eyes flicked toward her, seemed to measure her worth and then dismiss her.

"The Renaults were minores only by decree of the Eger and the emperor, never by blood. We have the Talent." His voice lost its tinge of irony, its conversational quality, grew into something archaic, filled with a ritual power. "You know with what justice my Domus lost its place. We kept faith when it would have paid us to betray our emperor, and went down with him. We were minores under the Silvertrees, earned title and favor again under the first Oriana, died in her nephew's wars, were betrayed and destroyed again— so they thought—by his descendants. I was born a commoner, and I have ruled this empire. Can any other Domus state a better claim?"

There was a sudden silence in the room, a silence that echoed with Talent. Doran, looking from one face to another, saw only confusion and hesitation. None of them had dared to state their families' claims in such a fashion, not for generations. That pride had been bred out of them under the last three Silvertrees. Keira's claim was the only clear one—not blood relationship, but the desire to hold power, and the empress's legacy to give him more legitimacy than blood. As for the others. . . . Doran calculated quickly. De Terranin could make a claim, as could Vladimir St. George, the count of Rohan; there had been many links between the Silvertrees and the majores of Verii Mir. There was Lasca FitzMary as well, descendant of an illegitimate child of a Silvertree Admiral; she had been in the empress's household for years, at least half as a hostage, but she was only a minore, ineligible unless she could produce majore children. The de la Mars, too, had bloodties to the earlier Silvertrees through the FitzMary line, but the claim was very weak. Hamm'tt, Audry Xie, the land-minores Shastri and Ayakawa, and perhaps a few others could claim that the blood of the Alexanders, the first emperors, ran in their veins and could take precedence over that of the usurping Silvertrees. It would not matter, for the purposes of making the claim, that the usurpation had taken place over five hundred years before.

Not all of those would try it, Doran knew, but if even one did, there would be civil war. He glanced dubiously at the Federal ambassador, Denisov-Graham, who wore the expression of a man who has just discovered a new antagonist. Could the Federation pass up the chance to bring its old colonies under its wing? Would it dare ignore the opportunity to control the sources of its desperately needed raw materials? More than that, could Denisov-Graham resist the chance to create a puppet emperor? I'll put my trust in what I know, Doran thought. He brought his hands together and bowed over them.

"Your Majesty."

From under his lowered eyelids, he saw the nobles move away from him, disassociating themselves from him.

"General Doran," Keira acknowledged. "You were Doran min-Silvertree?"

Doran kept his head down, managed to match Keira's calm tone. "I am the emperor's minore, Majesty. Doran min-Renault."

"Rise, General."

Doran lifted his head, and found himself looking directly into the Renault's pale eyes. He could not read the expression there—his Talent lay in the physical realm, not the psychic—but he found the cool stare perversely reassuring.

Keira nodded slightly, and turned his attention back to the nobility. "My Lords?"

Hamm'tt opened her mouth, but de Terranin waved her to silence. "My Lord," he said abruptly, compromising on the made-minore's title. "The Domi Council will consider your claim."

"Not good enough," Keira said.

Doran felt a momentary twinge of fear. The Renault was pushing too fast, Talented or not. And Doran had committed himself.

"There is no other legitimate claim," Keira went on, almost casually. "The others are of blood only, bastard blood or cousinage or alliance marriage, none valid under law, without birth or book to support them. And you forget that I have ruled for the past ten years." He nodded to the portrait of the empress that was set into one wall of the room. It was almost too real for comfort—the brown Silvertree face drawn into an irritable scowl, Oriana's natural expression in later years. "Do you want another like her over you? She was a capricious fool. Without me guiding her, we would have been plunged into war twice over—with the Federation or the Council, or even with the MarchWorlds, our own colonies. You bred too cautiously, my Lords, looking for the safe Talents. We never did, and I am not afraid to gamble. You only play games."

Denisov-Graham breathed softly, "Oh, yes, that's a Renault."

De Terranin hesitated, then said, slowly, "A gamesmaster . . . as all the Renaults were . . . does not necessarily make a good ruler."

Keira laughed. "I could spend an hour listing those who were."

"Your Majesty." Royd Lovell-Andriës, the Elector of Somewhere, made the ritual gesture, bowing over clasped hands. Keira's eyes fixed on him, and there was an almost audible crackling of Talent.

"My Lord Elector."

"Come, de Terranin," Lovell-Andriës said, his rough voice breaking the formality. "Admit it. There's no one else, and your son won't see the Quarters without a ten-year war. That holds for you, too, Hamm'tt." The hyper-awareness of Talent widened his eyes as he swung to challenge the rest of the nobles. "I'll back this with my life and soldiery, if I must."

The room was silenced by his outburst. After a moment, a few of the lesser nobles—von Sarazin, Kovar, Xie—lowered their heads and muttered their acknowledgements. Then St. George brought his hands together and bowed. De Terranin and Hamm'tt bent their heads stiffly. One by one, then in a last rush, the others followed suit. Keira rose from his chair.

"My Lords, I thank you. Duke Matto, I am sure the Council will be free to consider the will in the morning. I will attend."

"Of course . . . Majesty." The words came very hard to de Terranin.

"Then you may return to your quarters, my Lords." There was such a note of assurance in the favorite's voice that no one even thought of disobeying.

*   *   *

Outside the Imperial Quarters, the Guards looked questioningly at Doran. The general stood aside to let the nobility past, remaining discreetly close to the young sergeant who commanded the detail. The nobles were mostly silent. A few whispered together—Doran made a mental note of those as ones he would have to watch—but most paced quietly, eyes empty as they calculated the odds. No one bothered to mention the shame of being ruled by the dead empress's favorite; that would be for raising the minores, if it came to rebellion. They all knew too well what the last empress could have been, and what her father had been, to complain about anyone's morals.

"General?" the sergeant said tentatively.

"Um?" Doran collected his thoughts. "Sergeant, the Empress Oriana, having no heirs of body or blood, exercised the imperial prerogative and bequeathed the Imperium to Keira Renault, first of that name and line." He had made that speech before, in the army council, but this time there was more to add. "The Emperor Keira has my full loyalty, and is worthy of yours. You will protect him with your lives."

"Keira?" the sergeant echoed involuntarily. "A Renault?" The other soldiers exchanged stealthy glances, but said nothing. Then the sergeant's face showed sudden decision. Doran could almost read her thoughts, though he was not a telepath. *The general trusts him; I trust the general. I'll serve this emperor.* She saluted crisply.

"Very good, sir."

"Well done," Doran said gently, and turned away toward his own quarters.

"It's a good thing they trust you, isn't it?" a voice said at his elbow.

Doran controlled the impulse to reach for his shielded blade.

"Ambassador?"

Denisov-Graham smiled. "I'm sorry, I didn't mean to startle you. I wanted to ask you a few questions, if I might."

"About his Majesty?"

"Yes, about him." Denisov-Graham looked oddly troubled. "It doesn't interfere with Imperial interests. I give you my word."

Doran liked the Federal ambassador against his better judgment, and had been given reason, some years back to trust him. He gestured to the door that gave onto his own spartan quarters. "Come in, have a drink."

Denisov-Graham shuddered almost imperceptibly, but allowed himself to be led inside. A serbot brought drinks, and Doran leaned back in his chair.

"Now, Ambassador." The general took a long swallow of the heady liquid and regarded the Terran over the rim of his glass. "What is it you wanted?"

Denisov-Graham toyed with his glass; Doran could not tell if the gesture was from nervousness or simply because the Terran didn't like Imperial wines. "I don't know quite where to begin," he said. "I suppose—yes. You know my family's had dealings with the Imperium for a long time."

Doran nodded.

"We keep diaries." The ambassador grinned suddenly. "Oh, don't bother hiring someone to search my rooms. We never write anything down until we're safely home, I promise you that. Anyway, those records show we've also had quite a few encounters with the Renaults. They were all power-hungry and they were all Sighted—Readers—and a few of them were very, very good." He sighed faintly. "At any rate, Elidi, who lived during the reign of Alexander IV, predicted once—in a private conversation, of course—that the Renaults would take the throne one day. And they made a bet on it. Naturally, I didn't take it too seriously when I read the account, but now . . . I begin to wonder. Kay Renault knew of the bet—"

"It's quite a jump from Alexander IV to Oriana I," Doran commented, pouring himself a second drink.

Denisov-Graham nodded. "I know. That makes me think the whole family knew about it. And that brings me to my question. Could anyone plan for that long, just to win a bet? For a game?" He looked at Doran, all at once serious. "You're an imperial noble, or at least a minore, which I sometimes think means you know the high nobles better than they know themselves. Would they do that?"

Doran considered the thought for a long moment, watching the bubbles rise in his glass. It wasn't possible to see so far into the future, or so he had always been taught. The Readers didn't really foresee; they extrapolated from current events and past practices, added intuition, and gave their prediction. The farther ahead they tried to go, the greater the uncertainties. But the best Readings came from intuition and sudden revelation. "I suppose it's possible to predict something that far in advance," he said slowly. "But to act on it? That must have been five hundred years ago. No Domus can keep to a plan like that, not even a family of gamesmasters." But as he said it, he doubted, and Denisov-Graham read the doubt in his eyes.

"Or could they?" the Terran whispered.

Doran shook his head, driving the thought away. "What were the stakes?" he asked instead.

Denisov-Graham's expression was rueful. "I don't remember. I read the account long ago."

Doran raised an eyebrow, unable to hide his skepticism, but the ambassador met his gaze without flinching. After a moment Doran looked away, reaching for the bottle on the serbot's tray. "Be that as it may," he said, "Keira's the only man for the job."

"Oh, indeed," Denisov-Graham agreed, and added, so softly that Keira could pretend he didn't hear, "but did the Renaults engineer the whole thing?"

Keira sat again on the edge of the immense bed, staring at the smaller, informal portrait that was set in the far wall. The empress stared back at him, her eyes puzzled as they had often been when Keira tried to explain the necessity of actions.

"My poor lady," Keira said aloud. "You never knew if you loved me or hated me, and never enjoyed yourself more than when you had me fearing for my life, but you had the sense to know that I was right. I'm sorry about what I said to the nobles ... you were nothing like your father, or your grandfather. You knew you didn't have the makings of a monarch, and hated me for speaking from instinct and making a better choice than you did after days of thought. But you had the strength to use me. I respect you—I honor you for that."

He looked up at the heavy-bodied portrait, seeing in it the shadows of the great monarchs of the line. The Silvertrees had gambled, trading genetic flaws, a weak heart, crippling diseases, and ultimate sterility, for the psychic Talents needed to control their impossible empire. Oriana had been the final result of this process, and despite her faults, not entirely unworthy.

I don't know if you really understood the necessity for ending the line, he thought, but I think you felt it. You knew it was time for new blood. And there was the bet, his conscience reminded him. He winced. Yes, the bet. *How many generations ago did Elidi make it, and my father's father's fathers plan for my becoming emperor? This would've happened without it.* But the portrait scowled down on him as though to give the lie to his denial.

"Oriana," he whispered, as though ghosts of emperors had nothing better to do than hang around and listen to vows. "Oriana, I swear the bet was nothing. You didn't even know the story. I heard it as a child, and hardly listened. This was necessary for the Imperium, I swear that to you. You trusted me before; trust me again. You know my Domus's fault. We love the wrong people, and I did love you, despite everything you did, and despite myself. I wouldn't have denied you anything except for the Imperium." He knew he lied, but he seemed to see the lines ease a little on the portrait's stern features.

The spybox clicked and said uneasily, "Majesty?"

Keira whirled. He had forgotten, he who had been so careful for so many years, all about the security devices. "Yes?" he snapped, his mind searching frantically for an explanation.

"I heard voices. Are you all right, Majesty?" The voice was that of the Guard sergeant, and the Guard, at least, could be trusted now that Doran had declared himself.

"I was talking to myself," Keira said. He knew he was taking a risk, but he had kept his voice down. "I'm quite all right."

"Very good, your Majesty. Sleep well."

"Thank you, sergeant," Keira said to the box. *Oriana, I'll see that they tell the truth about you. That you were an indifferent woman and a bad ruler, who had the sense to use any tool to preserve her empire.*

"I promise," he whispered. Then he leaned back against the stack of pillows, waiting. He was not tired yet, buoyed up by his Talent, but it was better to wait, to be sure that the last of the nobles had retreated to their own rooms, before he went to the computers. He touched the part of the headboard that controlled the room lighting, drawing his hand down the hidden path until the lights dimmed. He would wait an hour; after that, there was work to do.

Chapter 2

The Federal ambassador had joined his fellow diplomats an hour before. Doran lay in the comfortably narrow darkness of his bed, feeling the drinks churning in his stomach. His thoughts wandered aimlessly, through his years of service at court and off-world, and through his childhood, with complete impartiality. Then, with suddenness like Talent, Doran remembered.

The court had gone to the MarchWorlds barely two years after Oriana's coronation. Trouble was brewing there, as always; the Barbaries, greatest of the MarchWorlds, had been imperial colonies for generations without gaining the privileges of the inner worlds, and were growing restless under the rumor of a new tax assessment. The empress's personal council had suggested that the presence of the new and relatively popular empress might relieve some of the pressure until the Eger and the Commons' Councils could decide on the proper response to the Barbaries' complaints. The March-Lords, on Diana and Far Havens as well as the two Barbaries, had seen the occasion for what it was, and had feted the empress in the grandest style, while being careful to show her how much more they could have done had they been granted full imperial privileges. Only the Overlord of the Barbaries, Canefar Andros, had been unable to win Oriana's friendship, but his heir Vasili had won back the favor Canefar had lost, and had even gained the empress's interest enough to be invited to accompany the court to Low Barbary. Krysten Caimile, Low Barbary's Lord, had welcomed the court, and, as the final event of the long tour, had brought them to the rigging station that swung in orbit above Low Barbary's tiny capital. Doran sighed at the memory. Lord Krysten's obsession with the solar schooners might cost her people a small fortune, but neither she nor any of the other nobles who shared her fondness for the sport would give up the prestige it brought them. And while her people might grumble after years of rejection, they no longer bothered to bring those complaints before their Commons' Council.

Oriana had stood bored among her courtiers, watching idly as Lord Krysten exhibited her prize ships. Lord Vasili, sensing the empress's inattention, began whispering snide remarks to his neighbor. Their voices were calculated to reach the empress's ear; Oriana smiled and edged closer. Krysten heard, too, and color flamed on her high cheekbones. She controlled her temper, however, and checked the screen of the keyboard that swung at her belt, saying sweetly, "But your Majesty has often seen the ships. Perhaps I can offer a thing that you haven't yet experienced. My technicians are rigging a ship even now. They're a Hellmouth crew, one of the best. If your Majesty would care to watch?"

Oriana's attention snapped back to her host. Even now, Hellmouth had an unsavory reputation, though that was derived more from its past than from any present-day behavior. If anything, Doran had thought, the Hellmouthers who had served with him, in the planetary armies and in the Guard, had kept more strictly to Convention than people from any other world. The empress nodded slowly. "I confess, I haven't seen the rigging," she said, with an attempt at polite disinterest. "Please, lead on, my Lord."

Krysten bowed, however, and motioned for Oriana to follow a floating serbot—the niceties of Convention, if not its spirit, were rigidly observed on the Barbaries. As she took her place at the empress's left shoulder, Doran caught a swift, triumphant glance at young Andros.

The corridor ended in a glassed-in observation booth. Doran, with the suspicion mandatory in his position, checked the glass and was relieved to find that it was treated plastis. Krysten ignored his action—she had no choice, unless she wanted to give her enemies an opening to call her traitor—and moved to the controls set into the wall.

"This is the crane control station," she said, in the slightly pedantic tones of a tour guide. "The crane is used to move the schooner into position at the start; after that, everything is done by hand."

Oriana stepped forward quickly, to stand with her palms flat against the plastis. There was something unforcedly eager about her stance that made Doran edge forward to see better.

The rigging room was huge, a zero-g chamber occupying nearly a third of the station's volume. A schooner, a smooth oval of drive casing topped by the tiny bump that was the pilot's bubble, hung motionless just above the "floor." Two human figures clung to that floor, apparently waiting to steady the ship when the time came to pack the sails.

"This is my own private schooner," Krysten said. "They aren't doing anything fancy, just changing to a new set of sails. The old ones wear out after about two months' use." She touched a stud on the control panel, and Doran, craning to see between her shoulder and the empress's back, saw a screen light up. In the rigging room, work stopped, and one figure floated away from the rest.

"My Lord?" The voice that crackled through the speaker was pleasantly tinged with the Hellmouth drawl.

"Master Keira, you have visitors." Krysten's tone was light, but sounded a little forced: the strain of the empress's visit, Doran decided. "Where are you?"

The figure apart from the others glanced at the schooner beneath him. "We've packed the x-sails, Lady. We're just beginning the y."

"Very good," Krysten said, and took her finger off the button. The screen faded, and the man in the room turned back to his work. At a signal from him, two of the others pushed themselves to the far wall—now that they were moving, Doran could see that they wore a-packs, running on compressed air—and caught up a bundle that lay there, secured by blue-glowing forcebands. Then they sprang free of the wall, dragging the sail behind them. They had judged the force needed with uncanny accuracy: they floated to a stop exactly as the sail came fully extended behind them. There was a gentle murmur of admiration from the court, Oriana's voice louder than the rest. The sail, an intricate web of iridescent threads, lay between the four sailworkers. At some signal, all four a-packs were triggered, and the sail, still completely extended, began to travel toward the waiting schooner. Again, there were murmurs of admiration for the teamwork. There was not even the hint of a wrinkle in the sail; it travelled as though it had been made of iron.

"That's the y-prime," Krysten said, quietly, not wanting to break the mood. "A mainsail, providing power, rather than maneuverability."

Oriana nodded impatiently, her eyes glued to the scene in front of her. As the sail approached the schooner, the two sailworkers beside it raised the handlers' poles they carried, and deftly swung the ship, so that it presented the lower surface of the oval to the advancing workers. The leader released the sail and, with the lightest blast from his a-pack, dropped to the ship. He had not judged his weight as perfectly as before, and the schooner subsided a little, to be brought back by the two handlers.

The three who still held the sail now shifted it, in response to hand signals, until the corner was perfectly aligned with the slot that now opened in the schooner's hull. The leader caught the corner and, with infinitely delicate tugging and stretching, worked it into place among the complicated gears and hooks of the winding mechanism. When it was at last adjusted to his satisfaction, he beckoned for the nearest sailworker, who dropped over to examine the attachment briefly before nodding. Then the leader touched a button and walked backward on the schooner's hull, away from the sail opening. The sail began to be drawn into the casing, the two sailworkers who still held the corners keeping the material taut between them. The leader, his feet seemingly glued to the hull—he probably wore ship-shoes, with their thin, flexible, magnetic soles, Doran had thought—watched them intently, occasionally gesturing to signal a correction.

Finally the sail disappeared into the body of the ship, and the four who had brought the first sail started for the far wall.

"I want to meet them," Oriana said abruptly. "Aren't they done?"

"Not—" Krysten checked herself, and continued smoothly, "I'll speak to them, your Majesty." She worked the communications equipment again, and the sailworkers stopped short of the wall, milling aimlessly while the leader brought himself back into camera range.

"Yes, Lady?"

"Can you stop work now, without damaging anything? My guest would like to meet you."

The leader hesitated, glancing over his shoulder at the schooner, then shrugged slightly. "Certainly, Lady, as you wish. We'll be right up."

"No," Krysten said, with a quick glance in Oriana's direction. "We'll come down to your quarters."

The empress looked pleased and Doran spared a moment's admiration for Krysten's handling of the situation. If she could parlay this into something that Oriana would really remember, she would be made at court.

"As you say, Lady," the leader said, and Krysten blanked her screen.

"If your Majesty would come with me?"

Once again, a serbot led the way through the corridors and down an elevator shaft to the lower quarters level of the station. Here the station was less antiseptic, brighter, with posters and hand-lettered notices giving the place a new feeling of individuality. The sailworker team was waiting in their own tiny common room, standing awkwardly around a low Hellmouther table. The temperature had been raised to accommodate them, and Doran could feel a wave of heat from the open door.

The serbot made a tapping noise within itself and announced, "Her Majesty Oriana, third of the name, empress." The sailworkers bowed deeply.

Oriana swept in, followed closely by Krysten. The room was too small for most of the others to enter. Doran, glaring, forced his way through the crowding nobles, whispering, "Security!" to anyone who seemed about to object. Andros was left outside, to Doran's satisfaction.

Seen close up and in gravity, the sailworkers lost their inhuman grace, gained human beauty. They wore tight-fitting bodysuits, dark against sun-darkened skin. Doran could not help raising an eyebrow at the low cleavage of one of the women, but it was the leader who had caught Oriana's attention. He was unusually fair for a Hellmouther, red-haired, and his suit was tight enough to outline every muscle of his well-made body. Oriana looked long and hard before demanding, "Which of you is the foreman?"

The red-haired man stepped forward and bowed again, seemingly oblivious to the empress's scrutiny. "I am, your Majesty." He was less overawed by the imperial presence than Doran had expected.

Oriana smiled. "Your name?"

"Keira, your Majesty, a master of the Sailmakers' Guild."

"And these others?" Oriana continued.

Keira presented the others, smiling faintly. Each bowed as Keira introduced him. They were less sure of themselves than Keira, and Doran wondered again where the guildmaster had learned his courtly graces.

"Your group is very skilled," Oriana said. "It was a pleasure to watch you work."

Keira answered with a stock courtier's phrase: "I am honored to have given pleasure to your Majesty."

For the first time, Oriana looked at him frankly, eyes travelling from the guildmaster's high-boned face to his shapely legs, and back again. She appeared to come to a decision, and said abruptly, "You will come with me."

Keira bowed again. "Your Majesty does me great honor, but I'm bound by Guild contract to serve Lord Krysten."

"I will compensate her for her contract," Oriana said. "Is that agreeable, my Lord?" Her tone brooked no argument, and Krysten bowed.

"Certainly, your Majesty." As she straightened, Doran caught a glimpse of her half-pleased, half-rueful smile. She was losing a skilled technician, but it was possible she was gaining an ally at court.

"Then I can hardly object, your Majesty." Only Keira's abjectly grateful tones saved him from the accusation of insolence. "May I say goodbye to my team?"

Oriana sighed. "Oh, very well, but be quick. I want to return to my ship."

Keira bowed again and backed away, murmuring something in the broad-vowelled Hellmouth dialect. One of the other sailworkers handed him a rolled-up bundle, and Keira tucked it under one arm, at the same time reaching to clasp the woman's hands. He spoke quickly to the others, and then, as he turned to a smaller, slimmer man, Doran saw his hand cross quickly to the pin above the breast pocket of his suit, where name and rank were indicated. The general strained to get a better look at that pin, but when Keira's hand came away it had disappeared. A moment later, as he clasped hands with the slighter man, Doran saw the hands move as though Keira had passed him something. Then Keira's eyes met his, and the general was unprepared for what he saw there. There was calculation—the advantage-weighing cunning that had made the last two favorites so hated in the court—but it was coupled with a sort of candor. Yes, the glance seemed to say, I took someone else's clothes to make myself desirable, but what else should I do? I will take advantage of any chance, and you should know I will. Then he followed Oriana from the room, and was lost in the crowd of nobles who followed them.

Chapter 3

Desolin Hamm'tt, Grand Duke of the Domus Hamm'tt, leaned back in her chair, fingers tapping idly against the bowl of her dead pipe. The computer showed the result of the past four hours' work, a series of probabilities, nothing conclusive. Certainly there was nothing on the screen to justify Lovell-Andriës, hailing Keira as emperor. The Elector's words had been prompted by Talent, then, but her own Talent told her less, and with far less certainty. A slight frown creased her forehead as she studied the screen again. The computers had done no more than confirm her instinctive knowledge: if anyone opposed Keira now, the Imperium would go up in flames. The question was, would anyone? She smiled, without humor. Almost certainly, but would she?

Without thinking, she tapped ash from the pipe, caught what she was doing, and decided not to refill it. She glanced instead at the sheaf of computer paper resting beside her on the broad chair arm. Her claim was diagrammed on those pages, black lines for full marriages, dotted ones for alliance-weddings, with the allied families carefully indicated, blue lines for consortship, red for companionage, and green for liaisons unsanctioned by any law. She had a certain right, but not through the Silvertree line. The connection with the Alexanders was an old one: a Hamm'tt had been Consort to Alexander II, though of course there had been

35

no children, and no solid claim could be made from that. The important tie was the alliance-wedding of an El Nath minore and Alexander IV, matched by the marriage of the Hamm'tt Duke and one of Alexander's minores. For her purposes, it did not matter that there were fifteen generations between the last Alexander and Oriana III, or that there was no Silvertree blood in the family. Oriana's father and grandfather had done their best to eliminate those houses with direct relationships to the Silvertrees. As far as she could tell, they had succeeded: the Heronaia were dead, the junior branch of the de la Mars extinct, the last descendant of the illegitimate FitzMary line too cowed—and lacking the necessary genes—to even think of making a claim. Her own claim might hark back to the Alexanders, but it was legitimate and direct. None of the others could state that.

However. . . . She sighed and put aside the computer paper. There were no legal difficulties; her claim would stand before the nobles assembled in the Eger. The question was not whether she could claim the throne, under law and Convention, but whether she would. And it was Convention that tugged at her: she did not know if she could win, or what the costs would be, and that put her under a restriction of honor.

With the will to bolster Keira's claims, she could see no way to defeat him without war, and outside of court Keira was a completely unknown quantity. She did not think he would be a great admiral—the war would be fought in space, under Convention, to protect the commoners—but he could hire good ones among the minores, even if the Navy supported another candidate or stood neutral. And Doran's throwing the Imperial Guard to Keira's side would weigh heavily with the admirals. According to the computers, she could win a naval engagement, and would probably win the entire

war—the odds were fractionally in her favor—but
it would be costly. She leaned forward to her keyboard again, clearing the screen, then began to set
up the equations again. She shifted the parame-
ters slightly, adding a few minores to Keira's forces,
compensating with majores of increased status on
her own side. The screen blanked itself and considered, the cursor hovering in the upper left-hand
corner, then spat its information.

The battle shifted location, toward the Council
border, and with that shift the results changed.
Keira won, at the cost of a third of his own minores
and even greater destruction of her side. She could
conceivably recoup her losses by attacking Avalon's
lunar station and the Palace itself—she keyed that
response into the computer, and got the expected
result—but too many commoners would be endan-
gered. The computer predicted at best a hundred
deaths among commoner service personnel. Inbre
constraints, and Convention, made such killing to
tally unacceptable. But she was not satisfied with
a Grand Duke's power.

She stood, feeling the thin metal spirals that
encased her legs from ankle to hip shift state to
take her weight. The wallscreens were still lit,
showing views of the palm-lined Grand Prome-
nade that ran from the ducal palace to the capitol
on El Nath. The feathery leaves trembled in a
vagrant breeze, and the road surface was slick
with heat haze. Hamm'tt glared at the picture and
moved to switch off the screen, only too aware it
was nearly dawn by Avalon's clock. She was tired,
and still undecided, and her Talent was still silent
in her. Reluctantly, she turned to face the portrait
that waited in its niche. Her father's face stared
back at her, and it was only too easy to imagine
disapproval in his expression.

She faced him anyway, as she had faced him
before, knowing what his response would have been.

It was that very predictability that had caused his
death. Attack, make your claim, let combat or a
game decide it all. Convention will stretch to justify the loss of life. And if you don't act, you are
not worthy to be Grand Duke. In spite of herself,
one hand stole to the thin brace coiling up her
thigh. She had not been her father's choice of heir;
an adolescent illness, aggravated by the genetic
complex that had given her her Talent, had left
her crippled, unworthy in his eyes. But she was
Grand Duke now, and she chose to wait, until
Talent or the computers could give her better odds.

She turned away from the portrait, putting aside
those memories until they could be useful again.
The Council of the Domi met—she glanced at the
time display built into her computer console—in
less than six hours. As head of a Domus, she would
attend, and that meeting should give her a better
idea of where the other heads of Domi stood. And
when she knew that, she would know what she
could do.

The sun had risen by the time the ambassador's
shuttle landed at the pocket field behind the Federal embassy at Government Center. Denisov-
Graham squinted into the new light and tried to
figure out if he would be able to get any sleep
before nightfall. The Eger didn't meet for another
eight hours, but there was the evaluation team to
brief and his report to the Board to draft. Those
could wait a few hours. At his elbow, Rubenstein
cleared her throat, and the ambassador turned
warily.

"Yes?"

The undersecretary smiled, a little maliciously.
"Shall I call out the evaluation team?"

"Now?"

"The sooner you brief them, the sooner you can
send the Board's notification," she answered.

"It can wait a few hours," Denisov-Graham said, and Rubenstein's smile grew wider. The ambassador sighed. "No, I don't want them to hear from the newsmedia before they get my report. All right, we'll meet—half an hour. If I have to be up, everybody else can suffer."

Rubenstein nodded, and vanished into the office wing. Left to himself, Denisov-Graham headed for his quarters, in the wing of the building that faced the city center. Someone had passed orders to his serbot: fresh clothes and a packet of wake-up pills were waiting. He shaved and showered, then dressed, hoping that the rest of the evaluation group were as miserable as he was. The pills took effect fairly quickly, and by the time he walked from his quarters to the smaller of the two conference rooms he felt almost able to cope.

He allowed himself a certain sour pleasure at the sight of the bleary faces ringing the long table, but as a serbot brought breakfast his mood eased. The meeting should not take long; he might even be able to sneak a quick nap before the Eger meeting that afternoon. He nodded to Rubenstein. "Kedma, do you want to begin?"

The undersecretary quickly set aside her coffee cup and shuffled a stack of hastily generated printouts. "All right, sir. Well, as you've all heard by now, Oriana died last night, and the will named her favorite as heir. I gather that our file on Keira doesn't show the important factor—" She tapped the stack of paper, and Kempe, who was responsible for compiling data on the Household members, made a face. "He's a Renault."

A junior liaison, a historian by training, whistled softly, then turned bright red and mumbled apologies as all eyes turned to him.

"Quite," Rubenstein said dryly, after a moment. "I know no one's had a chance to make any sort of detailed analysis of the situation—that'll come later—but I'm interested in hearing everyone's immediate reactions, and any guesses about what this is going to do to politics around here."

There was a moment of silence, then everyone spoke at once. Rubenstein opened her mouth as though to call for order, but Denisov-Graham motioned for her to be quiet. She subsided, an odd look on her face, and the ambassador leaned back, trying to listened to all the conversations at once.

"—never actively hostile to the Federation, the Renaults weren't," the historian was saying, "at least no more than they were to anybody—"

"Other claimants?"

"I'll prepare lists—" Kempe said.

"The Navy'll never have him." That was the embassy's own Navy representative, O'Farrell. The youngest of the political analysts was shaking his head.

"They might. They don't have a lot of choice—"

"What about ground troops?" another analyst broke in, and Denisov-Graham leaned forward.

"Doran—the general of the Guard—supports Keira."

O'Farrell nodded slowly. "That might change things," he said thoughtfully.

Denisov-Graham let the talk continue for a few minutes longer, then cleared his throat. A few faces turned, then all were quiet. "If you don't mind, I'd like to hear from all the sections now," he said. "This isn't for the record. I'd just like to hear your guesses before you get to work in earnest, and before I have to attend the Eger." He nodded to the Navy man. "O'Farrell?"

The captain spread his hands stiffly. "My immediate reaction," he said, choosing his words carefully, "is that their Navy won't stand for it. They're *minores*, all of them, and conscious of rank and station. But, then, he's got the empress's sanction, and that might give him Conventional support."

Kempe and the other political analysts were nodding. "That's just it," Kempe said. "Convention. Without more time, I can't predict how that'll affect things."

At the far end of the table, a gaunt woman with a faintly asiatic face raised her hand.

"Yes, Sakima?" Denisov-Graham said warily.

The cultural liaison folded her long hands on the tabletop and looked around the circle of faces before answering. "Convention," she said at last, "will determine everything."

Denisov-Graham opened his mouth to ask her to be more specific, but Sakima was already well launched into her lecture on Convention. He had heard it at least a dozen times before, as had all but the newest members of the staff, and he had learned that it was impossible to stop the lecture without cutting off the useful information that invariably followed. And Sakima was without question the most experienced of the cultural staff, well worth humoring.

The ambassador sighed softly, avoiding Rubenstein's accusing glance. The trouble was that they all knew—or should know, by now—what Sakima was saying. They had learned the origins of Convention in school: when the Old Federation was attacked by the Council eight hundred years before, the Federal Navy had been forced to pull back from the outermost federal colonies. The abandoned colonies had fought the Council anyway, with a navy made up of renegades from the Federal Navy, merchant captains, smugglers from the older border worlds, even ships from the corporate fleets, all of whom had been bitter rivals. Convention had begun in the loose agreements that kept those captains allied against the common enemy and, as those captains had become the absolute rulers of the planets they defended, evolved into the code by which the new nobles lived. The oldest tenet was still the central precept: "a noble exists to protect, and may never endanger, the commoners." Beyond that basic law, Convention provided the rules for the constant warfare among the Domi, permitting killing but, to keep as many nobles as possible alive in case of external war, assigning greater status to the use of finesse, bluff, and double bluff, to force surrender.

Status. . . . Denisov-Graham looked up as Sakima seemed to echo his thoughts.

"Status," she said, "is the key to Convention. Convention assigns status and moral value to all actions it does not prohibit. To say that one has acted 'according to Convention' is to say that one has weighed the moral repercussions—does this harm the commoners? is there unnecessary killing, killing that could be avoided by greater subtlety? do I break my word to someone who is in a position to shame me later?—and then calculated the prestige to be gained from the action."

That's true enough, Denisov-Graham thought, but not as true as it had been. Things are changing, have changed even in the seven years I've been assigned here. Oh, it's not the big things, not the rule that protects the commoners at the cost of nobles' lives—and the commoners' political voice—and not the ones that advocate finesse and surrender in the face of it. Even the laws that regulated marriage and defined Talent, forcing nobles to marry for Talent, remained more or less unchanged. It was in the little things that the line between cleverness and cheating was growing blurred. If the major rules were unbroken, and the gain was great enough, nobles broke the lesser rules with impunity.

"Keira will have to abide by the strictest Convention," Sakima said, and with an effort, Denisov-Graham dragged his attention back to her. "The other nobles—and I assume there will be at least one other claimant—will be able to bend Convention because of Keira's previous status. He'll be at an extreme disadvantage, unless he can somehow force them to obey the rules of their own accord."

"Is there any way he can do that?" Rubenstein cut in, and several of the others shot her grateful looks.

Sakima made a small gesture that in someone less formal might have been a shrug. "I can't think how. I anticipate a very short reign for this emperor, and a sorting-out period before the best claimants emerge."

"How long a period of instability?" Denisov-Graham asked.

Sakima frowned thoughtfully. "A year," she said at last. "Perhaps even longer."

"Less than that, surely," said Kempe. "They can't afford to be without some central power. The Eger isn't structured to maintain the government."

"The bureaucracy can always run things on an unofficial level," Rubenstein said.

"Not for a year or more," Kempe answered. "No mechanism for initiating policy."

"A number of emperors, holding power for short periods," the most junior analyst suggested, and was ignored.

Denisov-Graham let them talk for a while longer, until they began to repeat themselves. Then, with a nod to Rubenstein, he brought the meeting to an end by requesting the various department heads to have complete reports by the end of the week. "Preliminary reports by tomorrow, if possible," he added, and saw O'Farrell grimace.

"What do you think, Ioan?" Rubenstein asked quietly, after the others had gone.

"I don't know what to think," Denisov-Graham answered. "If you're asking me what I'm going to tell the Board—"

"Yes."

"—I'm going to tell them it's too early to tell them anything. What's next on the Imperium's agenda?"

Rubenstein touched buttons on her keyboard. "The Council of the Domi meets to affirm Keira's claim, then the claim is presented by the Council to the Eger—that's if the Domi leaders accept it, but I don't see how they could not accept it—and then the Commons' Councils on the separate planets are asked for their opinions. That's purely a formality, but it'll take a week or so before all the worlds can answer, given the screwed-up standard calendar they're still using here, and by that time any other claimants should have declared themselves."

"I'll wait for that before I send any recommendation," Denisov-Graham said. "We can afford to."

Chapter 4

A different sergeant was on duty when Doran presented himself at the door to the Imperial Quarters the next morning, a small, deceptively cheerful man. He saluted, and said, "General Doran, sir. His Majesty says you are to be admitted immediately."

Doran returned the salute with studied carelessness, long practice having taught him to walk the fine line between the devil-may-care attitude expected of a senior line officer and insult to the traditions of the minores and of the Guard. "Very good, sergeant. Carry on."

The outer door was already open; as he stepped into the short hallway, the ceiling monitors recorded his presence and the inner door slid back, admitting him to the small receiving room. Keira was seated there, already dressed in the severe tunic and trousers that were worn beneath a formal coat. A pot of coffee and an untouched breakfast tray stood on the table beside him.

Doran made a soldier's obeisance. "Your Majesty. I trust you slept well."

"Well enough." Keira's expression belied the Conventional reassurance. "Sit down, General. Help yourself to whatever you'd like. Do you take coffee?"

Doran shook his head. Coffee was addictive among the nobles, and a minore could not risk creating such a need within himself. "Thank you, I've broken fast already."

Keira grinned briefly. Doran had seen the expression before, usually when Oriana had not been looking. "The minore's life? Or at least the soldier-minore's?"

Doran bowed again, a fractional inclination of the head that indicated he understood, if he did not share, the jest.

"Come, General," Keira said. "We've known each other for some time now. I don't want to spend my life fencing with you. And if I wished to—I know the emperor can't survive without the Guard. No games between us."

Doran thought, *Unless the name of the game is "I will be frank with you,"* but said, "Certainly, Majesty."

Keira looked at him as though he had read the thought. "You never crossed me before, and you never crossed Oriana. Despite temptation, I might add. I repeat, I don't intend to play games. I need your troops and your influence with the minores, if I'm to survive long enough to establish my claim to the throne, much less consolidate my hold on the Imperium. You were the first to offer allegiance. Did you have conditions for your loyalty?"

Doran stared for a moment, staggered by this sudden candor. He collected himself hastily. "I had no conditions then."

"And now?"

Doran looked at his emperor, a white-faced man in drab grey. He could recognize neither the sailworker nor the royal favorite nor the last heir of a dead Domus Aurea in the sober figure. "Now . . . I would make only the usual conditions of any minore. I will serve you with all my heart, so long as you follow Convention."

Keira nodded. "I'd expected no less." He set his cup aside and leaned forward. "To business, then. I must go before the Domi Council this morning and restate my claim. After that, there's the presenta-

tion to the Eger Assembled. They've been here
since Oriana fell sick, waiting—" He shook himself.
"Are Oriana's usual security arrangements adequate?"

Doran considered it, his mind working nearly as
quickly as his computers as he reviewed possible
scenarios of assassination or insurrection, shuffling
his men to achieve maximum security without of-
fending the nobles' pride. "For visiting the Domi
Council, you can follow the usual procedure. I'll
provide you with a reliable escort, say, five men,
and I'll make the arrangements for the Eger and
report back to you."

"Excellent," Keira said. "How soon can I have
my escort for the Council?"

"Within the hour, Majesty." Doran recognized
the dismissal. "With your leave?"

Keira waved a hand, a gesture copied from the
dead empress. "You have leave. And thank you,
Doran."

Doran backed from the room, turning only when
the inner door had closed behind him. A second
later, the outer door opened, and Doran stepped
out.

"Sergeant."

The man saluted, and took a quick step forward.
"Sir?"

"His Majesty will attend the Domi Council this
morning. You, with these men—" he named them
quickly "—will attend his Majesty. Is that clear?"

The procedure was familiar enough; the sergeant
saluted again, and said, "Yes, sir." Doran returned
the salute, satisfied. A corridor escort, particularly
within the walls of the Palace complex, was easy
enough to choose. A rifleman or two, just in case
someone managed to sneak a projectile weapon
past all the sensors; a pair of swordsmen, since
shielded blades were the most common weapons;
and someone competent to command—for prefer-

ence, someone who knew unarmed combat. Doran
knew the Guard roster by heart: a simple matter.
The Eger was vastly more complicated.

His office was near the Imperial Quarters. There
were two rooms—one for interviews, and the other
for real work. The secretary unit sat idle in its
corner, the light that would have signalled messages unlit. Doran touched the replay button
anyway, and listened to the hissing static for a
second before switching it off again.

"I am not to be disturbed for the next few hours,"
he told it, "except for priority three, two, or one
messages."

The secretary acknowledged that with a discreet
chirp, and Doran went on into the inner room.
Computer banks lined the wall, and a holotable
dominated the central space, darkened now except
for the occasional flicker of a reflection as a computer signaled some change of status. His worn
chair was set to one side, behind the master
keyboard. He had to squeeze past the holotable to
reach it. Once seated, he began flipping switches
methodically, linking the computers and holotable
one by one into the simulations net. At last the
entire row of telltales glowed green, and a hazy
cloud, just at the edge of the visible spectrum,
hovered over the table. But there were some routine checks to run first. He touched keys, watching
the code phrases form beneath his fingers: first,
the tapes from the hidden cameras. For variety's
sake, he played them on the table rather than on
the screen. An image coalesced, the colors wavering a little, and a miniature version of the workroom stood on the table. To mark the passage of
time, an inset—a trumpet-flower—stood in full
bloom, then closed back in on itself in the space of
minutes. There was no visible movement at all. It
was remotely possible, of course, that someone
had slipped in and out of the room between two

shots, but there wasn't much anyone could do in so short a time.

The intruder scans in the computer were next. First the important ones, the ones that told him if anyone had tampered with his secret files—no one had—and then the spot checks, the ones that recorded who had sought what information in the Guard's open files. To his surprise, there had been considerable activity there. He frowned and punched for a more specific readout, ignoring the unchanging scene on the holotable, where the room stood frozen and in the corner a flower opened, closed, then was revived to repeat the process minutes later.

Whoever had been using the computer the night before—the request time showed two in the morning—had had an abnormal interest in high-ranking officers. His own file—both the official short file and the Guard's own longer dossier—had been requested, and the codes indicated that they had been fed into a simulations computer. That in itself was somewhat unnerving, and so he set up a trace program. Someone wanted to predict his actions, or those of the Guard. He put the trace on hold long enough to punch in a check on several other topics—a few selected names and dossiers, an analysis of the Imperial Guard, an account of a recent police action—and found that all of those had been requested the night before. He let the trace continue and leaned back in his chair to wait. *I suppose it's only to be expected,* he thought, *someone wanting to see how we'd react to this situation. I wish to hell I could find out just what they wanted to know.* Well, if the trace were successful, if whoever it was had not put too complicated a lock on the files, if he/she had not erased all records . . . maybe he could get at the conclusions.

The computer beeped softly and flashed strings of letters onto the screen. He skimmed quickly through the details of time and place, looking for the user-name. It was encoded, of course, but for once he didn't need the index to identify it: *Malmedy*, the dead empress's private code. For a second, he felt hair rise on his neck, thoughts of ghosts and the more recent fantasy of dead brains hidden in live computers roiling through him, and then he knew the real answer. Keira had to have known the code, and must have used it the night before, after the nobles had left. Just to confirm the suspicion, he checked the terminal location and found it blocked: as good as an admission that the request had come from within the Quarters.

He touched the keys again, tongue pressed against his teeth, hoping that the emperor had not had time to erase all traces of his work. The first two paths he tried were blocked, but the third override produced a flash and a file identified only by the previous day's date. That's promising, he thought, and punched the go-ahead.

Twin columns of words marched slowly up the screen, followed by a win/lose percentage. Doran frowned and ran it through again, more slowly. Just what was it that had only a 29 percent chance of permanent success? The words were mostly nouns and adjectives, with only an occasional verb: a common simulations code, but one that Doran could read only with an effort. He ran it again, and thought he understood. It was a condensed dialogue between himself and Keira, the emperor proposing alliance, with an appeal to his minore's pride of caste and his position as Guard commander. The sim indicated Doran's acceptance, but hinted at distrust and the possibility of later betrayal. Doran nodded agreement. The machine's word/emotional response programming had him down correctly, at any rate. If the emperor had tried to push those buttons, he would not have reacted well.

There was more in the file. The next argument

was for the safety of the Imperium, playing on a theoretical fear of the Federation. The chance of success was recorded as less than 10 percent. Clearly, Doran thought, his liking for the Federal ambassador had somehow crept into his record. The third projection was essentially the appeal Keira had made, though perhaps without any admission of the emperor's vulnerability. Doran was not familiar enough with the code to pick up the subtleties of a bare-bones simulation. The machine gave it only a 40 percent chance of success, and Doran smiled. It was encouraging to think that he had so far kept the Heralds from compiling a foolproof dossier. It was to a minore's credit not to be absolutely predictable from his files.

The argument in the last simulation was based on a combination of fears for the Imperium, if civil war should break out, and fears of what the Federation might attempt with a weakened emperor on the throne. The computer had liked this one, rating it at a 67.4 percent chance of success, but Doran, studying the coded words, could see the weaknesses too easily. Still, it was odd that Keira had not chosen that one. It argued—Doran hesitated over the keys and did not call back the second sim. It meant two things. First, Keira knew his general of the Guard much better than Doran had thought. Second, it was proof, if proof was needed, that Keira was enough a majore to pick up the patterns of a conversation, and to shape it to get what he wanted.

Doran wiped the tape then, erasing all references to the projections from his own files, and settled down to the real work of the morning. Under his skilled hands, the Eger chamber, with its long central aisle, royal dais at the end, and the steep galleries opposite where the minores sat, grew on the holotable and filled with shadowy ghosts of the nobility. The emperor and an escort group, arbitrarily set at nine men, moved down the aisle, while he programmed attempt after attempt on the emperor's life. Most of them failed, as he had known they would; when one did not, he rearranged his guards and began again. At last, he had reached a plan that did not involve too many men, but was flexible enough to take anything he threw at it. There remained, of course, the chance that an assassin willing to accept his own death could penetrate the screen, but that would always exist. And anyway, he thought, there's a 61 percent probability we'd get that one, too. Then he sobered. The computers had been wrong about his reactions. They could just as easily be wrong about this. He shook the thought away as quickly as possible. He was not a majore, with inbred instincts to calculate the human factors even the best computers could not fully reproduce. He would rely on his machines, as the minores had always done, until his master told him otherwise.

He closed the computers down, letting the carefully-wrought picture fade, watching the lights blink out, until the room returned to its original dimness. Keira—the emperor, he reminded himself—had chosen a 40 percent probability over a higher one, and had been right. What would it be like to have that certainty himself? He smiled ruefully. It would have to be enough to have an emperor who knew. Straightening his shoulders, he went into the outer office to give orders for the afternoon.

Chapter 5

Left to himself, Keira felt for the control panel concealed beneath the wood of the chair arm. As his fingers probed, the wood seemed to change in shape and texture. His hand slid past a dozen different control points, each subtly different from the others, before he found the ones he wanted. He pressed gently, and a panel slid back to reveal a cubicle jammed with machinery: the emperor's private workspace. The central screen was empty again, but the paper from the printer had spilled onto the miniature holotable. He sighed and stood staring for a moment, before crossing the room to tear free the folded sheets. Frowning, he seated himself before the main keyboard, but did not unfold the papers. They would contain nothing new. It was not a question of whether or not to take the risk—any action, including inaction, was risky now—but whether this was the time to take this chance.

He set the papers on the narrow shelf to his left and reluctantly folded back the top sheet. A familiar face stared up at him from the obligatory photograph—a face doubly familiar, because in Lasca FitzMary he could see the ghost of Oriana. FitzMary was a Silvertree, illegitimately descended from a Silvertree Admiral, younger sister of the emperor David III, and as such was dangerous. At the same time, she was only a minore, unlikely to produce children with major Talent even through

53

a major husband. And she had been Oriana's connection to the Navy.

Keira leaned back in his chair, sighing. That was the real key to the matter. Lasca FitzMary had been Oriana's navy liaison, had commanded her own ship before being given the post at court, was the only Navy minore with whom he had had enough contact even to think of trusting. But she had also come to court as a hostage for the good behavior of her maternal relatives. Keira flipped through a stack of papers, past FitzMary's official dossier, until he found the records of the case.

It had not been a pretty affair: Oriana's father had feared rivals with a paranoia surprising even in the late Silvertree line. With Oriana's birth, late in her father's life, David VIII had lost all reason, and proceeded to eliminate any survivors of the Silvertree collateral lines. Andor FitzMary had been one of the first to go, on a blatantly false charge of mismanagement; his wife had followed on general principles, but her sister, an Eneas of Jerra, had succeeded in saving Lasca, then a child barely two years old. The Eneas woman had claimed the child as her own, and put her into the Navy as soon as she reached adolescence. That was a clever move, Keira thought, to put her where the notorious independence of the Navy-minores would give her automatic protection even against the emperor. But then Eneas had over-reached herself. On David's death, she had revealed the existence of a FitzMary heir, and seemed ready to use her as a weapon. Oriana, no less fearful of rivals than her father, though somewhat more rational in her methods, had quietly ordered Lasca to court. A few weeks later, Eneas had been informed of her niece's "promotion", and shortly after that had sworn a particularly rigorous Oath of Allegiance. Keira wished he knew precisely what negotiations had gone on there—there had been threats and counter-threats, he was quite certain—but the Heralds had recorded only actions.

He sighed and refolded the stack of papers. There were no answers in that line of thought. All right, he thought, I'll look at it from another angle. I must have the Navy's support. Lovell-Andriës may have offered allegiance, and he has a fleet at Somewhere, but it can't match the Navy. The Admirals won't want to commit themselves at this point, and once someone else makes his claim, they will be in a position to push both sides for greater independence. An old anger stirred in him. The Navy's loyalty had once been proverbial; now the Admirals, technically mere soldier-minores, had used the weakening of the Emperor's control to turn their fleets into fiefs, and posed as arbiters of majore quarrels.

Keira closed his eyes, forced calm. That was the situation; he would change it when he could, but for now he had to work within it. And he needed the Admirals—even one of the three fleets would make a major difference in his situation. And because the Navy would only listen to one of its own, he needed FitzMary. The question was, could he trust her to speak for him? Logic held the options neatly balanced—past friendship, loyalty to Oriana, her minore status, poised against the temptations of power. Talent, and it was less full Talent than a hunch, said she could be trusted. That would have to be enough.

Keira pushed himself away from the computers, went to the corner secretary. He touched the botton that summoned the duty Herald, and waited for the response. When at last a young man answered, Keira said, "Summon Captain FitzMary to the Quarters. And confirm that the Domi Council meets at eleven."

"Yes, your Majesty."

Keira broke the connection and touched the button that resealed the panel concealing the computers, then settled himself to wait. It was not long before the door signal lit, almost as though FitzMary had been waiting for the summons. Keira touched the intercom as he seated himself again.

"Yes?"

"Your Majesty, Captain FitzMary is here, at your request."

"Send her in."

Keira waited while the outer door was opened and shut, and was not surprised when the inner door slid back to see FitzMary escorted by one of the troopers. That will never do, he thought, and smiled, Talent stirring.

"Welcome, Captain." To the Guard, he added, "You may go."

The young soldier-minore stiffened, seemed on the verge of protest, but Keira raised an eyebrow. "Very good, your Majesty," the Guard said formally, and backed from the room.

"Be seated, Captain," Keira said.

Warily, FitzMary settled herself in the chair nearest the door, her face very still. They stared at each other in silence for a long minute.

"You take chances, Keira," FritzMary said at last.

"Do I?" Keira watched her, not moving, seeing beneath the mask of calm the shifting tensions, the millimetric movements that betrayed her intentions. She was ready to attack. She had every reason to attack—to avenge her dead parents, possibly to gain a throne. He slid his left hand along the chair arm, feeling for the slight bulge of the concealed blaster.

"I could kill you now," she said, unmoving. Then: "This is a test."

"I'm at your disposal, Lasca," Keira said. This was not how he had intended to handle her, fighting on the minore's level; he was not entirely sure he could kill her before she reached him. Then the minore laughed sharply, her whole body relaxing.

"No, your Majesty, I will not try. Not even to oblige you. I've seen your games too often."

"I never played games with you," Keira said.

FitzMary bowed her head slightly in acknowledgement. "No, Majesty. You did not."

"Then will you join my household?"

Instead of answering immediately, FitzMary made an odd grimace. At last, she said, "I've been thinking since the empress died what I would do. I'm not majore, and my children will never be majore. I've no taste for being anyone's puppet. I'll serve you as I served her—so do I swear, on my honor as captain and minore."

Keira nodded his thanks, knowing better than to do more. "Good. Now, I want at least one of the three fleets. Can you get it for me?"

FitzMary leaned forward slightly, but her long-jawed, Silvertree face remained still. She had learned that wary mask early in life, Keira thought; he had never seen her face unguarded.

"You want me to persuade the Admirals to follow you?" she asked.

"Can you do it?"

She appeared to consider, her hands going as still as her face. "With proper credentials," she said at last. "Yes, I can."

"You'll have them," Keira said. He stood, waving her to be seated when she would have imitated him, then crossed to the secretary. There were blank tapes in a storage niche; he chose one at random and inserted it into the machine. Quickly, he dictated a brief message, couched in familiar formulae, naming FitzMary as his representative, then placed his hand on the warm guardplate to seal the tape. He handed the disk to FitzMary, who bowed more deeply than she had before.

"Thank you, your Majesty. Shall I leave at once?"

"That seems best," Keira said.

The woman bowed again, and backed to the door. Keira touched the lock switch and the door slid open. He let it close behind her, and then the intercom buzzed.

"Yes?"

The duty Herald said, "your Majesty, I've just spoken with the Duke de Terranin, and the Domi Council will see you at eleven hours, local."

Keira raised an eyebrow, even though there was no visual link. "Gracious of them," he murmured. "Tell His Grace that I shall visit the Council then, and that I wish to see the full Council present."

"Very well, your Majesty." The light blinked out on the intercom. Keira sighed, then clapped his hands for the serbot. One appeared almost instantly, floating from a hidden recess by the door, and he sent it for his formal gown. The machine returned almost immediately, and he turned to let it drape the stiff fabric across his shoulders. Then he glanced at the time display projected onto the wall above the secretary. He had half an hour, though their lordships could await his own pleasure, and it would take most of that time to get from the imperial suite to the Eger Hall. He touched the intercom.

An unfamiliar voice answered. "Majesty?"

"The Herald, please."

"A moment, your Majesty. He is speaking to the Duke de Terranin."

There was a long wait, then the Herald moved into the pickup range. "Your Majesty?"

"You gave my message to His Grace?"

"Yes, your Majesty." Keira could hear the ghost of a smile in the Herald's voice. "He was—not sanguine, Majesty. About the full Council."

"I see. Very well. Tell the sergeant of the Guard that I am ready to leave for the Eger. Is there an escort for me?"

There was a pause and a scuffling noise, and

then the duty sergeant answered, "Yes, your Majesty. The General left us orders."

By the time he reached the edge of the red circle, the top security area of the Palace complex, a hoversled was waiting beyond the checkpoint, four Guardsmen and a pilot crowding it. The sergeant extended a hand to help him into the low-slung craft, then climbed in beside him. Keira felt himself wedged securely between the soldiers, as safe as he could be in the event of crash or attempted assassination.

The sled moved quickly, even through the narrow corridors of the approaches to the Quarters. Once they reached the broader outer corridors, the pilot advanced the throttle. The sun shone through the skylights that topped most of the corridors, flashing green or amber as the color of the glass changed with the different areas. There were few other landcraft in evidence—their use was restricted to the majores within the Palace—and the pedestrians hurried to get out of their way. Keira was conscious of their stares as the sled swept by, and straightened his spine. You've been looked at before, he told himself, and you will be looked at again. *But I never claimed to be emperor before.*

The sled slowed as it approached the main gate that led from the Palace proper to the Eger buildings. The original nine buildings, one for each of the original planetary systems, had long ago been welded into a single structure by an ever-growing maze of corridors, tunnels, and extra wings, but tradition—and practicality—had kept the seats of the nobles' assembly, the Eger, almost completely separated from the buildings that held the emperor's quarters. Guards, members of the Imperial Guard, and armed retainers of the Domi Aureae watched the gate, Guardsman facing retainer across the glossy white strip of a shield generator plate.

"Who goes there?" the retainer in de Terranin green and gold challenged sharply.

The woman beside the pilot leaned from her seat to give the retainer a closer look at her uniform. "The Emperor comes to speak to the Council of the Domi."

"Yes, were were informed of your request," the retainer said. He was a big man, with a scarred hand and a clever cast to his face. "Pass, friend."

Keira scowled, and saw matching expressions on the faces of his escort. The soldier-minore's words were just short of actionable but, since he spoke for his master, no one could challenge him. The pilot stamped on the accelerator, kicking up dust and light pebbles that had drifted in from the garden strip on either side of the gate, and the sled shot ahead with more force than was necessary. Keira leaned forward, and the woman beside the pilot said, "Ease up, Jerr." The sled steadied.

The Domi Council met in a smaller chamber off the main hall of the Eger, a room with ornately chased bronze alloy doors and a matched pair of soldier-minores—de Terranin's retainers again, and Keira hid a frown at the sight—on either side of it. The corridor narrowed, went under a brushed steel roof, and artificial amber light replaced the blued sunlight of the main corridor. One of the retainers touched the keyboard at his waist, the other advanced to meet the hoversled.

"Dan Keira," he said, raising his voice to carry over the noise of the hoversled's engines and, Keira thought, to make sure his words reached the recorder pickup in his companion's keyboard. "The Council is willing to see you now."

Keira controlled an impulse to comment on the sudden unConventional lack of courtesy among the Domi Aureae, and held out a hand for one of the Guardsmen to help him from the hoversled. The retainers swung the great doors open. Two of the

Guardsmen, one wearing the badges of an unarmed combat specialist, the other with the crossed rifles of an expert marksman, moved up to flank him as he stepped through the door.

The members of the Domi Council sat around an oval table, Matto de Terranin at the far end, the other great nobles along the sides. Liveried soldier-minores stood behind each chair, eyes blank with watching.

"Dan Keira," de Terranin began, "I bid you welcome to this meeting, but I must ask that you leave these men outside. It is against Convention to bring armed force—armed Imperial force—in the Council of the Domi."

Keira curbed the first three things that came to mind and said, "Your Grace, I know her late Majesty always brought a full Guard contingent; it was with difficulty that I persuaded General Doran to allow me to be escorted by only two." He advanced three steps, calculating his movement, and seated himself in the chair reserved for the emperor or his representative. He saw irritation in two of the faces, and admiration on a third, but he had moved quickly enough to forestall any protest. "Now, my Lords, I believe you've met to certify her late Majesty's will. What is your conclusion?"

He looked up and down the table. Desolin Hamm'tt was doing her best to hide a smile; amusement showed in her eyes. Nuriel de la Mar, Overlord of Oceanus and representative of that system in the place of his invalid mother, looked back to Keira, light glinting from the jewels embedded in his cheek. It was rumored that his Domus was very close to the de Terranins, that the two heirs had long ago come to some sort of understanding. Which was not surprising in itself, Keira thought, given that their systems are in the same sector, and together are the richest worlds in the Imperium. Of course, they'll cooperate.

Royd Lovell-Andriës, the Elector of Somewhere, sat at de la Mar's right hand, and as his eyes met Keira's he nodded fractionally, covering the gesture by adjusting a knob on the computer interface in front of him. Keira did not dare respond openly, but the promise of support was comforting. Still, he would need more than Somewhere's hold to win over the other Domi: Somewhere was an anomaly among the great systems, still not fully part of the Imperium. The Electorship was not hereditary to any one family, but were chosen from among the Talented of the three planets. The hereditary nobles would never follow Lovell-Andriës' lead.

The three new Domi lords—Santarem of Babylon, Channis of Hellmouth, and Xio-Sebastina of Mist—clustered together at Keira's left; he dismissed them with a glance. The new Domi—so-called because their lords were not members of the planet's original dynasty—were still heirs to divided worlds. Santarem and Xio-Sebastina would stay neutral, and Channis, though he might want to see the Renaults dragged down again, would never be able to win enough support among his own majores and land-minores to move against him. There were too many blood-feuds among the nobility. Keira permitted himself a small smile, knowing there was nothing he could do to win Channis's support, and saw the old man's eyes darken with anger.

Balint Ojeda, the Grand Duke of Castille, and his brother the Cardinal-Archbishop, primate of the Imperial Church, sat to either side of Matto de Terranin. Both Ojedas were angular, unattractive men, though the Duke's grim face was somewhat softened by large, nearsighted brown eyes. Luckily, their choice of seats had nothing to do with their choice of loyalties, Keira thought. Castille system was powerful, and the Church's influence, though only moral, could have great impact. The last of the Domi lords was Vasili Andros of the Barbaries.

He had little power of his own, but his system had long been allied with the de Terranins. His eyes were cold and watchful, and Keira realized with something of a shock that the Barbaries lord still hated him.

"Well, my Lords?" he said aloud. "I asked for your conclusion."

De Terranin said carefully, "We ... feel there should be more time for study before the Council reports its findings to the Eger."

"Then you've found some reason to contest the will?" Keira asked mildly.

"In the case of such a startling bequest, there's always reason to question," de Terranin answered.

"But you've no other reason to do so?" Keira asked. "The fingerprints are in order, of course, and the identi-scan that preceeds the tape?"

"Yes, your Majesty." Lovell-Andriës nodded quietly, ignoring the frowns directed at him.

"And the brain scan, the monitor that proves she was not acting under drugs or telepathic compulsion? These were in order?" Keira went on.

Again the Elector nodded.

Keira looked around ostentatiously. "Where are the Order priests who witnessed the will? Surely their testimony will decide this."

"They have not been interviewed," the Cardinal-Archbishop said.

"Indeed?"

The Grand Duke Ojeda said, with scholarly curiosity, "Do you say my brother is lying?"

De Terranin cut through the question. "Dan Keira, the Order has been contacted, and the witnesses are on their way. Of course, until they arrive, we can do nothing."

"Of course." Keira leaned back in his chair, though every muscle protested. "Your Grace, I'm sure only your concern for the affairs of the Imperium has made you speak with such unConventional discourtesy. However, I must remind you that, even if my inheritance is disputed, I am still noble, by the Eger's decree. It would be more courteous to address me by my proper title."

De Terranin raised an eyebrow. The gesture showed, more plainly than words, his contempt for an imperial pretender who relied on the title of made-minore to bolster his claim.

"It's no more than courtesy, my Lords," Hamm'tt said softly. She fixed her eyes on the Ojedas. "Surely the arbiters of Convention agree to that?"

It was neatly done, Keira thought, though he could not guess her motives. The Ojeda Domus kept rigidly to Convention, and had done so since their ancestor had betrayed the last of the Alexanders. They had still not buried that shame.

The Cardinal-Archbishop's mouth twitched, and the glance he directed at Hamm'tt was poisonous. His brother merely nodded, his face showing, if anything, only respect for a clever gambit. "Indeed, Lady," he said, "the point is well taken."

Andros opened his mouth to say something, but at a signal from de Terranin he kept silent. De Terranin spread his hands. "We would not wish to give even the appearance of acting against Convention. I trust my Lord will forgive my preoccupation?"

Keira matched the light irony of his tone. "Certainly, your Grace." He had won the first skirmish, but he was far from safe yet. The real test would come when the Order priests arrived—and not even Talent was reliable in predicting the Order. The Order—there were no other neo-monastic organizations in the Imperium—had been the first to define and train Talent to serve the majores, and to articulate Convention to serve Talent. They knew more about Talent and related psionics than any other human beings, and guarded those secrets jealously. The earliest emperors had maneuvered them into the Imperial Church in a vain attempt to bring them under imperial control, and had only made them more independent, giving them the protection of clerical rank. Now, untouchable, they guarded the nobles' secrets as well as their own, and gave judgment in matters of Convention. They were said to be incorruptible, but Keira had learned early that nothing was that any longer.

The room lapsed into sudden silence, broken only by the occasional click of fingers on the keys of computer links. Keira, still leaning back lazily, regarded the majores from under lowered eyelids, taking stock. These were the most powerful nobles in the Imperium, and three of them—de Terranin, Andros, and Channis—were firmly against him. That was balanced by Lovell-Andriës, but he still needed the support of one of the uncommitted lords. He looked carefully at them—de la Mar, Hamm'tt, the Ojedas, Santarem, and Xio-Sebastina. The old Domi—Ojeda, Hamm'tt, de la Mar—were the only ones who really mattered.

I've no reason to think that any of those three like me, he thought, and I've given them no reason, in ten years, to dislike me. Except, of course, that the Church cannot approve of me, since Oriana gave me no status, and my promotion was unConventional. Which means that the Ojedas—either one—will be hard to persuade despite the evidence of Talent. Hamm'tt has always kept her own counsel, and I will work on her. And as for de la Mar. . . . If only his mother were well enough to come to Avalon. I liked the old woman, and I think she trusted me, as much as a majore ever trusts a favorite. But Nuriel will side with the de Terranins, will help them no matter what his mother orders.

The overhead speaker chimed once, and everyone jumped. Keira flushed at his reaction, and saw Lovell-Andriës trying to hide a sheepish grin. De

Terranin sighed and said, pitching his voice to carry to the pickups in the ceiling, "Yes?"

"Your Grace, the representatives of the Order request admittance."

"Send them in," Keira said. In spite of himself, his back tensed as the door slid open. If the de Terranins had planned an attack now, if the Order had been corrupted . . . . But there was no hiss of flame, only the heavy rustling of priests' robes as the Order's people entered the room.

"I ask your pardon, your Majesty, for the delay," said the spokesman, a tall woman in the shapeless grey robes of the Order. "And yours also, my Lords. The Governor-General wished to certify the evidence himself."

Keira allowed his eyes to flicker closed, one concession to his relief. Whatever the real reason for the delay—and for all he knew, the priest's explanation was genuine—the Order was acknowledging him. "Thank you, Sister," he said. "I am certain there could be no quibbling over your testimony."

De Terranin swallowed hard, and Keira wondered again if there had been some conspiracy. "Sister, we are grateful for your presence. Tell us what you know of her late Majesty's will."

The woman bowed, though not as deeply as before. "Your Grace, I am Valma. This is Brother Akiva. Together we witnessed the will." She reached into the wide sleeves of her robe and brought out a small tape cartridge, shimmering from blue to red to black even in the indirect lighting. "The Governor General sends this to certify that we are indeed the persons named as witnesses by her late Majesty, and to say that the Order will stand behind our testimony."

"Thank you, Sister," de Terranin said. His mouth twisted bitterly, and he added, "If the witnesses would view the tape?"

The Order priests bowed silently. At de Terranin's

gesture, his minore, who had been standing impassively throughout the meeting, touched buttons on the board hanging from his belt. The lights dimmed, and a small holoprojector rose from the center of the table. De Terranin lifted the tape that had lain beside his personal viewer for the entire meeting and displayed it ceremoniously. "My Lords. Her Majesty's will."

He inserted it into the machine and the lights went out. A glowing fog formed on the small table of the projector, then coalesced into a new shape. The empress, small and brown, stockily built, leaned on her cane and glared into the cameras. By a trick of the projection, it seemed that the empress was looking directly at her former favorite, and Keira winced. The portraits in the Imperial Quarters were bad enough, but the holotape, made only a few weeks before Oriana's death, was almost too painful to watch.

"I hope Dan Keira will not be too upset," Andros said spitefully, and the words helped to steady Keira. He ignored the gesturing figure, already showing the last signs of the disease that killed her, and concentrated on the telltales at the bottom of the projection. The harsh voice droned on, gasping now and again for breath as Oriana misjudged the length of a ceremonial phrase, and Keira contrived to ignore the words as well. Only the tone of voice, the anger at the failing body and the lack of Talent that forced her to rely on a favorite rather than her own skills, was too familiar to push away. The tape ended at last, and the minore brought up the lights again.

"Well, Sister?" de Terranin asked.

Both priests nodded, and Akiva said, "It's the tape we saw made, your Grace."

"You testify that these are your signatures and seals, here on the tape?" de Terranin pursued, but

his eyes showed that he had already admitted his
defeat.

Akiva examined the cartridge closely, then passed
it to the woman. She said, "We both so testify."

"And you see no signs of change? Nor were there
any signs of interference, mental or physical, when
the tape was made?"

Akiva shook his head, and the woman said softly,
"This is the legitimate will, made under the controlled conditions demanded by Convention and
the Charters, while her late Majesty was sound
and uninfluenced in mind."

De Terranin turned to the other nobles. "My
Lords, you have heard the testimony of the Order.
Is there anyone who would deny the will?"

"Not the will," Andros said. His eyes were angry,
and one hand was out of sight beneath the table.
"But could she—her Majesty—expect this to be
binding?"

"That is not a question for *this* meeting," Keira
said, stressing the word "this". "My Lords, you
met to certify the will. Can you deny the legality of
my claim?" He waited until each had shaken his
head, staring at de la Mar until he moved with the
rest, and continued, "Unless there is another claim
to be judged, my Lords, I think this meeting is at
an end. My Lord de Terranin. As Speaker, will you
commit yourself to informing the Eger Assembled
of the Domi's decision?"

De Terranin's eyes sparked with rage, but he
kept his face impassive. "I will do so," he answered,
biting off each word. Keira waited; the formula
stated there should be more. De Terranin mastered himself, and continued, "And so I give my
Oath, that you are a candidate of the Council."

"Thank you, your Grace," Keira said. He had de
Terranin, at least temporarily. The Duke would be
unable to support anyone else until the Domi Council could be persuaded to acknowledge another's

claim. "My Lords." He rose, collecting his Guards
with a look, and stalked from the room. After a
second's hesitation, Lovell-Andriës followed him.
Santarem and Xio-Sebastina stood as well, and
they and the grey-robed priests left together.

As the door closed behind them, Hamm'tt smiled
to herself and leaned back in her chair. It had been
a neat bit of maneuvering, she thought, but Keira
had had help from the Order—something de Terranin had not expected, either. She filed that knowledge for later evaluation. But that mattered less
than what de Terranin would do now. She glanced
around the circle, broken now by the departure of
the three majores. They had no quorum, and de
Terranin could not be sure enough of himself to
try to get himself—or, more probably, his son and
heir Edouard—named as a second legitimate candidate. By the same token, of course, she could not
press her own claim, but she had not intended to
do so—yet. In spite of herself, she sighed gently. A
hundred years ago, two hundred years ago, it would
have been easy: under the old interpretation of
Convention, the claimant emperor was obliged to
declared a challenge period—a week, two weeks,
perhaps even longer—during which every noble
had the right to attack the claimant, in reality or
simulation, without fear of reprisal, win or lose.
But those days were long past, the challenge no
longer a Conventional part of the interregnum between death of the old ruler and the coronation of
the new. She would have to wait to state her claim
until she could collect support on the Domi Council.

"That bastard," Andros said suddenly, drawing
Hamm'tt back to reality. "Shabai!"

The Cardinal-Archbishop looked down his nose
at the Barbaries Lord. "You should not speak so.
We can none of us judge another."

Andros bit back a retort—there was an audible

snap of teeth—and said directly to de Terranin, "You can't let him be crowned."

"His claim must be acknowledged," de Terranin said heavily. "The will has been proved."

"But it's not right he should be emperor, with no blood claim, and only half a name to him. I remember him a sailworker on Low Barbary, and Oriana's gigolo after, and now I'm to say 'Majesty' to him? It's not to be borne." Andros checked, glanced around, and seemed to come to some resolve. "I warn you, there are some who won't bear it."

There was a moment's hesitation. Hamm'tt glanced around quickly, saw her own wariness reflected in the others' faces. De Terranin's oblique move had been well made, but he would get no support yet, either.

"That's enough, Vasili," de Terranin said. "I tell you now that neither I nor this Council would countenance such an action."

Andros bridled. "There would be no Convention broken, just a challenge—"

"No." De Terranin was frowning deeply.

Andros has gone further than Matto wanted, Hamm'tt realized suddenly. *That last wasn't planned—it makes too clear how things stand between the two Domi.* Her lip curled slightly. *As if everyone didn't know that the richest system was backing the promising colonies.*

De la Mar said, "My Lord, I would hate to think that you would break Convention."

"I would not," Andros protested. "My Lord, I give you my word that any action taken by me would come within the bounds of Convention."

"See that it is," de la Mar said.

Andros stood quickly, hand slipping beneath his formal coat. "How dare you—"

"Enough!" Hamm'tt shot to her feet. "This is the Council of the Domi, my Lords. Lord Vasili,

Overlord Nuriel, this does not serve either of your Domi."

"Our work is done," Ojeda observed. "Perhaps we should adjourn."

De Terranin nodded frostily. "I agree. I here declare this meeting ended."

The imperial party entered the Eger Hall with all the pomp Doran could provide, though Keira had forbidden the use of any of the imperial panoply. Thus there were neither trumpets nor serbots to announce him, but the slam of ceremonial spears, the only visible weapons carried by the Guard in these Convention-protected areas, was enough to make his presence felt. Keira, his eyes fixed on the dais where the throne stood empty, felt the eyes of the nobility on him, majore and minore alike straining their Talents to deduce their place in the game. His own Talent responded, reaching out to look for the connections he knew must be there, the patterns of alliance and interest and enmity and love that webbed the Hall.

The walk to the dais seemed endless, but he did not allow himself to look at the faces surrounding him until he mounted the three steps and stood at the throne's right hand. Gauging the gesture, he let his hand rest lightly on its arm. The hundred, hundred and fifty faces staring back at him did not lose their expressions of watchful reserve, but to his Talent it was as though a murmur rose from the crowd. A few patterns showed starkly, as though in a flash of lightning, but there was not enough to read completely. He waited.

Doran had taken his traditional place behind and to the left of the throne. Now he stepped forward and slammed the butt of his spear against the sounding plate. The Hall echoed to the hollow crash. "My Lords of the Imperium, the Eger is met. Speak now." He had shorn the traditional formula of its final phrase: to have added "in the Emperor's name" would only have alienated potential support.

Matto de Terranin, seated at the Speaker's console in the first rank of the assembly, rose slowly to his feet. His family was present in force, Keira noted, as he knew the Duke had wanted him to notice. The Heir, the Overlord Edouard, was there, and beside him was his younger sister and her husband, young Lovell. Lovell's presence was the main message, Keira knew; he was in the position to undercut the support his cousin Lovell-Andriës could provide. Keira inclined his head in grave acknowledgement, and was rewarded with a jerky nod.

"Lord," de Terranin began, "and Lords of the Imperium. The Domi Council has seen her late Majesty's will, and offer you our conclusions. The terms of the will are as follows . . . ."

His voice droned on, a lawyer's precision coloring it, but Keira was only half listening. His Talent probed without success at the assembly; the rest of his mind was caught in memory. He had never spoken before the Eger himself, of course, but he had once dictated Oriana's address. The troubles on the MarchWorlds had broken out again, over taxes, but this time the Barbaries' anomalous status had become an issue, changing the stakes from a Treasury balance to the Imperium's survival. The MarchWorlders, led by Vasili Andros, newly come into the Lordship of the Barbaries, had forced the question before the Eger despite everything he had been able to do to stop them. Oriana alone could never have handled the debate; her temper would have betrayed her before the first hour had passed, and there would have been war. I honor your memory, Oriana, Keira thought, you admitted that. You let me deck you out in the imperial jewels, the Old Regalia that holds the little transmitter and the earrings that let me speak to you, and you yourself put the microphone around my neck. I dictated every word you said, that day, and we stopped the war. He had watched on the public holochannels, whispering into the filament mike, as grudgingly the Eger had agreed to Oriana's suggestions, and then, as solution and recompense became fully clear, they had stood to hail their empress. Oriana had been delighted, even as she had hated knowing that she herself had not earned it.

The memory sparked another train of thought, and Keira glanced toward the gallery that ringed the rear of the Hall. As he had known they would be, the commoners' crews were there, recording the assembly for the public holochannels. He fixed their presence in his mind, another variable that he would have to manipulate, and looked away. He could judge his success with the commoners later, when he had time to find out the odds the public bookmakers were giving.

De Terranin stopped speaking, and the corner of Keira's mind that had been monitoring the speech prodded him out of his reverie. He hesitated, reviewing the Grand Duke's words—he had done little more than state that the Domi Council accepted the will as a genuine expression of Oriana's wishes—and then lifted one hand in an imperial gesture.

"Lords of the Imperium, you have heard the Council's conclusions. They have accepted that I am a Renault, by blood and birth, and that her late Majesty did intend for me and no other to follow her."

He saw the impassivity of some of the faces begin to fade, and his Talent began to trace some of the patterns in the crowd. He went on, choosing his words with care and with Talent, fitting them to the patterns he saw, to build bridges between friends, to buffer enemies from each other, to convince each one that he, Keira, and only he, could control the Imperium. Talent noted the connections: de Terranin and his allies; Lovell, who could negate the support of Somewhere's Elector; the lesser majores of Verii Mir; Nuriel de la Mar, hampered by his status as his mother's representative. A looser web of land-minores, mostly from the Federal borders, wove through the back of the Hall; they might or might not support the de Terranins, but certainly would not support an ex-favorite. Hamm'tt and Ojeda sat quietly, linked only to their vassals, waiting. Lovell-Andriës seemed much alone, but Keira knew his improbable ties to the lower minores and the merchant classes.

Talent turned him to the other nobles who shared that tie, the old Renault allies from Hellmouth and Mist. Channis of Hellmouth seemed already diminished, the majores falling away from him, and Keira could sense the old man's sick hatred of the Renaults, returning from the dead just when it seemed that Channis could finally control his own world. He needed the Hellmouth majores—Elorin, Gunner, Ransom-of-An-Deth and Ransom-of-Hoybilai, Slavik, and perhaps even Castellar of Hell. He could win them and shock the rest out of waiting, with a single, simple move.

"But there will always be those who doubt my right," he went on, Talent-born intuition shaping easily into words, "no matter how poor their own claim. To you I offer a challenge. I declare interregnum on the old, the strictly Conventional terms. You have three days to challenge me, winner take all. Answer me who dares!"

He had expected surprise—it had been generations since any imperial candidate had openly invited challenge—but the sudden outcry startled him. Edouard de Terranin shot to his feet, shouting through the noise, "I accept, Dan Keira. Name the time."

Others echoed him, Ojeda raising a languid hand until he could attract Keira's attention, the rest baying their answers. St. George stood, heavy and martial—he was one of de Terranin's vassals, Keira thought, so who was this challenge from?—and he was followed by a block of land-minores. Ayakawa was among them, and she was dangerous.

Keira waited until the first burst of noise had died away. "Convention declares that such challenges shall be fought in simulation, to spare the nobility's lives for more important tasks. Does anyone wish to waive that right?" No one did, and Keira did not bother to hide his smile. If a noble "died" in simulation, it meant merely that he was obliged to obey the victor. If an ex-favorite should "die" in a game, his actual death was sure to follow, and very quickly. "Good enough." He searched the faces in front of him until he found the Order's representative and pointed to him. "Brother, will the Order certify the challenge tapes and oversee the combat?"

The grey robed man rose slowly, light spearing down from the balconies to record him on the multiple tapes of the holo-cameras. Keira risked a second glance at the commoners, and was gratified by the excitement there.

"Yes, your Majesty, we will oversee." The priest's tone implied that there had been no need to ask: such matters had always been the Order's business and always would be.

"Thank you, Brother." Keira turned slowly, found Ayakawa among the rear ranks. "You, Ayakawa, you challenged *en masse*. Do you wish to fight so?"

"Yes." She did not bother with any title.

"Then to even the odds against you, you may fight last. You of the majores can decide among yourselves the order of your challenges and inform

me. We have met, Lords of the Imperium. You
may go." Without waiting for any response, he
swept from the dais, the Guards falling into position around him. Only when he reached the door
did the noise blaze up again behind him.

In her own quarters in the majores' wing of the
Palace, Desolin Hamm'tt dismissed her attendants,
minores and serbots alike, and locked the door of
her workroom behind her. Only then did she let
herself collapse into the specially-built chair, and
reach to loosen the spiral braces. The too-familiar
pressure eased, and she touched the lever that
moved the chair closer to the simulations console.
She flipped the switches activating the linked
machines, but when the last, largest screen came
to life she did not reach for the keyboard. Instead,
she leaned back against the heavy pillows, staring
at the unlit wallscreens.

I don't trust it when things work out so neatly,
she thought. This was the chance she had been
waiting for, the chance to oppose Keira without
having to risk breaking Convention in war. But it's
too easy. She sighed again, and reached for the
keyboard, wondering what Keira had intended to
gain. Support from the ultraConventional, she
thought. No, probably not; he must know he'd
never get them. Maybe the border worlds? Well, it
didn't matter now. She typed a code phrase into
the main computer, then turned to the research
console and began calling up files from the University records. A third keyboard, tied directly to the
master machine in the basement of the House of
the Gordiae, the gaming house she patronized in
Government Center, provided both backgrounds
and the solitaire control program.

The last data fed into the main system, and she
settled to work. She generated a fleet simulation,
ships from her own worlds against ships from

Hellmouth, but tested it for less than an hour before rejecting it as too simple. A realtime, realistic scenario was discarded almost as soon as she had generated it. Over the next three hours, she created perhaps half a dozen simulations, and rejected all but two as utterly unworkable. The two that remained were marginal at best, and, after another two hours' work, it was clear that only one had a chance of beating Keira. And even that was not good. She ran the program a final time, knowing that she had to have at least a thirty-point victory margin to compensate for unknown factors and the inevitable imperfections in the program that projected Keira's actions. Once again, the margin was less than fifteen points.

Frowning, she tightened her braces again and stood, wincing at the stiffness. She had intended to turn on the wallscreens, but she stopped instead at the end of the bank of computers, reaching for the statue that stood just above the keyboard. El Nath was famous for its woodwork, and the statue was remarkable even by their high standards. It was the figure of a slender girl, carved from jeta, the stone-hard wood of the islands—a black girl armed with a man's black weapons, back taut with pride. The face was her own. She touched the wood, velvet smooth beneath her fingers. It had been her father's last gift, his dream of her, and she kept it even though she was not the Duke he had been, or had wanted.

Her eyes went from the statue to the computer screen, avoiding her father's portrait. The screen still displayed its figures, and she crossed the room to shut it off. But her hand hesitated over the switch, and she found herself scanning the numbers one more time, hoping to see some way around them. Damn it all, she thought, I'd make a good emperor, maybe even a better one than Keira. And at least I'd make him a valuable ally, well worth rewarding—maybe even with the Chancellorship, and to hell with Matto de Terranin. Then the answer hit her with the force of the lightning that struck the Great Mountain by Kaula Town. Her hands shaking a little, she fed the new data into the computer, too eager to sit down. The results flashed on the screen and, rough as they were, she grinned. This plan would work, she knew with Talent as well as from the machine.

"I have him," she said aloud. If Keira survived the challenges he's called down on himself, she would make her offer: her support, ships and men and the wealth of her Domus, in exchange for the Chancellorship, and full marriage between them to seal the bargain. Oh, the plan wasn't perfect yet, and there were rough edges that she would have to smooth over—marriage between two lords of Domi, much less between a Domi lord and an emperor, was unusual, for one thing, but not completely unprecedented. She smiled at the screen, where three of those precedents were listed in the Heralds' drastically abbreviated notation. Two of them had been made by Renaults. "I've got you now," she said again, and settled to the long job of refining her plan.

Chapter 6

The official challenges arrived early the next morning, before Keira had finished his meager breakfast. The Guard sergeant, the same dark woman who had been on duty the night of Oriana's death, escorted a slender woman in severe livery into the receiving room, announcing, "Kypria Ojeda, Overlord of Castille System."

Keira, only just dressed, momentarily regretted allowing Ojeda immediate entrance, but he gestured for her to be seated. His other hand stayed on his half-empty coffee cup: he was not about to let his one vice grow cold while he fenced with the nobility. "Please, be seated, Overlord Kypria. Will you take breakfast with me?"

"Thank you, I have eaten." Her tone implied that she had been up for hours already. Keira repressed a frown and studied her more closely. The Ojeda Dukes had not come to Avalon often during the previous reigns, the Grand Duke having stated publicly many times that the growing industries of his worlds required all his attention, and his vassals followed his example. Perhaps the excuse was real—it was true that new industries were being created, unConventionally under majore supervision, in the MarchWorld systems—but it seemed more likely that the Grand Duke preferred to stay out of politics, out of harm's way. Keira was still surprised that Balint had accepted the challenge. Kypria, Balint's heir, had her father's stern, hard-planed face, but lacked the mild eyes that warmed the man's ugly countenance. In compensation, she had a precarious beauty that seemed only to exist because she was not aware that she could be unattractive: a woman to watch closely, as the Duke grew older.

"Be seated, Overlord," Keira repeated.

Kypria shook her head. "Thank you," she said, and hesitated just noticeably before adding, "my Lord. I am here on a matter of Convention. Those who have accepted your challenge have elected me to bring you the respondent tapes." She dug into a purse that swung from her belt. The sergeant tensed, relaxing only when the Overlord brought out a handful of tape cartridges. "These have been certified by the Senior of the Order on Avalon."

Keira accepted the tapes, noting the double marks, the Order's soaring bird superimposed on the marks of the nobles' seals. The cartridges shimmered oddly where the Order's seal had been placed, guaranteeing their authenticity.

"I was also to inform you of the order of the combats," Kypria went on. "It was decided that my father the Grand Duke would fight first, as his is only a simple scenario, and then the Count of Rohan, followed by the Overlord of Verii Mir. The minores agreed that they would fight last."

"That is perfectly acceptable," Keira said gravely.

"I was also asked to confirm that the duels could take place on the third day," Kypria went on, and Keira nodded. "And I will need the names of your seconds."

I am slow this morning, Keira thought. "General Doran, Ivor Doran min-Renault, will be one," he said, "and the Elector of Somewhere." He did not think Lovell-Andriës would refuse—and it was not a catastrophe if he did—but he did not like to think what the Elector's help could cost him.

"I will inform their lordships," Kypria said. "My

father's seconds will be myself and the Lord of
Kusan Plains. I fear I do not know the others'."

"Surely the names are on the tapes?" Keira asked.

"It is Conventional to include them," Kypria
said primly.

"Is there anything else?" Keira asked, sharply.
The Ojeda heir, with her meaningless games, and
the worthless but infuriating victory she had just
scored, irritated him intensely.

"No, my Lord." The Overlord bowed, more deeply
than she would bow to a made-minore, but not as
deeply as to an emperor. The Ojedas were expert
in the nuances of protocol, of the millimetric shad-
ing that made the difference between respect and
insult. "If I may go now, my Lord?"

"You have leave." Keira touched the controls
hidden in the chair arm, then waited while the
doors closed behind her. The tapes were heavy in
his other hand. Four simulations in a single day
would be tiring, but he knew his Talent could
compensate. It was not his Talent that worried
him. It was ironic, he thought, that unlike most
nobles, majore or minore, he had learned to wield
his Talent in real-world situations, rather than in
simulation. And now his real-world fate depended
on the outcome of the sims. He was not completely
inexperienced in simulations play, of course; on
the other hand, he had never been able to join one
of the gaming clubs—to do so would have betrayed
his Talent as a majore's—and was unfamiliar with
the subtler tricks that could be programmed into a
game. The Order would eliminate anything blatantly unfair, but his Talent would have seen any
such distortion in the pattern of the game-world.
What he needed now was someone to check his
analysis, someone who frequented the clubs and
was highly enough rated to counterbalance St.
George's status as Magus of the Inner Circle. Or
Edouard de Terranin's place on the Board of Direc-

tors of the First Sector Gaming Society. Which meant Japhet.

He looked up, meeting the sergeant's quizzical eyes. They were the only living things in her professionally discreet face. "Sergeant—Lilika, isn't it?"

"Yes, Majesty. Anj Lilika min-Renault."

"Have the duty Herald locate Japhet—his code should be in the system, if you don't know it—and then I want gaming equipment."

"Yes, Majesty." Her face did not change, even though he knew that she must have recognized the name. Japhet was one of the most notorious of the Palace courtesans, a man who had made his fortune in any number of noble beds, and then lost and won it back again a dozen times in the gaming clubs. He was a commoner, unTalented under the Conventional definition of Talent, but the modifying, patterning programs provided adequate compensation. And he knew the games.

Lilika bent over the locater phone, speaking quietly into it, then sent the suite's serbots for the gaming tables. "Will you want AP helmets, Majesty?"

"No, I don't think that will be necessary," Keira answered. Or very practical, either, in a room not designed for such games. There were too many possible distractions to break the helmet's illusions: practice under those conditions would be worse than useless.

"I'm having the serbots set up in the inner room," Lilika said, "if that pleases your Majesty."

Keira nodded, still absently juggling the heavy tape cartridges, and set palm to the door that led into the emperor's personal rooms. The serbots were still shifting the equipment, pulling the players' consoles to opposite ends of the room, setting the simple projection plate in the center, opposite the judge's table and its overrides. The other furniture, heavy first Federal revival work, overlaid with gilding and stones in the ornate

Dresdener style Oriana had loved, had been pushed against the walls, out of the way. They nagged at his conscience: he did not care for the style, and would have them removed, but it hurt to think of doing it. . . . Oriana's portrait, a smaller version of the life-sized panel in the receiving room—there were similar portraits in every room of the Quarters—seemed to sneer at him, and he put those thoughts firmly aside.

The serbots had finished setting up the equipment, and vanished back into the storage wells. Settling himself at the judge's table, Keira broke the seals on the first tape, St. George's, blue with a silver dragon embossed on the smooth plastic, and fed it into the machine. The outline unreeled on the screen, and he frowned, watching. As he had expected, the Count of Rohan had specified a full-scale simulation, using the AP helmets, but the setting had been chosen to be as disconcerting as possible. St. George was a member of the Sorcerer's Guild, and he had followed their usual practice, choosing a world that used magic in place of normal science. There was a complicated political/historical summary, and Keira skimmed through that. St. George was using a world with which he was familiar, in which he had set other games, and that would give him a real advantage. But the situation itself seemed standard enough: war between barbarians and city-dwelling wizards, with St. George playing the barbarian side. The outline continued with a technical summary of the rules that would govern the wizards' special powers. Keira read through them, but decided to wait until Japhet arrived before making any decisions.

As though the thought had conjured him, a Guardsman's voice sounded in the receiving room. "Your Majesty, Dan Japhet is here."

Keira heard Lilika answer, and a moment later the door slid fully back.

"Keira?"

"Dan Japhet, your Majesty," Lilika said, following him in.

"Your Majesty, I should say now," Japhet said. "I beg your pardon."

Keira pushed himself away from the judge's console. "Of course. Come and take a look at these."

"Game tapes?" Japhet came cautiously forward, leaned over Keira's shoulder as the other rewound the tape.

"It's interesting," Japhet said at last. "You play the wizard-king."

"What else?" Keira answered. "How does it look to you?"

Japhet glanced warily at him. "It seems perfectly straight-forward, your Majesty. It's a common Sorceror's game; I've played in that world."

"Good." Keira reached for the rewind button, hit it, then waited for the tape to be ejected. He picked up the next tape, this one purple with the Ojeda tower stamped into it. As he slipped it into the machine, he said, "I need your help."

"How may I serve your Majesty?"

"I want help choosing the input factors for these games, and figuring out the possible biases. And finally, I need someone to give me some practice." Keira looked up, but Japhet's face was shuttered, presenting only his official and correct emotions. He wished that he knew the correct word, the key that would break through the other's reserve and return them to the easy friendship of a few days ago. . . . And then he knew. "Here, pull up a chair. Do you want to take notes?"

Japhet did as he was told, but declined the offer of a scratch pad. He bent close to the screen, one hand resting on the keys of a notewriter. Keira, watching out of the corner of his eye, his attention only half on the screen, kept his tone casual, and was relieved to see the lines of tension fade from the other's face. By the end of the first hour, Japhet had shed his formal manners along with his loose coat, and the two men were working easily together.

"All right," Keira said at last. "Is that everything?"

Japhet scanned his screen. "Did you specify the power level of the screens—oh, yes, I'm sorry. It's in."

Keira nodded. "So Ojeda challenges first, yes? Then St. George, then Edouard, and finally the minores."

Japhet nodded. "Yes, Thorsson, Devereux, Frehalt, Ayakawa, and Nayati. Who has the blood?"

"Ayakawa, through the Alexanders. And she could breed majore children, if she married right." Keira smiled. "I doubt, however, that she could make her own claim stick. Now. Ojeda wants a standard sim, a straight fleet action, run out of the control panels with a judge to monitor. St. George and Edouard both want full-scale sims, with AP helmets and illusory settings, and agree to give the judge full control of the scenario. St. George wants a Sorcerors' sim, on Verii Mir, and Edouard wants a scoop-ship race, through the old Oceanan courses."

He grinned, and caught Japhet's sympathetic nod. It had been ten years, or longer, since he had last flown any small ship, except in simulation. A full-scale sim would not be the same as space, but it would be the closest he was going to get. Edouard was trying to be clever there, he thought. The Overlord was gambling that his opponent would become overconfident, would trust too much in the Renaults' legendary shiphandling abilities.

"And the last is a simple ship-to-ship," Japhet said. "Have you rechecked the tapes?"

"Yes." Keira reached for them, then hesitated. He had no personal seal—a minore, particularly a made-minore favorite, was not allowed one—and he did not want to use Oriana's crowned tree and stars. Well, they would have to go to the Order blank-sealed. He pulled the tab on each tape, and quickly set his thumb on the soft plastic. It would do for now. "Lilika. Give these to the duty Herald, and see that they're sent to the Order House in Government Center."

That ended his Conventional obligations: the Order, and his opponents, would receive the tapes specifying the attributes of the various parts he would play. He was ready now to begin the game.

Chapter 7

The Order had coopted The House of the Gordiae, the oldest of the gaming societies on Avalon, and one to which none of the combatants belonged, for the four duels. Doran, as Keira's second, protested bitterly—The House of the Gordiae was outside the protected quarters of the Palace, across the Narrow Straits in Government Center—but both the Order and the other seconds had remained adamant. So it was that on the morning of the duel that Keira found himself wedged between Guardsmen in the rear compartment of his aircraft, circling over the Straits while the first of the three chase units landed at the main field behind Government Center. The other two hovered just above and behind the imperial craft, just visible as white dots against the brassy clouds.

The field was declared safe at last, and the three ships descended, following the line of the coast and then cutting west along the edge of the Table Mountains, rather than passing over the city. Keira, knowing the delays this would cause in commercial flights, wondered if all the precautions were really necessary. It seemed somewhat premature to conceal soldier-minores, or, just conceivably, Assassins and missiles in the city, breaking Convention to do so, when four different nobles had a perfectly Conventional chance to kill him that morning. It would be time enough to be careful after he'd won. If he won . . . he touched a piece of decorative panelling for luck, hoping it was real wood.

The craft landed easily on the cleared field, followed almost to ground level by the escort units, and taxied slowly along the treated concrete until it finally drifted to a stop in front of a secondary terminal. A groundcar, the passenger compartment covered with an armorglass dome that gleamed faintly gold with shield-fire, stood waiting, flanked by Guardsmen armed with blastrifles. The shields flickered and died. Keira was hustled out of the craft and into the groundcar, and then the shields sprang back into place. Doran breathed an audible sigh of relief as the car rumbled out of the port and onto the ramp leading to the elevated driveways.

Only majores and a few businesses were allowed to operate groundcars within the city limits, and Keira's machine was made doubly conspicuous by the imperial tree and stars stenciled on every available surface. Commoners and nobles alike stared avidly from the sidewalks and malls. Keira ignored them, watching the buildings that surrounded him. The elevated driveway gave a magnificent view of the city, and it had been a long time since he had been outside the Palace, free of the presence of the empress and the entire court. In spite of the duel ahead, he found himself looking for the familiar landmarks: the Guild Row, for one, just flashing by beneath the car. The identical Old Federal buildings could be distinguished from each other only by the banners of the individual Guilds above each set of white-painted steps. A fugitive glint of sunlight lit momentarily the clear plastis dome of the old City Hall, now the commons' court; under the Federal governors, it had controlled traffic for the entire sector.

Beyond the sturdy buildings of the Old City, dating from Avalon's days as a sector capital, rose the stubby towers that dated from the Great Council War and the interregnum governments that had preceded the Imperium. They were ugly buildings—slit-windowed, functional fortresses—designed to withstand both the Council and any local rebellions. Beyond them, the city opened up a little, a few lacy spires surrounded by the varied greens of parkland marking major or land-minore villas. These were interspersed with blocks of cheaper housing. Keira looked for the Tiberian Park, and found it by the weak lights of the imported Faber's Trees, but he could not see the low-slung building at its center that housed the Federal Embassy.

The groundcar slowed a little, and turned onto a ramp leading off the driveway. A tall, windowless building cut off his view of the city before he could look for the other embassies, and Keira saw more faces staring down from the greenhouse at its top. The car turned onto the mall below the driveway, rattling over the uneven paving, and pulled to a stop at the door of a pink-stone building, the garish color of the local stone only slightly mellowed by the years. It was an old building—Keira shuddered to think what the color must have been like when it was first constructed—probably dating from the colonial period, and there was no sign over the door. Then he looked more closely, and saw the tiny, intricately woven golden knot placed in the very center of the door panel.

The door folded in on itself then, opening a well-lighted passage into the building. At its mouth stood three figures, flanked by the hovering globes of serbots. The central figure, a tall, androgynous person swathed in the Order's grey robes, bowed deeply. Doran frowned, and reached for the switch that controlled the outside speakers.

"—your Majesty to The House of the Gordiae. I have been sent by the Governor General to oversee the combats. My name is Ahira Forster; I am priest and gamesmaster." The voice was a woman's, as was the thin hand that emerged from the folds of the sleeve and gestured gracefully to the left-hand serbot. "This unit will escort you to the rooms reserved for your party, and from thence to the sim tank."

"Thank you in the emperor's name," Doran said, and cut the speakers before he began giving orders to his men. Keira narrowed his eyes, trying to read the livery badges that dangled above the shirt pockets of the technicians flanking the priest, but he could only make out the Order's double moon, shadowy disk poised in the brighter crescent, worn by the left-hand tech. Which meant that the other was probably a tech employed by The House, he thought. He could not resist sneaking a look as he went into the building. As he had expected, a gold knot dangled from the man's pocket flap.

The serbot, flanked by watchful Guards, led the way through a maze of identical narrow corridors, then up a series of ramps, and finally stopped in front of an open door. The Guards darted inside even as the serbot announced, "My Lord's rooms."

Keira shifted position a little to see past the shoulder of the machine. The rooms seemed small, with heavy table and chairs, and a miniature gaming table in one corner. There were no windows, but an unlit viewscreen hung above the table. Doran, with an apologetic murmur, pushed past to inspect; he returned and issued quick orders that sent most of the Guards scurrying to take up positions inside the room or along the corridor outside. Keira was left with only three Guards, and Lovell-Andriës and Doran as seconds, for an escort.

"Is my Lord satisfied?" the serbot asked. Its vocalization was not good; only the order of the words distinguished its question from its statement.

"Yes," Keira said.

"Will my Lord follow me to the lobby, and from there to the tank?"

"Lead on."

The serbot rose gently on its antigravs, then rotated its body so that its main sensors pointed directly down the corridor. A hiss of compressed air sent it floating easily along the carpeted hall. Keira followed it, aware both of the Guards at his back, and of the fact that there were only four of them. The serbot led them down a spiralling ramp, past silk-sheathed walls decorated with Delrwa sketches of famous gamesmen, and then, with startling suddenness, they were in the lobby.

The House of the Gordiae had spared no expense in decorating their building. The carpet strips were outrageously thick, and the blond-and-mahogany parquet was made of real wood. The tables, the sort of small-scale gaming machines that rich commoners bought their children, were nevertheless the best models. Looking at the display, Keira had no doubt that the gilding that edged the doors and circled the ceiling was real as well. The others were waiting for him in the center of the room.

He saw Forster first, her grey robes remarkable in the middle of the vivid livery colors surrounding her. At her elbow stood Desolin Hamm'tt, wearing not her own red and gold but a creamy tunic and wide, dark brown trousers. Her simple coronet bore a pattern of intricate knots. What is she doing here? he wondered, nodding with all the calm he could muster to the Ojeda party waiting on the opposite side of the room. Hamm'tt didn't challenge me—and I was sure she was not going to—but. . . . He shook the thought away, trying to ignore his Talent as it flared to life, seeking some pattern in which Hamm'tt presented an active danger.

Forster bowed, as did Hamm'tt, though the Grand Duke's bow was shallower. "Welcome, my lords combatant," the priest said. "As I told you both, I am here under the Governor General's seal to oversee these games. Her Grace, as Presiding Secretary of The House of the Gordiae, will also oversee, though only I will have powers of intervention. Is that acceptable to you, my Lords?"

"Yes," Ojeda said, without hesitation.

I should have known that Hamm'tt was more than a member here, Keira thought. I should have checked that, or had the Heralds inform me of relevant information. Talent seized the face, juggled it deftly, and fitted it into the pattern as more than coincidence, but not actively dangerous. "I have no objection," he said.

"Excellent. If the lords combatant and their seconds would follow me to the chamber?" Without waiting for an answer, she turned toward a short, dimly lit corridor, Hamm'tt silent at her shoulder. Ojeda, followed by his heir and the land-minore who was his other second, fell in smartly behind them. Keira, not yet prepared to argue over precedence, followed in silence.

Forster paused in front of the padded door that led to the sim tank and laid her palm flat against the lock plate. She beckoned Hamm'tt with her other hand, and the Grand Duke joined her, setting her own hand on the plate beside the priest's. The lock gave with an audible click, and the door sighed outward a few inches.

"My Lords, these machines were inspected and certified by technicians of the Order of The House, working under my supervision," Forster said. "The room was then sealed to my palmprint and that of the Grand Duke Hamm'tt. Does anyone wish to claim tampering?" There was no answer. "Is there anyone who wishes to withdraw? Or to postpone the combat, if there is sufficient reason to do so?" This time, Ojeda shook his head slowly. "Then enter, my lords combatant, and may the best man win."

They entered in silence, each group of three going

to the assigned console. The room was grey—walls, padded tiles, ceiling all the same pearly shade. Only the consoles and the chairs were different, one a dull red, the other a dull blue. Both colors seemed to absorb what little light there was in the dim room. Keira settled himself behind the blue console, his hand reaching automatically for the test circuits, before Lovell-Andriës' glance reminded him that that was his seconds' task.

The judge's booth was a box suspended from the ceiling, walled in plastis and steel. The judge himself, an Order priest rather than the usual minore professional gamesmaster, was already there, busily adjusting his controls.

"Are the seconds satisfied?" Forster asked.

"Yes, Sister," Lovell-Andriës said.

"I am satisfied, on my honor," Kypria answered, bowing.

"Then the non-combatants will leave the chamber," Forster said. She looked toward the box on the ceiling, touched two fingers to her forehead. "Roker, the game is in your hands."

The door hissed shut behind them, and Keira was left alone, facing the Ojeda Duke across the length of the hazy room. Not quite alone, he reminded himself. The seconds, his and Ojeda's both, would be watching on the monitors, ready to intervene if something went wrong. However, it had been over twenty years since mechanical failure had made such intervention necessary.

"My lords combatant," the judge said from above. "You may put on your headsets, unless one of you wishes to withdraw. This is your last opportunity to do so."

"No," Keira said, and picked up the headset, adjusting it until the earphones fit comfortably. At the other end of the room, Ojeda had done the same, and then both men made a last check of their boards, and signaled the judge that they were ready.

The lights dimmed, and the color of the walls seemed to darken to the dead black of dust-occluded space. Faint pinpoints appeared in the air between the consoles, grew until a hundred thousand tiny suns danced in the chamber. A single, larger star hung exactly in the center, surrounded by nine planets.

One turn for assessment of setting, the judge said, his voice projected directly into their ears.

"Acknowledged," Keira said, his hands already busy on his keyboard. New readouts appeared in his screens: the solar winds, the gravity lines, information on each of the planets, all were extracted from the game's master tape and fed into the battle map he was creating.

Turn ends, the judge said. Colored lights flared in the holo of the system, each one representing a warship. Keira's fleet was depicted in shades of blue, each variation in color indicating a different class. The little projections were perfect copies of Imperial ships, but it was hard to see the details at a distance. The code of shadings was more useful. A second fleet, this one red, formed in front of Ojeda's console.

One turn for fleet placement, the judge continued.

Keira's hands moved rapidly across the controls, turning the rough plan he had developed while studying Ojeda's challenge tape into modified reality. It was a commonplace among gamesmasters that, if the player were skillful enough, speed and maneuverability were considerably more valuable than mere firepower, and cost fewer gamepoints to build. Keira had taken that advice to heart: his fleet contained nearly ten more ships than Ojeda's, though the blue ships carried lighter weaponry. His largest ship was a single cruiser of the old Federal Bitch class; he grouped half his corvettes around her in a defensive screen, and sent the others out hunting ahead of the fleet. Clippers, lightly armored, expendable missile carriers, lurked on the flanks, and a pair of schooner tenders waited within the escort screen until the time came to drop their circuses. He looked up to see Ojeda's fleet fully formed, two, no, three cruisers in a line formation, buttressed by three frigates and a brace of corvettes. Clippers screened the flanks, but there were only a few of them.

Turn ends, the judge announced. *Combat may begin.*

Keira was already busy with his controls, sending his scouts, clippers backed by a corvette, flying down the gravity curve toward the Ojeda fleet, their own power augmented by the pull of a gas giant. The Grand Duke moved his fleet as a single unit, using the sun's radiation fields to help screen his precise moves as he advanced toward firing range. Keira touched buttons, and missiles flew from his advance ships. The Duke's ships parried the attack, but his riposte fell short as the blue ships sped away again. A second force of clippers dove in. Keira pressed the attack, and managed to score a series of minor hits on the opposing corvettes and clippers, but lost one of his own clippers in exchange. So far, Ojeda had not attacked, had done nothing more than respond to the other's attacks, and Keira studied his own readouts, frowning. He could not see Ojeda's plan, yet, and did not know how to counter it. Then a light flashed on the subsidiary screen, Ojeda's ships' velocity shifting again, another acceleration ... and his Talent saw it.

Ojeda hoped to keep his fleet together, to stay on the defensive until he was on top of the other's single cruiser, and then overwhelm it by sheer weight of numbers. Keira touched keys, sending the rest of the scouting corvettes against the other

fleet, then added the clippers to the fray. He
hesitated, his hand hovering over the buttons that
controlled the second, screening group of corvettes.
Did he want to risk them yet? he wondered, then
stabbed the buttons, hard. He would need room to
stop Ojeda's advance, and he'd need all the ships
he could bring in. He hit the key that released the
schooners, and saw new bright points open on his
own map as the oversized drive units tore holes in
the local space-time fabric. They would do little
real good, except to confuse the other's sensors
and maybe trap an unwary clipper, but everything
helped.

The steady advance slowed, the acceleration numbers falling again, as the red fleet became the
nucleus of a whirling mass of blue ships that dove
and ducked in and out of the ordered lines, leaving
the white flashes of missile fire in their wake. Here
and there a brighter flash marked a successful
counterattack, but Ojeda's ships were too slow to
catch most of the harassing ships. And then, as the
hits mounted, the cruisers became more vulnerable.
A corvette drifted away, steering jets crippled. Then
a frigate, the target of six missiles, lost its screens,
and a seventh shot finished it. The corvettes pressed
the attack, supported by those clippers that had
not fired all their missiles. Another corvette exploded—a red one—and a second frigate dropped
from the red line. She had lost maneuvering power,
but her guns kept firing even as the gravity curve
pulled her inexorably away from the fighting. The
two ships that remained could no longer fill the
gaps in the line. Keira brought up his cruiser.

I concede, Ojeda said calmly.

Instantly, the scene froze, catching the tiny cloud
of gas and debris from an exploding clipper before
it had time to unfold fully.

His Grace concedes, the judge repeated. *Do you
accept, my Lord?*

I accept, Keira said.

Then I declare the game over, the judge said. The battle scene and starfield faded away into the dull grey of the room's real colors and the lights came on again. Ojeda wrenched off his headset, and Keira copied him, frowning. There was something odd about this, he thought. First he obeys all the old rules of courtesy, even to the extent of sending me a full tape, which he was not obliged to do, and then he concedes when there was still a good chance for him to win.

"So you didn't intend to win," he said. Ojeda raised an eyebrow, and Keira stared him down. "You were testing me, making sure that I really was majore—which is rather presumptuous of you, your Grace, since both the late empress and the Order swore to my Talent. Oriana is dead, but the Order might be insulted by your lack of confidence."

The Duke bowed over his console, more deeply than he had before. "I have admitted my defeat, your Majesty, and acknowledge you as my emperor."

There was the faintest hint of irony in his voice, more Read than heard. He thinks he's won, Keira thought, but how? Unless . . . yes, there could be something else. He wanted to be maneuvered into this position. He wanted me to be able to accuse him of the ultimate sin against the Church, doubting the honor of the Order, because he does not want to take sides. Castille, Aragon, the other affiliate worlds would also be immobilized—be protected, Keira corrected himself, by Ojeda's inability to act. It was not a bold tactic, not one a majore would brag of, but it was—just—within Convention and, more to the point, it would work. *But I know what you've done, Balint Ojeda, Grand Duke of Castille System. I know.* He smiled dryly at the other man, allowing his knowledge to color his smile. *And you know that I know it, and that will truly hold you in check for as long as I wish.*

Chapter 8

The Order and the various seconds had agreed on a rest period of one standard hour between each simulation. Keira did not feel the need of it, and returned to his room in the upper levels of the House reluctantly. He would much rather have continued with the games while blood and Talent were hot, and he said as much to Doran, who listened with such obvious patience that Keira was forced to be silent. He settled himself irritably on one of the half-unfolded pillow-chairs and waited for the Guard to bring him the drink he had requested.

"Excuse me, Your Majesty, General." It was the senior of the two Guardsmen detailed to watch the corridor, a diffident, scarred woman with a technician's badges as well as a senior sergeant's cord-of-rank. "May I speak? There's something I think you ought to know."

Keira sat up quickly, his drink forgotten. "Speak."

"The Count of Rohan has an Assassin with him," she said. "We saw his group arriving, and you couldn't miss the mask. I think it may be his second, even."

"An Assassin," Keira repeated. Was the Guild taking sides in this conflict? Unlikely, he decided a moment later. The Assassins' Guild occupied a far too precarious position for it even to think of interfering in politics on its own initiative. Which left two possibilities—either St. George had acquired an Assassin as a regular member of his household, or he had hired the Guild for some other purpose. He put the question to the Guards, cutting across Doran's staccato orders, and stopped the General in his tracks.

"Does the Count keep an Assassin on retainer?" Doran repeated. "I don't know, your Majesty. He didn't the last time he was at court, and he wasn't reported to have one this time."

"Well, I think we can assume that he does now," Keira said.

"Majesty?" Doran looked sideways, not knowing how to respond.

Keira opened his mouth to explain, then realized that he could not. It was Talent, operating outside the realm of logic, that chose one rational alternative over the other, and Talent was less than convincing when explained. To hire an Assassin to kill a noble was a commoner's trick, not the work of a majore who had already agreed to a formal duel. Doran might argue that it was both plausible and within Convention for St. George to have ordered the Assassin to strike only if the Count were to lose his duel, particularly since Rohan County was one of the richest holdings on Verii Mir, the major de Terranin world. The fact that St. George would then be acting for his own immediate liege lord would take away any lingering shame of having refused to accept the outcome of the duel. But that was not why the Assassin was there. "Enough majores keep ties with the Assassins," Keira said. "They're good protection. I don't think it's important, sergeant, but thank you."

Doran looked dubious still, but nodded in agreement. Which was good, Keira thought, because this time he was right. There was no fuzziness about this conclusion; it had the diamond brilliance of absolute truth. The certainty remained with him even when the serbot returned to lead him back to the lobby and his waiting opponent.

The Assassin dominated the little group, even though he was smaller than both Hamm'tt and St. George. He—she? the bulky tunic and wide trousers effectively hid gender—stood politely at the Count's shoulder, light glinting from the flexible silver mask that hid identity. The face on the mask was remotely feminine, thin-featured and predatory, and totally at odds with the Assassin's heavy, straddle-legged stance. The others, even St. George and his other second, stood a little apart from him, as though afraid of touching the dead grey robes, only a half-shade lighter than true black. Keira could feel his own Guards tense.

"Your Majesty," Forster said. If she was upset by the presence of the Assassin, it did not show in her voice. "And my lord Count. This combat will be held in the Gold Room. If you will follow the serbot?"

The machine brought them down a longer stretch of corridor to a door sealed with the formal lock of the Order. Two overseers laid their hands on its sensor plate, and the orange light of the field died away. Forster twisted it off, then manipulated the door controls. The door slid reluctantly back, and she motioned for the combatants to enter.

This tank was much smaller than the first, and furnished in monotonous yellow-brown from floor to ceiling. Only the twin helmets, resting ominously on the double couches, were a different shade—a misty indeterminate metallic grey, like impossibly weathered steel. There was a new judge in the ceiling control box, a younger priest with the faint shadow of a moustache. He swept his hands across the control boards and the tank hummed, a sound so deep as to be a vibration in the bones. Keira winced, feeling the noise strike through him, and then, disconcertingly, Hamm'tt smiled. It was not a smile at his own discomfort, he was sure of that. Rather, her face showed delight, a fleeting admission of pleasure. He made a mental note to check her gaming reputation as soon as the duels were over.

"Sister, your Grace, the tank is alive."

"Very good," Forster said. "Seconds, you may test the chamber."

Lovell-Andriës crossed to one of the heavy couches, pushed buttons at random, and nodded when the tiny checklights all showed green. At his side, the Assassin mimicked his actions.

"Are the seconds satisfied?"

"Yes, Lady," Doran said, and the Assassin nodded.

"Then the noncombatants may leave," Forster said. She looked up at the box. "The game is in your hands, Seves."

As the door closed majestically behind them, the judge said, "Please take your places, my lords."

Keira settled himself in the left-hand couch, resting the heavy helmet in his lap as the cushions shifted, adjusting themselves to his body. The footrests rose gently, and the arms lengthened. Beneath the fingers of his right hand, he felt the worn grip of the escape switch. Gingerly, he took hold of it, not wanting to clasp it too tightly and end the duel before it had begun. If anything went wrong with the projection equipment, or if he proved unable to handle the illusory worlds, he had only to pull the switch and the machine would instantly disconnect from the main computers. Theoretically, it was impossible for an involuntary movement to move the switch, but Keira, like everyone else, had heard the stories of various young and nervous gamesplayers who had flinched at some imagined menace, hit the escape, and lost their fortunes and even their lives. He loosened his grip until his fingers were barely touching the plastic.

"My lords combatant, you may don your helmets. If one of you wishes to withdraw, you may do so now," the judge recited. "This is your last chance."

Keira lifted the helmet awkwardly—it took two hands, and he had to let go of the safety to manage it. He settled it on his shoulders, the padded edges only taking part of the weight, and let the inner lining reach out to his face. It was as warm as blood, softly firm like flesh, and Keira could not repress a shiver as it fitted itself closely to him, curving around nose and mouth to feed him the mildly hallucinogenic gas that would make him more receptive to the machine's illusions. His scalp prickled as delicate sensors attached themselves, burrowing through his hair. His left hand dug deep into the padded arm, and it was only with a great effort that he relaxed the other hand enough to curl his fingers around the safety.

"My lords, the combat begins," the judge announced, and Keira was suddenly aware of a faint odor, sharp but not unpleasant. It was gone almost before he could recognize its existence; the gas was working its way into his system. A heartbeat later, a world exploded into existence.

He was surrounded by a sea of white, white ground, white sky, white trees and bushes. His breath hung white before him, and the furs he wore were white. The air was bitterly cold, biting in his lungs.

Assessment turn begins now, the judge said. He was no longer even a voice, merely words scribbled hastily in his mind, fading as soon as they were understood.

Keira pulled himself together, trying to make sense of what he saw. There was another set of thoughts in his head, a disordered jumble of emotions and understandings that made his head ache. It was only the pseudo-personality, he told himself. Ignore it. He looked around, remembering what the tape had promised. Close behind him, but farther down the slope, stood frozen figures in white fur: his seconds, or rather, the projections of their personalities and gaming records. Beyond them, still nebulous, waited the army. Even farther out, he could see the stiff pennants and poised arrows of the barbarian army, almost at the edge of the plain. So this is Rohan County-of-Verii Mir, he thought, and behind me is the Bergman range. But it's not quite Verii Mir, he reminded himself, it's Verii Mir as Verii Mir might have been if humanity had evolved there and given it legends and a mythology of its own. This was a world of magic, where good and evil wizards fought for control of the plains.

But enough of that. His lips quirked upward as he allowed the pseudo-personality to come forward. His own personality and the talents he had requested had made him into one of the evil wizards, but the persona sharing his head was more evil than he had expected. The persona's goal was to defend his city—turning, Keira could see it outlined against the grey-white sky, a thick reddish tower flanked by lesser towers of a muddier stone—from the attack of one of the plains lords. That would be St. George's persona, of course, a brave, clean-hearted barbarian come to deliver the city from its vicious ruler.

Assessment turn is over, the judge announced. *Begin play.*

"Most High," the Doran-projection said, stepping suddenly out of his immobility. All around him, things began to move naturally again. "Your people await you."

The pseudo-personality supplied the projection's name. "Go before me, Sarngin. And you also, Alauda."

The two figures bowed and moved off down the narrow trail, Alauda holding back branches that threatened to slap his master. At last they came out from under the trees and reached a spot where the ground sloped gently away to the plains. A thousand men, maybe more, were gathered there, most of them infantry armed with the heavy pikes and short axes that were the principal weapons of the mountaineers. Cavalry clustered on the wings, too few to do more than protect the flanks. Only the slightly indistinct faces of the background figures betrayed that this was a simulation.

Farther out, the barbarian skirmishers, lightly armed cavalry, were advancing at an unhurried trot, arrows already nocked. The main army, following more slowly, looked more disciplined than he had expected. "Sarngin, you will command the van," Keira began. "Alauda, take the right wing." That was only a guess, but at the moment St. George's troops looked a little stronger on their own left.

"Yes, Most High," Alauda said. "Will you command the left, Most High?"

I don't like my pseudo-personality very much, Keira thought. "No. I will remain here, where I can exercise my arcane powers."

"Then may I remain, Most High, to lead the Household Guard?" Alauda asked, cringing as though he expected some terrible outburst of anger.

I definitely don't like my persona, Keira thought. "Very well. You, there—" he did not know the projection's name, or the etiquette involved in addressing an unfamiliar simulation-figure, but he pointed to the brutish-looking captain, and hoped for the best. "—you will have the right wing." Before the Doran projection could say anything in protest, Keira lifted his hand. "No more, Sarngin. Do as you were told."

The general closed his teeth over whatever he had been going to say, and turned down the slope. Keira's persona protested the lack of courtesy, but

Keira ignored it. Instead, he reached out with his magical senses, testing the power inherent in the sky and land around him. In the judge's booth, outside this world entirely, a computer juggled numbers, came up with a random factor that fed into another equation: the land was weak here, and the sky drained, the storm fading quickly. There was very little arcane power for the combatants to draw on. Keira made a face, and discarded several plans, half-formed.

There was a sudden sinister hiss, and the sky was full of arrows. Keira made an abortive gesture of protection, then realized that the missiles would fall short. Gaps appeared in his front lines—the barbarians, wheeling away before his own men could work their heavier mechanical bows, raised an ironic cheer—but men stepped forward quickly to fill them. At the same moment, the barbarian infantry broke into a run, their shorter spears lowered, some swinging axes or double-handed swords, but the gaps in the other line were filled, and the pikes lowered into place, before the two armies shocked together.

"Sound the advance for the cavalry," Keira told the trumpeter at his side. The man lifted the curved instrument and produced a braying wail. The small cavalry units, glittering with armor, moved forward at a trot, lances lowered. The barbarian cavalry retreated a little, thwarted in its flanking maneuver, and settled down to a steady harassment. His people would hold, for now; Keira turned his attention to the larger pattern.

The opposing lines writhed as though they themselves were sentient beings in pain, but it was not that macabre dance that drew his Talent. Beyond the lines, a knot of men, mostly wizards guarded by a few warriors in furs and dented armor, clustered about a tall standard. It was not a banner, though strips of bright cloth fluttered from it, but rather a thick staff topped by the figure of a bird, its wings spread, on whose head rested a sphere of clear crystal. The pseudo-personality recognized it as the magical talisman of the barbarian clans, the incarnation of their luck. It was also their one major weakness—his Talent made that clear—but for now he saw no way to seize it. There was simply not enough arcane power available for him to risk it, at least not until things got a lot more desperate. If he tried to take it physically, he and his people would be cut down by cavalry long before they could reach it.

Drums rattled along the barbarian line then, and Keira heard the voices of his own officers over the rumble of the fighting. The fighting slowed a little at the center of the tangle.

"What the hell?" he said, half aloud, and Alauda leaned forward.

"Most High, the generals will fight."

"I can see that," the persona snapped, but Keira bit back the rest of the tirade. Sure enough, Sarngin faced St. George's persona, both men wielding heavy mountaineer's axes. Fighting continued on the wings, the barbarian archers still wheeling in and out to harass, but there was a space of quiet around the generals. Keira cursed, barely able to see, then decided to risk using some of the land's limited power. A muttered command brought him a crystal sphere, similar to the one on the barbarian standard, but smoky, and another word created a picture in its depths. Sarngin and St. George's persona stood chest to chest, axe-hafts straining against each other. Then, with a mighty shove, St. George thrust the other away. As Sarngin staggered backwards, St. George swung his axe down and across. Blood fountained from the other's chest, to freeze pink the instant it touched the snow. The barbarians screamed their triumph and surged forward.

The pseudo-personality knew the solution, and Keira executed it. He drew power from the thinning clouds, and lightning leaped from his hand. It sped toward the barbarian general, who raised his axe in a futile attempt to ward it off. Fire flared about him, and a charred corpse hit the snow.

And nothing else happened.

Keira swore once. If the general had really been St. George—and he had been sure he was—the scenario would have ended, and he would have won despite the "death" of one of his seconds. But now . . . With a second eliminated, he would have to "kill" St. George to win, and the heavy-featured majore was nowhere in sight among the barbarian officers. Where the hell could he be hiding?

His own lines were wavering, and already a few stragglers fled from the wings. The pseudo-personality pointed those out to the Household archers, who took turns cutting them down. The desertions stopped, but the lines still sagged backward. They would soon break, Keira knew, and St. George was still nowhere in evidence. His Talent insisted that the talisman was vulnerable, and reluctantly, he turned his attention to it. The clans could do nothing without it, according to the terms of the scenario; St. George would have to concede a draw if it were destroyed, and perhaps the attack would force the count to reveal himself. It would leave him with very little power, but then, the barbarians would be in the same position.

With a thought, he gathered raw fire from the clouds above, shaped it into a spear, and drove it against the talisman. The standard's defenders fell away, but the staff did not crumble. The stone at the top glowed angrily, and flung back the fire as though it were alive. And then Keira recognized it, almost forgetting to block the rebounding attack: St. George. He had taken the persona of the talisman. He flung lightning again, followed it with

sheeting rain and wind that threatened to tear the
standard from the ground. The ribbons shredded
immediately, but the standard itself remained
whole. Keira's pseudo-personality suggested a hundred different dark and twisting spells that could
be used to bring certain victory, but Keira ignored
it. There would be defenses against those, his Talent said. There was no more time to think: not
knowing why he did so, he matched the other's
strength, wrestling for control of the cloud fire.
For a long moment they hung there, mutually
repelling, and then Keira forced the other away.
The defensive shield shattered under the strain of
Keira's attack, and the standard tottered. He struck
again—there was very little power left now, he
realized; rents in the clouds showed clear sky—
and saw the staff snap, throwing the now-darkened
crystal to the snow. There was a cheer from his
own troops, and the scene faded to darkness.

Keira loosened his cramped finger's hold on chair
and safety, and lifted the helmet from his shoulders.
He blinked at the sudden light, and saw, through
green clouds, that St. George had also taken off his
helmet and was pushing sweat-soaked hair out of
his eyes.

"Neatly done," he said. His voice was tired, but
perfectly cheerful. He seemed almost completely
untouched by his defeat and "death".

"Thank you," Keira said. *I wonder why you're
so calm. If you really wanted to be emperor, I
would have expected you to be more upset. And if
you challenged for Matto de Terranin, I would
have expected at least chagrin, and maybe fear. Or
were you testing me?* His Talent was obstinately
silent on the question. *But,* he thought, *against all
reason, I like this man.*

Chapter 9

The feel of the helmet lining closing in over his face was less startling this time, and Keira found himself welcoming the judge's litany of questions and orders. The voice was oddly accented, lisping: the judge was an ÿHalvith, small and sleekly furred, and his/her mouth was not well shaped to speak the Common Tongue. There were not many ÿHalvithi in the Imperium, but the few who ventured off their own swampy planet were said to be superb gamesmasters.

"My lor's, the com'at 'egins," he/she announced, and Keira dragged his attention back to the combat at hand. The sharp scent of the gas filled the helmet. He took a deep breath, and was propelled into a new world.

There was no disorientation this time, now that he knew what to expect. Keira found himself seated before a scoop-ship's control panel. He himself was swathed in a cumbersome radiation suit that the pseudo-personality found comfortingly familiar. He prodded nervously at the new persona: a racing pilot, an Oceanan native, and a certified member of at least three different spacefaring guilds. There was a confused flash of emotion as well, pride/confidence/arrogance mixing with cooler competence and the glittering streak of a born gambler. It had all the traits he had requested, but there was more to it than that. The persona had a life and coherence of its own, as though another person shared his head, but was still a being he could work with. The ÿHalvith was a true artist in his/her profession.

Satisfied, he turned his attention to the scoop-ship itself, and the reality surrounding it. The hull curved up to cradle him, opaqued against radiation, and without thinking he reached for the switch that would clear it. He hung suspended in the center of a spider's web of armsteel girders, each one tipped with the cup and saucer of a Tanyason generator. Below his feet, he could just see the mouth of the grappling unit, flanked by the smaller muzzles of the twin blastcannons. Beyond the girders blazed the stars.

Assessment turn 'egins, the judge said.

Keira tore his mind from the illusory stars, and forced himself to review everything he knew about the Old Federal sport of scoop racing. It had been the predecessor of the great schooner races, he recalled, the game of hot pilots before the Delrwa-Terra contacts that had produced effective solar sail rigs . . . . Then the pseudo-personality took over. The object of the game—and to the persona the purposeless danger was a marvelous sport—was to recover a target satellite from the convoluted radiation and gravitational fields of Oceanus's triple suns. The target ball moved about at random, just to make the situation more interesting, and the competing ships were allowed to use their light blastcannons on each other. As an additional incentive to the pilots, the ships' screens could only absorb a certain amount of radiation, and therefore any attempt to recover the target had to be made at a high velocity, before the pilot fried. There was rarely time to make a second attempt. The Daimnoe course—and they were running that track—was the most difficult of the three famous courses in the Oceanan system, starting on the up-side of the orbital plane, sweeping down and through the inner asteroid ring, skirting the heavy-r zone, and finishing below the orbital plane on the fringes of the dust clouds that shrouded the area g-south of Oceanus System. Of course, the dust was barely thicker than usual, but the scoop-ships were fragile enough that even that minuscule increase in density could prove fatal. Velocity control was the key to Daimnoe, the persona thought. Too fast, and you broke up in the dust clouds of the Swamp; too slow, and you fried.

Turn en's, the judge said. *Stan' 'y for com'at.*

A voice crackled in the illusory headphones. "All systems show green here. Do the pilots confirm?"

"Roger," Edouard said. He sounded as confident as he had looked before the duel, as though he had piloted these ships a hundred times already, in reality as well as in simulation. But then, Keira thought, I am a Renault. We've always been pilots, and damn good ones. And I learned to fly schooners when I was ten. He checked his own board a final time—there wasn't much to check, four major indicators and a small row of maintenance lights—and set his hands on the twin throttles.

"All green."

"Pilots confirm all green," the starter repeated. "On my mark . . . countdown from five . . . begins now."

A small screen in the corner of Keira's board lit up abruptly and began flashing numbers. He tensed, then forced himself to relax and let the pseudo-personality guide him.

". . . two . . . one . . . mark!" the starter intoned, and on the last word Keira kicked the ignition pedal and advanced the main throttle. Light flared around him. The pseudo-personality reminded him to semi-opaque the bubble, taking one hand from the primary controls to do so. Then acceleration slammed him against the backrest. A course correction was necessary almost immediately, and

that saved him. The little ship was nothing like
the graceful schooners; maneuvering was quick
and tricky, the controls deceptively simple, but
heavy-handed, without the sensitivity of a schooner's
multiple sail lines. Keira fumbled with the second
throttle, the one that controlled both the power
and the direction of the maneuvering jets, and the
ship faltered badly despite the pseudo-personality's
knowledge and assistance. He could not feel the
currents through the controls. He twisted the secondary throttle again, too hard, and the ship yawed
wildly. Then Edouard's ship flashed past, and the
sight steadied him. The pseudo-personality took
over, pulling the ship back into the optimum
attitude, and advancing the main throttle slightly.
Velocity built as his fuel ticked away. He glanced
quickly at the limited readouts, calculating overhaul time from the relative velocities. He would
catch Edouard just as they came into the radiation
fields, and he considered greater acceleration, but
decided against it. He would be better off saving
fuel for later maneuvering.

Time passed—he could not tell if the judge used
his/her prerogative and speeded the effect—and
the asteroids loomed larger in the bubble. Do I go
through, or go around, Keira wondered, but there
was little choice. To go around the belt meant fuel
expenditure for both the maneuver and for acceleration to compensate for the lost time. And Edouard
was going through. Keira watched the scoop-ship
ahead of him, a roman numeral ten with an extra
bar through the central point, weave through the
maze, new lights flaring here and there on the
structure as Edouard dodged the drifting rocks.
Then his own ship was among them.

Before, everything had moved with deceptive
languor; now he could see his real velocity. Percep-
tion narrowed as he submerged himself in the
pseudo-personality, narrowed further to his hands

on the two throttles and his eyes glued to the view in front of him. The secondary throttle twisted a millimeter one way, and he rolled away from a rock; an immediate correction saved him from becoming one more minor crater on the scarred surface of its companion. Despite himself, he hit the main throttle, decelerating, gaining more time to react to the giants' dance around him. A reckless spin, a final challenge declined just in time, and he was out.

He checked his readouts hurriedly. He had not used as much fuel as he had feared, but the gap between his ship and Edouard's had widened considerably. He would overhaul well within the light-radiation zone, even if he increased his velocity. He touched the primary throttle briefly, watching the matched scales—velocity rising, fuel falling— and settled himself to wait.

The convoluted suns approached so quickly that it seemed certain the judge had once again speeded the scenario. Keira barely remembered to flick on the receiver that would track the target and to opaque the bubble completely before the first tongue of radiation licked the ship. He could see it advancing across the projection on the inside of the bubble, a wave of dull green-black light, barely distinguishable from the black space around him. Then the entire bubble seemed to glow with eerie lights, and he felt his skin prickle with atavistic fear: he was fully in the radiation zone.

He shook it off and concentrated on the projection. It showed radiation as washes of green light, variations in strength and type showing as different shades, while gravity showed as a neat blue grid, going from blue-violet at the edges to an electric hue that hurt the eyes in the center. The flare of Edouard's engines registered as a dead bronze spot in the center of the glory. A light flashed on a side panel, and he glanced at it. It was the locator light, so the target had to be near. Edouard was leading, but his speed would hamper any efforts to retrieve it. Which means I have a chance, Keira thought, and swept his eyes across the projection.

He saw it only because he looked away. The dot was only a little brighter than the deep olive-green background of the secondary radiation zone, and it was falling deeper into the suns. Edouard had seen it, too, and the bronze dot glowed again as he changed course in order to pursue it. Keira glanced at his minimal readouts, guessing at Edouard's remaining fuel and the relative velocities. There had to be a way to take advantage of the intricate gravitational fields of three suns, so obligingly displayed in almost textbook fashion, by the projection.

And then he saw it. His Talent read the pattern, drew on the "memories" of the pseudo-personality— the rules of the simulation—and moved his hands on the throttles before he was consciously aware of the solution. The scoop-ship leaped ahead, found a gravity curve and held to it. A tiny flick of the secondary throttle, and the ship was positioned perfectly. He shouted wordlessly as the velocity meter started to climb, then swung the ship and kicked the cannons' trigger as Edouard's ship flashed by "beneath" him. A second later, the target loomed in the projection, the meter on the panel going crazy. He hit another pedal. The grapple fired, and an orange light flared on the board. He could not spare it more than a glance, but he thought that the target was at least partly in the pod. He waited a little longer, hunched over the controls, counting the seconds and gauging his position relative to the other tongues of gravity that snaked out to bar his way, then slammed the main throttle and twisted the other viciously. The ship moaned under the stress, but held together, then pulled free. The velocity meter twitched madly, then settled: high, but not too high—he hoped. His fuel was low, and the Swamp was not too far ahead at his speed, but he was running parallel to a higher-g line that should help slow him. . . . I've cut it too fine, he thought, I'll be dragged in and I don't have the fuel to pull free. But the g-line curved away even as he reached for the secondary throttle, and the scoop-ship slid past. The greenish glow of the radiation faded from the inside of the bubble. He pulled the main throttle toward him for the last time, and held it there until he felt the braking engines stagger and burp as the last of the fuel went through them. Only then did he clear the bubble and twist his couch to look back at the suns.

A single white dot—the white was the engines, firing at full power in a futile attempt to break free—dove toward the swollen surface of the ternary sun. A moment later, the dot was gone. I hit him, Keira thought. That one shot must've knocked out a couple of control jets. A lucky shot . . . no. Not luck at all.

The sky around him faded, the stars winked out, and then he was back in the close, sweaty universe of the helmet. It was heavy on his shoulders. He lifted it off, his hands shaking. Edouard lay quiescent beneath the other helmet, his hand limp on the safety. For a moment, Keira feared he was truly dead; then the Overlord's arms twitched, fumbling momentarily with the helmet before he gained enough control to lift it off. He was very pale, and his eyes flickered closed again as soon as the helmet came off. Why didn't he hit the escape, Keira wondered, staring frankly at the other. He was beaten, couldn't pull free; he could've spared himself the nightmare of "dying". But he didn't, and that might well be significant.

"Your Majesty," Lovell-Andriës said softly, and Keira realized that the main doors were open, admitting the seconds. He allowed them to lead him back to his room, to feed him coffee and the mild Xanadan stimulant h'rai. For the first time, he was grateful for the rest period, and he lay back against the chair's firm cushions, watching the scene the Guards had selected for the wallscreen. For some reason, they had chosen the channel that displayed exotics, rather than the more mundane view of the city around The House. This hour, it showed a stretch of beach on one of the resort worlds. Empty black sand glittered as though sprinkled with diamonds, and green foamed waves struck and receded under the vivid sun. Their rhythm was the rhythm of his heartbeat, of the drugs moving through his body, restoring his strength. He let it carry him away, drifted with it, until the call came for the final duel.

Chapter 10

The final simulation was to be held in the largest of the House's tanks, where as many as twelve couch-and-console units could be tied into the computers. This particular game would use only six—five on the far side of the room, and the single unit where Keira sat, facing the minores who had accepted his challenge. Ayakawa sat at the central unit, flanked by the Tyrian land-minores Freyhalt and Nayati, and two Vinlanders, Thorsson and Devereux, at her right. Above them, in the judge's booth, a grey-robed priest signalled, and the speakers came to life.

"My lords combatant, are you ready?"

Keira adjusted his headpiece a final time—this was a standard simulation, not the full-scale game set up by St. George and de Terranin—and said, "Ready."

The minors echoed him, and the judge worked his controls. The room lighting went out, and stars began to form in the space between the couches.

Then, nightmare. Greyness became palpable, with a fresh scent all its own. Lightning flashed without thunder. Infinity appeared, with neat red flags marking its edges. . . . A ship swept out of nowhere, so close overhead that Keira ducked to avoid it. He swore at it, and his words foamed from his mouth in long streams of blue and purple bubbles, broken only by the brighter pink flash of a hard consonant. He fended off a swarm of terwillies,

117

and groped for the nonexistent console. He knew it was there, but his hands moved through hot glue that smelled of roses, and a false-hawk's musk. The air went grey and liquid, while an Oceanan in full diving gear swam blithely through him, and then the entire world whirled away into space, stars flashing past at impossible speed. Then his hand closed on the emergency cut-off, and the lights came on in his half of the room.

Under the lights, only a few pale ghosts played against a dense grey fog, but even as he watched, they faded. He shook his head to get rid of the blurring ache.

"What the hell is going on?" he said, directly into the headpiece's microphone. There was no answer from the fog-shrouded judge's box. A malfunction, he thought, and the minores were hit hard. The status boards showed green: the machinery was functioning, but neither tape nor human operator controlled it. Then the pattern of lights changed, and something dove at him out of the clouds. He shied away before he realized that it was only an illusion. Something, human or tape, was exerting control after all; he reached for his own console and tried to abort the program.

The fog drew back slowly, the judge's box emerging first. Keira caught his breath. The judge was slumped over his console, arms outstretched, forehead resting on the atmosphere controls. He looked dead—but there were more important things to worry about. The fog refused to fade further, forming a stubborn wall that blanketed the minores' consoles. He reached for his keyboard, but before he could link his console to the opposing computer, something flashed from the wall of fog. He thought it was another illusion, but then it cut through one of the drifting phantoms: reality—a real knife—spinning end over end. He dove from his couch, one hand still clawing for the controls, and the knife slammed against the array of switches, bouncing from his hand to the soft tiles. Blood welled along his knuckles—his right hand, too, his weapon hand. He slapped at the buttons that controlled the lights, plunged the tank into sudden darkness, and heard Ayakawa, her voice distorted by the padded walls.

"Fool! Now he's armed."

"I thought I could get him," someone—Freyhalt? Devereux?—whined in answer.

"Shut up," Ayakawa said, and was obeyed.

Now what? Keira thought, still crouched beside his chair. Somehow they've managed to kill the judge and put me at a disadvantage, a physical battle at five to one. And I missed the possibility. I didn't see it at all. He shuddered, then forced himself to think more clearly. The minores could not be armed with more than knives: the automatic scanners would have picked up either blasters or projectile weapons, and no blades larger than knives could have been concealed in their coveralls. He collected the thrown knife from the tiles where it had fallen, laid it to hand on the console. He risked rising, protected by the fog, and scanned the multiple keyboards. As he had hoped, it was possible to tie into the House's main computer, and through that he could reach the power plant and the environmental controls. It took him precious seconds to find the proper overrides, but at last he had the patch-through. Gravity was variable in the House, to accommodate visiting aliens; he activated the generators beneath the central flooring and ran them up to their full three-g capacity. Beyond that, he set up a band of light, and ran that machine up to its highest setting as well. Even from his side, it was dazzling, and he blocked it with an illusion of utter darkness. With luck, the minores should be dazzled, too.

The pedestal beneath the console—the pack that

powered the various projectors—whined briefly,
and warning lights flashed across the console. The
minores, or some of them, were trying to override
his arrangements. The strain was high, too much
power channeling through the circuits, but he
locked the program anyway, feeding power directly
from the main power plant. It was dangerous, but
the pedestal and console would blow before the
minores could break through. Keira smiled wryly,
lifting the knife left-handed. All minores were
soldier-trained, even the land-minores. They would
come for him as soon as they realized they couldn't
break his programming. And the seconds would
already be breaking into the tank, alerted by his
use of the escape switch. Everything depended on
how long that took.

Keira heard the minores struggling against the
weight of their own bodies long before he could
see them, could hear their breath rasping and the
shuffle and drag as they pulled themselves along.
Someone whimpered and fell painfully. Then, in a
sudden rift in the fog, he saw Ayakawa stagger out
of the curtain of dark, hands over her eyes. She
was followed a moment later by Devereux, still on
hands and knees, eyes screwed tightly shut. Ayakawa
blinked, trying to shake away the afterimages, then
peered through the fog. Devereux took three tries
to get to his feet, but once up, seemed to shake off
the dazzle more quickly.

"Keira!" Ayakawa shouted. "Come out and fight."

Keira glanced at the console a final time. The
warning lights were flashing steadily, but the strain
seemed to have steadied. "I am here, Ayakawa.
Come and get me." The fog closed in again as he
backed away from her voice. A swirl in the fog
caught his eye, and he dodged blindly. Devereux's
blade cut only fog, and Keira fell backwards to
avoid the return stroke. The console was beneath
him, buttons giving beneath his back. A whooping

alarm sounded, and Keira risked a glance at the indicators, though Devereux nearly skewered him in the process. All the warning lights were on, a steady, angry red.

Devereux thrust again, and Keira parried by instinct rather than design, trapping the blade on the dagger's crosspiece just long enough to fight free of the console. Devereux followed eagerly, trying to force him to turn toward Ayakawa, hidden somewhere in the fog. The alarm was still sounding, and a deep vibration rose from beneath the floor. There was an acrid smell of metal smoke. Keira retreated a few more steps, then broke and skipped back farther. Devereux grinned at him through the fog, and moved to follow.

"Get down, Arne!" Ayakawa screamed. "The whole thing's going!"

Keira dove for the nearest corner. Behind him the room erupted in flame. A pillar of fire rose where his console had been, and the links set off other consoles as well, clearing the fog as though it had never been. The judge's box was filled with white fire. Whether Ayakawa had killed him or merely stunned him, the priest was dead now. Keira picked himself up from the floor, bruised but otherwise not hurt, and raised his knife warily. The safety systems cut in, liquid and gas spurting from the ceiling nozzles. The consoles sizzled as the chemicals hit, but the sparks died.

"I've still got you," Ayakawa said. She was still on her feet, coveralls singed, face bloody where a flying splinter had laid open her cheek. Devereux lay huddled beside the ruined console, just outside the blackened ring where the flames had struck.

Keira dodged away, cold with fear. The far door slid open a few centimeters at last, then jammed, then slid a little farther. He could just see armored hands tugging at it, but they were too late. Ayakawa saw them too, and swore. She launched herself at

him, avoiding his knife with contemptuous ease.
Keira fell backwards again, twisting to keep her
from landing directly on top of him. The minore
was fighting from anger, not with Talent; Keira
struck at her wrist. She lost the knife, but clawed
fingers reached for his eyes, raking cheek and
forehead. Keira knew one throw from his time as a
sailworker; she was badly balanced, so that even
his clumsy execution was good enough. They rolled,
and he came up on top, desperately trying to pin
her hands and hold her with the weight of his
body.

"Your Majesty," Doran said. "We have her."

Keira glanced over his shoulder—a tensed part
of him expected a trick, but the long room was full
of Guardsmen—then slowly released the minore.
Doran offered him a hand, and the emperor was
suddenly glad of the support. Two other Guards
dragged Ayakawa to her feet; several more leveled
rifles at Freyhalt. A guard was bending over
Devereux, but after a brief moment abandoned the
corpse. There were two more blackened bundles
near the remains of the minores' consoles. Doran's
face tightened at the direction of Keira's gaze.

"Dead," he said shortly.

Keira nodded. "Get the others to the medstation."
He looked around the shattered room. The thin
padding was peeling from the walls, and the consoles were little more than melted piles of slag.
The judge's booth—and he winced at the thought
of what must be inside it—had been partly torn
from its anchors, tilted at an angle. Water and gas
still trickled from the nozzles, but the fires were
mostly out. Only a few pieces of tile still smoldered.

"And then?" Doran asked, after a moment.

"The judge is dead," Keira said. "I declared
interregnum, but they've killed an innocent by-
stander. Convention's been broken—"

"Innocent!" said Ayakawa, and somewhere found laughter. "The judge was bribed, bribed to give us the advantage. There were special circuits running to my console that gave me as much control of the environment as he had."

"It didn't help you," Keira murmured, but his heart wasn't in it. If one member of the supposedly incorruptible Order could be bought, others could be, and their apparent support was worthless.

I have to get back to the Palace, he thought. The Guard will get answers from Ayakawa—I know she didn't lie—and then I can confront the Governor General.

"I offer you a clean fight," Ayakawa flared. "Which is more than you deserve, usurper." She spat on the warped tiles between her feet. "I'll still meet you, if you're noble enough for it. Here and now, your choice of weapons."

Keira shook his head. "You had your chance. Doran, lock them away somewhere until the Eger can pass sentence. I'll have orders for you."

"She should be shot now," Doran said. "Majesty."

"Oh, no," Ayakawa jeered, her voice tinged with anger and madness. "Oh, no, that wouldn't be Conventional, would it, Dan Keira? And you want to look like the perfect majore, until you bring the house of cards down on them all." She swung against the Guards' grip, looking wildly from face to face. "You don't know this one, he's sly. He'll destroy everything if you put him on the throne."

"Oh, get her out of here," Keira said. His hand stung violently, and his back and ribs hurt from the minore's blows. Doran gestured to his men, and they pulled her toward the door, shoving Freyhalt along behind her. Keira followed in their wake, stepping carefully over torn patches of tiling. In the center, where the gravity generators had been turned on, the tiles were warped and compressed, and there were deeper indentations where

Ayakawa and Devereux had crawled across it. A third trail ended in the middle of the band: Freyhalt's.

"You'll want a doctor to look at those cuts, Majesty," Doran said. "I took the liberty of warning the House's doctor—she's a Hildiv, and reliable."

Keira nodded, but his mind was elsewhere. If even a part of the Order chose to side with his challengers—but this had to be an isolated case, one corrupt priest among a thousand or more. If nothing else, a well-organized conspiracy would have killed him. But if one priest could be bribed, then others might be ... For a moment, anger threatened to overwhelm him, anger at a priest who had broken Convention—the Convention that his own order had helped to shape, the Convention that protected him, let him indulge in political games without running any of the risks taken by the nobility. He shook himself, wincing a little. At this moment, he had only Ayakawa's word that the priest had been bribed; he needed more proof than that before he could act.

The Hildiv doctor was waiting in the corridor, the leash of her anti-grav-buoyed medical kit wrapped around one slender wrist. She was quite tall, and painfully thin to human eyes, like a short-muzzled, bi-pedal greyhound. A froth of ribbons fell from her gilded torque and from the belt riding her hips, hiding nipples and genitalia. She extended one velvety paw, claws ostentatiously retraced, and bowed.

"R'rtai, Majesty," she announced. The name was a growl ending in a medium-pitched yip. She brought the medical kit up beside her, the top rising automatically to reveal miniature scanner and a tiny pharmacy. "You, me this permit?"

"Yes."

Her touch was very gentle, almost imperceptible. Keira stood patiently while she pointed scanners

at him, then deftly cleaned the cut and covered it
with a coat of thin medical plastic. She reached
into the pharmacy, but Keira shook his head. The
doctor hesitated, then shrugged faintly.

"Majesty, as pleases."

Lovell-Andriës cleared his throat. "Pardon, Majesty, but the lords are waiting."

Keira nodded. Doran gestured to the Guard
contingent—there were more than there had been,
Keira noted, and mentally commended the general.
At the entrance of the lobby, he checked slightly.
St. George and Ojeda were there, backed by their
seconds and the ubiquitous Forster, but de Terranin
was missing.

"Edouard?" he said quietly, not daring to stop.

Lovell-Andriës said, "He was ill. His people took
him back to the Palace." He made a face. "The
judges had the authority to let him go."

"Later, then," Keira said. "Well, your Grace, my
Lord?"

Ojeda bowed, calculating the depth to the millimeter—you are emperor and I acknowledge you,
but you have not yet been crowned and more would
be improper—and St. George copied him less
precisely.

"You are willing to swear?" Keira asked.

"We are." That was Ojeda. St. George nodded
agreement.

"I am listening."

Ojeda raised an eyebrow at that, and Keira stared
him down. "Your Majesty," the Grand Duke began.
"I, Balint Ojeda, Grand Duke of Castille and Aragon,
Overlord of the High Haven and Jant', pledge my
life, land, and service to the maintenance of Keira
Emperor, restricted only by the demands of Convention. I swear this on my honor, and seal it with
my word."

"And I, Lucas Vasil St. George, Count of Rohan
on Verii Mir, pledge myself, life, land, and service,

to the maintenance of Keira Renault, within Convention. I swear this on my honor as a majore."

Keira nodded, carefully forming the proper formula words. "And I, Keira Renault, first of my dynasty, pledge to you, Balint Grand Duke, and you, Lucas Count, together and severally, to support and maintain you and yours to the limit of Convention, on my honor as majore and emperor."

It was done. Bowing, majores and minores moved aside, leaving him a clear path to the door that had suddenly opened in the far wall. A serbot painted in the House's distinctive pattern waited there, flanked by Guards. The sound of a hovercar was clearly audible. Keira climbed aboard, still closely followed by the Guards, and settled into the middle seat. Lovell-Andriës hauled himself into the forward seat, directly behind the driver's pod, and leaned forward to be heard over the sudden whine of the fans.

"Shall I have Edouard brought to you as soon as we land?" he asked.

Keira hesitated, then shook his head. "No. Time enough in the morning. Ayakawa—that priest is more important now." A warning voice pointed out that not to take Edouard's oath was sheer stupidity, but Keira ignored it.

Lovell-Andriës nodded. "Very well, Majesty."

Chapter 11

Edouard de Terranin knelt in his tiny chapel, eyes fixed on the triptych before him. Tripartite God looked out from the center panel, the galaxies clustered at His feet—Father, Son, and Spirit, crowned with the fires of creation. In the right-hand panel, the Donna stood amid snow, looking up to the stars flung across the arch of heaven. The crescent moon was at her feet, and a shaft of clear light touched her wondering face. To the left, Michael raised his sword, a beacon against the roiling clouds, to strike the Dragon that coiled and clutched at his armored legs, great wings spread to bring down the Archangel.

He whispered, "Almighty and everlasting God, I thy needy creature render thee my humble praise, for the preservation of my life to this day, and especially for having delivered me from the dangers of the past hours." The words went on, slipping through his mind like well-worn beads, too smooth and polished from constant use to find any grip. He had come through the dangers, yes, but he had lost the game, and in losing had lost his chance for real power. Soon, too soon, the new emperor's men would be coming to demand his Oath, and he was honor-bound—no, he told himself, Convention-bound—to give it. But the game, and all the other simulations he could run, were not absolute indicators of the future. Nothing, not even his sister in the Order, could give a definite prediction, though she could see farther than most. It was still possible that he could win a battle with Keira. The Renaults were not invincible. If he moved now, while things were still unsettled, other nobles would join him, if only in the hope of later deposing a de Terranin emperor. He would risk that: he needed more than his own people to defeat the usurper.

He crossed himself automatically, having come to the end of his prayer, and blushed as he realized he had paid no attention to his words. Lord, forgive me, but You know what's on my mind. Do I break Convention? Do I dare, when all my life I've been told that to break Convention is to break honor, is to bring down the society that has served us so well? That society is already changing, for the worse. . . . And is Convention the same as honor?

The serene stares of God and the Lady promised little help; his eyes turned, as always, to Honor's Hawk stooping above the Dragon. The clean fierce eyes looked through him, and he lowered his head. Oh, Michael-who-keeps-our-honor, I know the price if I lose. I'll be hunted from one end of the galaxy to the other, through Federation and Council if I get that far, until I'm dead and the Imperium safe from a Convention-breaker. But will my honor be gone? Will I spend eternity in a darkness far from you? Doesn't honor also demand I try? I am the last of the true Silvertree line, though the claim is somewhat tangled. Am I not obliged to keep this total stranger, a favorite, a Renault with none of the blood of either Silvertrees or Alexanders, from the throne? Is Convention the same as honor? Michael, most honorable, help me know what to do.

He knelt a while longer, methodically addressing himself to one saint after another, until he was calm enough to rise. The meditation had steadied him enough to reach a decision, wiping away the echo of his "death" in the suns. Convention and honor were not quite the same thing. He would leave Avalon now, before the Guard could be warned to stop him. He glanced at the wall-chrono, comparing the times on the three dials—local, Standard, and Verii Mir. It was nearly dawn by Avalon's clock; he would have to hurry. But if he could get off-world before the Navy was alerted to stop him, he could make it to Verii Mir with ease, and be safely ensconced behind the planetary defenses before the Renault realized what had happened. After that . . . time would tell, of course, but he guessed that the other doubtful Domi would join him. And if they did not, de Terranin was the richest of the nine Domi, richer even than the Imperial Domus, with the resources of Verii Mir and the industries of wind-kissed Altus to back his bid. Victory was more than possible.

He seated himself on the hard plastic chair that stood before his computer console, wincing a little. The chair might be worth a fortune as a genuine Old Federal antique, but it was damnably uncomfortable. What still had to be done—or, better, what did he have time to do? A message for his father, left in the secret mail file. His fingers flickered over the keyboard, couching a quick explanation in the family's private code, just in case Keira's people had tapped their system. The ship was ready, as it always was, waiting for just this sort of disaster. It remained only to warn the pilot.

He pulled the communicator table over to his side, the wheels sticking in the deep carpet. He activated all the security circuits, then waited, the screen fuzzing, until the pilot answered.

"VMR *Storm Lily*. Captain Maguire."

Edouard switched to the planetary patois. Though the emperor was sure to have the lines tapped, it might take him a little longer to decipher the strange language, and every minute would count.

"Hē, Maguire. I it is, Edouard. To blow this planet, by highlight before, canst do?"

"Hē, Edouard. Sure and certain, yes." The pilot grinned tightly. He was a soldier-minore who had served the Domus his entire life, waiting for this moment. "Storm's a-riding?"

"Maybe."

"Kor'sho. We waits."

"Going," Edouard said, and broke the connection. The ship would be ready; all that remained was for him to reach it. He glanced around the long room, divided into smaller areas by stiffened draperies. There was nothing here he really valued, except for the triptych. He ducked back into the blue-curtained chapel and lifted it carefully from its hook, folding the wings inward over the representation of God. From his own travelling chest, he extracted a commoner's shoulderbag and a couple of clean shirts, then wrapped the triptych well before fitting it into the very bottom of the bag. He added more clothes, then his signet, and put a clean pair of trousers over that. A touch of the concealed catch opened the safe compartment, revealing the commoner's ID papers and transit pass he had acquired on his first trip to Avalon. With them, he could travel to Government Center and the spaceport by untraceable public transportation, rather than having to take a majore's groundcar.

The soldier-minores turned a blind eye as he left the de Terranin quarters, and dropped down an empty grav-shaft to the first of the subterranean levels. From there, he worked his way deeper, toward the maintenance levels where the few commoners employed in the Palace generally worked. The lower the level, the less cautious he had to be: his face was not yet well known to the commoners, and while the number of commoners employed at the Palace was relatively small, the actual number was large enough to keep them from knowing each other by sight. The orange-toned lighting, too, worked in his favor, hiding details rather than revealing them.

He was lucky at the transport station. Though both Guards and planetary police were watching the boarding gates—he did not know if that was the usual procedure, or if Keira had gotten suspicious, and his fear nearly choked him—the night shift had just ended. Hundreds of commoners filled the platforms, their voices echoing dully from the curved walls of the tunnel, some arriving for work, some leaving, but all converging on the bank of gate-tenders. Edouard found a place in the line, trying to look half asleep, and shuffled forward until he was confronted by the barred gate and the bland face of the machine. There was a second's panic—he had never actually used his pass, and did not know if it still worked—but the scanner accepted it. Lights flashed and his card was jerked from his hand, only to reappear in a slot on the other side of the now-open barrier. Edouard hurried through before it could change its mind, snatching up his pass on the way, and found an individual pod marked as going to the spaceport. He settled himself in the comfortable couch, letting the servos adjust the safety netting over him, and waited tensely for the kick of the jets.

It came at last, but he could not bring himself to relax until the pod jerked to a stop. The trip had not seemed long. Even though he knew that the public transport pods were fast, he could not help fearing that, when he popped the canopy, he would see not the sky-topped trench of the spaceport terminus, but the dull concrete arch of the Palace tunnel. He was afraid, so he pulled the release at once. The dawn air poured in, damp and fresh: he had made it. He levered himself out of the pod and walked up the short ramp toward the terminals

and the majores' field. *Storm Lily* was waiting.
He had escaped.

Matto de Terranin curled one hand around the
miniature globe that hung suspended from his
heavy collar of state, fingers feeling for the control
points. One was in Rohan County, another in the
polar sea, another on the uninhabited southern
continent, where the archeologists had found the
pitiful remains of a mammalian species that had
died out just on the verge of intelligence. The
smoothly enameled surface changed under his
touch, one spot growing warm, another gaining a
faintly sandy texture. The changes followed a familiar pattern: the security devices behind the silk-
sheathed walls of the imperial receiving room were
blocking his own recorders, and probing the controls hidden in his jeweled collar. There was nothing
to fear; the collar was Man'net work, unbreakable.

"So your son has decided to leave Avalon, without my permission, and without having sworn the
Oath."

De Terranin jerked slightly, looked across his
intertwined fingers at the emperor's still figure.
Yes, he thought, and what will you do about it? He
said, "Your Majesty, that is news to me. Edouard
has left Avalon?"

Keira tilted his head slightly. "He has."

Calculating the gesture, de Terranin spread his
hands. "Majesty, forgive me, but this has taken me
by surprise. Where has he gone?"

"Verii Mir." Keira's face was split by a sudden,
wry grin, gone as quickly as it had appeared.
"Though of course this isn't completely certain, as
his captain neglected to file a flight plan. A dangerous procedure, your Grace."

"I fear so," de Terranin said, intensely aware of
the irony. "But, Majesty, what can the boy do on
Verii Mir? It is still my world. . . . But of course

Edouard is very religious. He's only gone to confer with his sister. She's a priest, your Majesty, of the Order."

"I have heard much of the Overlord's piety."

De Terranin looked up sharply, wondering if he had overstepped himself with that barb, if he had imagined the hint of anger in the emperor's voice.

Keira went on smoothly, "Surely such a pious man, intending no evil, would have waited to swear before leaving, if only to prevent misunderstanding."

Of course, de Terranin thought, and we both know that's just why Edouard didn't stay. "His 'death' upset him greatly, your Majesty. He's not used to losing. Even something so important may have slipped his mind."

"As you say," Keira agreed blandly, "or perhaps he deliberately overlooked it, so he might remain free to act. Unlike those of the nobility who have already taken the Oath."

Neatly done, de Terranin thought. If you had accused me openly of planning to break Convention, I could have taken half the nobles from your side. "Forgive me for saying so, Majesty, but it might have been wiser for you to have accepted his Oath immediately after the duel. Then this situation could not have arisen."

"Perhaps."

De Terranin wondered if that one word contained enough of an accusation to be actionable. Probably not, especially since his recorder was still jammed.

"But what situation is this?" Keira continued.

De Terranin bowed his head. "This unfortunate misunderstanding," he amended. Now we come to it, he thought, and his finger stole around the curve of the planet, reaching for the emergency signal. His minores couldn't do anything to save him, but they could warn the rest of his family.

"I trust it is only a misunderstanding," Keira

said. "Will you contact your son, your Grace, and ask him to return to Avalon? Once he has sworn, he will of course be free to do as he likes."

"I will certainly contact him," de Terranin said, "but I cannot order him back to Avalon. It is a delicate matter, your Majesty, I beg you to understand. If I were to order him, and he found that he did not have to obey, that I could not force him. . . ." He gestured again. "I don't think I have to explain the bad results."

"I understand completely," Keira said.

De Terranin bowed. Yes, I know you do, he thought. We've each said what we had to say—you that you know that Edouard's planning to move against you, if he can find support on the home worlds. I expect he can; they know their duty on Verii Mir. And I have told you that I will not side with the emperor against my son. Oh, I won't break Convention, that's not in me, any more than it's in Edouard, but I sure as hell won't lift a finger to help you—Oriana's favorite or a Renault, I don't care which. "You are most kind, your Majesty."

"Thank you, your Grace," Keira said. "You have leave." He waved a hand in dismissal. De Terranin ground his teeth—it had been bad enough to take that from Oriana, but from this Keira!—and bowed with all the more courtesy to make up for the lapse.

His minores were waiting outside the Quarters, but de Terranin did not speak until he was safely inside his groundcar, the dome drawn tight over the passenger well. Only then did the most trusted of the minores say, "How was the interview, Lord?"

"Is this secure?" de Terranin asked.

The soldier-minore looked hurt. "I debugged it myself this morning. And Katya—" he gestured to the pilot, who rode outside the bubble, her eyes fixed on the crowded corridors "—was with the car the whole time you were in the Quarters."

"Ah. It went as expected," de Terranin said. "Keira carefully refrained from accusing me of anything—though he made clear what he really thought of Edouard, damn the boy—and I carefully refrained from saying whether or not I'd support his dubious Majesty."

"And will you?" the minore asked.

De Terranin shrugged. "I am bound as a lord of Domus to support only the candidates of the Domi Council." The words were still bitter, and he added quickly, "However. . . ."

The minore nodded. "I see. You can't support Edouard, but you'll leave the rest to the planetary nobles' discretion?"

"If they have any," de Terranin snapped. "No, I shouldn't say that. My minores know their duty."

"Thank you, Lord," the minore said, with only the faintest hint of a smile.

"You know that was no slur on you," de Terranin said irritably. "God's blood, will you people stop being so sensitive? But Edouard should find enough support for this venture of his, and—God willing," he added, more from superstition than as a result of his children's pious influence, "—we'll pull down the usurper. Or he will, rather."

"Yes," the minore said. "Lord, shall I pass the word, very unofficially, of course, that you wouldn't be too displeased if your people followed Edouard? Even if you have to issue contrary orders?"

"I don't intend to order my people to stay here. That would be a gross tyranny, against Convention. Minores must always have free access to their homeworlds." De Terranin smiled. "I think you may reassure any minores as to that."

The soldier-minore nodded. "I will do so, my Lord."

"And one more thing." De Terranin leaned back

against the cushions, not really seeing the people who crowded the corridors. "Get in touch with Vasili Andros. I have some things to discuss with him."

Chapter 12

Desolin Hamm'tt arrived on de Terranin's heels. She had not been expected. Keira and Doran, studying the preliminary results from Ayakawa's interrogation—her failure had destroyed what little stability the land-minore had ever had, and the tape made little sense—exchanged glances, and then the emperor shrugged and set the tape aside. "Very well, admit her."

"Your Majesty, her Grace is accompanied by the Governor General."

The leader of the Order. Keira hesitated, heard Doran's quick intake of breath. "Admit them." He waited until he was certain that the circuit was closed and glanced toward the Guard sergeant, standing silent by the door. "I assume you're armed, Lilika?"

"Of course, Majesty," the sergeant answered, sounding rather hurt.

Keira nodded, and felt along the chair arm for the button that controlled the inner door. As it slid back, he said, "Welcome, your Grace, Governor."

Hamm'tt gestured courtesy; the elderly man in the Order's grey bowed more deeply.

"Be seated, your Grace, good sir," Keira went on. He waited until Hamm'tt, at least, had obeyed, and the Governor General had taken a stand to the left of the Grand Duke's chair. A subordinate's position, Keira thought. Does she have the Order, then? "What brings you here, your Grace? Have you decided to challenge me after all?"

The Governor General stiffened nervously at the suggestion of insult, but Hamm'tt tilted her head to one side, not quite smiling. Keira studied her, a handsome woman whose brown skin had a suggestion of velvet. Her brown eyes were hooded, as though she were peering out through the holes in a mask. Her loosely draped, gauzy tunic was a pleasing contrast to the gleaming metal of the leg pieces. She was aware of his scrutiny, and smiled.

"No, your Majesty, I haven't come to challenge you. But before I explain my business, I believe you know my client, the Governor Alau?"

The Governor General bowed low, and Keira nodded acknowledgement. He had met Alau before; it had been the Order, and ultimately Alau, who had certified his Talent. But he had not known that Alau was a Hamm'tt client—a Hamm'tt vassal, probably the child of an El Nath majore, removed by his office from the Conventional political game, but still under some obligation to his former lord. It was not a pleasant thought. If Hamm'tt could tap the power of the Order. . . . Out of the corner of his eye, he saw Lilika tense, though her hands remained motionless at her side.

"You will note I have not challenged you," Hamm'tt said, with a sidelong glance at the soldier-minore. Her lips twitched again, though whether in humor or irritation Keira could not be sure. "In earnest of that, I understand there is some question about the impartiality of the last judge."

"So it has been said," Keira answered, "and there is proof of it."

Alau shifted uneasily, and Hamm'tt quieted him with a look. "As you know," she went on calmly, "I am Presiding Secretary of The House of the Gordiae. Such an accusation touched my honor, as well as the Order's. And I will not have that."

Keira sat very still, Talent flaring to life. Her statement did not fit the pattern; there were none of the imperceptible shifts that betrayed true anger. She was using this, he felt certain. It simply fell in with some plan she had already made.

"I have spoken to Alau, who assures me that the Order did not—does not—sanction this. And he has also given me, his patron and the wronged party, assurance that any more such unConventional behavior will be sought out and punished by the seniors of the Order."

Keira nodded. He did not need to ask why Hamm'tt, rather than he, was considered the injured party: the interregnum he himself had declared could be held to legitimize almost any trick. So now the Order is a card in her hand, he thought. Highly unConventional for them to take sides—he glanced at Alau, who nodded, as if to confirm his thought or her words—but they are the arbiters of Convention. Who can question them?

"I offer this in earnest of my intentions," Hamm'tt went on, smiling faintly, "because I wish to speak frankly. You know that I am a danger to you, perhaps the most dangerous of the undeclared Domus lords."

True enough, Keira thought, and why are you flaunting that? "You would be a dangerous enemy," he said aloud.

"I follow Convention," Hamm'tt went on. "I cannot see my way to a certain victory, and therefore I am hesitant. But I want power, more power than the third of the four old Domi can wield."

"You are already very powerful," Keira said. "El Nath, Simba, Sahara, Cape Fear all under your personal control, and the Doldrums and St. Katherine and New Jerusalem all pay your taxes. What more do you need?"

"Hamm'tt is shadowed by de Terranin and de la Mar," the Duke answered simply. "If I cannot be

empress—and that is not altogether clear—I would
be first among the Grand Dukes. I offer you my
full support, with all the influence at my command,
under Oath and Convention, in exchange for two
things. First, the Chancellorship, so that I am first
noble of the Imperium. Second, to seal the bargain, I want our Domi joined by marriage—true
marriage."

Keira dropped his eyes to hide his shock. Marriage between the senior members of two Domi
Aureae was unheard of. Alliances were sealed by
the marriage of majore and minore, each ally mar-
rying the minore vassal of the other party in the
alliance. That kept any one Domus from gaining
too large a holding. Convention dictated that not
only to protect the emperor from too-powerful
vassals, but also to keep majore holdings manageable. It also limited the number of majores, vital
for peace in the Imperium. Second children, non-
heirs, existed only to insure the line of descent
should something happen to the heir; they were
allowed neither to bear nor beget children, for fear
of founding a collateral line that might ultimately
prove dangerous. He shook himself, smiled.

"The Imperial Domus already controls two full
systems, Avalon and Citadel, and I intend to exert
my rights over Hellmouth," he said. "It would be
unConventional to join El Nath to the Imperial
holdings."

"Only slightly more unConventional than joining Hellmouth to Avalon," Hamm'tt observed.
"However, I agree. It wouldn't do at all for you to
take my system. May I remind you of your own
family's solution to the problem? The first child
belongs to the parent of higher rank, the second to
the lower."

Hamm'tt had done her research all right, Keira
thought. The Renaults had followed that system in
the earliest days, when the family confined its

alliances to its own system. But the imposition of Convention, and Hellmouth's new ties with the other worlds, had made the old ways of no importance. Still, it would work. "And our Talents?"

"Are compatible," Hamm'tt said. "It's a safe match, genetically, with all the right Talents dominant."

And at what price? Keira thought, but said nothing. She could not lie too blatantly; the inevitable minor defects could be adjusted during gestation. He glanced at the braces strengthening Hamm'tt's legs. That at least would not matter, except as one more genetic factor: no majore carried her own children. And Hamm'tt's support would be valuable—doubly valuable with the Order behind her; it would be dangerous in the same measure to refuse. The whole proposal was of questionable Convention, but with the Order bound now to Hamm'tt, the marriage would be sanctioned. And when had the Renaults worried about bending Convention? His Talent was silent, and he took that for assent. "Very well, Lady, I agree. We can draw up a detailed contract later, I trust?"

"Of course, but I think we should swear to the bargain now." Hamm'tt was smiling, but Keira could sense the steel behind it. They would swear now, and on her terms, or she would join Edouard, no matter how much she disliked him.

"Certainly." Keira framed the ritual words, binding himself to marry Desolin Hamm'tt and make her his Chancellor, first among the Domi lords—if their Talents proved compatible. Hamm'tt, in her turn, made the proper gesture, invoking divine and Conventional censure if she broke her given word, and swore her loyalty, in return for power and marriage as a symbol of that power.

Such an unConventional arrangement could not be kept secret for very long. The Heralds who manned the University's archives and handled the routine functions of government were trained to cross-check requests for information, and the tapes were indicative of only one thing. The Heralds were also human: within a local day, rumors of the marriage had spread as far as the Federal embassy. Denisov-Graham stared at the reports that appeared on his desk, sighed, and erased the taped report he had been working on. Rubenstein smiled down at him, the expression humorless.

Denisov-Graham sighed again. "I assume Keira is buying support," he said. "But I thought this kind of marriage was illegal."

Sakima, standing at Rubenstein's shoulder, shook her head fractionally, but said nothing.

"Have a seat," Denisov-Graham said, after a moment. "Why isn't it illegal, Sakima?"

The cultural liaison seated herself primly in the straight-backed chair to the left of the ambassador's desk, folding her hands neatly in her lap. Rubenstein perched informally on the arm of a second chair.

"It isn't illegal," Rubenstein said wearily, "because the Order says it isn't."

Sakima shifted uneasily. "There are precedents for this sort of marriage—Hellmouth precedents."

"Hellmouth." Denisov-Graham shook his head. "That shouldn't surprise me. All right, give me a coherent analysis."

"No such thing," Rubenstein muttered.

Denisov-Graham ignored her. "How accurate are these rumors?"

"An eighty-three percent probability, Ioan," Rubenstein said.

"Are those the bookmakers' odds?" Denisov-Graham asked.

"Yes," Rubenstein said.

Sakima sighed.

"So Hamm'tt's allied herself pretty conspicuously with Keira," the ambassador said. "Why—and why this way?"

Rubenstein shrugged. "Strengthens her position, probably. She didn't take advantage of the interregnum, so maybe she didn't think she could win any other way."

Sakima raised her head, and Denisov-Graham could almost hear the click of steel on steel as she met the undersecretary's gaze. "I disagree. The Grand Duke is controlling the Order—"

"How?" Denisov-Graham wanted to know.

"The Order's leader is an El Nath majore by birth—the Grand Duke's vassal. I think she forced Keira to accept her support, rather than him winning her to his side."

Denisov-Graham seriously doubted anyone could force Keira to do anything he didn't want to do, but decided not to say anything. "You think Hamm'tt's trying to be a power behind the throne?"

"Possibly," Sakima answered. Rubenstein made a face, but said nothing.

"All right, we'll wait and see," Denisov-Graham said. It was typical, he thought. Sakima always made statements like that, then backed down without committing herself.

"It's Talent," Rubenstein said suddenly, with the expression of someone making a concession. "Probably that influenced her decision, and we'll pick up the pattern in a few weeks—maybe a month, local."

"Talent," Sakima muttered.

Denisov-Graham nodded. Not even their most sophisticated computer programs could always pick up the patterns followed by the Imperial nobles; any analysis always had a huge chance of error. But still.... "Run a study," he said. "See what you can pick up. Put the full staff on it. Am I right in thinking that Hamm'tt's support strengthens Keira immensely?"

Rubenstein nodded. "She's rich, has rich worlds, and a private fleet. Plus she has a lot of influence among the minores from gaming."

"All right." Denisov-Graham looked down at his reports, making sure he had not forgotten anything. "Sakima, I want that full analysis as soon as you can get it to me. I also want everything we have on Hamm'tt."

Rubenstein nodded, sliding up off the chair arm. "I'll get right on it, Ioan." Sakima echoed her.

Left alone, Denisov-Graham swung away from his desk, staring out over the parkland toward the buildings of the Government Center. He had received word from the Federal Governing Board that morning, dumping the question of official Federal acknowledgement of Keira back in his lap. He had expected that, but it made his job no easier. Certainly Hamm'tt's support improved Keira's chances, if the unConventionality did not alienate the more conservative nobles. And no matter what the Order decreed, this sort of alliance was unConventional, at least as he understood Convention.

He stood up nervously, leaned against the sun-warmed glass of his window-wall, not really seeing the mechanical graders that moved through the park. I don't like the way things are heading, he thought. Though of course this is nothing new. Convention has been less and less binding, at least in the borderline cases, ever since I was assigned here. And my predecessor said the same thing. But to control the Order, which controls Convention, and to control it openly.... That's too blatant. And the majores have a second candidate.

He turned back to his desk, touched keys on the desk display to call up the list of Commons' Councils that had acknowledged Keira. The acceptance was more or less routine, or should be, the commoners having bargained their political voice in true feudal fashion, rights given up for protection.

The Councils should not acknowledge Keira until their overlords had declared themselves. For the most part, that was the case. The Ojeda clients led the list; Avalon and Citadel, the worlds of the Imperial Domus, had answered, while the de Terranin worlds stayed mute—but there was one notable exception. Hellmouth had acknowledged Keira within days of the announcement. Given the time lag, Denisov-Graham thought, they must have met and decided within hours of getting word that Keira was the heir. And that was completely unprecedented. It meant that the commoners, at least on Hellmouth, were moving to take back their political rights—or did it? After all, Keira was a Renault, the rightful overlord, and those loyalties were almost inconceivably strong in the Imperium. It could also mean that Keira had more support among the Hellmouth majores than they had expected.

He blanked the display, seated himself, and pulled the voicewriter closer. The news changed his assessment of Keira's position, and he had to report that to the Board. But he could not shake the conviction that things were changing in the Imperium, that the system itself was shifting, and that the winner would be the claimant who could best predict those changes.

Chapter 13

Keira returned to the Imperial Quarters well after midnight, tired from negotiating with the Eger to set Ayakawa's trial. He dismissed even the serbots, stretching out on one of the couches in the innermost room. It was the first time he had been alone in days, but he was too tired to appreciate it. He was also too keyed up to sleep. He considered calling a serbot for a sedative, but he had been depending on stimulants for the past three days. Three days ... three days since he had accepted Hamm'tt's offer, three days of setting things in motion, of consolidating one kind of support and reaching for others.

It was clear Edouard was plotting something—I made a bad mistake there, Keira thought. I should have made sure he gave me his Oath that night— but at least his father was unable to help him openly. Vasili Andros was active in the March- Worlds, not getting very far—and neither was Edouard. But the emperor could not act until they did something overt. Keira knew all of the Conven- tional reasons for waiting, and detested all of them. But whoever moved first would be in the wrong. There was too much to be gained from portraying Edouard as the aggressor. And if nothing else, wait- ing gave him more time to win the neutral Domi.

The supposed neutrals were not all undecided, though. De la Mar was effectively hostile, with the Grand Duke too sick to control her son. Ojeda balanced that, having deliberately maneuvered to force his Domus into political impotence. Kypria and her agemates might not thank him for that, but they would not break Convention by joining either side. Two of the new Domi, Xio-Sebastina and Santarem, would stay equally quiet. Their vassals, divided by old feuds, would decide on the basis of those local enmities, and there was little he could do to influence their choices. De Terranin and Andros against, Hamm'tt and Lovell-Andriës actively for him, four more neutral or nearly so . . . eight of the nine Domi Aureae were accounted for, but the ninth was the one that mattered most. Or, rather, it was the system that mattered; the Channis Domus was doomed regardless.

Keira sighed, closing his eyes against the star-scattered darkness displayed in the wallscreens. If Channis were doomed, and he himself could not go to Hellmouth to exert his rights, the next most important majore in the system was Owen Castellar, Lord of Hellmouth's moon. And naturally Castellar, after reluctantly acknowledging Keira to be a Renault, was waiting to sell his support to the highest bidder. Lovell-Andriës, distant kin to the Castellars, was on his way to the Hellmouth system with an offer; however, Castellar was closer kin to the de Terranins, and the de Terranins could offer him the lordship of the entire system, raising the Castellars to Domus status. And there was still no word from FitzMary, or the Navy. The Admirals sent their reports on the usual schedule, but made no overtures.

Keira could see the strands of his plotting, alliances, offers, and counteroffers, FitzMary and her mission, starkly outlined by Talent. The possibilities ran together, each so dependent on the others that the lines seemed to knot together, the tangle bulking so large he could not see beyond it. He could only wait, his moves made, for the others' action to clear his path.

Lasca FitzMary settled herself in the wardroom's most comfortable chair, thoughts tinged with a righteous pride. *Land Searcher*, smaller and faster of the two Navy ships assigned to the emperor's personal use, had a reputation as a temperamental ship with a touchy crew. She had found neither to be true, and had also found her skills as captain were still sharp. Best of all, she had made tentative contact with Dai PenMorgan, Admiral of Blue Fleet, and had set up a rendezvous. The Admiral had not seemed unreceptive, even though he must have guessed her mission. . . . The buzzer sounded, cutting through her thoughts. She started up, but the captain of marines stuck one long arm out of the recreational kitchen and touched the intercom plate.

"Wardroom."

"Captain to the bridge. Captain to the bridge, please." The first officer's voice was carefully neutral. "Message from the fleet, sir. Direct and personal."

FitzMary sat up quickly. "What the hell now—?" She cut herself off and scrambled for the door, kicking off her magnetic-soled slippers as she went. With the gravity on, they served only to slow her down. She swung herself up the ladder and the three-leaved hatch spiraled open at her touch. The first officer turned to face her, swinging his heavy crash column away from the banks of exterior controls. He had pulled the combat board into place across the arms of the padded chair: trouble ahead.

"What's up, Rabbie?" FitzMary asked.

"I don't know." Rab Quiric's tone was oddly flat, and he looked away from her. "The tape's there."

And what's got into you? FitzMary thought. Why the first-stage alert if you don't know anything? She settled herself into the captain's column, kicking the power on as she did so. The faint vibration that came through the chair cushions was not as comforting as it usually was. A tape was sitting on the flaring arm of the chair.

"What's the trouble?" she said again.

"Change of rendezvous point," Quiric said.

FitzMary whistled softly, and pulled her own combat board into place. At the same time, a miniature viewer swung into place, servos whining gently. She fed the tape into the machine, and waited until the screen flashed white. After a moment, letters appeared—routing codes—and then the glaring screen softened into the grey of a Navy ship's padded bulkheads. PenMorgan stared out at her, frowning behind his heavy beard.

"Captain FitzMary, due to circumstances, I am forced to change our rendezvous point. Time and coordinates follow." The screen blanked abruptly, filled with numbers.

"What the *hell*?" FitzMary muttered, and touched buttons to freeze the coordinates. Then she activated the navigation tank, plugging in the numbers from the screen. The tank lit, tiny stars flickering on, and a red dot blossomed, marking the rendezvous point. It was very close to a jump point, not a standard military rendezvous, and her frown deepened. What's he up to? she wondered. That's a multi-exit jump. It'll take the fleet to the MarchWorlds, or into the Central Approach Chain and maybe Avalon. The first rendezvous he gave was defensible. . . . She was suddenly conscious of the waiting silence.

"Rab, can you get the numbers from my tank?"

"Yes, captain." There was a pause, and Quiric said, "Plugged in."

"What's the time differential?"

Quiric's shrug was evident in his voice. "Almost nonexistent."

"All right," FitzMary said. "Plot me a course that gets us there a little early. I'll take a long jump if we have to."

"Yes, sir."

FitzMary leaned back in her column, flipped switches to slave the combat board to the exterior controls, and watched as lights and numbers shifted in the navigation tank. After a few minutes, the lights steadied. Three jumps, none over two minutes, to a total of twelve hours transit time . . . "It looks good," she said.

"Yes, sir." Quiric looked to the pilot, leaning half out of his own column to reach the more sensitive main controls. "Helmsman, execute."

"Sir." The pilot touched buttons, moved the throttle a fraction of an inch, and the clipper shuddered delicately to the thrust of oversized engines. Mimis Jan was a Talented pilot; FitzMary found real pleasure in watching him shift from one course to the other. In the navigation tank, lights changed a final time, the tiny triangle that represented the ship shifting from one broad course line to another.

"ETA for the first jump, two hours, forty-three minutes standard," Quiric announced. "ETA for the final point, eleven hours, forty-eight minutes standard."

"Thank you," FitzMary said. "Nonessential crew stand down." She leaned back against the oil-cushions, staring at the cramped bridge. *Land Searcher* had been built after the plans for a Terran Exploration Service ship—possibly from the remains of just such an Old Federal relic, though most of her parts would have been replaced two or three times since those days. Her bridge had never been designed to hold the bulky crash columns. They sprouted from the deck in front of each major station, designed to protect essential crew from everything short of a direct hit. Ugly things, she thought, like the unbranching tuber-trees of Jerra, but bronze-brown rather than the waxy apple-red of the trees. She made a wry face. All very well, she thought, but it doesn't answer what PenMorgan's up to. He didn't trust Keira, of that she was certain, but she could not see the threat in a single ship. Of course, at the rendezvous, off MJ1106b, PenMorgan could reach the leaders of either side quickly, in a maximum of five jumps. He was hedging his bets, of course—as she would in those circumstances— but it didn't make her any happier. PenMorgan would have had offers from Edouard, and she did not like to think what would happen to the losing messenger.

Land Searcher reached the rendezvous point on schedule, ahead of the fleet. FitzMary pulled the ship out of the usual transit plane, shut down the non-essential systems, and ran the sensors up to their highest capacity, waiting for the Admiral. They had barely had time to adjust to the new quiet when the alarms sounded: PenMorgan, too, had arrived early. FitzMary swore, clawing for the ID switch, and relaxed a little as she recognized the familiar blips on her repeater screen.

"Rab, turn those things off!" she yelled into her microphone, and a moment later the alarms shut down.

"*Tyr* acknowledges us," Quiric announced.

At the same time the communications man said, "Captain, message from *Tyr*."

"Put it on my speaker," FitzMary said.

The system crackled for a moment before the technician caught the carrier wave, and than an unfamiliar voice said, "Captain FitzMary. Varnaud, commanding *Tyr*. You're to report aboard *Tyr* immediately, for your meeting with the Admiral.

I've already dispatched a gig. It'll reach you in ten minutes standard. *Tyr* out.''

FitzMary touched her own mike. "FitzMary, commanding *Land Searcher*. We've got the gig on our scopes.'' She glanced quickly at the repeater, but it was still dark. Oh, well, let him assume we're really efficient. No, there it is. "I acknowledge, docking in ten minutes standard. *Searcher* out.'' She sighed. The years at court had made it no easier to function as both captain and imperial representative, subordinate and equal to the Admirals. "Rab, you'll have the con until I get back. If anything happens, you'll find a tape in my cabin. Get it to Avalon.''

"Yes, sir,'' Quiric said, face wooden. If anything happened to her, they both knew it was unlikely the ship would survive to pass the message.

The gig linked with them on schedule, and FitzMary swung herself down to the lower deck. The marine captain was waiting outside the lock, too casually.

"Need some company, captain?'' he asked, his hand resting on the butt of his holstered blaster, the blaster he almost never wore shipboard.

"No, Tyree, if I needed you, I'd've told you so,'' FitzMary said. Deep inside, she wished she could say yes, but to bring a marine, to imply that she needed protection, was an insult, would jeopardize her cause. Taking a deep breath, she cycled the lock, waited for the doors to close behind her and open again in front, then swung herself out of gravity and into the transfer tube. Another marine was waiting at the far end, ostensibly to help her into the lighter gravity of the gig. His grip was disconcertingly strong.

The gig's crew did not speak, except to ask her to move out of the way, and the same thing was true when she reached *Tyr*. The junior lieutenant who met her at the lock said only that he would take her directly to the Admiral, and lapsed into an impenetrable silence. He stopped in front of a red-painted door, and touched the outside speaker. "Delsin here, sir. I've brought Captain FitzMary."

The door slid open instantly, revealing a slim albino lieutenant, who stood to block the other lieutenant's view of the cabin. "Please come in, Captain," she said. "That will be all, Delsin."

The albino—an Oceanan or a Far Havenite, probably, FitzMary thought—stood aside just enough to let the other woman into the surprisingly spacious cabin, and Dai PenMorgan swung around to face them. FitzMary had seen him before, but only among crowds and from a greater distance. He was smaller than she had remembered, shorter and fractionally thinner, but his beard still looked as though small rodents had been nesting in its depths.

"So. FitzMary." PenMorgan looked angry, but his face rarely relaxed from a scowl. "Sit, Captain."

FitzMary did as she was told, perching on the edge of the chair the lieutenant indicated. PenMorgan glowered at her, then lowered himself carefully to the chair beside his massive console.

"FitzMary," PenMorgan muttered again, drawing his eyebrows together in a frown that made canyons of the deep lines of his forehead.

After another long silence, the flag lieutenant cleared her throat and said tentatively, "The tape's not running, sir."

"Oh, be quiet, you. It's not that simple." PenMorgan brooded for a moment longer, eyes fixed on nothing. Then he said slowly, as though thinking aloud, "FitzMary. Or the last Silvertree. . . . Damn it all, he's pushing me, and I don't know why."

FitzMary sat very still, appalled by a new thought. The Admiral was seeing her as a possible claimant to the throne, not just as Keira's messenger. She cleared her throat, but PenMorgan seemed not to hear her.

"She's not majore?" he demanded abruptly, wheeling to confront his flag lieutenant. Unmoved, the pale woman touched buttons on her own keyboard.

"No, sir."

"You're sure? Not like this Renault, is it?"

FitzMary felt her cheeks grow hot with anger at being discussed as though she were no more than a piece of furniture. She said evenly, speaking through the lieutenant's answer. "I'm not majore, sir, nor can I breed majore children."

PenMorgan seemed to see her for the first time. "Lucky for someone," he said.

FitzMary seized the moment. "I have been sent by the emperor, sir. Will you see my credentials?" She waited until PenMorgan had given her an impatient nod before reaching slowly into the inner pocket of her coveralls. She offered the tape to the Admiral, who tossed it without looking to the flag lieutenant. The pale woman caught it neatly and inserted it into a viewer.

"Sir?" she said, and offered PenMorgan the earphones. The Admiral took them with a grunt of thanks, and swung the machine so that he alone could see and hear. The flag lieutenant waited with no sign of impatience while PenMorgan played the tape once, rewound it, and played it again. FitzMary tried to copy her stillness. At last PenMorgan pulled off the headphones and tossed them onto the console. The flag lieutenant caught them before they fell, but the Admiral did not notice.

"So you've decided to serve this Renault, have you? And he wants my service, too?"

"Yes, sir—" FitzMary began, but PenMorgan kept talking as though he hadn't heard her interruption.

"So why does he put the Silvertree heir under my hand?"

In the sudden quiet, the flag lieutenant cleared her throat. "Excuse me, Admiral, but I ran a projection of Keira's possible motives while we were on our way to the rendezvous."

"Why didn't you tell me before?" PenMorgan snarled. Before the woman could answer, he turned away. "Never mind, give me the tape."

The lieutenant obeyed, saying expressionlessly, "The risk isn't so great—the captain isn't majore—and it makes you declare yourself earlier."

The Admiral stared at her for a moment. "Your Renault plays dangerous games, Captain," he said at last. "Maslin, I'll want a detailed analysis later. For now, my compliments to Captain Varnaud, and I want a course to Avalon. Then find Captain FitzMary a place to sleep."

"Yes, sir," Maslin said. Her white fingers moved rapidly over her keyboard, noting down the orders.

"Avalon?" FitzMary said.

"Yes, Avalon." PenMorgan grinned briefly, an expression more dangerous than any of his frowns. "I want to meet with this Keira. You have the authority to arrange that?"

"I do. But I'll travel on my own ship, thank you, Admiral," FitzMary answered.

"As you please," PenMorgan said. "Maslin, I'll want to talk to Varnaud about the escort. See Captain FitzMary to the gig."

"Yes, sir," Maslin said again. She rose, switching off her console. "If you'll follow me, Captain?"

"Certainly," FitzMary said. Half of her mission accomplished, at least, she thought. Knowing Keira, he had probably planned it to end this way. I just hope he knows what he's doing.

Chapter 14

For the meeting with the Admiral, Keira took over the orbiting schooner station, temporarily displacing the pilots and rigging crews who made their homes there. It had taken a great deal of negotiation to choose the station: Doran had wanted to hold this meeting on Avalon itself, where Pen-Morgan and his delegation would be cut off from the awesome firepower of their ships, and the ships from Lovell-Andriës fleet could be effective. Pen-Morgan had wanted to meet on the Navy's station on the Tor, Avalon's single natural satellite. The commercial stations were the logical compromise; the schooner station, where the wealthy minority who indulged in schooner racing stored and repaired their fragile ships, was the smallest and most defensible of the group in orbit. It had been Keira's first choice.

Lilika shifted suddenly, pointing to the lit view-screen that turned one bulkhead into an illusory window on space. "Pardon, Majesty, but the cruiser's dropped its shuttle."

Keira turned to face the picture, holding back his excitement only with an effort. The gig, banded by a single red stripe running from nose to tail fins, floated leisurely toward the station's main dock. *Tyr* hung just out of camera range, the underside of the great bow filling one corner of the screen. Though the Navy would deny it, all her guns would be trained on the station. And the great guns from the Tor, now firmly under control of the Guard, were trained on Tyr: stalemate.

"Thank you, Lilika." Keira spoke absently, still watching the screen as the shuttle edged toward the dock. It disappeared at last from the camera's view, and a moment later a thin chime sounded.

"The Admiral has docked," Lilika announced.

"Very good." Keira leaned against the bulkhead, his mind running down the list of key points and phrases, through the channels of the simulations he had run over and over again. The essence of fifty games was distilled into a single tape, waiting in the console in the far corner, humming to itself. It should convince, where his own words might fail.

The doorchime sounded, and Keira pulled himself upright, nodding to Doran. The general passed a hand across the door controls, and the naval delegation entered, flanked by a squad of empty-eyed Guardsmen. The Admiral had brought his own guards, Marines from the cruiser, but only two were with him now, their holsters empty. He had also brought his officers, and the Guards had not dared take their weapons. The bulky Admiral was shadowed by a fragile-looking young woman who must be his flag-lieutenant, and by Varnaud of *Tyr*. FitzMary walked both behind and to one side of the others, visibly disassociating herself from them.

"Good sirs," Keira said. The group moved almost as one, bowing over their clasped hands, only FitzMary apart. Then they straightened, and Keira felt PenMorgan's eyes upon him. The emperor stared back, knowing he could stand the scrutiny. He had dressed with calculated simplicity, tunic over trousers, grey over black, and he had wrapped a black scarf around his head in place of a coronet. His hair flamed straight to his shoulders beneath it. He waited a moment longer, then gestured to the waiting chairs. "Be seated, please."

PenMorgan hesitated, then nodded thanks and lowered his bulk into the central chair. The other officers followed his lead, FitzMary still keeping subtly apart, and the Marines positioned themselves behind the Admiral's chair. Keira waited until they were settled, then sat in the high-backed chair Doran had found somewhere. It was not quite a throne.

He let them wait, studying each one carefully. PenMorgan was furious, that could be seen in his scowl and the set of his jutting beard, but his eyes were more calculating than angry. Varnaud was merely watchful, observing for the fleet. The flag-lieutenant was Talented: her reddish eyes were empty and unfocused, seeking new factors for her equations. FitzMary was very quiet, her hands folded in her lap.

"It's good to see you again, Captain FitzMary," Keira said at last. FitzMary bowed gravely.

"Thank you, your Majesty."

"Enough," PenMorgan said roughly. His normally ruddy cheeks were even redder with suppressed anger. "You've summoned me, let's get on with it. What do you want?"

"You will address his Majesty by his title, Admiral," Doran said quietly. "If you please."

PenMorgan snorted. "You've not been crowned, General. Nor has his—Highness." That was an ambiguous title, no longer a legitimate part of the Imperial hierarchy, but so old that no one could really find fault with it. "I asked an honest question, Highness."

"And will get an honest answer," Keira said. I know this game, he thought. He means to startle me by being blunt. He thinks me too subtle, too much the calculating majore to be able to handle that. But I can meet him on his own ground. "I am quite certain your flag officers have already analyzed all possible meanings of my invitation. Primarily, of course, I wanted to see what you would do. And I sent you Captain FitzMary to—raise the stakes." As he said that, Keira let his eyes slide to the flag lieutenant, and was gratified by the sudden focusing of the young woman's stare.

"And now you've seen, Highness." PenMorgan's anger was a shield, Keira realized suddenly, damping out all other emotions.

"Yes. You're here," Keira said. "And you brought a battle cruiser."

After a moment, when the emperor said nothing further, PenMorgan growled, "The Navy protects itself."

"Of course," Keira said. "And yet you weren't ready to challenge me."

PenMorgan went briefly still, and scowled more deeply to make up for the momentary lapse. "My loyalty is to the Imperium," he snapped.

"And you see no better alternative than myself," Keira agreed mildly.

"So far, Highness," PenMorgan said. He was surprisingly calm, suddenly, flirting with treason. "All my projections tell me that you will set off a wave of unrest, and that you won't survive a year beyond your coronation."

"And what options has that left you?" Keira asked. The Admiral merely looked at him, mutely refusing to respond. "To join me, bettering the odds in my favor. To do nothing, to wait out the crisis, and swear loyalty to the winner. To join any other claimant. I've played this game already, Admiral. And I'll make you a wager."

PenMorgan still said nothing, but his entire being seemed to stiffen, like a hunting beast freezing onto the scent of its prey. The albino lieutenant shook her head, lost.

"There is a tape in the viewer," Keira went on.

"The results of many hours' gaming. I'll wager we've guessed and answered all your options."

PenMorgan shook his head. "I'll see the tape."

"Make free."

The Admiral hoisted himself out of the chair and crossed to the console, his footsteps ringing heavily even on the soft tiled decking. He cocked his head at the controls, then touched keys, leaning forward so that his body blocked the others' view of the screen. Keira could read the progress of the tape, the flow of code-words that traced each possible course of action, in the Admiral's hands, flexing gently on the edges of the console. He followed the simulations' course from the dangerous, almost anarchy that could so easily follow the Navy's declaration of neutrality, as the individual minores took their ships out of service to follow their own masters, to the chaos and devastation that would follow the Navy's joining Edouard while the Overlord had no majore support. The tape ended there. PenMorgan's hands clenched tight, showing bone at the knuckles, then loosened. He switched the machine off.

"And can I trust this, Majesty?"

"On my words, as Renault and majore," Keira said gently. "This is true to the best of my seeing." It was the one oath no noble, not even a Renault, could break, even in the face of death. PenMorgan sighed slowly, then bowed.

"You have me, your Majesty. I will serve you."

Chapter 15

Desolin Hamm'tt floated easily in the pool, the faint currents caressing her bare arms and the skin that showed between the turns of the spiral braces, waiting. The diving mask fitted tightly over her face, comfortingly like a gaming helmet, and the weighted belt that negated her natural buoyancy was heavy on her hips. She was terribly aware of all these sensations, of the pull of her breathing as the mask filtered oxygen from the water, and the quickened beat of her heart, of the way the currents moved against her, and of the glimmer of the surface two meters above her head.

There was a sudden chill in the water, a tendril of current curling up from the colder layers at the bottom of the pool: the remote. She doubled quickly, curved hands cutting the water, twisted and dodged as the torpedo-shaped machine bored through the space she had just occupied, its motor leaving a sudden flurry of bubbles. The computer quickly located it again, and the remote swung in its tracks. She threw herself to one side, dove deep, hands pulling her hard toward the tiled floor of the pool. The machine followed, unaffected by the depth even though her ears ached from it. At the last minute she spun, flipping head over heels, and her braced feet slapped the tiles. In one smooth movement, she crouched and leaped at the machine as it bore down toward her. It made an abortive attempt to follow the movement, but her palm struck the padded casing, and the remote died. It sank slowly past her, toward the wall of the pool.

She had gotten disoriented again, she realized. The light "above" her that she had half-consciously identified as the surface was really the glass wall of the observation room, presently unoccupied and unlit. The "floor" became a wall, and the wall where the remote rested, moving sluggishly to the current, became the floor. She shook her head, the water tugging at her mask. That was part of the problem of learning to swim in natural pools, rather than in the sporttanks that were merely rooms filled with water from floor to ceiling: you would always rely on the wrong signals. She would try again, and see if she could break the habit.

Orienting herself, feet toward the floor, head toward the ceiling, she dove for the remote, then swam toward the open mouth of the projector. Before she could insert the machine and call up another attack, there was a dull buzz and the glass wall suddenly blazed with light.

That was even more disorienting, to have an entire room suddenly materialize beside her, so that she hung suspended like a technician on EVA. Hisako, the senior minore of her personal household, was bending over the control board, a microphone at her lips.

"Lady." The word came slowly and somewhat distorted from the phones set into the corners of the tank. "The contract has arrived, and Dan Aisan has given preliminary approval."

Desolin had asked to be notified when that happened. She nodded—the mask kept her from speaking—and jerked her thumb at the ceiling: "I'm coming up."

But instead of rising, she dove again, angling her body toward the far corner of the pool, where the oval of the lock casing made a faint shadow against the pale walls. She caught at the inset handholds beside it, hooked left hand and foot around the grips. With her free hand, she groped for the lever that controlled the door, and forced it down. The door popped outward, and she swam through into the lock chamber.

Lights flashed on inside as sensors registered her presence. She reached for the handholds on the inner walls, not inset here but standing out like the rungs of a ladder, and anchored herself again by hand and braced leg. She caught the inner lever on the second try and pulled the door shut behind her, throwing all her weight on the bar to make sure the seal was tight. Water spurted backward from the sealing, and lights flashed red on the panels above both near and far doors. The seal was good, and the transfer sequence was activated. The water around her shuddered with the faraway beat of the pumps, and then the currents changed, swept down past her shoulder to the drains beneath her feet.

After a little, the water had ebbed enough to that she could raise her arm and touch the surface. As the water dropped further, gravity returned, and she eased herself slowly into an upright position, her feet resting lightly on the soft, tightly woven gridding that covered the drains. She touched the braces lightly, adjusting the metal to provide more support. Her head broke the surface, and she ducked to bring her face back under the water, breathing through the mask, until her feet were firmly anchored. The suction tickled gently, pulling at the soles of her feet. She straightened, her face fully out of the water now, and pulled off the mask. The air was warm even on her damp skin, and held the spicy scent of recirculation.

The water level dropped more quickly now, from her shoulders to her waist, then crawled down her legs. The last centimeters lapped at her toes and vanished with a deep-throated gurgle. The sign above the far door turned green: sequence complete, exit permitted. She popped the door, and winced as she stepped out through the curtain of hot rushing air. It dried her efficiently, however; she left no puddles as she unlatched the weighted belt and handed it to the waiting serbot. Another serbot handed her a robe, and she shrugged it on, hugging it tight across her breasts. The skin-tight bodysuit was already dry, the Delrwa-woven material shedding water even more quickly than her skin under the dryers.

Hisako was waiting for her in the outer dressing room where the cold metal walls gave way to the muted colors of plaster and paint. A third serbot, the general Palace glyph prominent on its bulging top casing, hovered beside the minore, the Grand Duke's clothing held in multiple extensors. A fifth arm reached for Desolin's robe as she discarded it, and the Duke reached for the gold-scattered strip of silk that formed her usual loose tunic. She wound it quickly about her body, adjusting it so that the broad band of gold embroidery formed the hem, then tossed the excess length over one shoulder. The weighted end balanced the drag of the material perfectly. Hisako held out the lockbox that held the ducal coronet, and Desolin passed her palm across the sensor to release the catches. The top sprang up, and she lifted out the golden helmet.

"Beautiful, Lady," Hisako said softly.

Desolin smiled, rather wryly, but Hisako had cared for her since adolescence, and was privileged. "Let's go up."

Aisan Lavras min-Hamm'tt was waiting in her receiving room, his hands folded in the sleeves of his official gown. The padded shoulders were too wide for him, making him look even older and more shrunken than he actually was. He had served both her father and grandmother before her, as a judge in the Doldrums' courts, and as their advocate on Avalon.

He rose and bowed as she came in, wincing as Hisako lit the wallscreens and he found himself suddenly surrounded by the hot sands of Sahara. The harsh light struck reflections like sparks from the black satin of his gown, and flashed off the scarlet sleeves that marked him as a judge as well as an advocate. Desolin acknowledged his greeting with a wave, and settled herself on one of the stacks of cushions that served as chairs. A square of carpeting slid aside, and a computer link rose from the floor at her elbow; she ignored it for the moment and accepted the sheaf of papers proffered by the robe-minore.

"This is the final draft, Dan Aisan?" she asked, after glancing over the flimsy pages. As best she could tell, there had been no changes from the previous copies, except for minor turns of phrase, and Lavras would tell her if those made major legal differences.

"Yes, your Grace." Lavras might have served the Hamm'tt Domus for nearly three generations—minores tended to outlive majores, and the commoners outlived them both—but he had never lost the robe-minore's formality of language. "If I might point out, there has been one significant change regarding your children by this marriage." He came diffidently to look over her shoulder, found the passage he wanted, and pointed to it. "Originally, both you and his Majesty were entitled to remove your heir from the common dwelling—presumably Avalon Palace—at any point in the marriage. The emperor suggested, and I saw no reason to oppose him, that for the children's sake, neither one of you be allowed to remove your heir until the child has reached the age of seven standard years."

Desolin considered the question, then nodded. "I see no difficulties there."

"Thank you, your Grace." Lavras bowed gravely. "I anticipated none, so I had the formal contract prepared."

Desolin's eyes strayed from the text in front of her to the advocate's document case, which rested beside his seat, the lock glowing balefully red. The contract itself would be within, hand-typed on individual sheets of paper, not recorded onto tape or even machine-printed. There would be taped copies, of course, to be filed with the Heralds in the University archives and distributed to the various bureaus and the Eger, but those would be made only after the contract had been signed and witnessed.

"Excellent," she said. "Hisako, have the Heralds inform his Majesty that I am ready to sign the contract."

Hisako rose from the cushion where she knelt, and went silently to the screen that concealed the secretary. Rather than speak aloud to it, she unreeled the wire of a filament mike and murmured softly to it. When the acknowledgment came, it was equally muted, and she folded the wire neatly before relaying the message. "Pardon, Lady, but his Majesty will be able to see you in an hour, local."

"Thank you, Hisako," Desolin said. "Will you see that Dan Aisan has everything he needs for the ceremony?"

Recognizing the dismissal, both minores rose and bowed, then slipped away, leaving the Duke alone in the receiving room. Desolin lay back across the cushions, staring up at a ceiling draped with heavy velvyn in imitation of a Saharan nomad's tent. The wallscreens radiated warmth as well as strong light, but she found herself shivering nonetheless. The contract was an irrevocable step, committing both political and person life to one man, and she could not help wondering if she were doing the right thing. Perhaps she should wait, but the chance would not come again. There was never gain without risk: that was the oldest adage of the majores, older than Convention, and one she would need to remember.

And marriage need not affect her personal life that deeply, she reminded herself. Law and Convention both recognized that marriage was for a majore a political act; both provided other institutions for love. She could take lovers if she chose, provided only that she produced no children to complicate the succession. She could even acknowledge a lover as her companion, in effect naming him her partner of choice, and no one could stop her. Even Keira would have to accept that.

Keira had made all the Conventional arrangements for signing the marriage contract, calling three members of his household to witness his signature, and notifying the Order as well, so that a neutral party would register the document and see that it was safely filed with the Heralds. He had posted Guards, but only at the door of the reception room, not inside. Desolin smiled, and ordered her own escort, El Nath soldier-minores, to remain outside with them.

Keira rose to greet her, another good sign. The furniture had been changed at Keira's order, Oriana's gaudy Dresdener things replaced now by an eclectic mix of pieces united only by a serene severity of line and color. The wallscreens were dark, and covered by sheer curtains. That was enough to make her slightly edgy—she had never liked enclosed spaces, preferred at all times to see at least an illusion of open air. Her peculiarity was probably well documented, she thought, and the screens left off deliberately. I won't give him the satisfaction of making me nervous.

"Welcome, your Grace," Keira said. "I hope the occasion will prove auspicious." The words were formulaic, and Desolin could see mischief in his eyes as he recited them. "May I present my household witnesses, Lasca FitzMary min-Renault, Anj Lilika min-Renault, Erik Havener min-Renault. If any of these is not to your liking, speak now."

Desolin murmured the response, scanning the three minores waiting to the right of the emperor's chair. FitzMary she knew, from Oriana's day, and she recognized Lilika; Havener was an unknown quantity. She filed his name for later investigation. He was young, but his gown, scarlet with the black sleeves of an advocate, was badged with the cords that marked scholastic honors. He would be equal in status to her own advocate, and Lavras would probably be able to give her more information.

She introduced her own witnesses, Hisako, Lavras, and the captain of her private cruiser, and waited for the Order priest to complete the short invocation. When it was done, the two advocates stepped forward and unlocked their cases. They exchanged copies of the contract, flipped through the pages a final time, even though the copies had been prepared from an identical tape, then turned to their respective masters.

"This is the contract agreed upon, your Grace," Lavras said. Havener echoed him. Keira nodded, and signalled a serbot for a writing table. The machine rolled one out of a corner, and set it between the two parties, locking the wheels into place before it retreated.

"Your Grace?"

"Yes, I'm ready." The Hamm'tt seal was suddenly heavy around her neck. Desolin fished beneath the draped cloth of her tunic for the clasp, snapped it open, and drew out the seal on its thin chain. It was old, though not the original mechanism, dating from the reign of David V, but it was unquestionably an heirloom. The slim cylinder was as long as her forefinger, the golden casing inlaid with a delicate tracery of vines. The tip was engraved with Hamm'tt's saltire-crossed spear and double crescent. The touch of generations had worn down the inlay around the control points and dulled the finish. She felt for those points, and the seal grew daintily warm in her hand.

She advanced to the little table, set down the contract, chose a pen. Before she could think any more about it, she scrawled name and titles at the bottom of the final page. She set the tip of the seal to the paper beneath the signature, and waited for the puff of smoke. She lifted the seal away, leaving a perfect imprint of the Domus's symbol burned into the paper. She exchanged contracts with Keira and repeated the process, signature, and seal. Keira's mark was new. The symbol of his Domus had always been a wheel; Keira had added a wave to that, rolling over it, but not conquering it. Change and stability, she thought, setting aside the contract, the balance of the Imperium.

The witnesses signed then, and the priest came forward with the official recording camera clamped in the palm of his hand. Solemnly, he photographed each page of each contract, then pronounced a blessing. As always, the sense of ceremony dissolved instantly, leaving majores and minores alike standing awkwardly, not knowing what to do next. Keira clapped his hands, breaking the spell, and serbots appeared to carry the table away. Lavras deftly rescued Desolin's copy of the contract.

"So, your Grace." That was Keira, gathering himself with a shake. His face was very still, too still. Desolin wondered suddenly what he thought of their marriage, after the years with Oriana. If he had loved the empress. . . . Then Keira cleared his throat, and the moment was gone. "We'll meet soon, to consider our strategy?"

"I'm at your disposal," Desolin answered. Whatever Keira thought of this, she realized with an odd feeling of shock that she had what she wanted. Love had always been a remote possibility for her. By this marriage, she would be second in the Imperium, the most powerful of the Domi nobles. And that was good enough for her.

The news that the marriage contract had been signed arrived on Denisov-Graham's desk along with the long-awaited dispatch from the Board. Reading both together, the ambassador could not restrain a wry smile. As always—as was inevitable, even with near-instantaneous communications systems—the Board was a little behind the times: the computers on Terra were predicting that the marriage was merely a rumor, some sort of ploy in the power games, and that Denisov-Graham should disregard it.

Then his smile faded. That prediction was the most concrete piece of advice the Board had sent him. The other eight pages of closely spaced printing were filled with hints and conditional statements disguised as long-range forecasts. Reading between the lines, he knew only too well the message the Board was trying to convey. If you succeed, they were saying, if you put the Federation on the side of the winning candidate and keep us from looking like fools, then we'll support you. If you blow it, we'll recall you and renounce your actions. The situation had been no different in any of the other appointments he had held, but this was somehow different, not least because he had been on Avalon for a few years, long enough to have his own favorites among the nobility. And that, he told himself firmly, was dangerous. He could only

rely on his sense of which one of them would be
most useful to the Federation.

He leaned back in his chair, letting the heavy
piece of furniture bob gently against its stabilizing
coil. The Federation's aims were simple: peace along
the borders, Council and Imperial, for as long as
possible; protection of trade; and, finally, the maintenance of the tacit understanding that Federation
and Imperium, if attacked, would stand together
against the Council. All three were important. These
days, with the Council somnolent, it was no longer
possible to give any one clear priority. His job was
to further all three, by whatever means necessary,
including a discreet bit of king-making if it came
to that.

Denisov-Graham made a face at that thought.
He had a proper confidence in his own abilities,
but no Terran, unTalented and raised outside
Convention, could hope to play at Imperial politics with any success. It shouldn't come to that, he
thought. In fact, as things stand now, there's really
nothing I can do except lend Federal presence to
the coronation of the first Renault. The only possible other claimant is the young de Terranin, and
he doesn't seem to be doing anything at all. So my
job is to persuade Keira that he, too, wants peace
and the unspoken alliance. The question is how to
do it.

Carefully, he laid out his arguments—the advantage of peace and trade, the dangers of the Council,
murkier matters of prestige and previous commit-
ments—then balanced them with the Imperial
counterarguments, and the ancient resentment that
the Old Federation had abandoned the outer worlds.
The inducements were too equally weighted. There
was nothing terribly compelling among the Federation's arguments, nothing to catch Keira's imagination and make him willing to cooperate with
Terra.

Denisov-Graham sighed. There was one thing he could add, one thing he felt almost certain would bring Keira to a bargain. He reached for his keyboard, typed in the series of codes that gave him access to his private files. Even when the security system released the proper file, the words were cryptic, drastically abbreviated: his notes on the bet his ancestor had made with Elidi Renault. That would intrigue Keira, he felt certain, if Keira were anything at all like his Renault ancestors, and he could use that interest to bring Imperium and Federation back to their old, uneasy cooperation.

He checked the schedule projected on one of the console's minor screens. Oriana's funeral was only a day away, Keira's coronation two days later. The day after that, the ambassadors would formally present their credentials. He could spring the bet on Keira then.

Chapter 16

Edouard de Terranin sat on the terrace of his house, the Overlord's Eyrie that dominated Peter's Port on Verii Mir, watching the cloud shadows race across the city beneath him. It was autumn on his world, the best season of the year, when the pungent odor of burning Stevenson's Plant filled the entire northern continent, and the sun gilded the edges of the towering clouds, throwing yellow-white fingers across the horizon. It was cloudy again today—it almost always was, in autumn— but the day was late enough for the eastering sun to break free, dropping below the ramparts of steel blue clouds. Every so often the tiny orb, painful to look at directly, would be obscured by a racing cloud, and the air would suddenly grow chill. When the light came again, it was as though a dying fire had flared up.

Edouard lifted a mug of hot wine, set it down without drinking, and pulled his fur-trimmed jacket about him more closely. The mountain wind, already heavy with snow, knifed through it, cutting him to the bone. He sighed, shivering, but did not go in. There was no other place in the city that was safe enough for him to meet with Vasili Andros; he could suffer a little for security's sake.

"Overlord?" Andros said politely, and Edouard forced himself to turn.

"Welcome, Lord Vasili. Please be seated."

Andros, wrapped in a floor-length cape that seemed to be fur-lined, sat down gratefully, choosing the side of the table where a potted dwarf m'kay's branches broke the full force of the wind. His hands, reaching for his pipe, were white with cold.

"May I call for some wine, Lord Vasili?" Edouard asked solicitously. "I forgot that you are not used to this weather; let me get you a brazier as well."

"The wine would be welcome, the other's not necessary," Andros said. He drew on his short pipe, carefully shielding the bowl, then released a cloud of slightly narcotic smoke. The odor of Stevenson's Plant was suddenly overwhelming, and Edouard could hardly restrain a cough. He suppressed it, and called for the serbot, which rose silently from the elevator hatch and floated across the terrace to the two men. The wind caught at it, making it dip and sway, but the gyros compensated. Lights flashed on its belly, indicating that the computer had stored the new factors of wind direction and velocity. Of course, Edouard thought as he gave it its orders, if the wind dies down or changes direction before it gets back, it'll be in trouble.

"I think the major difficulty is coming from early summer on Avalon," Andros said idly. "My own world, High Barbary, is roughly in step with Avalon, so that at least we're experiencing the same seasons. And most of the other worlds I've visited have either been in step, or completely the opposite. Somehow it's easier to go from one extreme to the other, than from summer to autumn."

"Yes, I agree," Edouard said without listening. He stared out over the sharply slanted roofs of Peter's Port, and the broad expanse of treated concrete beyond that, the spires of control towers and tending stations rising at regular intervals from the pale grey surface. Their shadows moved and danced across the scarred field. Andros was looking at him oddly, and the Overlord collected his thoughts hastily. Before he could continue, the

serbot re-emerged from its housing, carrying a tray
with two more mugs in its wells. They each took a
mug, and Andros leaned forward.

"Well, Overlord, you know I come from your
father."

Edouard felt his mouth tighten in spite of himself.
"What does my father want? He has made it clear
that he will do nothing to help me." He held up
his hand to forestall Andros' immediate protest.
"Forgive me, my Lord, I know I was being unjust.
Having sworn, of course he cannot think of breaking his word."

"As you say." Andros leaned forward even more,
lowering his voice so that Edouard had to strain to
hear over the wind. "But, Overlord, his Grace has
given you all the help that is possible within
Convention, and has done all he could to delay
Keira—again, within Convention. His minores have
been given leave to return to Verii Mir, and nearly
all of his household has come here to pledge their
service. I confess, Overlord, I don't understand your
difficulty."

Edouard looked away over the city, trying to
gather his thoughts. The sun had slipped even lower,
and was now a pale red dot poised directly on top
of one of the port towers. "The difficulty," he said
slowly, "is not a simple question of loyalty."

"No doubt," Andros murmured, and Edouard
looked at him with a sudden hatred he did not
bother to disguise.

Oh, my Lord of the Barbaries, your title's the
right one for you, he thought. You and your sector
are bringing back all the things the Silvertrees
tried to stamp out—that they succeeded in destroying, damn it, until the expansionist lords tried to
revive the old ways. Slavery for criminals rather
than prison, the tight feudality, with the commons
so closely under your control that they have no
recourse, not even to the Assassins. . . . Those were

the things even the Alexanders wanted to see ended. And, since you only have to snap your fingers to bring your petty land-minores groveling to your side, you can't understand why it takes me time to convince the majores to follow me.

"My Lord," he said, stifling his anger, "you must realize two things. First, my father, not I, is Grand Duke. Second, I have been beaten by Keira once already; the majores do not want to see that happen in reality. Especially if they're supporting me at the time."

"Haven't you shown them the projections?"

"Of course."

"And they said?" Andros seemed impervious to the other's dislike.

"My Lord, there is another factor involved here," Edouard said. "If you remember, the Count of Rohan also accepted Keira's challenge. He has sent word to his people, and through the Guild, that he approves of Keira and is giving him his full loyalty. As the Count is the second most powerful landholder on Verii Mir, his opinion divides the northern continent."

"His Grace thought that might be the difficulty," Andros said, quite mildly. He drew deeply on his pipe, and said around the smoke, "He suggested that you consult your sister."

"Alesia?" Edouard frowned. He had hesitated to contact his sister, telling himself that he was worried about the security of any communications, but he knew perfectly well that he had waited for fear of her disapproval. If she, a Sister of the Order, told him that his actions were against honor, he did not know what he would do.

"Yes, Overlord," Andros said. "His Grace suggested that, if she gave you a favorable Reading—and if she were willing to help you, if the Reading were good—the majores would be much more willing to follow you."

Edouard nodded. "That's true." If Alesia gave him a favorable Reading—and he would not admit that she might not—the majores would have to agree that the simulations were not always accurate. You'd think they'd remember that, Edouard thought. They're Talented, they should remember the times that their Talent whispered "no" to a result, not just the times it said "yes." "All right. You may tell my father that I'm going to New Canterbury. He's right. I have to break this stalemate somehow."

Andros stood stiffly, huddling inside his cape. "I'll tell him that, Overlord—your Majesty, I should say now."

"Quite. You'd better stay away from Avalon until after the coronation," Edouard said. "I don't want to lose a loyal servant if you're forced to swear the Oath."

"No, Overlord, I'm afraid I have to go back to Avalon, if only to carry your message." Andros grinned, his teeth white and feral in the dusk. "And I have private business there. If you'll excuse me?"

"Of course." Edouard said automatically, then wished he hadn't. But Andros was already gone. I wonder what he meant by "private business"? he thought. God, please don't let it be some harebrained barbaric plot of his own. That would be just like him, to act like an ancient hero and throw away his honor to win me an empire. I couldn't come to the throne that way. It would hurt my own honor too much.

He stood up quickly, determined to follow the Barbaries lord and have it out with him, but sat down again, defeated. It was only a day's flight, a long jump, but a day's flight, standard, from Verii

Mir to Avalon. Still, if Andros had such a plot in mind, he would never admit it—and my father would never allow it, Edouard thought, so I can rest easy. Always, he's kept Vasili on a short leash. He can continue to do so.

Chapter 17

Oriana's funeral was held two days before the coronation, over two standard weeks after her death. The stasis-held body had lain for that time in the Cathedral, generally ignored by nobility and commoners; it would have lain there for as long as it had taken for a definite heir to appear. The ceremony was widely broadcast—by tradition and Convention only majores attended—and the rites were observed. All over the Imperium, the nobility wore mourning white, and Domi banners were lowered. In the Palace and across the Straits in Government Center, all work stopped for eight hours, the formal holiday welcomed without much regard for its cause.

In the darkened Cathedral, the walls still opaqued in mourning, Keira knelt in the chief mourner's place, closest to the glowing bier. The icy glare of the stasis field was the only light in the long nave; the priests moved like ghosts at the altar, even their droning chant distorted by the field. Within the enclosure of the light, Oriana's broad features seemed unchanged, pale and angry even in death. Keira, the memory of the marriage contract he had signed the day before still heavy in him, could not take his eyes from her. She would have killed him, had she suspected such a move. Had she lived, he would neither have dared nor wished to make such an alliance.

The priests moved close again, surrounding the

bier and momentarily dimming the cold light.
Smoke billowed from their censers, casting new
and shifting shadows across the front of the nave.
The stuff dissipated quickly enough, but even so,
Keira caught a choking breath of the thick, cloying
incense. He smothered his cough, heard other muted
noises among the majores behind him. The sound
was drowned quickly by renewed chanting. Keira,
with the others, made the proper responses, speaking the words that ended the ceremony. The priests
formed into a final escort, two by two, censers still
smoking, and the chief celebrants touched the controls that lifted the bier and sent it floating solemnly in the wake of the procession of lesser priests.
The Guardsmen that lined the aisle, their formal
armor mourning silver rather than the gold of
celebration, snapped to attention. Keira rose, folding his hands into the wide sleeves of his coat, and
took his place directly behind the bier. He was
close enough to feel the faint tingling chill that
radiated from the field. Doran and another of the
senior Guards took their places flanking him, and
the procession moved slowly to the door, the other
majores joining it one by one.

The first priests reached the end of the nave, and
the massive doors rolled back with a low rumbling.
The midday sun struck in, cruelly bright, erasing
the cooler light of the stasis field. Keira winced,
blinded; he stumbled slightly on the low threshold
and the jarring seemed to shake free his Talent.
The funeral was not merely Oriana's, a still voice
whispered as his sight cleared, and he saw the
path of the cortege neatly marked across the im-
maculate lawns of the Palace. Already the ground
gaped wide, polished steps leading down into the
blackness only emphasized by the brilliance of the
sunlight: the Silvertrees, as the Alexanders before
them, were buried beneath the foundations of their

own palace. Oriana's body was going down there, and with it went the Imperium.

"No," Keira whispered, and the sound of his own voice broke the spell. Things have stagnated, yes, but I can change that. I'm more Talented than the last three emperors, and I've hardly been pushed yet. I'll shake things up, I'll bring them back to life. But there had been a black certainty about the first vision, the absolute certainty that came from unsummoned Talent. He groped for a fresh sight, but the first steps of the vault were already beneath his feet, and the sudden shadow drove away the last vestiges of Talent.

FitzMary, with the other minore members of the Imperial household, was not allowed to attend the funeral herself, but rather than watch with the others, she retreated to her own suite of rooms, where she could watch the commoners' broadcast. Especially in the last few years, the commoners' channels had given a better analysis of imperial events than had the Heralds' coverage. At the end of the ceremony, the bookmakers came on: of late, even the commoners liked to think they were playing the nobles' games. Unaccountably depressed, FitzMary switched the channel until the holoscreen showed the Dragon Peak beyond Government Center, snow-capped and serene in the afternoon light.

For the first time since Oriana had died, she felt haunted—by Oriana's ghost and the ghosts of her parents and the aunt who had pushed her to claim the throne. I was—I am unsuitable, she told them silently. Isn't this the next best revenge? To see the Silvertree line extinct, and a total stranger on the throne? There was no answer, and she switched on music to cut the silence. And you, Oriana, she thought, knowing she would never have dared speak so to the Empress while she lived. You terrified me for years, held me hostage, but I've made this choice of my own free will. And you lie in your vault and rot.

The intercom buzzed sharply and she started. "Who's there?"

"Japhet. May I come in?"

"Oh, Japhet." She sounded more relieved than she had intended, and grimaced as she worked the door controls. "Come in, and welcome."

He strolled in, the youthful swagger belied by the tight lines at the corners of his eyes. Seeing those, and remembering how much he knew of past courts, she found herself wondering just how much longer his career would last. She dropped her eyes to hide the thought, but he had seen, and the ghost of a smile crossed his pale lips.

"His Majesty's returned?" she asked quickly.

"Oh, yes."

There was something in Japhet's tone that made her stiffen slightly. "Is everything all right?"

"A good question," Japhet answered. "Something happened during the funeral, and his Majesty won't say what. He saw something, I think, and he's shut himself up with his Readers to see what they can find." His voice was faintly tinged with the bitterness of the unTalented.

FitzMary shivered, wondering if the reflected sense of the emperor's major Talent had sparked her own imaginings. "Will it be all right, do you think? Is it something serious?"

Japhet shrugged. "How can I tell? But unless I miss my guess, he'll spend tomorrow gaming."

"Not a bad thing, I should think," FitzMary said. "The General won't be happy, though."

Japhet grinned, his temper restored, and looked suddenly years younger. "No. I'll be interested in seeing the security arrangements for that."

"So will I." FitzMary crossed to the wall console,

dialed a drink for herself, then turned to Japhet. "What'll you have?"

"Whatever you're having, thank you."

FitzMary grinned evilly and shook her head as she repeated the order. She handed the glass to Japhet, who cocked an eyebrow at it, then glanced up at her and shrugged, equal to anything. He sank gracefully onto a cube of stiff foam, unconsciously arranging himself so that his long limbs showed to advantage. The captain sat less gracefully. "This Reading of his Majesty's," she ventured after a moment. "Do you think it's a true Reading, or emotional?"

Japhet hesitated fractionally. "I couldn't know."

"But he did care for her," FitzMary said.

"Certainly," Japhet said. "There's a Renault for you. What is this, anyway?" he asked, nodding down at his glass.

"A Navy man's drink. Not up to it?" FitzMary answered.

"Not at all," Japhet said carelessly, taking another cautious sip, then holding the glass up to the light.

FitzMary watched him curiously. She had not thought him callous before now. Then, with the unpredictable insight that was like but was not Talent, she understood. His words, the careful pose, the way he had turned the knot of mourning ribbons so that the dangling ends were hidden by his body, all of this took on a new meaning. She smiled, and he looked up. Their eyes met, and then Japhet smiled back, ruefully.

"Forgive me, Captain," he said. "Yes, I did come here with a mind to seducing you. But I'm lonely, and I've slept alone for too long."

FitzMary nodded. "Well, stay a bit."

"Yes." Japhet knew, from his years at court, and before on Mist and New Amsterdam, that he had won. The potential for power shimmered in his mind, possibilities for manipulation and control, and then he killed the idea. I'm growing too old for this, he thought. I'll need friends soon, more than lovers. Be content with what is offered, and don't scheme for more.

As Japhet had predicted, Keira summoned both him and the robe-minore Reader, Erik Havener, early the next morning, to announce that a game had been set up at the University's facilities. They would not use the full projection units—the University did not really have the equipment for the more elaborate games—but instead would rely on the simple code-and-central holo units Keira had used in his duel against the Ojeda Duke. At some point in the past days, the emperor had found time to set up the bare outline of a game simulating the war he expected between himself and Edouard, and Havener found himself assigned the Overlord's part. Seeing the stacks of tapes, copies of Edouard's records from the University archives, and Havener's martyred expression, Japhet was glad he was only acting as referee.

They left the Palace by the wide Upper Sallygate, and the pilot turned the hovercar onto the meticulously clipped lawn that separated the Palace and the University buildings. To the right, across a similarly well-kept green, was the Cathedral, forming the third point of the triangle of buildings on the Palace continent. Its clear walls were still opaqued, this time to hide the preparations for the next day's ceremonies.

The Dean in charge of the Library facilities was waiting under the squat arch of the Quadrangle gate, his brown academic robes blowing wildly in the sudden wind that swept through the long tunnel of the gate. He bowed courteously, then pushed back the cowl of the robe to his shoulders.

"Welcome, your Majesty. I am Otman Rai min-U,

in the service of this place. If your Majesty would follow me, the computer rooms are on the lower levels."

"Lead on, Dan Otman," Keira said. The robe-minore bowed once more, less deeply for fear of disarranging his robes yet again, and turned back into the gate. The hovercar followed him at a decorous pace.

The gate gave way onto a paved courtyard, from the painted lines usually used for parking the various masters' vehicles. There was no ordinance that said they had to live within the University compound with the students; indeed, it argued a certain amount of status for a master to be able to reside in Government Center. The pilot steered the car to a place usually reserved for the senior Librarian, and Rai waited at an ostentatiously safe distance while Keira dismounted. The double steel doors opened at his touch, and emperor and escort followed him inside.

The University buildings were fairly new, built of local stone and wood, but they followed the lines of the pre-Alexandrine house that had been built by one of the local governors for the remains of the Telen Institute for Psionic Studies. The corridors were deliberately labyrinthine, to give the telepaths who had once studied there at least the illusion of the privacy they needed so desperately. They passed a number of rooms, even a few housing suites, and Keira could feel the wariness of the Guards. Each time they passed a brown-robed master or tan-robed student, the soldier-minores tensed, hands straying to their weapons, but nothing untoward happened. Students and masters alike shrank back against the corridor walls, or dropped to their knees to prove their harmlessness.

The computers in the main library, and the gaming rooms attached to it, were buried on the lowest level of the University, perhaps four levels down,

and cut off from the rest of the building by airtight
doors and a layer of reinforced concrete. Only senior masters and Heralds were allowed to use these
consoles; all others used terminals on the upper
levels. One gaming room was reserved for the
emperor, designed so that it could be defended by
a small contingent of Guards. Rai led them to its
armsteel doors and bowed again.

"The chamber, your Majesty." Without waiting
for an answer, he stepped forward and laid his
palm against the lockplate. After a momentary
hesitation, the room's computer accepted the identification and the door slid back. The Guard in charge
of the escort cleared his throat, half-unslinging the
sensor unit he carried slung over one shoulder.

"Your Majesty, shall I check things out first?"

Keira hesitated, and saw the sudden set of the
robe-minore's face. To order a check would be to
insult the University, and he could not afford to
alienate them now. "I don't think that will be
necessary. Thank you, Dan Otman. You have been
most gracious."

The dean could not have ignored that dismissal
even had he wanted to. "Your servant, your Majesty," he murmured, and backed out of sight.

When he was gone, the escort captain, Elsu min-
Renault, stepped forward again, and this time Keira
did not stop him from making a quick scan of the
equipment. After a moment, he signalled that all
was in order, and the players entered. A single
Guard accompanied them; the others arranged
themselves outside the chamber, rifles and communications keyboards ready to hand.

Keira settled himself at a console, feeding tapes
into his machines, and watched the other two set
up their own programs. Japhet, for all that he
would act as judge, worked casually, almost carelessly, choosing tapes seemingly at random and
feeding them into the memory without pausing to

confirm the contents. Havener, on the other hand, proceeded more slowly, scanning each tape briefly before committing it to memory. Of course, his task was in some sense more difficult than Japhet's, Keira had to admit. The judge had to make the moves he thought Edouard would make in a similar situation, based on the Overlord's files, rather than choosing the solution he himself thought the most logical.

"Are you ready?" Japhet abandoned all formality in a game room.

"Yes," Keira said.

"Just a moment, please." Havener hesitated between two final tapes, then darted forward to seize the longer of the two. He slammed it into place, and said, "Yes, I'm ready."

"Then we'll begin." Japhet's hands moved across the primary control board, and the overhead lights went out. They were replaced at once by individual cones of light enclosing each console. A fourth, dimmer cone covered the silent Guard by the door. At the same time, the air between the consoles thickened perceptibly as the holoprojectors came into play. Japhet touched more buttons, glancing from screen to screen, then touched a final sequence of keys. Supplementary screens sprang to life on the players' consoles, and quickly filled with numbers and drastically abbreviated words.

"This is your first random factor," Japhet announced. "Solar weather shifts by a factor of five on the Moänin scale in the indicated systems with the appropriate results."

Keira scanned the screens quickly, noting the areas where he would have to revise any military strategy. The disturbances affected Babylon primarily, and with Babylon her sister worlds of Nineveh and Tyre. These worlds were among the greatest resources of military power in the Imperiums, Babylon for her shipyards, Nineveh and Tyre as the homeworlds of highly trained soldier-minores and unrestrained by a strong Grand Duke. But now, any assistance from those worlds would be delayed by weather. The other disturbances were in the Marches, affecting Diana and Far Haven, and were far less important to him.

Keira turned his attention back to the main boards, concentrating on building up his own alliances and disrupting "Edouard's". From his screens, Havener was doing the same thing, but with a greater emphasis on Church support. Occasionally, Japhet interjected a new factor, but more often his role was to decide the reactions of the other "characters", the nobles and commoners whose support both players sought. At last, they had reached the brink of war, maneuvering cautiously just short of open hostilities, each hoping to force the other into the first act of open aggression. Keira loosed a fleet of partially allied minores from the fringes of Somewhere and ships hired from the Independent Worlds to harass "Edouard's" commercial shipping. "Edouard" retaliated by stepping up his Church-aided propaganda campaign.

"Dialogue," Havener said suddenly.

Keira looked up. He had been so lost in his calculations that the sight of the room beyond his little cone of light was startling, the other two consoles only partly obscured by the hazy light from the holoprojectors.

Japhet consulted his board. "On what terms?"

"A peace mission, an attempt to resolve our differences without bloodshed," Havener answered.

"Acceptable," Keira said without waiting to be asked. "Where?"

"Verii Mir," Havener said promptly, and Keira shot back, "Why not Avalon?"

Japhet laughed aloud. After some sparring, they settled on Babylon, where the solar disturbances would hamper any military action in the system.

"The players have agreed to a dialogue," Japhet said formally. The cones of light faded, though enough remained for each one to be able to read his console, and there was a sudden change in the central haze. Colors came into existence, solid structures bloomed in the depths of the cloud, grew and strengthened until emperor and robe-minore faced each other across the expanse of the New Palace ballroom on Babylon. For some reason, Japhet had chosen planetary night for the scene; the twisting pillars that marked the edges of the windows glowed with pearly fire, and the gleaming blue-black floor seemed to hold the reflection of a million stars. Beyond the windows, one of the Thousand Rivers leaped up and rilled, a vagrant wave now and then flashing white under Babylon's cold moons.

The colors changed and merged again, tiny swirls of pale fog spinning out to form ghostly shadows of people, shadows that quickly coalesced into holoshapes almost indistinguishable from the real things. Most of the Imperial court was there, allies of either Keira or Edouard. Keira identified them quickly, checking their listed political stance even as he marvelled at Japhet's skill. There was Hamm'tt in her armor, unshakeably held by her bargain; Nuriel de la Mar, with his pure white skin and hair, the inlaid wire and jewel decorating one cheek, equally loyal to Edouard. The Somewhere Elector was beside Hamm'tt, his ugly face frozen in one of his broad smiles, and Castellar and the two Ransoms, An-Deth and Hoybilai, were behind him, their heavy overcoats pulled tight over their flowing desert robes. That was a mistake, Keira thought. The Castellar were Lords of Hell, Hellmouth's airless moon; they would not wear desert dress.

Then a new figure winked into existence, and at the same time the other figures broke out of their stasis. Edouard stood at the far side of the room, dressed in ostentatiously plain clothes, with a plain coronet confining his severely clipped hair. Keira jumped a little, even though he knew it was only Havener's projection, and punched keys to call up his own image. A shadowy figure appeared, but this one remained transparent, little more substantial than a tinting of the air. He knew, though, that from Havener's point of view, the projection would be as solid, as complete and compelling, as the figure of Edouard.

"My Lord Keira," the projection said. "I am very grateful that you have agreed to this meeting. I hope we will be able to settle this matter without bloodshed. In fact, I am prepared to make only reasonable demands, and to listen to all reasonable requests." Havener was speaking into a vox humana that caught his voice and transformed it into an approximation of the Overlord's. It was doing a good job of it, too, Keira thought. It failed to capture the burred timbre of the long vowels, but the rest was perfect.

"I am also glad that we are able to meet here in peace, Overlord," Keira answered, "and I am certain that we will be able to come to some agreement."

The sparring went on, each man choosing his words from a relatively limited list that the computers were able to accept and assign a numerical value, on which Japhet's calculations would be based. After the first few exchanges, it became clear that "Edouard" was gaining ground. Keira had expected that. "Edouard" had gained points merely by asking for the meeting; now he was able to exploit that by posing as the champion of Convention. The readings of the allies, fed directly to Keira's board as Japhet calculated them, showed that Edouard was winning even their sympathy. A change of strategy was in order, he thought. He would have to force Edouard into open battle, and soon. If it meant losing some of his supporters, he would give them up, and could survive the loss—provided that they did not go over to the Overlord. He monitored the conversation with that in mind, taking every opportunity to nudge it in the right direction, until at last the opening he wanted appeared. He used it, bringing out the speech he had been shaping, packing it with emotion-laden words that would register high points on Japhet's computers. When he had finished, Havener, faintly visible through the hologram between them, nodded, and said in his own voice, "I'll withdraw."

"Dialogue ends," Japhet announced, and Keira quickly checked the results. He had lost a few of the inner-sector land-minores, and St. George with them, but none seemed inclined to support Edouard. He had not done as badly as he might, but it had not gone as well as it could have.

The battle, when it came, was something of a disappointment. The twin fleets formed amid the sea of stars off Vinland, swarmed together in accelerated time, spat drones and missiles. Keira knew there would be no resemblance between this and any real battle between himself and Edouard: Havener was no soldier, and he lacked the majore's Talent that might have compensated for the lack of training. After what seemed an impossibly short time, the last of the Overlord's fleet had vanished or was fleeing, and Japhet faded out the scene.

Chapter 18

The gaming chamber was comfortable enough, but by the end of the game Keira's back was aching and his eyes were gritty from peering at the flashing characters on the multiple screens. Still, he thought, as the caravan of hovercars made their way from the university buildings to the Palace, it had been a useful enough day. Admittedly, the victory had been contingent on Castellar's joining him—and the latest word from Lovell-Andriës promised only that the Hell-lord was listening to his offers. But if that one factor were resolved, as Talent told him it must be, he felt confident that he could defeat Edouard.

The hovercar slowed, and Keira glanced up to see the first of the hovercars enter the Sallygate. Overhead, the larger of the monitor drones pulled up and away. The smaller, suited to the low clearance of the Palace corridors, dropped lower still, swooping close to the cars as they and it passed together through the gate. The light of the setting sun deepened even further as the caravan left the gate and turned into the glass-topped perimeter corridors. The Guard commander—not Lilika, though she rode with him in the central 'car—was taking them by the seldom-used outer roads. That route avoided potentially dangerous congestion in the main corridors, though it skirted the base of the clustered towers where the visiting majores were housed. An acceptable trade, Keira thought.

Lilika, seated opposite him on one of the fold-down seats, was frowning, half perplexed and half uneasy. Keira leaned forward, intending to ask her what was wrong, then the corridor was filled with an unnatural purple light.

With the light came a sound like static, clearly audible even through the thick plastis of the 'car's dome. The 'car bucked, then the fans shuddered and died, even as the driver tried to swing the machine around. The 'car fell heavily, and slid forward a meter or so, crumpling the fan skirts. Activated by the crash, the escape systems rolled back the dome.

"Gas!" Lilika yelled. She and the other Guards clawed for the filtermasks that hung with the rest of the emergency equipment along the top of the panelling. Someone slammed one into the emperor's hand, and Keira got the thin plastic into place just as the cloud of gas washed over them. A few second later, its chill was gone: one of the unstable battle-gases, he guessed, fast-acting and equally quick to break down into harmless compounds.

Lilika caught his shoulder, pulling him over to the side of the 'car to crouch with the other Guards against the buckled fan cushion. At the same time, darts rattled overhead and against the body of the 'car. One struck the corridor floor less than half a meter from Keira's hand, and stuck quivering for a moment before the weight of the drug cartridge toppled it, snapping the needle. Keira stared at it, feeling time slow about him. He reached for the controls of his shield belt, tuning it high to override the influence of the trapfield that had grounded the hovercars, then drew his own dart gun. Farther down the corridor, he could see the wreck of the monitor drone, and beyond that the third hovercar, seemingly not too badly damaged. Its crew of Guards huddled in its meager protection, but even as Keira watched, one moved forward quickly, sheltering briefly behind the wrecked drone before dashing forward to join the emperor's party. He held out a broken dart cartridge.

"Trumps, sir," he said.

The Guard commander took it, sniffed at the smear of liquid along the broken casing. "Right," he said, and gestured for his men to take up positions at either end of the slewed hovercar. A moment later, there was a muted snap of dart guns as the Guards returned fire.

Keira leaned back against the fan cushion, trying to stay out of the way as more of the Guards from the third 'car moved up to join them. Japhet and Havener, who had been riding in that 'car, were nowhere in sight—either still inside it, or hiding behind it—but there was no need to worry about their safety. This was a Conventional attack, using non-lethal darts—trumps. The object was his surrender, not his death.

"Elsu." That was the lieutenant in command of the third hovercar, sliding in beside the senior commander. "We're right at the edge of the trapfield. If you cover us, we can pull the 'car out and get his Majesty away."

"You're sure the fans are all right?" Elsu asked.

"Yes, sir, Jos got the wheels down."

"Right, then," Elsu muttered, and turned toward the emperor. "Majesty—"

"I heard," Keira said. "Do it."

"Yes, Majesty. Jafar, signal when the 'car's out and the motor's started. We'll bring his Majesty then."

"Sir." The lieutenant saluted, then, ducking and weaving, made his way back to the shelter of the third 'car. Elsu gestured to his own men, sending some out along the corridor wall, while others, dragging the heavily padded seats out of the grounded hovercar, moved forward in relays, pushing the seats in front of them to catch the darts. At the same time, their volume of fire increased.

Keira did not need to be told the tactical situation. The leading hovercar, its load of Guards overcome immediately by the gas, had crashed just before a bend in the corridor. The wells for the maintenance serbots were usually located at those points, and a determined man, once he had bypassed the multiple security devices, could conceal a good-sized force in one of those compartments. But the Guards had reacted quickly and well to the attack, holding off the immediate danger, and the failure of the monitor drone would already have alerted Doran to send help. The question now was who had set up the ambush. Keira leaned forward, touched Lilika's arm.

"Has anyone gotten a look at them?"

The soldier-minore, her attention focused on the third 'car and the dozen or so Guards—perhaps a third of the remaining escort—that struggled to move it, started at his touch. "Assassins, Majesty," she said, after a moment. "We haven't spotted their employer."

Keira grimaced. That told him nothing. He had hoped that a majore attacker would use his own Domus troops, rather than the professionals available to anyone. He would have to wait to find out if Edouard were at last making his move.

There was a shout from down the corridor: the third 'car was moving at last, the Guards oblivious to their danger as they rose to their feet to keep it moving. Two more fell, then a third, joining the growing number of unconscious bodies that littered the tiles. The 'car slid out of the trapfield. Its motor choked, then caught, whining angrily toward overload before the driver, ducking low, got it under control.

"Now, Majesty," Lilika said quietly.

Keira gathered himself as Guards pressed close

to him, shielding him with their bodies. One, the youngest of the group, waved him forward, but before he had taken two steps toward the waiting car there was a noise on the roof. Involuntarily he hesitated, looking up for the expected reinforcements. Then there was a blinding light, blued by the glasstex, and the roof broke into a thousand webbed cracks. A spot on the floor was red and smoking. The rest of the glasstex gave with a gentle crackling sound, and a woman dropped through the hole in a shower of sapphire glass. She landed with a feral grace, and brought up the blastrifle she had held at waist height. The closest Guards turned quickly, but she burned them down. Instinctively, Keira dodged away from his unshielded escort, back toward the grounded car. Elsu shouted something, orders or advice or a curse, but he could not spare the time to listen. Ayakawa—it was her, somehow escaped from the prison in the Iron Hills, looking for her revenge—smiled grimly and took careful aim, ignoring the darts that shattered against her combat armor. Keira brought up his own gun and fired twice, aiming for her unprotected face, but the darts broke against the far wall.

The first shot slammed against his own screen. He was unprepared for the force of it, and the searing heat that washed down his less protected arms. He fell away, biting back a cry of pain, and caught himself awkwardly against the fan cushion. Her second shot was high, scoring the corridor wall, and from the yelp of pain, the backwash had caught one of the Assassins. They came rushing forward as soon as the Guards' attention was divided. Faced with a minore holding an illegal rifle, the leader reacted from Convention. Throwing aside his gun, he dipped into the flowing sleeves of his tunic. Before he could complete the movement, Ayakawa's rifle hissed again, and he fell, clutching a smoking arm. The land-minore swung her rifle again, bathing the corridor in its scalding light, and guards and Assassins scattered back.

"By Convention, gas her!" Elsu shouted at the Assassins, and Ayakawa snapped a shot at him. Keira fired twice more, and hit only armor. Her return fire pinned him against the side of the hovercar, his screen pulsing as it struggled to absorb the energies.

Then the fire control system went off. Foam rolled from nozzles set in the baseboards, and a fine spray of chemical wash streamed from the ceiling pipes. Ayakawa leaped backward, momentarily distracted, her rifle automatically centering on the pipes above her. A small canister arched out from the shelter of the hovercar, splashed into the foam at Ayakawa's feet, and gas billowed. She fired a last shot, but it went wide, and then, as a second canister burst behind her, she collapsed. The Guards rushed forward to secure the prisoner.

Keira pulled himself upright, leaning heavily against the stained metal of the hovercar. "What the hell happened?" he demanded of no one in particular. Then he saw the young Guard who had waved him forward slumped against the far wall. One arm dangled awkwardly, but in the other hand he held a small piece of metal. Broken wires trailed from it.

"You pulled the fuse," Keira whispered, suddenly aware of the pain that flared along his arms and across his chest. He clung to the car for support, wondering vaguely why he was afraid now. Then a new figure moved behind the line of Assassins, a man dressed in plain battledress badged in familiar Domus colors: Vasili Andros. Keira pulled himself upright quickly, pain forgotten. The Barbaries Lord looked surprisingly shaken, glancing uneasily at the blastrifle one of the Assassins was studying.

"I'll take that," Keira said. To his surprise, his voice was steady. The Assassin removed the charge, then passed the emptied weapons across. Keira underestimated its weight and misjudged his own strength, but saved himself from dropping it by resting the butt on the floor, grasping it by the still-warm barrel. "Well, my Lord Andros?" he continued, afraid to let the other seize the initiative. "Is this your celebrated honor? Conspiring with a Convention-breaker, doubly so for bringing an energy weapon into the Palace? Are you going to bring the commoners against me next?"

Andros was pale. "No, my Lord, I. . . . This was none of my doing."

"Oh?" Keira forced himself to ignore the pain, to speak as calmly as he would before the Eger, with the same Talent-led choice of words and phrase. "You admit no connection between these two attacks?" It was obvious that there was none, but he hoped the accusation would keep Andros off balance for a moment longer.

"No!" Andros caught himself and said, more carefully, "I have no relations with her." He gestured to Ayakawa's motionless body, Guards busy beside it.

"Yet you attacked now, against Convention. That's a very large coincidence," Keira said.

"It's hardly against Convention to attack before you're crowned," Andros answered. The surviving combatants, until now busy with the wounded, looked up at the new tone of the majores' voices. "The amenities were observed," Andros continued, without a glance at the Guards who moved to stand beside their emperor. "And you yourself declared that the interregnum was open season."

"The tradition is three days of challenge—long since past," Keira said, "and in simulation."

"Originally, under true Convention, the heir was fair game until he was crowned."

The mention of true Convention, original Convention, sparked Keira's Talent, which had remained silent and unhelpful throughout the fighting. The pattern formed almost instantly, despite the pain that he had feared would cloud his thoughts: a way to neutralize Andros, perhaps dubiously Conventional, but a way the Order could be made to sanction. "You keep to the old ways on the Barbaries, do you not?" he said.

"We do," Andros answered, half proud and half wary.

"Then you'll remember the first purpose of Convention: to keep rivals allied against a common enemy. In those days, it was made a principle of law that fighting together implies an oath of alliance. That law still applies."

"You can hardly say we fought together," Andros protested.

"Your men answered my men's appeal for help," Keira said. At his side, Elsu nodded, and, after a brief hesitation, one of the Assassins stepped forward.

"In honor, my Lord, that's so."

"If you deny the alliance," Keira went on, not giving the Barbaries lord a chance to answer, "I can have you arrested for treason. If you accept it, I am here to accept your formal Oath. Which will it be?"

Andros's eyes went distant, and Keira did not need to be a telepath to guess his thoughts. There was actually a third course of action, to refuse to swear, giving notice that he intended to repudiate the implied alliance. But that required an act of the Eger, and could not be done in time for him to be of any use to Edouard. Andros had made his best shot, and lost.

"Your Majesty," the Barbaries lord said, "I give you my Oath."

"Without reservation," Keira prompted.

"Without reservations, except those of Convention," Andros said. He looked suddenly old.

"Your Majesty." Doran was suddenly standing with the other Guard officers, and there was a second, combat-armored squad filling the corridor. Keira looked up, startled. He had been so absorbed in trapping Andros that he had not seen the general arrive. "What— You're hurt," Doran went on, beckoning to one of the robot medics that had arrived with the second squad. Keira waved it away impatiently.

"Later."

Doran nodded. "Very well, Majesty. What do we do with her?" He jerked his head toward Ayakawa, still unconscious on the corridor floor.

"Kill her."

"Majesty?" The general looked surprised. "Shouldn't she be questioned first?"

"You've done that," Keira said, more harshly than he had intended. "All you could tell me was that she was mad. This is my right, under Convention. Do it."

Doran looked as though he wanted to protest further, but then bowed slightly. "As you wish, Majesty."

He gestured to one of the Guards, who drew a thin-bladed knife and knelt by Ayakawa. He inspected her for a moment, then replaced the first knife in its sheath and chose another, finer-bladed one. This one was thin enough. He slipped it, casually, through a crack in her armor into her heart. He wiped the blade carefully on the tiles, and put it away again.

Keira was conscious of the Guards' sidelong looks, knew what they were thinking: that he had killed Ayakawa out of anger and fear, and would regret it later. That's not it, he wanted to say, but knew he could not explain his decision, made out of Talent and in an instant. He knew, from Talent, from unconsciously seen and noted clues in Doran's first report, and in the subsequent reports, that Ayakawa was no longer rational, no longer a serious threat to him. He knew, too, that to pursue the matter would result only in bloodfeud, Ayakawa's most distant kin aligning themselves with whatever powers opposed him throughout his reign. Besides, as Andros had pointed out, he was not yet crowned. There was no need to implicate others in Ayakawa's crime, particularly when it was more than probable that they would obey strict Convention from now on. Ayakawa's unConventional behavior would shock them into that.

"Majesty." Lilika came toward him, bowing. "The car is waiting. And a medic."

Keira turned, wincing. The Guard might not understand his motives, but they would obey him.

Chapter 19

The dawn was a pale line on the horizon when Denisov-Graham took his place in the section of the Cathedral gallery reserved for foreign dignitaries, nodding gravely to the other ambassadors, and to those attendants whom he recognized. There was an unusual tension among the ambassadors, though not among the nobility: word of the assassination attempt had spread rapidly, though all the accounts were vague, and the bland official reassurances had done nothing to allay suspicion. The usually reliable sources among the Heralds had been unable to provide more than confirmation of the attempt and the information that Ayakawa had been killed. Denisov-Graham had ultimately been forced to bribe his own pilot, a New Victorian with relatives on Imperial New Wales and half a hundred contacts among the space-faring population, minore and commoner alike, but even the promise of a seat in the ambassadors' gallery had been unable to produce anything new. The official announcement had stressed that things would proceed as planned; the Federal delegation, increased by one, could do no more than attend, though Denisov-Graham found himself wondering even now if Keira would really be there.

The Cathedral was crowded, and the cool air was filled with whispered conversation, a hissing that swelled and ebbed like the beat of waves. In the darkened Cathedral, its pure glass still opaqued against the darkness, the sound bordered on the unearthly.

Only the faintest green-glowing line marked the edge of the gallery, and Denisov-Graham was careful to plant both hands firmly on the rail before he leaned over to survey the assembly. The nave was packed with the nobility, mostly majores, and there would be millions more—commoners and minores—watching the ceremony on any one of the holo networks. Here and there a discreet light flashed among the packed bodies: the Heralds were at work, making sure that everyone was in his proper place. Those lights flashed briefly on the polished steel of military formal armor, on the clotted richness of velvets and rough silks, struck fire from heavy jewels and satin gowns. It was as though the Cathedral floor were smoldering, needing only a single spark to set it ablaze.

"My God, but I feel drab," Rubenstein murmured at her elbow.

Denisov-Graham glanced dubiously at her, seeing how the archaic uniform flattered her strong figure. The tight, dove-grey jacket molded itself to her body, while the heavy matching skirt flared sharply over her hips, settling in wide folds about her knees. The formal cloak, vivid blue lined with white, was draped with seeming carelessness over one shoulder. Hidden weights and a single chain and clasp of fine gold held it in place. She wore no other jewelry, not even the signet to which she was entitled as a senior diplomat, but her capable hands and strong face had no need of it. The ambassador smiled.

"My friend, you could never look drab."

She turned, startled, but a single trumpet shivered the air.

Instantly, there was utter silence, without even a rustle of silk to break it. The Heralds, forewarned, were gathered by the door in neat rows, the most

senior clutching their rods of office. The trumpet
sounded again, and the senior Heralds lifted their
rods. The great doors, of the same bronze-like metal
as the frame of the Cathedral, swung majestically
open. The trumpet sounded a final time, this time
breaking into a long run of notes that was at once
solemn and rejoicing.

The first procession passed under the mighty
lintel, their robes still greyed by the early light.
Two Knights of St. Michael led the way, both
young, both carrying lit shielded blades, the fields
glowing intolerably in the dim Cathedral. The
Cardinal-Archbishop followed several paces behind
them, a small, erect figure who only just saved
himself from being dwarfed by his elaborate robes.
The Governor-General of the Order, tall and stately
in his black and white formal vestments, walked a
few paces behind him, hands clasped and head
bowed. Denisov-Graham knew a telepath when he
saw one, and mentally approved the courage that
sent an unshielded mind out among so many people.
Behind him came the rest of the attendant clergy,
walking three abreast, carrying the regalia. Two
more Knights of St. Michael brought up the rear,
these in full battle armor. They carried axes instead of swords, but the curving blades gleamed
with the same shield-fire as the swords.

The head of the procession reached the transept,
and the Cathedral choir burst into song. A hundred and fifty voices soared high, the clean, clear
notes of the boys' voices competing with the
women's trained treble, a full voice above the soprano line. The result was not quite human, an
angelic quality that raised the hairs at the base of
the neck. Then the deeper voices of the men answered the soprano chant. The Cardinal-Archbishop
had reached the altar. His party genuflected as
one, and turned to face the doors, the Knights and
attendants collecting at the corners of the dais.

New music, a choir of trumpets this time, cut through the last note of the choir's chant, and the Cathedral doors rolled back as though blown open by the music.

The Domi Aureae made their entrance, representing all the nobility. Matto de Terranin led them, almost unrecognizable in his regalia. His grey hair had been tamed, and was held in place by a thick, plain coronet studded with stones that would flame in the sunlight, but now were white, cloudy, sleeping. His gown was covered by the tremendous floor-length cloak, sweeping to a short train in the back, that marked the senior members of the Domi. His was dull gold in color, real gold overlaid on gold-colored cloth, marked with the single green disk that was the de Terranin symbol. It was a simple design, Denisov-Graham thought, but it was far from plain. Even from the gallery he could recognize New Erin silks, imported from the Federation at exorbitant prices, and then sent to the workshops on Man'net. The work of the Man'net craftsmen would triple the value of the material.

Nuriel de la Mar followed him, standing in for his invalid mother. His family's blue-and-white livery, seven wavy stripes representing their single watery planet, stitched with the design of an antique sailing ship, complemented his fine-boned, albino features. Except for a very plain coronet—he was not yet the Grand Duke, only his mother's proxy—he wore no jewelry beyond the stone-and-wire design set into one cheekbone.

"Hey, boss, is his mother really sick?" That was the pilot, leaning forward so that she could speak directly into the ambassador's ear.

"Later, Martine." But once the question had been asked, Denisov-Graham found it hard to dismiss the suspicion.

Desolin Hamm'tt, gaudy in red and gold, an abstract brocade, strode behind pale de la Mar, eclipsing him. Her coronet was a gold helmet, and she wore gold bracelets that reached almost to her elbows, defiantly matching her braces. The Grand Duke of Castille followed her. His gown was in his Domi's colors, as was required by Convention, but he had taken as much liberty with the design as possible. Rather than the single castle, gold on purple, that was the Domi's sign, his cloak was covered with tiny golden castles, each one picked out with jewels and embroidery. The purple was so dark as to be almost black, the darker color favoring his complexion.

He was the last representative of the true Domi Aureae. The other families who had governed the original nine systems were either extinct or, like the Babylonian Domi, had lost its nobility under David I's reform of the nobility. But the tradition of the nine Domi, including the imperial Domus, had been preserved: four more nobles, one from each of the border sectors, walked behind the first group of majores, but only two wore the great Domi cloaks. Denisov-Graham narrowed his eyes against the growing light, trying to identify the tiny designs strewn across the blue background of the next man's cloak. They were dolphins, so trimmed with red and green gems as to be almost unrecognizable, so the man had to be Santarem, the titular Grand Duke of the Babylon System. It was a pity that everyone knew the corporations were the real rulers; the man made an impressive entrance. Xio-Sebastina of Mist System, the successor to the deposed Fabians, was vivid in green and white, the cloak studded here and there with a complicated sort of knot picked out in glittering red cord. Her face was worried beneath the tall coronet, though, and Denisov-Graham could not blame her for her concern. The Renaults and the Fabians had been traditional allies. Now that the

Renaults had returned from the dead, Xio-Sebastina
might well worry about her Domi's status.

The final two figures wore formal robes, but not
the Domi majores' cloaks. They represented the
least-populated sectors in the Imperium and were
included in the general procession, so Denisov-
Graham suspected, only to preserve the Conventional numbers. The Elector of Somewhere, whose
system was practically the only inhabited one in
the rimward sector, was the more senior, and
walked first. Vasili Andros followed him, his pal-
lor evident even from the gallery. There was a
murmur of surprise, rippling from the doors to the
dais, as the assembled nobles caught sight of him.

Rubenstein leaned close. "Ioan, what's he doing
here? All our contacts swore he was involved in
the attack."

"Yeah," the pilot continued, "but it was Ayakawa
who got killed for it, and there's no way a Barbaries lord and a Tyrian land-minore would work
together."

Denisov-Graham shook his head helplessly. "I
don't know. He's here, at any rate."

The last of the procession reached the transept.
Lovell-Andriës and Andros bowed to the altar and
to the Cardinal-Archbishop, and took their places
to either side of the corridor. Only de Terranin
remained at the foot of the altar, his rod of office
ready in his hand.

There was a moment of silence. The sun was just
rising, turning the blanked windows behind the
altar to milk. Then the glass cleared, and the sun
leaped into the Cathedral with a shout of trumpets.
Keira stood alone, framed in the doorway. The sun
gleamed off robes that reflected the light like snow,
made his unbound hair a halo of flame. He posed
there for a moment longer—savoring the effect,
Denisov-Graham thought, not without admiration
and envy—then came forward into the now bril-

liantly lit Cathedral. He was followed by a squadron of the Imperial Guard, headed by Doran, all looking immensely capable behind the heavy formal breastplates. The polished metal had been neatly painted with the wearer's rank signs and decorations. The choir chanted triumph as he paced toward the altar.

At the foot of the dais, de Terranin blocked his way, at the same time signalling to a greying, plumply handsome man who had been sitting quietly among the first rank of the majores. Standing, he looked completely out of place among the glittering nobility: rather than a majore's robe or even the uniform of a soldier-minore, he wore the short coat and trousers that were a commoner's formal wear.

"That's Tanazy A'asta," Rubenstein murmured. "The Commons' Speaker. And Jenny A'asta's son."

Denisov-Graham nodded. A'asta Corporation had once been a noble Domus, but the line was not Talented, and they had been reduced to commoner status. The family had continued to participate in commoner politics, though, and had held the higher offices of the Common's Council an unseemly number of times. A'asta's position made the commoner's challenge more than mere formality.

"What of the common man?" A'asta recited. "You are heir to this empire, but without us, you are nothing, no matter what the majores plan and the minores fight. What do you say to us?"

Keira answered gravely, "I say to you what I say to all my people: serve me well, and I will serve you. That is the ancient compact. I do not revoke it."

The Commons' Speaker bowed deeply. "Then rule with the Commons' free consent." He stepped aside, and Keira nodded courteously to him before turning to face the altar again. De Terranin, too, moved aside.

"What brings you here, Keira Renault?" the Cardinal-Archbishop intoned. His voice was better than Denisov-Graham had expected, clear and carrying.

Keira gesture to the regalia that now lay on the altar. "I come to claim my rights."

"Before you take up such a heavy burden," the Cardinal said, "do you not wish to seek guidance and strength from our Lord, who is greater than any emperor?"

Keira bowed agreement, and attendants came forward to lead him to a chair set aside for him. The Cardinal-Archbishop crossed himself, and began the service. Denisov-Graham found himself listening to the sound rather than the substance of the words; he dragged his mind back to the service, but found himself once again wondering just what had happened the night before. Keira looked completely unharmed, as indeed the report had claimed, but the ambassador found that hard to believe. Weaponry was simply too sophisticated these days for an assassin to get that close to the emperor and fail to leave some mark behind. He peered down at the emperor's slim figure, sitting very straight in the ornate chair. The long robes would hide many things.

Rubenstein nudged him gently, and the ambassador hastily collected his thoughts as they knelt for the final prayer. The response, when it came, had an oddly fervent sincerity. Then attendants came forward to help Keira from his chair, and he rose with a magnificent air, graciously allowing them to assist him. They slipped off the outer robe, which was actually more of a long coat, Denisov-Graham realized, leaving the emperor in plain grey shirt and trousers. There was something odd about the skin that showed at Keira's wrists. Looking closer, the ambassador realized that he was seeing the edges of sani-skin bandages.

Melissa Scott

The Cardinal-Archbishop glared out over the assembly, his fierce black eyes roving from one face to another, and demanded, "Is there anyone who would challenge this man's right?"

There was silence, and then Hamm'tt stepped forward, bowing. "Your Eminence, I may testify that challenges have been made and met, and there is no other to be made."

"Then kneel, Keira Renault," The Cardinal-Archbishop said, "and answer: are you prepared to give yourself, heart, body, and soul, for the good of the people?"

Keira came forward to kneel before the altar. When he answered, his voice was subdued. "I am."

"Then the blessing of God be with you, His light to guide you, the Spirit to inspire you, and His Heart to give you rest at last." The Cardinal-Archbishop signaled to the two attendants who held the robe of state. They brought it forward and laid it with a flourish across Keira's shoulders. There was a subdued gasp from the nobility, and Denisov-Graham echoed them. The robe was a simple cloak, of the same pattern as the ones worn by the Domi nobility, full in the body and spreading to a short train in the back. The material was black and satin-like. It gleamed dully in the sunlight, striking fire from the thousands of diamonds scattered across the cloth. They formed a pattern that seemed vaguely familiar to the ambassador, like stars in the sky . . . the constellations of Avalon? He had seen too many star patterns to remember those of the individual worlds. Only Terra's remained distinct.

"Accept, Keira, this robe, in token of the worlds you will rule," the Cardinal-Archbishop said. Two more attendants approached the altar, and returned to kneel beside Keira, one holding an old-fashioned sword in an ornate sheath, the other holding a light gilded rod perhaps half a meter long. The

Cardinal-Archbishop touched them in blessing, then said, "Accept, Keira, the sword of justice and the rod of mercy, that you may use each in their seasons."

Keira took them easily, holding them in folded arms, the shafts projecting over each shoulder. Now there was only the crown, sitting on a velvet cushion in the very center of the altar. The Cardinal-Archbishop approached it reverently, followed by two acolytes bearing strangely shaped basins, one gold, one silver. In silence, the Cardinal-Archbishop turned to the silver basin, sprinkled its contents over the crown. Then he dipped a finger into the golden basin, and traced a symbol on the upswept band where a single clear stone gleamed. The acolytes withdrew and the Cardinal-Archbishop, still silent, held out the crown as though offering it to the deity. Then, bowing, he turned to Keira.

"With this crown I, Sevilin, primate of this Church, do certify that you, Keira Renault, are true and only heir, worthy of the throne and of our loyalty." He lowered the crown slowly, prolonging the moment, until at last the glowing circle rested squarely on Keira's head.

"May it please your Majesty to rise," the Cardinal-Archbishop said, bowing deeply.

Keira rose, not really needing the help of the attendants who moved to steady him, and turned to face the nobility. Instantly, the acclamation rang out, "The emperor! Keira!"

Matto de Terranin stepped out of the ranks of the majores, bowing. "Your Majesty, accept our oath, and with it the hearts and minds of both us and ours."

Denisov-Graham leaned forward a little. De Terranin had not precisely sounded as though he meant it, and had already sworn the oath of loyalty some weeks before. Then he remembered the tape he had read that described the coronation ceremony. The Majores' Oath was for their systems and families as well as for themselves, and, being so general, was not as binding as their personal oath. In fact, this oath would not necessarily hold Edouard if Edouard chose to ignore it.

The other Domi nobles came forward to join de Terranin, forming a line across the foot of the dais. "We, the leaders of the Domi Aureae, do pledge our lives and our lands and our people to the service of Keira Emperor, that he may preserve and increase our honors, within the bonds of Convention."

Keira looked each one of them in the eyes before answering. "I, Keira, Emperor, Master of Avalon, Overlord of Sander's World and Jerra and Hellmouth, Grand Admiral and Guildsmaster, do swear to maintain your honor and that of your people with my life, if need be, within the bounds only of Convention."

There was a moment of suspense as the faint echo of Keira's words died in the cool air, and then the Domi nobles moved. As one, they loosened the clasps of their great formal cloaks, swung them from their shoulders and reversed them in one graceful movement. The inner linings, a deep blue that, like Keira's, sparkled with a hundred thousand diamond pinpoints, were now outermost, the star-like patterns dwarfing even Hamm'tt's strength. Keira inclined his head to them—that was not part of the ceremony, Denisov-Graham thought, but it should have been—and the Cardinal-Archbishop stepped forward to pronounce the final blessing.

Even before he had finished, the Heralds were moving among the nobility, bringing them forward to swear their individual fealty. Denisov-Graham heard the pilot stir behind him.

"They all pledge loyalty now?"

"Yes," the ambassador answered shortly.

"There are thousands of them," the pilot said. She surveyed the assembly mournfully. "Maybe more."

"There are only about two thousand noble families," Rubenstein commented, smiling, "and most of them are minores, who don't have to attend. Their lord's oath binds them."

"So where does what's-his-name—"

"Edouard?" the undersecretary asked.

"Yes—get his army?"

Rubenstein said patiently, "Edouard is himself Overlord of Verii Mir, as the Duke's heir. The minores there are directly responsible to him, and he hasn't sworn."

"But his father did," the pilot said.

"Matto isn't directly their lord," Denisov-Graham said.

"So what about that one from Verii Mir, St. George, the one who challenged and lost. Do his people follow Edouard, even though St. George swore?"

Denisov-Graham shook his head. "Martine, I just don't know."

The pilot turned her attention back to the scene below. While they had spoken, two majores had given their oath; as she watched, a third man knelt before the emperor. "Do we stay for the whole thing?" she asked. "I mean, you don't present your credentials now, do you?"

"No, thank God," Denisov-Graham said, glancing around. Njru had left as soon as the Cardinal-Archbishop pronounced the blessing; the ambassador from Dixie was just slipping out the door. As he watched, the Delrwa representative rose quietly to her feet, gathered her loose vest about her, and began to edge through the crowd. Catching Denisov-Graham's eye, she gestured delicately, the Delrwa equivalent of a wink.

"I think we can leave now," the Terran said. "We've witnessed all the important things."

There was a Herald waiting at the bottom of the narrow stairway to direct them to a side entrance, where the embassy airsled was waiting. The pilot climbed into the forward cockpit, then popped the main canopy. Rubenstein slid in across the heavy cushions, then waited for the ambassador to follow her and close the canopy after him. Denisov-Graham clambered in, but instead of reaching for the control lever, he leaned back against the cushions and closed his eyes. Rubenstein leaned across his body for the lever, meaning to comment on his abstraction, but the look on his face stopped her.

"When we get back in, maybe you should get some sleep?" she said instead.

"Hmm?" Denisov-Graham looked up, his train of thought broken, and forced a smile. "No, I'm not tired, really. It's just . . ." His voice trailed off in defeat. *I don't have the words to express it,* he thought. *The whole thing was a lovely piece of theater, and somehow I'm sad. Is it just because it's over?*

To his surprise, Rubenstein nodded. "I know," she said. "Have a cup of tea, then, it'll help."

Yes, the ambassador thought, *it might just do that. I need something ordinary, after all that.* He settled himself more comfortably as the sled motors whined, lifting the machine above the manicured lawns of Avalon Palace. The pilot pointed her nose at the sea, grey touched with white, and Government Center, beyond.

Chapter 20

Keira announced that he would receive the ambassadors' credentials the day after the coronation. Arriving at the edge of the red circle, Denisov-Graham was shocked by the drastically increased security, then impatient with himself for not having anticipated it. FitzMary was waiting for him, to offer the emperor's excuses for his having to pass through the scanning devices, but even so, the Guards seemed more nervous, ready to challenge even the Federal ambassador.

Things were different in the reception room, as well, though here Denisov-Graham found the changes pleasant. The last traces of Oriana's reign had been removed, and Keira had replaced the overly ornate chair of state with a wide, square-cushioned chair covered in soft, dark leather. Only the slightly raised platform beneath it marked it as the formal center of the room. They exchanged greetings, and then Denisov-Graham settled himself in an antique plastic-and-metal construction whose odd angles conformed surprisingly well with the contours of the human body.

"I've been meaning to talk with you, anyway, ambassador," Keira said.

Denisov-Graham looked quizzically at him. "I hope your Majesty is not displeased with me."

"If I had been, I would not have accepted your credentials so quickly." Keira seemed unusually on edge—probably because of the assassination attempt and the increased security, the ambassador thought. He watched with interest as the emperor fiddled with the small stack of tapes that stood on a low table beside the ever-present coffee set.

"No, this is a personal matter."

"Indeed?" Denisov-Graham murmured. The bet, he thought. Not the assassination attempt, but that bet. And I still don't know what the stakes were.

"Yes. It's a question of a debt," Keira went on. He poured himself some coffee, and the ambassador thought he saw a trace of a smile as the other turned back to face him. "It is a tradition in my family—one that my mother told me before she died—that there was a longstanding wager between an ancestor of mine, and an ancestor of yours. The terms were, roughly, that we intended to become emperors, and your ancestor bet that we could not. I think the terms have been fulfilled."

"As you say, the terms of such a bet have been met," Denisov-Graham agreed. He kept a careful eye on the other, and was not disappointed to see the fractional slump of shoulders, instantly controlled. Parry, he thought, and riposte. "But I'm afraid—" he spread his hands "—our records aren't as good as yours."

"I find that difficult to believe," Keira answered, "knowing that you've told others that your family diaries are most complete."

The ambassador smiled to hide his surprise, at the same time kicking himself for not having realized that Doran would have passed that information along. "Diaries? We have them, yes, but I can't recall having come across more than the mention of a wager with someone in the Imperium. I'm afraid I'm not familiar with the details." He tensed, waiting for Keira to impose some impossible forfeit. The blade was poised, ready—and at the last moment deflected.

The emperor said, "Perhaps you had better look through those diaries. I wouldn't want there to be any disagreement on the stakes."

"They're in the archives on Terra," Denisov-Graham said quickly. "I'm afraid I don't have copies here—you understand why not. The information isn't classified anymore, but we wouldn't like to embarrass friends and allies." Attack, he thought, and feint.

"I do understand," Keira said. "But I suggest that it might be best for you to consult them, the next time you're on Terra."

—And strike now. "Certainly, your Majesty. But my next leave is some time away. Might I ask what the stakes were?"

There was a moment of silence, and then Keira said, "I would prefer that you read them for yourself."

"You don't know them yourself, Majesty?" Denisov-Graham was careful to phrase it as a question, but the emperor's eyes went bleak. Straight through the guard, he thought. That drew blood. He was hard put to restrain his exhilaration, even knowing how dangerous this small victory might be.

"No. I do not. And I wish to." Keira forced a smile, tried to recapture his earlier tone. "Surely even a Conventionless Terran must admit I'm owed my winnings."

Denisov-Graham said quietly, "I don't deny it, your Majesty. But it will take me some time to find out the stakes. I don't know them either."

"I hope you'll make every effort to find out." It was not a request.

"Certainly, your Majesty, but it will take time," Denisov-Graham said again. Don't risk anything more, he told himself. You've won. "I'll have to send word to my relatives, maybe even go to examine the documents myself, before I can tell you anything."

"Very well," said Keira. "Take all the time you need."

"Thank you, your Majesty. If you will excuse me?"

Keira made an effort to control his temper. "Forgive me, ambassador, of course you may go. Things are still so uncertain."

It's not the uncertainty that bothers you, Denisov-Graham thought, but the waiting. I remember hating that from my Navy days. "I quite understand. And I will send to Terra." He bowed, and left the room before he heard Keira's muttered thanks.

Left alone, Keira lifted his cup, but the coffee was cold. He barely restrained himself from throwing the entire set—cups, pot, sugar, and spoons—against the wall. He forced himself to breathe slowly and deeply, calmly, holding his hands folded in his lap only with an effort of will. I have no reason to be so angry, he told himself. It's not surprising he didn't know the stakes. Even Mother had forgotten, or didn't know, so why should a Terran remember? He will find out eventually. But he needed that bet, needed something to keep himself busy, to take his mind off the waiting. If only there were something I could do to force Edouard's hand, he thought. But I've been through all that, and there's nothing at all. I'd only lose allies, no matter what I did.

"Majesty," the secretary unit by the door said. "The ambassador from Dixie is here."

Oh, hell, thought Keira that's the one whose name I can never remember. "Name?" he asked.

The secretary, at least, wasn't affected by memory blockage. "Ambassador Torrey, your Majesty."

Keira took a deep breath and poured himself more coffee. "Admit him." At least he didn't have to worry about insulting Torrey; there was nothing Dixie could do to injure the Imperium.

* * *

Despite Keira's desire to let Ayakawa's plot die with her, Doran was able to discover which of her kindred had arranged for escape. In a midnight raid, three land-minores, all from Ayakawa's home world of Tyre, were arrested and taken to the Imperial fortress buried in the hills beyond the Palace. Keira was awakened with the news of the arrests, and was waiting when Doran returned to the Palace. The emperor had lit only the wall screens, and the inner rooms were filled with a chill grey light. The soldier-minore's face was tired, but had lost the look of strain that had marked him for the past few days, and he laid the stack of tapes on a table with an air of satisfaction.

"There's the proof, your Majesty. These are the ones who conspired with Ayakawa."

"Who were they?"

"Tetsu Aleyns, Nathu Rai, Ressa Kwan," Doran answered.

No more titles for them, Keira thought. He said, "Why?"

"Ah, there's the question, Majesty." Doran looked troubled. "Ayakawa swore she was only wanting to escape before she could be tried, and they provided her with the rifle and the breakout gear on that understanding."

Keira stared at the holo screen, watching the gardening machine moving silently across the broad mall between the Palace and the Cathedral. The mowing machines were followed by smaller craft that gathered the clippings into bags that gleamed ghostly white. "Do you believe that?"

"They were scanned." Doran's tone gave no indication of whether the minores went to that questioning willingly, and Keira shuddered.

"And?" he said, more to banish that thought than because Doran needed prompting.

"According to it, they're telling the truth," Doran said. "The other evidence tends to confirm it,

Majesty. It's hard to say, but I doubt Tetsu Aleyns or Nathu Rai would've allowed her to bring a rifle into the Palace. If she'd told them her plan, they might've supported it, but they'd have given her other weapons—something Conventional, like gas."

Keira nodded. "All right. And the other—Kwan? What about her?"

"There's the trouble," Doran answered. "She's Ayakawa's cousin-german by marriage twice, and they were close anyway. She might well have gone along wholeheartedly. But Rai swears he was the one who provided the gun."

"I see."

Before Keira could go on, the secretary by the door buzzed for attention, and both men turned to face its array of lights.

"Santarem?" Keira said softly, and Doran nodded.

"I'd not bet against it."

The general touched the response buttons, admitting image without triggering the machine's cameras. One of the wallscreens faded from the greys of the pre-dawn landscape to the pale brown of an inner Palace wall. Raman Santarem had dressed for the occasion, in semi-formal coat and full trousers of a severe blue that flattered his complexion. He wore his coronet, and Keira signaled a serbot to bring him his own informal coronet and a decent coat. He settled the coronet carefully in place before gesturing to Doran, who started the cameras.

"Yes, my Lord?"

"Your Majesty." The majore's bow was the minimum demanded by courtesy. "Three of my minore—my land-minores—have been arrested by your Guards, without any declaration of intent."

"There was no need to declare intent, my Lord," Keira said. "The minores who were arrested were involved in Ayakawa's attempt on my life."

"Majesty, I must ask to see evidence of their guilt," Santarem said.

"I'll see that you get it." Keira gestured sharply to Doran, who cut the speakers. "Are the tapes in shape to be transferred?"

"Yes, Majesty."

"Good." Keira waited until the speakers were reactivated, then said, "The evidence is ready now. Can you accept a tape transmission?"

Santarem looked to someone off-screen, then nodded. "Yes."

"Then stand by." Keira looked to the minore, then winced as the high-speed tapes squealed thinly. When the noise stopped, he said, "Have you gotten all that, my Lord?"

"Yes, your Majesty." Santarem seemed to remember the amenities, and bowed awkwardly. "I will review the accusations, and prepare a tape for the Eger."

"If you accept the reality of the tapes, there'll be no need for a trial," Keira pointed out. "But you can witness that justice has been done. You may go."

Without another word, the majore broke the connection, the screen going dark. Keira set the coronet aside and ran both hands through his sleep-snarled hair. The pulling helped him focus his thoughts. "Doran."

"Majesty?"

"What would you do?"

"Execute them," Doran said promptly. "You saw what happened with Ayakawa. There's too much chance of creating a blood-debt."

"Mmm." Keira curled himself into a pillow-chair, staring at the still-lit screen to his left. The sun was just rising, a line on the horizon, red and brighter orange staining the drifting clouds. One spot glowed brighter than the rest, first yellow, and then, as the yellow light spread across the screen, white. Then the edge of the solar disk broke the horizon, and the first hints of color crept into the scene. It rose inexorably, and, as the lower edge pulled free of the horizon, the world was suddenly bright and green. The gardening serbots had disappeared into their silos; the mall stretched, fair and empty, sparkling with dew. Keira shook himself and reached for a tape viewer. Doran handed him the stack of tapes and then, without being asked, punched for coffee.

The secretary rang again, two hours later. Keira reached for the remote-control unit beside him, signaled to accept the call. The wallscreen shifted views again, and Santarem appeared, his whole attitude one of resignation.

"Your Majesty, I have read the tapes you sent me. I give the minores into your jurisdiction, and ask that your Majesty submit the case to the Eger."

"No." Keira touched other buttons, and Doran's face appeared on the secretary's smaller screen. "Doran, have the Herald get me a holo-link with the Iron House, and patch His Grace of Babylon into the circuit."

"Very well, your Majesty." The secretary's screen blanked again, and Keira reactivated the speakers.

"Your Grace, I will pronounce sentence myself."

Santarem swallowed his protest. "Yes, your Majesty."

The door opened then, to admit a coveralled technician-minore with a Herald's badge clipped to her belt. She bowed quickly, then settled herself at the control console built into one wall, her small hands darting over the boards. After a moment, she nodded, and Keira stepped into the cone of light from the ceiling camera. At the same time, the air before the door fuzzed, forming a brown, indistinct picture. The Governor of the Iron House, a soldier-minore hand picked from the Guards, bowed low.

"Your Majesty."

"Colonel Aniol," Keira acknowledged. "I want to speak to the prisoners."

The Colonel bowed again. "Yes, your Majesty."

There was a long pause while half the room was filled with the projection station of the Iron House, where indistinct figures moved around out of focus objects, and Santarem's image fretted on the far wall. Then the Colonel appeared again, jumping sharply into focus. The three land-minores stood behind him, flanked by Guards with levelled blast-rifles. Their imprisonment had drawn harsh lines across once-proud faces; only Ayakawa's cousin held her head up, though her cheek bore a livid bruise. Rai's eyes were empty; he seemed to have withdrawn from himself, leaving only his body to face his punishment. Aleyns lowered her head in grudging acknowledgement as the emperor's image appeared in the reception circle.

"My Lords," Keira said quietly. He let his voice trail off, deliberately prolonging the suspense. He did not have to tell them he intended to judge them himself; that was evident from his appearance in the viewing platform. "I am told that though you intended to help Lord Ayakawa escape her deserved fate, you were not informed of her intention to attack me. However, to have helped her escape is treason, and her attempt only compounds your offense. Your treason is proven under scan, and your overlord has acknowledged your guilt. Your lives are therefore forfeit to me. Do you deny this?"

He waited until Aleyn's head dipped, and Kwan said, "No."

"But you did not intend to kill me," Keira went on. "And I was not yet crowned. I will not collect your debts now, my Lords. Go home, keep out of politics—and know that your next error, however slight, will be your last. You are already dead to me."

Kwan's mouth fell open. Rai did not seem to have heard, but then his eyes moved, questioningly. Only Aleyns seemed to have understood the full significance of his words.

"Your Majesty," she said softly. "I accept your sentence, as do these others." Kwan nodded slowly.

"Very well," Keira said. "You'll remain at the Iron House until I have settled matters with the Overlord de Terranin." He held up a hand to forestall the protest from Santarem. "This will not be strict, and you will be allowed communication with your families. After that, you may return home." He turned to face the Grand Duke. "Do you agree that this is just, your Grace?"

The majore bowed. "I do."

"So be it," Keira declared. At his signal, the Herald cut both linkages and the room faded to its normal colors. Doran appeared in the doorway almost immediately.

"You're going to let them go, Majesty?"

"Yes," Keira said. "There's not much chance of a blood-debt now, since they all owe me their lives, and not much chance of rebellion. You yourself admitted that their main motive was to help Ayakawa."

"As you say, Majesty."

Keira turned away, dialed for new scenes on the wallscreen. A view of Government Center from the top of the Dragon Peak flamed into existence, and he turned back to the general. "Now, that's ended—I hope. You can call off your extra watchdogs."

Chapter 21

The Order had held New Canterbury for generations. The first Order House had been built there,
near the blasted ruins of the Old Federation's Telen
Institute's farthest outpost. Over those generations,
the Order's control of the planet had expanded
until nearly two continents were under its rule,
and there was reason for this. The true telepaths,
few as they were, and the Great Readers and lesser
Readers who entered the church, needed space
and privacy in which to practice their arts, more
space even than the most ascetic members of the
older religious groups. The most recent expansions
had preserved the rule of ten square kilometers of
open land for each member, but even that had not
been enough for some. The Stylites had taken to
space itself to gain the ultimate privacy, living
alone with their thoughts deep within hollowed
asteroids, coming out only reluctantly when confronted with a duty they could not avoid. They
were healers, empathic to such a degree that contact with ordinary undisciplined humanity was
physically painful. They could learn to block out
others' thoughts only at the price of their unique
healing Talent. Therefore they fled to space, ac-
cepting contact with the sick only when the patient had exhausted all other options. Most members of the Order were not so sensitive, but all,
telepathic to a degree, relished the solitude of New
Canterbury.

Edouard hated it. He was city-bred, reared with the thoughts of a hundred thousand other minds always subliminally present, and he could feel the emptiness of the Order's world like a physical emptiness in the pit of his stomach. Had he been a true telepath, the silence would have been easier to accept; as it was, though he could never be consciously aware of "hearing" those other minds, the lack disturbed him on a very fundamental level. Space travel was simpler, the close contact helping to compensate for the relatively small crews. Besides, space was supposed to be empty; an uncrowded planet was unnatural.

He delayed his landing for as long as possible, talking to various Order functionaries by holophone, but at last he could put it off no longer. Armed with the coordinates of his sister's retreat beacon, he cast off from *Storm Lily*, his shuttle skimming easily along the upper edges of the atmosphere. Once he had made it down to normal flight levels, he switched to jet mode, and flipped on the targetting computer, looking for Alesia's beacon. The air was crowded with signals, from other marker beacons, navigational warnings, and the idle chitchat of a widely scattered populace, but the computer was sensitive enough to filter them out and home him onto Alesia's beacon with little effort. Less than an hour after he hit the atmosphere, he was well out into the central pampas, and bringing the shuttle to an anti-grav-only landing near a stand of trees.

He sat for a long moment in the cockpit, the only sound the ticking of the cooling metal. On three sides, the faintly lavender grass stretched to the horizon. The utterly cloudless sky was like a dome. New Canterbury's sun, hotter than Verii Mir's but farther away, was a pinpoint that dazzled; the sickle of a moon rode the opposite horizon. On the fourth side rose a stand of trees, thick pulpy stalks crowned with leaves two meters square. Then there was a movement in the shadows, and a grey-clad woman stepped from among them. Instantly, Edouard jerked the canopy release and swung himself out, sliding down the warm metal of the shuttle's side, careful to avoid the blackened heat shield.

"Alesia!"

"Welcome, Edouard." Her voice blew down to him on the constant wind that disordered her long hair and plucked at the hem of her sleeveless jumper. They embraced, then held each other at arm's length. Edouard was first to break the silence.

"You look well."

"As do you." Alesia caught him close again. Her voice was slightly hoarse, as though she had not spoken in some time, but otherwise she did indeed look fit. Her arms and legs were deeply tanned, and the circles had vanished from under her eyes. She looked much less tired than Edouard remembered, and he said so, knowing that he was merely postponing the inevitable.

"It shows you what a month of nothing but sleep, meditation, and books will do for you," Alesia added. "It's been good to rest, I must say, but . . . I'm no Stylite. I need to be *doing*, as well." She took Edouard's hand, twining her fingers through his the way she had done since they were children. "Walk with me, let me show you my preserve."

Edouard nodded. They would have to get away from any recording devices planted either in the beacon or on his shuttle, before he could broach his plans to her.

The grass grew deeper as they walked away from the trees, rising from their knees to waist-height, and in places growing even higher, but Alesia threaded her way by invisible paths. Edouard followed, fascinated. The air was cool—this was New Canterbury's autumn—but the wind was paradoxically warm. They had walked nearly a kilometer before Alesia spoke again.

"What brings you here, Edouard?"

"I need your advice," he answered simply.

"As a Reader?"

"Yes," Edouard said again. It's strange, he thought. I've never found it hard to talk to her before. But she'll understand. "You've heard all about our new emperor?"

Surprisingly, she laughed. "Less than you'd think, I'm ashamed to admit. Why?"

"He defeated me in a simulation." Edouard looked at her, eyes pleading. "Alesia, you know it isn't just sour grapes when I say I still think I'd be a better emperor, that I'd serve the Imperium better."

Alesia looked down at the darkly purple soil beneath her bare feet, which were stained equally purple by the chemicals in the pampas grass. At last she said, "No, Neddya, I don't think it's sour grapes. I trust you more than that. But what about your Oath?"

Edouard shook his head. "Allie, he never made me swear. After the duel, he just let me go back to my quarters."

"I see." Alesia looked relieved, and Edouard felt hurt. The Reader seemed to sense that, for she said hastily. "No, don't misunderstand. I do trust you— that's why I asked. You might be strong enough to do right no matter what you'd sworn, but I'm glad it didn't come to that." She was silent again, then said, "So you want a Reading."

"Yes."

"Then we'll go to my chapel."

She led him through more channels in the grass, until they came abruptly into a clearing. It can't be natural, he thought, overwhelmed by the sudden emergence of order in the formless sea of grass. The purple-stained ground was bare of dead or broken stalks, the dirt raked into neat patterns. A slab of rock rose from the very center of the circle. The rich brown stone looked warm beneath the cool steel of the sky. There were hollows worn in its surface; water had collected in one of them, but the other was empty. A familiar crystal sphere sat beside it: Alesia's focus for her Readings. There were no other symbols that Edouard recognized, but he could feel the power of the place. He walked very lightly when his sister beckoned him to enter.

"I've been tending it since I came here," Alesia said. "I went for a walk and . . . here it was."

"Yes," Edouard breathed, feeling his word ridiculously inadequate. Alesia genuflected, then collected her crystal, cupping it in both hands. Without turning, she said, "I will Read for you now, Neddya."

Edouard heard the Talent in her voice and crossed himself. He settled himself at the edge of the clearing and watched the shadows lengthen on the stone.

It was night before she was finished and rose to face him. Edouard looked up at her incuriously, the urgency of his mission drained from him by the long wait. Her voice was flat, tired.

"I have Read. I see victory, I think, or the chance of it. I see more strongly that you must try."

Edouard bowed his head. "Thank you, Sister."

She set her crystal aside and turned to look at the rising moon, full and blue-stained with craters. "Let us pray, then, that He may guide us."

Edouard bowed his head, crossing himself. He knelt beneath the twin moons and alien constellations, not knowing whether he prayed for success, for guidance, or merely that he not bring Alesia down with him if he failed.

When the service was finished, Alesia led the way back to the shuttle, its heat-reflecting paint glittering blue-white in the moonlight. Edouard stopped beside it, narrowing his eyes against the dazzle.

"Won't you stay the night?" Alesia asked.

"Would it be proper?" Edouard asked. "I thought I'd sleep shipboard tonight."

"It's too long a flight," Alesia said. "And it would be wrong not to offer hospitality." Her tone brooked no argument. Edouard followed silently, through the stand of trees and into the grass beyond, heavy with a bitter scent. A few clouds had formed now that the sun had set, and the moons edged them with molten silver. Even as Edouard watched, a thicker cloud than the rest obscured the smaller satellite; the shadows danced and reformed around him, so that the grassfield seemed to move suddenly against the wind. Then the cloud had passed, and the light was normal—as normal as moonlight ever was—again.

Alesia's retreat was dug in beneath a low hillock, visible from the surface only as a plain metal circle set into the hillside. She knelt and slid the cover aside, then motioned for Edouard to precede her down the ladder. Following him, she slid the door closed, and he heard the click as she pushed home the bolts. He stood patiently in the darkness, sensing her presence as she slipped past without touching him, and then she activated the lights. A glow built and grew until the whole chamber was bathed in an amber-tinted brightness. He was standing in a tiny entrance hallway, crammed with the machinery that monitored the retreat's automatic functions. Alesia beckoned, and he followed his sister into the main room.

The floor was carpeted with woven grass matting, but the bitter odor of the living plant had mellowed into a faint muskiness. There was a portable shrine in one corner, the fretted grill pulled across the images. The furniture looked spartan, but the thin pillows and the chairs, whose seats were woven leather, were surprisingly comfortable. Alesia touched buttons, and a serbot emerged from its alcove. The leaves folded back from the internal tray to reveal gleaming steel cups that smoked faintly in the sudden warmth. Edouard took a cup, handling it carefully to keep from numbing his fingers, and waited while Alesia chose one before seating herself.

"So what are your plans?" she asked, rubbing her chilled fingers against her jumper.

"My plans?" Edouard repeated. He looked down into the cup, watching little rivulets of dark liquor run off the sides of the ice-block. "To go home—to bring you home with me, if you'll come."

"Yes."

"And raise the minores. With your Reading to back me, to certify that I have a chance, they'll join me. Certainly they have no reason to love Keira."

Alesia turned her own cup gently, watching the ice melt and subside. "I'll miss it here. But. . . ." She sighed, and sipped gingerly at the liquor. "I'm needed, yes?"

Edouard nodded.

"Ah, you don't bring me the easy ones, do you?" She rose stiffly, setting her cup aside. "I'll tell the Sisters in the morning—if they haven't guessed already. In the meantime, I'm for sleep. There's a mattress in the closet, Neddya, and a noise-maker for the quiet." She smiled. "I've not forgotten how much you hate that."

Chapter 22

On Avalon, the time passed in an aching tedium. Keira had done everything he could, made his moves, blocked or tapped every possible line of communication for Edouard, and now he could only wait. The daily business of government was far from demanding; the Heralds and Havener could handle it alone, and viewing every tape did not occupy his Talent for very long. The news from Hellmouth was encouraging, but Castellar still refused to commit himself, waiting for a higher offer. Keira still held long gaming sessions, and convinced himself that the Hell-lord would eventually join him, but he could not suppress all worries. He grew irritable, and the household moved warily in his presence.

Desolin regarded her emperor over the remains of a planning breakfast, careful to hood both eyes and thoughts. So this was the reverse of the Renault Talent, she thought, this jittering impatience. It was no wonder they had been considered so dangerous: in this mood—balked, inactive—they were capable of anything. But his Talent was in proportion to his present stifled fury. When the time came for action, he would see farther and more clearly than could she. It was not yet time to regret her bargain.

The thought of the contract between them, and the power she would gain from it, reminded her of the power she had hoped to hold. What would have happened, she wondered, if she had challenged him, then forced him to wait, until he made too many moves simply out of boredom? Could she have won then?

"Majesty. Are you interested in a game?"

Keira looked mildly startled, though she could not tell if it was because of the abrupt change of subject, or because she had been reluctant to do any gaming for some weeks now. "Certainly, Lady. Name your world."

"This one." She had his interest now. His eyebrows arched, one higher than the other, adding two more angles to his already angular face. "I am curious, Majesty, to know if our agreement was necessary."

She held her breath. It was a risk, saying it in that way, but if it did not infuriate him, it was just the sort of statement that would appeal to him. His light eyes stared at her for a long moment, their expression unreadable, and then he relaxed subtly. "Are you indeed? So you want to play out a contest between the two of us?"

"Yes."

Keira smiled with genuine pleasure, and the recent lines of temper disappeared. His face resumed its old elegance and, irresistibly, she found herself smiling back. "Very well, Lady," he said, "you'll have your chance at me."

Without waiting for her answer, he reached for his pocket secretary and sent serbots for the Quarters' gaming equipment and for Japhet.

Keira hunched forward in his chair, hands busy on the controls. Around him, in the makeshift tank that was really the larger of the private rooms, the lights were fading, to be replaced by individual pillars of light around each control station. The mutiple screens filled and refilled as he calculated new patterns of alliance, this time binding Edouard reluctantly to his cause, having him swear immediately after his defeat, taking the de Terranins out of contention. He saw Desolin smile knowingly, caught in her column of light, and looked away quickly. The alliance with Edouard, however reluctant, freed St. George to support him immediately and wholeheartedly. Ojeda remained neutral again, but this time Xio-Sebastina was enlisted on his side, though Lovell-Andriës and the majores of the Federal border sectors joined Desolin. Frowning, he exploited Hellmouth commercial ties by bribing Castellar, and set up a program that would drain Desolin's military strength by affecting the commercial lines from which she would draw half her ships.

She in turn attempted to enlist the Federation, and Keira countered by appealing to Denisov-Graham. He was only partially successful: the Federation agreed only not to interfere.

Suddenly, his interest in the game deserted him, and he was left staring at a row of screens. The symbols that they displayed were only symbols, meaningless. The whole thing was irrelevant. He knew the ending already, starkly clear in the opening moves.

"Desolin."

She looked up curiously, her hands still entering data culled from one of her tapes into the machine's memory.

"It's over," he said. "I've won."

"How can you say that?" she protested. "You've hardly begun."

"Look." Keira glanced at Japhet, and the commoner transferred control of the room to his machine without being asked. Fueled by Talent, Keira shaped both campaigns, his and hers following each to its logical conclusion, and his inevitable victory.

Desolin looked as though she wanted to protest,

but his projection mirrored her plans too exactly for her to do anything but admit defeat. Keira nodded and rose, his face suddenly despairing.

"Why won't Edouard *move*?"

Desolin watched him stalk from the tank, stunned by the display of Talent. Now more than ever, she was glad she had chosen alliance. She would have been defeated, just as the sim had predicted, and her own people would have suffered for the attempt.

But that was not the main thing she had learned from the game. Keira was tired of sims; they could no longer hold his Talent. Edouard, boy, I hope you hurry, she thought. Because if you don't, he's going to start playing games with our allies. Or just playing games.

Chapter 23

Storm Lily reached Verii Mir on the day of the first snow. From the port, they could see the city buildings crowned with white, the red tiles visible only in irregular patches. In the city itself, the unplowed streets were ankle-deep in the stuff. The day was a traditional holiday, and the streets were full of people, wrapped in bright woolens and black-dyed furs. Children, released from school, dragged saucer-sleds through the streets and flung themselves down hills with a fine disregard for pedestrians. The city had been closed to groundcars since the snow began. From the first approach to the planet, when the traffic control officer had sent a suspiciously cheery message, Edouard had known what would be expected of him. Once they landed, he dug out his warmest clothing, topped that with a borrowed fur coat, and set out on foot for the Eyrie. Alesia, her robes drawn so closely about her that she looked almost like an Assassin, walked at his elbow, a scarf protecting her face from the biting wind.

Despite the cold and the wind that held a promise of more snow as it sliced off the Bergmans, the city was out to celebrate. Street vendors sold hot sausages and baked maya-apples. Nearly every family had made its own saphir-wine, and those few who had not were assailed by offers from those who had. Edouard, easily recognizable, was pressed to accept cups from nearly every household he passed. The usual formality was gone; the commoners pressed close, cheering him, offering food and wine as visible symbols of their loyalty. It was a heady feeling, especially combined with the saphir-wine, and by the time he and Alesia reached the base of the Eyrie, Edouard felt as though he were walking on top of the snow, not wading through it. The lift was heated, and Alesia sighed in the sudden warmth.

"Ah, that's better. First snow is fun, but Donna! you have to be dressed for it."

"I should've thought," Edouard said. "I knew it was getting on toward that time." He couldn't help remembering his own school days, before he had gone to Avalon to finish his education at the Academy. For the first weeks of autumn, everyone hung on the weather forecasts, waiting for the meteorologists to say the magic word. There would always be one or two false alarms, days when there was the merest possibility of snow and the juvenile population of the planet held its collective breath and hoped, but no one could mistake the real thing. It would almost always begin in the late afternoon, with a wind off the Bergmans and a milky sky, and by full dark everyone would be busy putting out the jars of saphir-wine to freeze. And then there was the next morning, waking up to snow-light and the heavy silence, before everyone was out in the streets. There were parties, the street festivities in Peter's Port, and the nobles' banquet in the Eyrie. Edouard grimaced. He would have to attend that, of course, and he was hardly in a mood for celebration. Then he brightened. At least it would give him an excuse to meet with some of the majores.

As Edouard had expected, his household had already made the preparations for the traditional banquet. His steward relinquished control of the proceedings, and provided him with a tape of the guest list. Edouard took this into his study, and by midafternoon had taped and sent cautious supplementary invitations to those land-minores to whom he had already mentioned his plans. By evening, they had all answered: most were willing to listen again.

He had just finished erasing the last of the acceptances when a serbot appeared at the office door. "Lord Mihas's pardon, Overlord, but it's six hours."

Edouard glanced quickly at the time display above his computer screen. The alarm light was flashing, but he had been too immersed in his work to notice it. "My compliments to the steward, and I will be down directly."

He dressed hurriedly, pulling his formal long coat directly over the clothes he had travelled in. The heavy brocade hid a multitude of sins. He paused in front of the mirror just long enough to adjust his coronet, and rushed to the banqueting hall. The serbots had an elevator waiting for him, a mute reproach for his tardiness.

Mihas, the steward, was waiting for him at the far end of the hall, just inside the double doors. The tables were impeccably set, snowy cloth beneath bright-painted china and ruby-toned crystal, serbots hovering silently in the background, ready to bring out the first courses.

"I'm sorry, Lord Mihas," Edouard said.

The steward bowed, unsmiling. The wire of an earphone was just visible along his jaw before it disappeared into the furred collar of his coat. Edouard winced at the thought of requests and reproaches that would be flooding in over that channel.

"With your permission, Overlord?" the steward asked.

"Of course, my Lord."

Mihas touched hidden controls, and the door swung open sharply, admitting the guests, who had been waiting in one of the smaller halls. Edouard endured the formality of greetings with what he thought was commendable patience, and presided over the banquet with what he hoped was appropriate mirth. When the meal was finally over, he announced the dancing, and looked for a suitable minore to partner him in the first figure. As always, the steward was ready with a suggestion.

"My Lord, the Lord Nashira's husband is ill. It might be courteous to ask her to dance."

It was a good choice, Edouard thought as he approached the lanky northerner. No one can say that this is any evidence of my choice in consort or wife, and Nashira is suitably neutral in local politics. She can dance, too.

They danced, under lights made brighter by the presence on the balconies of the cameramen for the commoners' networks, taping the event for later broadcast. Edouard knew that Keira would have agents among those crews, and spent nearly a local hour on small talk before he dared slip away from the festivities. Alesia was waiting for him in a screened cubby off the hall, flanked by Ragnar Faldan, Count of Istvan's Meer on the southern continent, and Takenya Morgan, the most important of the northern continent land-minores. A third man, Tor Mairin, Lord of The Rais and one of Edouard's oldest supporters, waited in the shadows.

Edouard flipped back the top of the desk, revealing both a computer link and the controls of the room's security fields, and switched on the machines that deadened sound and sight. Once he was sure everything was functioning properly, he said, "My Lords, I think you know why I asked you to meet with me tonight."

Morgan nodded. "You spoke to us once before about the emperor. We gave you our answer then."

"You said you weren't convinced that I could win," Edouard said. "I went to the Order, to my sister, and had her Read for me. She sees my victory."

"Definitely?" Faldan cut in.

Alesia looked at him from under her cowl. "Nothing is ever definite in a Reading, my Lord, as one with Talent should know. The odds are in our favor, strongly so."

Faldan gestured his apology.

Morgan nodded. "But even if you win, my Lord, what do we gain from supporting you?"

"The certainty of having someone you know you can trust on the throne," Edouard answered. "You know me, you know I'll always follow Convention. Keira Renault—the name alone should make you nervous. That family has always lived just on the edge of Convention, never quite breaking it, but they've bent it badly when it suits them. It is said on Avalon—by everyone, even the commoners—that he's made a pact with the Hamm'tt Duke, for a full marriage between them." He did not add—he did not need to add—that a Hamm'tt ascendancy would mean money and business diverted from Verii Mir and Altus to the mines and factories on Sahara and St. Katherine. The commoners would be hurt, and the nobles would suffer with them.

Faldan said, "You said to me that our honor was at stake, Overlord. Not a merchant-minore's bank account."

Morgan bristled at that, and Mairin ducked his head to hide a grin.

Edouard said, "My Lord Ragnar, not everyone is fortunate enough to hold self-supporting, majore lands. Nor are the contributions of those land-minores who concern themselves with manufacturing inconsiderable. But yes, honor is at stake, as well as our prosperity. Doesn't it tarnish our honor to be ruled by someone who is not only unConventional but anti-Conventional? It's our duty to op-

pose Keira. And my sister's Reading promises us
victory."

"I will follow you, Overlord," Faldan said grimly.
"I know my duty, and I will serve you to the
death."

"As will I," Mairin said promptly.

"And I," Morgan said, but he sounded a shade
less enthusiastic than the others.

Edouard bowed to all of them. Mairin had been
committed for some time. Faldan he could rely on;
Morgan, he was sure, would come over wholeheartedly when he compared the industries on Sahara with the Altus businesses whose stock he
owned. He made a mental note to have his steward mention those Saharan properties in Morgan's
hearing. "Thank you, my Lords, I am grateful for
your support."

Faldan bowed even more deeply, and Morgan
said, "Our honor is at stake, Overlord." Edouard
pretended he did not hear the touch of irony in the
land-minore's voice. He deactivated the security
fields and bowed them out. Mairin hesitated, and,
at Edouard's nod, stepped back inside as the Overlord switched on the screens again.

"Is there more?" Mairin asked. "I thought I was
to pass the news on to Bernard."

"That can wait for a few minutes," Edouard
said. "Alesia, what did you think of this? Were
they sincere?"

"When is Ragnar Faldan anything but sincere?"
Alesia answered. "And Morgan will come around,
I'm sure of that."

"Good enough. What's the word from Hellmouth?"

Mairin made a face. "What do you expect from a
Hellmouther? Castellar wants to be Grand Duke."

"That's very unConventional," Alesia said.

Edouard nodded, but his heart wasn't in it. If
that was the price of Owen Castellar's support, so

be it. He wasn't fool enough to think a Castellar would oppose a Renault for anything less than a dukedom. He caught Mairin's eye, and saw the other majore nod slightly. Mairin would make the offer.

"What about military support?" Mairin went on.

"Mine remains much as it was," Edouard said. "We have ground troops in plenty, mostly from the southern continent. Ships are more of a problem, but if Castellar joins us, we'll have capital ships and schooners in plenty."

"And if he doesn't?" Mairin asked.

"We will hire transport from the Guilds," Alesia answered. "The Overlord de la Mar will also be providing warships."

Edouard activated the computer link, displayed a summary of his most recent projections. Without waiting to be asked, Mairin leaned across to view the screen more closely.

"So you can see," Edouard went on, "we think Keira's strength will be in space. He has Lovell-Andriës' fleet—schooners and a few small warships— Hamm'tt's warships, and naval support."

"We're still hopeful of the Navy," Alesia interjected. "We have high-ranking clients among the Navy minores. They'll join us."

"Even so, we're weaker in space," Mairin said.

"Yes." Edouard touched buttons on his keyboard, displaying a second screen of figures. "But look at the ground strengths. Even if Hamm'tt can bring in her minores from El Nath—and none of Keira's backers have many soldier-minores among their vassals—we outnumber Keira's ground troops nearly two to one. And if we cut him off from El Nath, since Somewhere hardly has a ground force, that leaves only the Guard. An elite, I grant you, but a small force."

"I see." Mairin studied the screen.

"There is a way to turn this to our advantage," Edouard said. "If we can avoid a space battle, and decoy Keira's fleet away, we can take Avalon. And if we win Avalon, that's more than half the war."

Mairin was nodding. "Yes, I see it."

Edouard could hear the Talent in the other's voice, and nodded gravely. "Thank you. We'll talk more later, but for now, I think we'd better rejoin the party."

Chapter 24

The command station, cut deep into the base of the mountain that held the Eyrie, had not been used in several generations, but the maintenance robots had kept the place spotless. It had been the work of hours, not days, for Edouard's technician-minores to put the equipment into working order. The computers there, their memory temporarily linked to that of the main house computers, fed data into the simulation tanks, where Alesia was hard at work. She cast and recast her scenarios, produced new data for the others to interpret, until finally she declared that there was no more for her to learn.

The station had been designed to be the nerve center of a defensive battle, from which any seige of Verii Mir could be broken. It had never been tested in actual combat—no one had yet been foolish enough to try taking the de Terranin home-world—but the strategic analysts agreed that the listed capabilities of the center were unsurpassed even by the imperial installations on Citadel. Edouard felt a glow of satisfaction as he took his place at the head of the communications table. From here he could contact his allies on distant worlds, without fear that Keira would intercept the T-drive transmission. He looked around complacently at the blank white walls, envisioning the elaborate computer-controlled scrambler that lay beneath the gleaming panels. In fact, all the technical details of the system were handled by computer, eliminating the chance of treachery from a human operator. He touched a button on the table, and his keyboard rose in front of him. He was ready.

"Initiate sequence blue."

"Acknowledged." The computer vocalization was deep-toned, rasping.

Around him the lights dimmed, then came up again, but there were differences. It was as though the room had been divided into neat segments, perfectly dovetailed but still distinct. Shadowy figures began to appear, their shadow-tables overriding and meshing with the one at which he sat. They grew clearer; Edouard could now put a name to each shadow, though the connection was not complete. Nuriel de la Mar was at his right hand, tense and frowning. Alesia—her image was the sharpest, coming only from the southern continent where she had gone to negotiate with a recalcitrant majore—was at his left. Gregor Burian, Altus-Lord, came into view next to Nuriel, but at the final place there was only a haze, as though that part of the room were slightly foggy. Edouard frowned, but before he could touch the keyboard a picture began to form, static-blurred but discernible. Clearly the commodore was having trouble making contact: a spaceship could only carry so much projection equipment, and it would take the full power of the engines to run it. Even so, Edouard was sure his own machines were doing most of the work, catching, amplifying, and shielding the faint signal.

"Contact is complete."

"Acknowledged." Edouard looked around the composite table, making eye contact with each of the projections as though they were actually present. "My Lords, commodore, I am glad we were able to arrange this meeting."

There was a polite murmur in response.

"I assure you," he continued, "I would not have asked this of you if it were not important. Your reports indicate that each of you is ready to move against Keira. Am I correct?"

Again the polite murmur, more positive than before.

"Then the sooner we act the better." Edouard looked around again. "You already have tapes detailing your roles. Does anyone foresee difficulty in coordinating with anyone else?"

There was silence, a few heads shaken, nothing more. Then Nuriel cleared his throat.

"Overlord?" Edouard prompted. Damn you, he thought, if you think you can back out now, by God I'll give you to Keira myself. He suppressed his anger and concentrated on the deep purple sea visible over Nuriel's shoulder until he was calm again.

"My Lord, my mother is still on Oceanus, and she is very unreceptive to this plan."

"We've discussed this before," Edouard said. "Will you be able to declare yourself military regent when our ships appear in the system?"

Nuriel nodded, light winking on his jeweled cheek. "I can do it," he said, "but you'll have to make me permanent regent if you want to keep Oceanus."

"That will be taken care of," Edouard promised.

Burian lifted a hand. "With my ships," he asked, "what are our naval forces?"

"Three frigates, three corvettes, and the schooner circus—and, of course, the hired caravels, but I don't think we need to count them," Alesia said, speaking from her Reader's memory.

Burian nodded.

"Does anyone else have questions?" Edouard asked. The others were silent. "Then it seems we need only set a date for the rendezvous." He glanced down at the keyboard and its figures, though he had calculated the various factors so many times already that he hardly needed to see them written out. "Ten standard days from now—ides minus five August, Standard, at the agreed coordinates. We'll show on your sensors at Portaprima dawn, Lord Nuriel."

There was a general rumble of agreement, then Valin's image rose to its feet. The picture wavered, but the computers compensated quickly.

"My Lords. The emperor Edouard."

Around the table there were nods, and a ragged chorus: "Long live the emperor!"

Edouard bent his head graciously. "Thank you, my Lords. If there's nothing else, then I declare the meeting ended." To the computer he added quietly, "End sequence blue."

All around him the colors began to run together, fading into a uniformly grey haze that hid the walls for a moment, then dissipated like mist in sunlight. Edouard took the paper with the rendezvous date out of the printer and shredded it methodically, listening with only half an ear to the muted noises of the computer as it shut down the communications room. When the chimes sounded the clear, he rose and left by a door that opened abruptly in the featureless wall.

The Assassin was waiting in the antechamber, his hands tucked into his sleeves. He bowed deeply.

"Dan Natesa," Edouard said. "Are you ready to carry my message to Keira?"

The Assassin bowed even more deeply. "I am at your lordship's disposal."

"Then let's get on with it," Edouard said.

Chapter 25

FitzMary was dining alone for the first time in weeks, and wondered irritably why she felt so lonely. It had become a pleasant habit, she would admit that much, having company while she ate, and Japhet had been well trained to be an entertaining companion. But this sudden empty feeling when he wasn't there was completely unexpected. She had ordered enough food for two, and ate both portions in a fit of morose frugality. After the serbot had cleared away the dishes, she settled herself on the couch and stared at the wallscreen, sipping a glass of cordial she did not really want. The screen showed a bleak seascape, low waves rolling in against the barren coast of Sparta, that matched her mood.

She had just finished the cordial and was trying to decide whether she would have another when the intercom chimed. Surprised by her own eagerness, she hit the response button. "Who is it?"

"Japhet." He sounded harried. Something went wrong, she thought. That's why he didn't come.

"Enter."

"I apologize for not making it to dinner," Japhet began, with an attempt at a smile.

"It's all right," FitzMary said. "What happened? Is there trouble?" She motioned for him to sit, then turned to the kitchen console. "Can I get you anything?"

Japhet was momentarily stunned by the barrage

of questions. "Nothing—well, tea? And a sandwich?"

"You haven't eaten?"

He shook his head, and then, as FitzMary began
punching in a request for a full meal, said, "I'm
really not very hungry. Just a sandwich, please."

FitzMary hesitated, but reprogrammed the machine.

"In fact, I think what I want most is sleep,"
Japhet went on, "and I'm too tired for that."

There was such a startled note in his voice that
FitzMary could not help smiling. "Tea will help."

"Yes." Japhet arched his back, wincing, and
FitzMary could hear his muscles crack. "I've been
with his Majesty all day."

Oh, have you? FitzMary thought. Her stomach
twisted, and she forced her voice to remain neutral.
After all, what right did she have to be jealous?
"Were you?"

"I was. Keira took it into his head that he wanted
to be entertained."

FitzMary grimaced, and hoped that he would
take it for sympathy and not anger.

"So we played sims all day," Japhet went on,
oblivious. "He's really bored with them, anyway,
and I'd just be getting used to the scenario when
he'd decide that he'd won already and want to
move on to something else. I'm not majore, I can't
keep up with that."

FitzMary hid her sudden intense relief. "He's
been that way lately. I'm sorry he was taking it
out on you."

Japhet looked up from the tray of sandwiches
proffered by the serbot. "Better me than someone
else."

"I suppose." FitzMary joined him on the couch
and poured tea for both of them. The serbot closed
its leaves over pot and food and squatted beside
the low table.

"He acts almost as though he's losing his grip on things." She was only just able to repress her own bitterness, the frustration of the past weeks. "Is this another of his games?"

Japhet curled his hands around his cup, seemed to draw into himself. "I don't know."

"You don't think so."

"No." Japhet sighed deeply. "I think I've seen this before. Keira's scared, that's all. He doesn't really know how to wait. Especially now that any move he makes will only hurt him."

FitzMary had not expected to be forced into this sudden intimacy with the emperor, an intimacy that was tempered by such detachment. Japhet sensed this, and shrugged. "It isn't helping with the uncommitted nobles."

"Nor with the Federation," FitzMary said. She stopped abruptly, not wanting to be any more indiscreet than she had already been. Then, Japhet was certain to know as much as she did, she consoled herself. Maybe more, these days.

"Yes." Japhet shrugged. "And I admit I'm worried about my own status. I don't want to be just a gaming partner, not even to the emperor, and I'm not getting any younger."

"Of course," FitzMary said. As they spoke, her subconscious had been busy; now it presented her with a decision. "You've a place—status—with me, if you'd accept it. Surely his Majesty wouldn't object to that."

Japhet looked up suspiciously. "I wasn't angling for that."

"I was offering—asking. You're a good friend, more than that. I hoped you felt the same." In spite of herself, the words came out stilted, and she knew she was blushing.

"I do." There was no calculation in his voice, just acceptance.

"It's settled then?" FitzMary asked, and the other

nodded. She did not quite know what all the implications of this would be—would she be patron, mistress, lover, companion, consort?—but that could be decided later. What mattered now was that their friendship would be official and evident, that he would have a claim on her.

Chapter 26

Keira woke suddenly, uncertain what had disturbed him. He lay still for a long moment, listening. There was nothing out of the ordinary, only the soft hiss of the ventilation system and the humming of the spybox at the head of the bed. He tested the air, but there were no unfamiliar smells. He listened a moment longer, unable to see a thing in the absolute darkness of the bedroom, then, carefully, he reached for the bed controls.

Something moved in the blackness, came rushing forward with a hiss of displaced air. False hawk! he thought, even as he remembered that the species had never been taken off Hellmouth. He rolled away, dragging the pillows across his face to avoid the false hawk's skunk-like spray. The thing coughed twice, three times, and something hit the pillow. Keira kept rolling, slapped his hand across the light controls. The overheads blazed on, and he saw it. A rounded metallic wedge, it hovered on black-glowing antigravs just below the ceiling. A tiny antenna swiveled until it found him, and a tube opened on its belly. Keira barely had time to drag the second pillow across his body before the sliver-darts thudded home. Oh, Donna, an Assassin, he thought, slamming the alarm key and snatching his hand back beneath the cover before a dart shattered against the bedstead. A gold liquid oozed where it had hit: poison, probably. The emperor huddled beneath the two pillows, not

daring to move. There was a nightmare familiarity
to the situation, as well there might be. It was the
sort that was all too common in simulation, but
there was no chance this time of being allowed to
concede.

The machine hovered overhead. As long as he
didn't move, he seemed to be safe. Stalemate, he
thought, but it can't last. Even as he thought that,
edging the pillow a fraction of an inch to one side
to get a better view, a new sensor rose from its
back. It began to sweep back and forth against the
ceiling in a search pattern. He watched it carefully.
Was it self-sufficient, or was there an Assassin somewhere running it? Probably the latter, he decided.
There wasn't room in its casing for fancy computer controls. By the same token, it couldn't carry
too many darts, so maybe he had a chance.

As if to deny his thought, the circles grew smaller:
the machine, or its operator, had determined that
he wasn't lying on the floor beside the bed. It
swept toward the bed itself, dropping lower. Keira
leaped to meet it, throwing off the bedclothes,
discarding one pillow and bringing the other viciously across the wedge. It spat a last dart that
shattered against the wall, and the pillow's weight
dragged it to the floor. Keira launched himself on
top of pillow and machine, stepping as heavily as
he could in the hope of crippling it, then ran for
the door. As he fumbled with the palm lock, he
saw the machine push the pillow aside and wob-
ble into the air, its external sensors bent and broken.
Then the door opened, and he slipped into the
outer room, slamming the lock behind him.

He stood for a moment, letting his heartbeat
slow, then behind him he heard the machine striking softly against the inside of the door, and then
against the lock plate. He tensed again, but the
machine was not equipped with the sensor heads

that could simulate the pattern of an authorized human hand.

Then the outer door snapped back, and the room was filled with Guards in battle armor. They relaxed slightly, seeing no immediate attacker, and Doran pushed his way to the front.

"Majesty, what's happened?"

"A floater," Keira said, and to his shock had to pause to steady his voice. "Throwing darts. It may be damaged, but not too badly."

"Right," Doran said. He gestured to one of the Guards, who carried, in addition to the projectile rifle, a heavy scanner pack. "Take care of that, Tulsi." The Guard saluted and moved toward the door, unslinging the heavy scanner, and Doran reached for his pocket communicator. "Arel, pick up your search. You're looking for a dart controller. See if you can spot transmission."

"It's still live, sir," a Guard reported from the door.

"Concentrate on picking up the transmission," Doran ordered immediately. "It'll be there."

Keira could not hear the acknowledgement. He stared instead at the Guards working by the door. Already, two had set up an improvised trapfield, bellmouthed field projectors aimed at the door, while the third manipulated his scanners.

"Transmission's stopped, sir," he reported, after a moment.

"Proceed with caution," Doran answered. "Majesty, if you'd withdraw to the command station?"

Keira nodded, then started as Lilika touched his arm to offer a pair of Guard's coveralls. "If you think that's best, Doran," he said. Adrenalin still filled his system, and beyond that there was the sheer pleasure of having survived, of having proved to himself that he could survive.

"In the interests of security, Majesty," Doran said.

"Very well." Keira pulled on the coveralls, then followed Lilika out of the emperor's suite. There were more Guards waiting outside, battle armored and heavily armed, to escort him to the command center within the Quarters. They surrounded him closely as they walked the length of the corridor, kept blastrifles leveled even after the command crew had identified themselves by the proper codewords. Only when Lilika was personally certain that the center was secure did the escort relax even slightly. Three followed them into the command room, crowding the cramped space even further; the rest took up positions outside the single door, rifles at the ready. Lilika sealed the door behind her, then gestured politely toward the only corner not jammed with consoles and scanning monitors. Keira moved gratefully toward it, dodging technicians, and leaned against the bare wall. Beneath his hands, the surface had the smooth silkiness of armorsteel.

The multiple screens flashed constantly shifting images—shots of corridors and rooms, public and private, and the network of serbot tunnels—and complicated strings of numbers and symbols. There was a constant murmuring as the technicians spoke to each other and to the Guards conducting the actual search, but Keira could not make out the words. Then a light flashed on one of the side consoles. The minore seated before its keyboard frowned sharply, his hands stabbing forward to adjust knobs and buttons. The single screen blanked briefly, then displayed an oddly fuzzed picture of one of the serbot tunnels. The minore made a further admustment, and the image split apart, revealing a ghostly, indistinct shape. A line of symbols crawled across the bottom of the screen.

"Got him!" the minore exclaimed, and instantly got his voice under control. "We have a contact." As the other technicians quickly adjusted their own instruments, focusing in on the disturbance, the minore who had made the first sighting read off a string of numbers. On one screen, the largest of the monitors, Keira could see symbols, each representing a team of Guards, moving through a plan of the Palace, converging on the point of contact. There was a sudden flurry on the screens, over almost as quickly as it had begun, and then the pictures cleared. Doran stood at the focus of the cameras. Behind him, Keira could see more Guards, and, securely held between two of them, a silver-masked Assassin.

"Your Majesty," the general said. "We've made the capture. We'll take him across to the Iron Hills."

"No," Keira said. One of the Guards immediately offered him a headset; Keira took it and adjusted the microphone. "No, Doran, I think Dan Assassin will have a message for me."

The Guards looked sidelong at him, and at each other: it had been generations since the rules of challenge and first blood had been followed. Keira smiled sourly. The Silvertrees had found that part of Convention inconvenient and had done their best to eliminate it, striking first and finally.

In the screen, the Assassin was stirring. Keira's smile widened, and he suppressed it with an effort.

"Put me on an external speaker," he ordered. "There is one?"

"Yes, Majesty," one of the technicians answered. "You're on, Majesty."

Keira nodded thanks, and said, "Dan Assassin. I expect you have something for me, since you failed?"

He could see no change of expression, of course, but he thought that the Assassin smiled behind the mask. "Yes, I carry a message," the Assassin said. His words were faint. Another technician frowned, and adjusted his controls to bring it in more clearly.

"State it," Keira said.

"Very well. Edouard, Overlord of Verii Mir,

Duke's Heir of de Terranin's system, declares war against you, Keira Renault, as a usurper of the Imperial throne. He calls on all those truly concerned with the welfare of Imperium and Commons to join him in deposing the false emperor." He made an abortive movement, and caught his breath in momentary pain. "I bear a tape of the same declaration, which the Overlord charges you on your honor to play before the Eger."

Keira grinned. "I see. The tape is where?"

The Assassin gestured with his chin to the front of his tunic.

"Sergeant," Doran snapped. "Fetch it out, but carefully."

The warning was probably unnecessary, but Keira held his breath until the sergeant had retrieved the cartridge. A senior technician touched his keyboard, and one camera zoomed in to focus closely on the cylindar. It was a full-scale holo, not just a voice-and-screen video, and a bright orange sticker warned that it had been treated to prevent tampering. It could only be played once; after that, the tape deteriorated too rapidly for even the most able technician to save it.

"Very well," Keira said. "General, see that the Assassin is well-guarded until we have recorded an answer to the Overlord's challenge. He can take my answer back to Verii Mir."

"Majesty, you aren't going to let him go," Doran protested. "I know strict Convention demands it, but it's not good policy to send Edouard back his pet killer."

"No," Keira said. "We'll play this by all the rules, general, not just the convenient ones. You may tell Edouard that, too, Dan Assassin."

"Very well, Majesty," Doran said. "With your permission?" He indicated the Assassin with a sweeping gesture.

"Go ahead," Keira answered.

* * *

Security within the Eger Hall was extremely tight, and Doran had insisted on tripling the usual escort. The attending nobles, majores and minores alike, passed through not only the usual unobtrusive weapon-detectors but through portable sensor gates manned by cold-eyed Guards. Those who failed the test were given the choice of submitting to a thorough search or not attending. Most chose the search, and there was surprisingly little grumbling.

In deference to Convention, the Guards who actually entered the Eger did not carry energy weapons. They did carry shielded blades, and not a few carried concealed dart-guns. Even after those precautions had been taken, Doran insisted that the imperial party travel to the Eger aboveground, not through the tunnels, and that Keira enter the Hall through the most secure door behind the throne. The assembly had been alive with conversation; at his entrance, all noise ceased, and Keira caught himself prolonging the moment before he took his place on the throne.

"My Lords." The chair itself was constructed to catch and project his words to every corner of the Hall, so that he barely had to raise his voice. "The Eger is assembled." He waited a moment, looking over the faces. There were fewer nobles on Avalon than there had been: as soon as it became clear that fighting was inevitable, many had returned to their homeworlds, either to raise troops or to protect their holdings.

"Lords of the Imperium. I have been presented with a challenge to my rule, under Convention. I have summoned you to witness the challenge and my reply." He leaned back against the chill ironwood, and motioned to Havener. "Dan Erik."

Havener came forward, touched his wand of office to a depression in the floor of the dais. There was a faint whisper of machinery, and a section of tile slid back, revealing the top of a holoprojector pedestal. It rose slowly and clicked into place, lights glittering across its surface. Havener took the Assassin's tape from a pocket of his glossy robe and displayed it to the assembly.

"My Lords, this has been certified by the Order as the original communication from the Overlord Edouard." His light voice fell dead in the silence.

He held up the tape for a moment longer, then dropped it into the central cavity of the machine. Lights flashed across the control board. Havener glanced at them, and made final adjustments before he touched the master switch. The Hall lights dimmed a little, and a strong column of light sprang into existence on the speaker's platform before the dais. At first it was empty gold, and then colors leached in, forming a shadowy figure. A ghostly Edouard stood there in the gold-and-green formal coat of his Domus, a coronet finer than an Overlord's resting arrogantly on his scarred brow.

"Lords of the Imperium." The recorded voice came through without a hint of static. "I, Edouard, Overlord de Terranin, proclaim the so-called emperor, the made-minore Keira Renault, to be an usurper with no right to the throne, by either blood or birth. I call on all those loyal to Convention and to the Imperium to join with me in opposing him by whatever means necessary. The Eger may then freely fulfill its duties and choose the rightful heir to Oriana's throne." The image looked around as though Edouard could see the assembled nobles. "My Lords, I have spoken."

The shape dissolved into a brief burst of static and then into the empty column of light. Havener touched the projector controls, and that winked out. Slowly the Hall lights came back to normal.

"My Lords." Keira did not rise from the throne, as strict Convention demanded. "I have fought the

Overlord once before, and defeated him. I see no reason to fight again. For the rest, I, Keira, have been acknowledged by Eger and Church to be the only rightful heir. I have been crowned, and I sit here as emperor. If the Overlord will not retract his challenge—and I offer him a final chance to do so—he must face the wrath of the Imperium. The emperor has spoken." He looked out at the faces of the nobles. None of them showed surprise: they had known as well as he that there would be trouble when Edouard did not attend the coronation. They had had enough time to choose their sides. He would see within a few hours who would be loyal and who would simply wait to see who won.

"My Lords, you have heard," Havener said formally.

The answer rumbled from the assembly. "We have heard, and witness."

Chapter 27

"So Edouard's finally declared himself," FitzMary said.

Desolin finished lighting her pipe and said, around the puff of smoke, "With a vengeance, one might say. But at least the waiting's over."

Keira nodded, and accepted a cup of coffee from the serbot, glancing over it at his household. They were gathered in one of the computer-filled planning rooms outside the red circle, under heavy security. Havener was busy at one of the many terminals; even as Keira glanced his way, he accepted a printout and came to stand beside the emperor's chair. Keira took it and glanced at the latest projection of his support. Havener, conservative as always, had listed Castellar as doubtful. Keira made a face, but said nothing. He was certain now, Talent-certain, that his final message would bring Castellar to his side. It had proved impossible to convince the others of that, though.

He glanced around again. FitzMary, Desolin, Havener, Doran, Lilika and other soldier-minores from the Guards and Desolin's household: a few faces were missing. Lovell-Andriës was in his own system, collecting ships and men. PenMorgan was with the fleet, patrolling somewhere between Avalon and the Federal border, waiting for orders and for any indication of the other Admirals' loyalties.

"Well, my Lords," he said, "You saw the tape

when I played it for the Eger, and you saw the reaction. What do you think they'll do?"

There was a silence, and Havener said, "I ran an analysis, Majesty. It's very rough, though."

"Let's hear it," Keira said.

The robe-minore consulted the sheaf of computer paper that lay on the table in front of him. "I don't think it'll make that much difference, Majesty. A few waverers—the de la Mar minores whose allegiance isn't direct to Nuriel, and Altusians for Edouard, some of the Mist and Council-border nobles for us—may move now, but the majority should stay neutral."

"I'm not sure how much Nuriel could do to bring over those nobles," FitzMary said softly. "There's the question of his Oath. . . ."

"Technically, you could get around that," Desolin said. "He swore as his mother's proxy, not for himself as Overlord. If you stretched the point. . . ."

Keira said, "Nuriel has never struck me as a person who takes risks easily."

"He and Edouard are close," Desolin said. "If he'd risk honor for anyone, it would be for Edouard." She leaned back in her chair, wreathing herself with clouds of smoke. "If he goes against his Oath, you'll have to count on him providing a base for Edouard."

"His mother would surely oppose that," Doran said.

"Indeed," Keira said. "Even though she's an invalid, she's still Grand Duke. My guess is that he'll wait until Edouard appears off-planet, and then 'surrender' and plead overwhelming force. That way he won't damage his honor or directly disobey the Duke." He looked to his left, and saw Havener nod and note new factors on a scratch pad. After the meeting, he would convert the discussion into data that could be used in simulation. Keira recognized the minore's skill, knew also that his own figures would be more accurate. "And what about the Navy, Captain?"

"Will any of them join Edouard?" she asked. "A few, possibly, from his home sector—especially people who've been stationed near Verii Mir for any time. It's a popular port, and the de Terranins have always treated us well. But most of his support will come from minore reserve commissions."

Keira nodded. "How many ships could he gather?"

Fitzmary shrugged. "Anywhere from two to ten, Majesty, from cruisers to corvettes. The Admiral and I think he'll get four or five big ships, but nothing larger than a frigate. At least one schooner circus from the land-minores—more, of course, if Castellar joins him—"

"He won't," Keira said.

FitzMary nodded. "As you say, Majesty. We also think he'll be hiring caravels from the guilds."

Havener cleared his throat. "It might be wise, Majesty, to consider sanctions against them. Commoners have no right to meddle in majores' wars."

"We can consider that when this is over," Keira said. "He'll get guild help for troop transport, regardless. The question is, is he hiring mercenaries?"

Doran shook his head. "Not among our people, and not outside the Imperium, at least according to Denisov-Graham, and I trust him. But he still has the advantage in infantry. If he reaches Avalon, we're in trouble."

"Majesty, why not wait for Edouard here, make him have to bombard, break Convention?" Havener asked abruptly.

"No." Keira's refusal was equally abrupt. "My honor is involved here. I can't afford to act against Convention. War has been declared, so the Court will remove to Citadel." He looked around for challenge, stared down the unspoken protests. Citadel was the old Silvertree stronghold, their homeworld before they had acquired Sander's World and Jerra. It was a barren ball of rock, honeycombed with tunnels and elaborate defensive installations. It commanded a network of jump points, too, and had always been a major fleet rendezvous point. It had long ago become Conventional for the emperor, during fighting between Domi, to leave Avalon and take up residence on Citadel, partly to protect the commoners of Avalon, and partly to give himself command of the spacelanes.

Desolin cleared her throat. "Do you plan to leave Avalon without any protection, Majesty?"

"Of course not," Keira said. "Some of the Guard will remain, and the Navy has doubled the forces on the Tor. And our projections indicate that Edouard will try to secure a base on Oceanus—to get control of extra ships, too, and an escape route— before he moves on Avalon. By the time he's done that, we can intercept him easily."

"Suppose he takes the risk and lands directly on Avalon?" Desolin asked. "You don't want to be forced into besieging the capital yourself."

"He'd have to take short jumps because of the troop transports," Keira answered. "If he takes a chance on not securing an escape route—and I say he won't move without one—we can intercept before he can break through the Tor's defenses. It's a single-day flight from Citadel to Avalon; there won't be a siege." He looked around the room again, waiting for further protest. There was none, though Desolin still looked unsatisfied. "Very well. The court will go to Citadel—I have a tape for the Eger. Captain FitzMary, I'll ask you to supervise communication with the Navy. Doran, you'll have to choose a cadre of Guards to supplement the troops already on Citadel."

"Let me bring all the Guard, Majesty," Doran said. "The Citadel troops haven't fought in fifty years."

Keira ignored his objection; they had been through that before. "Lady Desolin, are your ships ready to join us, or do you need more time?"

"I'm ready," Desolin said.

"Your ships will be under the Admiral's command when we join the fleet," Keira said.

"Of course," the Duke said. There was a note in her voice that suggested she did not intend to get very far from the center of power.

"Good." Keira looked around the room again, waiting for further comments or protests. "Then I suggest you see to your own plans. I want to be off-world in three days, local."

FitzMary was caught up immediately in the whirl of preparation, particularly in the naval arrangements. PenMorgan professed himself displeased with Keira's plans, but he had never given outright approval to anything proposed by the emperor. FitzMary suspected his objections were only a matter of form. Even after the basic outline had been more or less settled—there were minor details to be checked up to the minute of departure—she was dragged into the monumental task of preparing to move the imperial government. A number of minores and children of majores, motivated more by romance than by considered decision, had asked to join the emperor. FitzMary was assigned to help Doran decide which ones could be allowed to do so. Most were cleared easily. Several more were put under surveillance, but permitted to travel on one of the escort ships. Three—two from Aragon and one from a Dianan family with relatives on Altus—were refused under various excuses.

By the departure date, she was exhausted, but somehow she kept her temper until she saw her own belongings on board the caravel that would carry the emperor and the Household. Usually such ships were nothing more than spherical cargo ships

fitted with a single gun, but this one had once
been used as a decoy ship, and the concealed guns
had been replaced for this one trip, to the delight
of her elderly Guildmaster-captain. FitzMary had
been assigned to share a cabin with Lilika; mutual
agreement had replaced the Guard-sergeant with
Japhet, while the sergeant had moved in with another Guardsman. FitzMary waited until the ships
were moving out of the system, then turned off the
intercom, told Japhet to go away, and fell into her
bunk. She slept for a glorious twelve hours.

The trip, only two standard days long, was
uneventful. FitzMary divided her time between
sleep and long conversations with the Guildmaster-
captain, who, it seemed, had been everywhere, even
to Terra itself. He had flown his ships through
jumps himself, when his guidance computer failed;
had run through Somewhere's debris-strewn system under full acceleration; had been part of the
supply convoy at the relief of Dresden twenty years
before. He had served, as a young apprentice, in
the ships that had evacuated the Hildiv colony on
rAobath, during the last Council troubles, and had
been one of the few commoners ever to serve on a
combat ship. At first, she doubted his claims; by
their second conversation, she was taking careful
mental notes of everything he said, particularly
his descriptions of space off Oceanus. If they met
with Edouard's fleet in that particularly convoluted neighborhood, his words could prove inval-
uable. Japhet, to whom she returned each day
with a growing awareness of her own good fortune,
scoffed only until he met the man. All in all, the
trip was a profitable one for her, and she regretted
its ending only because it brought her that much
closer to parting with Japhet.

Chapter 28

Despite the messages, the governor of Citadel was not prepared for the arrival of the court. It took nearly two standard hours for the ground crews to bring the first ships, both escort ships, down the giant elevators from the landing pans to the well-protected bays beneath the planet's surface, a procedure that should have taken a quarter of that time. Most of the Guard contingent had travelled on those ships; by the time the emperor landed, the Guard had disembarked and was waiting with the governor's own honor guard. The local troops stood sloppily, showing signs of neglected training. Keira listened to the governor's greetings and excuses, smiled and nodded, and made plans to replace the man as quickly as possible.

The imperial suite was well below the dock level, far beneath the surface. The Silvertrees, whose home it had been for a hundred years before that Domus took the imperial throne, had done their best to make the dank, laser-smoothed corridors and hollowed rooms less cave-like, but the rich furniture and elaborate computer fittings only made the grey stone look bleaker. Looking closer, Keira could see that the elaborate carvings were worn, the bright colors faded.

The other fleets, Lovell-Andriës's squadron and Hamm'tt's cruiser, arrived a standard day later, but it was not until the third day that Keira was able to free himself from the trivial review and

planning sessions to tour the installation. The
Guards were busy with exercise, Doran trying to
work the Citadel force into some sort of shape in
case Edouard acted against all probability and
attacked the planet. Such a move would be stupid,
as well as uncharacteristic and unConventional,
and Keira knew as well as anyone that Doran was
merely worried about his own Guards losing their
edge. The emperor did not really care about the
cause: he was too grateful for the chance to slip off
alone. A serbot accompanied him, more because it
knew the access codes to areas that had been closed
off years before than because Keira was worried
about security, or the need to stay in contact with
his troops.

The corridors below the living level were dusty,
but showed little other sign of the years, though
Keira estimated that no human being had been
down there since the civil wars of the first Oriana's
reign. The serbots had kept the place relatively
clean, and the maintenance robots had been through
every year, until cost-cutting had forced the governor to turn off the unneeded machinery. Keira
found himself walking very carefully in the white-
painted halls, which lit up as he passed and then,
thriftily, went dark again behind him. Four hundred years since Oriana I's day, four hundred and
twenty-odd years since she had defended Citadel
against the Jerusalemer fanatics, while half the
Navy sat idle and mutinous. Four hundred and
twenty years since Keira's own ancestor had walked
these corridors. Those had been the best days of
the Imperium, something whispered in a corner of
his mind. Certainly, they had been the best days of
the Silvertrees. Now the Imperium was too settled,
the nobility blocked from its function by its own
inertia and the necessity of peace with its neighbors,
driven back on civil war for its amusement, for
those who dared to be amused. Colonization had

stopped: to add another world to the network might be the straw that broke the camel's back.

"No!" he said aloud, and the serbot, misunderstanding, froze in the act of opening another sealed door. "Continue."

The serbot whined obediently forward again, metal pseudofingers clicking as it pressed the sequence of buttons. Keira ignored it, fighting his own dark thoughts. I can handle more data, he told himself. The colonization can continue, somehow. I'll start looking for marginally Talented commoners—that'll shake up the minores and the majores, bring in some fresh blood. I can bring things back to life. I have to.

Those thoughts were less comforting than they should be, echoing the vision he had had at Oriana's funeral. No, he thought again, it can't end this way. Not just fading out from inertia. Rather than that I'll—The realization of what the unformed thought would have been shocked him into sudden stillness. He could not provoke a war that would bring an end to the Imperium. There could be no death or glory. He, the last Renault, last heir of the outlaw Domus whose members were bound by nothing, was compelled by Convention like any other noble. He tested the thought, and felt it ring clear and bitter-true. His Domus's greatest strength, the secret knowledge of their freedom, was denied him. The pain of it held him frozen, and Talent surged within him, showing him the futures, paths dreary with dust and the dying order. The Imperium was mortally old, Talent whispered, the decay as yet invisible but already irreversible, inevitable. All roads led to an end; his only hope was to ease the death.

All my family's plans and schemes, the games to bring us to this height of power, and we're made stewards of our own death.

The serbot had worked the door open at last,

leaning its full weight against the stubborn panel. It stood waiting, its stance seeming to Keira to be filled with mute reproach. Without certainly knowing why he bothered, he stepped through the door. Beyond was a conference room, the twin of one on the upper levels, except for the fact that here the screens were green and empty. The maintenance robots, and the serbots sent to clean, had been less than thorough here. Dust, fine and soft as velvet, lay centimeters thick on the table, and booktapes still lay discarded by one keyboard.

"Where is this?"

It was a long moment before the serbot answered, as though it had to dredge the information from some long-unused section of its memory. "This was the primary control center," it said at last. "It was closed off when the upper levels were made habitable."

Keira nodded to himself. That explained the dust. No maintenance robot could be allowed into such an area without a human supervisor, and, once the new conference room was made ready, there was no need to keep it in perfect condition. It would only be used in a dire emergency—the breach of the upper levels, perhaps. Telltales glowed at the corners of the screens: the center was not yet dead.

That cheered him somewhat, and he walked farther into the room, stepping carefully to avoid raising too much of the dust. Looking for more information, he seated himself at the great planning table, the top the transparent black glass of a holo display. Then he realized that he had sat in the imperial chair almost by instinct. He smiled, wondering what his ancestors would have said if they had seen him—or what the last few emperors would have thought, for that matter. Oriana would not have been happy. But this was where the Renaults had imagined their unknown descendant, sitting at the console that controlled an entire world, and, controlling that world, controlled the Imperium. Even more than the Palace on Avalon, this had been the seat of Imperial power. It was good that he had come here, good that he had at least filled that much of his ancestors' wishes, even if to head this table meant nothing any more.

"No," he said again, but so softly that the patient serbot did not move from its place by the door. Maybe this control room no longer meant power. But the Palace did, and he had ruled there, would rule there for quite a few more years. It was time he stopped allowing the age of the installation to affect him. His Talent had used him all day; it was time he used it. He was not a Reader by training, but his Talent was awake and restless. He reached into the depths of his mind and dragged it forward, forced it to become aware of the vision of the futures that had so frightened him. Then, as though he were running a simulation, he made it accept changes, made it modify the insight as he modified the present time. The Imperium as such would end—he could see that clearly now, beyond doubt or change—but there was a chance to make that end the beginning of another, greater—

The picture slipped away before he had grasped the final result of his changes, leaving him breathless. He sat very still for a moment, willing the taut muscles of his arms and thighs to relax without cramping. He had seen at least that there was an escape for the Imperium, a way to steer it away from the death of exhaustion, even if he could not yet trace the thread of that future to its end. He and his would be stewards—he could accept that now, had to accept it, however grudgingly—but not for death. There was something else coming—a new world that was not for his Domus or for any of the Domi. It was something new, a beginning rather than an end. It would be enough.

Chapter 29

The embassy felt empty, though the staff was as large as always. Perhaps, Denisov-Graham thought, pacing through the strangely quiet halls, it was the calm before the storm, the dead hush before the thunder. And then again, he thought, slapping open the door of his office, it might just be that the embassy has less work to do now that the emperor has left Avalon.

It was evening, and the office was almost dark. The Tiberian park beyond his window was blue and fuzzy with the twilight. Beyond the parkland, lights were coming on in the buildings and along the slidewalks. The chill light gave everything an odd look of winter; the leaves and living grass seemed almost incongruous.

Denisov-Graham settled himself into his over-sized chair and spun it to face the window, his back to his desk. Keira was on Citadel now, or had been at the last report. There was an unavoidable communications lag between Avalon and the emperor now: the court was the government, and there was no need to inform anyone else of the emperor's movements. No one would know what was happening until the battles were over and the victor found time to send dispatches. Keira could be dead at this moment, and they wouldn't know it until someone claimed power, and held it long enough to inform the galaxy of his intentions.

The bleak thought matched the bleak evening

only too well. He kicked the window controls. Instantly, the glass went opaque and the room lights came on. Tea would help, too, but the human kitchen staff had gone home for the night, and the ambassador did not trust the serbots to brew a truly Terran drink. Sighing, he unlocked the largest drawer of the desk, and rummaged in the debris until he uncovered the battered tin. He popped it open and sniffed at the contents.

The scent was unmistakably Terran. He closed the tin to avoid spilling any of the precious stuff, and crossed the room to the makeshift kitchen Rubenstein had had installed for him. Solemnly, he boiled water, measured tea, then brought the pot back to his desk, swaddled in a bright tea cosy. Rubenstein—and others before her—had noted that there were more efficient ways to keep the water warm while the tea steeped, but for Denisov-Graham the inefficiency was a reminder of home.

When it was ready, he poured himself a cup and reached for the most recent tape from home. The cover bore an official label, but the scribbled monogram beneath the diplomatic service's rose marked it as another letter from his little sister, thriftily sent through the diplomatic pouches. He had viewed it before, but contact with home might cheer him up.

Like all of the family, Irina looked young for her age, and was still young enough for that to be a handicap. She had filmed the letter sitting in the courtyard of the family's main house on Mars, the sands just visible through the haze of the atmosphere dome behind her, but her first words were to explain that she would be moving to Tiber within the week.

"Week local, that is," she went on. "I think that's about five days, standard—I'd need my almanac to be sure. Certainly, I'll be there by the time this reaches you."

Denisov-Graham closed his eyes momentarily, conjuring up the embassy on Tiber. He had served there, too, when he had been Irina's age. The house stood well outside the boundaries of tiny New Rome, only a few kilometers from the Great Ravine, separated from the other great houses by a wide tract of undeveloped land. Much of Tiber was like that. The colony had been one of the last to be settled before the Great Council War had put an end to Terran expansion, and it had been planned by a group at once practical and utopian. As a result, Tiber was one of the best-run and most beautiful worlds in the Federation, but after a few weeks there, the ambassador usually felt a longing for the lights and excitement of any of the great Terran cities. Still, there was nothing like a summer evening on Tiber, when the wind came from the south, bringing with it a hint of the exotic vegetation of the Ravine.

Suspiciously, he reached for the almanac-and-calculator that was a permanent part of the desk furniture, letting the tape run on without really listening to it. As he had half guessed, it was late winter on Tiber. If there was snow, it would be melting and the air would stink of that. In a week or less, the mud would be deep across the land.

The tape clicked to an end, and he thrust it back into its case. Rather than cheering him, the reminders of Tiber's quasi-spring had only depressed him more. He supposed he should at least take care of some business, and dictate an answer to Irina's letter—there was always the possibility it would put him in a better temper. He dug out a blank tape and switched the machine to "record", then found he had nothing to say. Well, he thought, is there any business I have to take care of at home? He ran down the mental list of things mentioned in recent letters from bankers and relatives, but there was nothing that Irina would not handle better without his advice. There was no point in sending for the passages from the family diaries until he was sure that Keira had won. It wouldn't do for the diaries to fall into Edouard's hands.

On the other hand, why not send for the excerpts? He thought Keira was going to win, why not put his own wager on it? If Edouard did win, it did not follow that he would find out about the bet, or even about the family diaries, and even if he did, it wouldn't make that much difference. Irina would understand, even if she would joke about her brother being corrupted by Imperial ways.

With new decision, he released the "hold" button and began to dictate the letter, smiling at the thought of Irina's reaction. When he had finished, he sealed the tape with his official stamp, and scrawled his initials beneath the ambassadorial diamond. He locked the letter into the box that already held his most recent reports for the Board, and opened the office door. The embassy still seemed unusually quiet, but the ominous quality was gone from the silence. He had committed himself irrevocably, even if only he knew of the commitment. If Edouard were to win, he would have to resign—in disgrace, to save the Federation's dignity—and the thought gave him new pride.

You really shouldn't get so involved in local politics, he told himself, but the voice of conscience was too bloodless to make any real impression. I am still the Federation's representative, first and last, he thought firmly. I support Keira because I believe that's in our best interests, as well as good for the Imperium. If I didn't think that, my liking him wouldn't stop me from supporting Edouard. Or resigning, he amended, more realistically. But I would resign.

Chapter 30

Owen Castellar, Lord Hell, stood before the screen that formed one wall of his office, staring at the city that was his demesne. The slender towers, mostly refineries and cracking stations rather than dwellings, were elfin in the bronze light from rising Hellmouth. The planet swung up over her moon's single city, dominating it as the Renaults had dominated the lives of the Castellars. The Hell-Lord grimaced at the facile comparison, but admitted, sourly, that there was an element of truth in it.

His family had been the most powerful on Hellmouth before the fall of the Old Federation, the most powerful group of transportees until the arrival of the first Renault. The Castellars had been the first to recognize her power, and the first to ally themselves openly with her; they had been well rewarded, remaining the second most powerful family on the planet until the deposition of Alexander X. The Ojeda Domus had foresworn itself then, and had never quite regained their reputation. The Castellars had not betrayed their lords, but had done nothing when the main branch of the Renault Domus was destroyed and the cadet branch degraded to minore status, and that was treason enough in the opinion of the other Hell-mouther nobles. The Renaults had survived, becoming the unofficial rulers, the Shadow Dukes to whom the taxes were paid before taxes went to the nominal Channis Dukes. The Castellars had ex-

changed their fief of Satansburg for safer Hell, but
the Assassins had gotten to the traitor Castellar all
the same. After that, Hell paid its taxes to both
Dukes. It had been hard to keep that up, the double duties, but in the end, they had prospered.

Castellar's gaze caressed the spires displayed before him, counting the cost in lives and money
that had been paid before Hell had taken its place
among the wealthy worlds. It had only been in his
grandfather's day that they had begun to build on
the moon's surface, rather than in the tunnels
below. And now, all that was threatened.

His glance strayed from the screen to his desk.
Two tapes lay among the litter of printouts, one
black-cased, one ochre, old and new. He had not
replayed the newer one—he hadn't needed to, to
know that he could no longer put off the choice
that had been confronting him since Oriana's death.
Sighing, he picked them up, one in each hand,
weighing them as though that could help him make
his decision. They were exactly the same, each
feather-light. The de Terranin seal was vivid on
one, the Renault wheel starkly plain on the other.
With a muttered curse, he slammed the ochre tape
into his viewer, not really looking at the little
screen. Edouard de Terranin, already robed with
the magnificence of the Silvertree emperors, looked
out at him.

"Hell-lord, I, Edouard, of my dynasty the first,
give you greetings and offer you the friendship of
my Domus. I call upon you and all those majores
who honor and respect Convention to join with me
in removing the usurper from the throne of the
Imperium."

There was more, but Castellar hit the stop button.
Join me, Edouard was saying. I can help you be
free of the Renaults once and for all. I can make
you lord in your own right, not just the master of

the Renaults' moon. I can make you a Duke, and your family of the Domi Aureae.

Castellar dropped into the visitor's chair that sat facing the screen, and sat sprawling, arms and legs outspread, chin dropping on his chest. He could see Keira now, as the tape showed him, standing in a chalked circle—the cameraman had been careless there—hands jammed into the pockets of his loose, embroidered coat, a coronet the only mark of rank. He had been more regal than de Terranin. I offer you a chance to serve my Domus, he said, and to redeem yourselves. You can still return to your old place, my family's most trusted servants.

Castellar's mouth twisted again. Three generations ago, things might have been different. His great-grandfather, his grandfather, even, might have been able to take Edouard's offer, to elevate the Castellar family to the Domus status, and to force the other nobles of Hellmouth system to accept it. It could not happen now. There was too much at stake—too much on Hell, and on Hellmouth, that depended on peace and keeping on the winning side. The system's nobility had changed, as well; it was no longer their way to push Convention to its limits. It was ironic, Castellar thought, that as the majores of the inner worlds began to evade Convention, the Hellmouther lords began to follow its precepts rigidly. And because of that, he could not follow Edouard. Memories were long on Hellmouth: his family had betrayed the Renaults by their inaction, in the eyes of their peers and by their own admission. He still owed Keira, was caught in the misty web of obligation spun by his own ancestors.

He stared at the rising planet, detail obscured as it so often was by delicate twists of clouds. And I'm not immune to that, either, he thought bitterly. I can tell myself it's because the other nobles won't back me that I won't try to become Grand Duke; I can tell myself it's because all the simulations I can run show that Keira will win. Both are true, but not the whole truth: I will support Keira because I know I owe him that. It was too long ago to matter, or should be so, but he's offering me the chance to return to what we once were—not the greatness of a Grand Duke, but a loyalty that was more important even than power.

His eyes dropped to the surface towers, wandering from building to building, thinking of the wealth and power they represented. That would have to be enough, he told himself firmly. Then he rose and crossed to the old control console set into the far wall. There was only a single panel there, three buttons, each covered by a sheet of clear plastis to prevent them from being pressed by accident. He hesitated a moment, then slid aside the central sheet and set his thumb on the button before he could reconsider. A strident, two-note hooting filled the air, growing louder as each station picked up and repeated the signal. It was the Alert, not sounded in fifty years, warning the entire population of an Assembly. He listened a moment longer, then called a serbot to bring his regalia.

Hell's upper corridors were empty by the time he was ready. Half-opened doors gave onto abandoned businesses, rooms in which machines still whined or teleprinters chattered, unattended. Castellar took the emergency routes, dropping down gravity shafts that seemed only just able to break his fall, ducking through double-thick doors that opened reluctantly for his palm print. At last he came to the corridor behind the main auditorium.

Oles Lonato, the commons' speaker, and Suzue Tate, the Castellar robe-minore who acted as his steward, were waiting for him there. Tate at least wore ordinary clothes, her judge's robes slung hastily over shirt and trousers, but Lonato had been caught about to go above-surface. His airtight coveralls bulged over an everyday shirt.

"Lord Suzue, Master Oles," Castellar said with a nod. "Is everything in order?"

"Yes, my Lord," Tate said. "The nobility is accounted for."

Lonato said, "The commons' assembly links are open, and extra monitors have been rigged for invalids and essential personnel."

Castellar nodded. The main auditorium was reserved at an Assembly for Hell's nobility and the most important commoners, the four speakers and the major guilds' local representatives. The rest of Hell's people could watch the meeting in any of the dozen lesser auditoria on the lower levels, and could register protests and opinions with their own speaker. "Good enough." Castellar could feel Tate's questioning look, but ignored it. She could find out at the meeting, like everyone else. This was not a matter for debate. "Let's proceed."

Tate bowed over her clasped hands, suddenly formal, and palmed open the door. She walked between the banks of holo-projectors, whose technicians glanced nervously about, dividing their attention between the robe-minore, Castellar, and their own readouts, and stepped up onto the projection circle.

"Lords and commons! Alert is sounded, we are assembled. Heed our Lord!"

She stepped from the platform. Castellar drew himself up, automatically balancing the weight of his coronet and the drag of the stiffly embroidered cloak, and took his place in the column of light. Blinded by it, he could not see the faces of the assembled population, but he heard the faint sigh, the collective intake of breath as they remembered Alexandrine portraits and realized what was to come. *Oh my people, I am sorry it has come to this,* he mourned, even as he held up his hand in the old, commanding gesture. At least I can spare you most of the fighting.

"Lords and commons! I bring you tidings. Everyone has heard that the succession has been contested on Avalon, that Edouard, Overlord of Verii Mir has declared Keira Emperor a Convention-breaker and usurper. I come before you to tell you of my choice." He heard a stirring in the audience, coming from the major seats to his right. They had not been consulted—no one had been—and they were not happy about it. But it was my right to choose, Castellar thought, and my responsibility. Even if I had asked each one what he would do, it still would have come down to my decision.

"My lords majore and minore, I ask you to ready your ships, schooners and tenders alike. We will sail under the Renault wheel." Again the sigh, but he spoke over it. "My commons, I must ask you to refrain from trading with the minores and commons allied to de Terranin and his followers. I recognize the hardships, but in war, all must sacrifice. Is there anyone who would speak in this matter?"

He waited, trying in vain to see beyond the light that walled him in. For a long moment, nothing moved, and then he heard someone rise from among the minores. Light lanced down from the ceiling, caught the man in a second column as the technicians brought portable cameras into action.

"Lord Hell."

It was the senior of the tender captains, and Castellar hid his frown. The two were much of an age, and had studied together at Sparta without aquiring a liking for each other. "Lord Hilario, you may speak."

"Lord, *Black Roger*'s Circus is at your command." Hilario Reeve sat down again, and Castellar raised an eyebrow. He had expected some opposition. But then, the man was noble, he reminded himself, and Convention was above personal feelings.

"Lord, *Honeybird*'s Circus is yours." The woman had spoken too quickly for the holocameras to catch her. The column of light probed vainly, and went out.

"And *Makepeace*'s Circus," a third voice announced.

Castellar held up his hand. "My Lords, I never doubted your response." Like hell I didn't, he thought, but kept his grave mask. "Lord Suzue."

The steward came forward, stopping just short of the stage. A second beam of light, narrowed and less intense, captured her. "My Lord."

"You will act as lord while I am gone. In the event of my death, my son Isak is next Lord Hell."

"As my Lord wills." Tate bowed deeply.

"And now." Castellar turned his attention back to the assembly. "Lords and commons, we are at war. There will be restrictions on off-world communications. I will expect you all to observe them, whatever they may be. The penalties will be those of wartime."

"My Lord." That was Lonato, stepping forward at Castellar's left hand. "I will answer for the commons."

"Thank you, Master Speaker. Is there anyone who would speak further?" He waited, but there was no sound from the nobles. "Then let the Assembly end."

It was a week's flight from Hell to Citadel, six standard days crammed into the tenders. Castellar, now no longer Lord but senior Circus Master, brooded over the plotting board in *Makepeace*'s control room. He had left Hellmouth in chaos behind him—quite deliberately, but the disorder pained him. His choice had split the Hellmouther majores, and his active recruiting ensured that, if Hellmouth did not come to Keira's aid, the Channis Duke would not be able to bring them into Edouard's fleet. But still. . . . It was a majore's duty to protect order, not to destroy it.

To reassure himself, he glanced again at the plotting boards. His own Circuses were there, in perfect formation with the three more from Hellmouth. The latter were the real accomplishment, he told himself firmly. Keira—the emperor—would need as many schooners as possible. Any disorder was justified if it brought men and ships to his cause.

A two-toned chime sounded above his head, and he looked up quickly. Li Hua, the Coordinator and Castellar's wife, had one hand to her throat, long fingers poised over the microphone controls embedded in her stiff collar. She smiled at him as she spoke, her voice perfectly modulated.

"All ships, attention. From *Makepeace* captain: final jump in fifteen minutes. I repeat, final jump in fifteen minutes. All confirm, please."

There was a lag while open channels hissed, and then the other coordinators began to answer.

"*Honeybird* captain confirms."

"*Gabriel* captain confirms." That was one of the Hellmouthers, a rich land-minore from St. Julian's County.

"*Bravura* captain confirms." Another Hellmouther, this one from the Dusty Sea—or was it Samara? Samara: Vondila Elorin of World's End, who held nominal lordship over the Dusty Sea minores, had forbidden her people to join either side. Keira, if he ran true to the Renault type, would not thank her for her caution.

"*Wild Hunter* captain confirms." Castellar smiled to himself. An-Deth's Lord, the sixth Monime Ransom, rode that ship, was in fact *Hunter*'s coordinator. Winning her support had been a real coup, but then, An-Deth had always been loyal to the Shadow Dukes.

"*Black Roger* captain confirms."

The jump went off as scheduled. The convoy—if it could be called that, six tenders and no true warships—flashed into existence again with Citadel a visible disk on the screens. Every alarm on board immediately clamored for attention. *Makepeace*'s captain lifted his voice to carry it over the yammering consoles.

"All ships. Identify, but take no other action. Repeat. Keep your screens down."

Li Hua spoke into her microphone. Her voice was sweet, with an overtone of sensuality that demanded attention; movement became purposeful rather than panicked. Castellar saw new codes crawl across his screen and knew that the identification was being sent. Gradually, the alarms stilled, until only one red light still flashed on the screen: a warship bearing down on them, as yet unidentified. Castellar hesitated, not knowing if he wanted to challenge it first. The ship-to-ship channel came on with a crackle of static.

"*Balance of Power* captain, Davin Iye min–Lovell-Andriës, sends greetings and welcome if you come in peace. Who's in command here, and who's Lord?"

That was a tricky question, given that Convention reversed many of the usual rules of precedence about a warship, giving a trained soldier-minore authority over an untrained majore. This time, it was Iye himself speaking, not the Elector. Castellar nodded to *Makepeace*'s captain, who reached for his microphone.

"*Makepeace* captain, Oloeron Barse min-Castellar, sends thanks for your welcome. I am senior captain of the Circuses. Hell-Lord rules, with An-Deth's Lord."

"My Lord extends his sincere welcome," Iye said, "and requests speech with the Hell-Lord."

Barse glanced to Castellar, who nodded. "Lord Hell agrees. Will you pass the code setting?"

"Of course. Stand by to receive." There was a long moment of silence as numbers flashed by at blinding speed across the screens, then Castellar heard the hissing of static in his own speakers. He turned the crash column so that his back was to most of his crew—the engineer, at the rear of the bridge, turned his own column away—and touched the button that activated his throat microphone.

"My Lord Elector."

"Lord Hell." Lovell-Andriës had a pleasant voice, hinting at a vast good humor. Castellar hoped this would be a good omen for the future. "His Majesty has asked me to extend his personal welcome, and to inform you that there will be a council session on planet as soon as you can take up a docking orbit. Do you have news of Edouard?"

Castellar took a deep breath, and stopped himself from touching the tape he had kept in his pocket all the way from Hell. "I have a set of fleet rendezvous coordinates."

Citadel was a depressing world, even harsher than Hell. The population was exclusively robots, of various types, and soldiers. The corridors were uniformly bleak, and the lighting archaic. Only in the command room was there any indication that human beings had been living on this world for any length of time. There, where Keira spent most of his time conferring with his officers and nobles, were the brightly colored coffee mugs and plastic tea glasses of nobles and minores alike. Computer printouts overflowed the disposal bags, and some-one had left a majore's scarf of rank draped across a chair.

Castellar settled himself in his place at the middle of the long table, a cup of thick, sweet coffee ready beside his console. The Navy representatives, PenMorgan and his flag lieutenant, sat at the far end of the table, PenMorgan scowling irritably at his stack of reports. The Admiral had arrived only the night before, bringing with him *Siva*, Blue Fleet's flagship, and a pair of corvettes as escort.

Tyr, the other cruiser, remained on station on the Federal border. With luck, her presence there would deter any more attacks on Federal shipping. Lacking other Navy support, that was all Keira could do; Castellar only hoped that Edouard's tape had not been a double feint, designed to lure the emperor's forces to Oceanus while the Overlord struck at Avalon.

A door chime sounded. Resolutely, he killed that thought, and stood as the emperor entered, followed by the rest of his household. Keira looked worn, with dark circles under his eyes, but no more so than usual. And there was something different about the way he moved this morning.

"My Lords." Keira took his place at the head of the table, but he did not sit down. Instead he leaned forward, both hands flat against the table top, one on each side of the computer link. "We'll sail tonight."

Castellar sat very still, and could see his shock reflected in nearly every other face. Only PenMorgan and FitzMary seemed unsurprised, and PenMorgan had a sour smile on his face, half concealed by his beard.

Keira seemed to see that, and one corner of his mouth twitched upward in response. "Admiral PenMorgan, Captain FitzMary, the Grand Duke Hamm'tt and myself extrapolated Edouard's probable course of action from the tape the Hell-Lord brought us. It seems clear that the Overlord plans to use Oceanus as his base of operation. If he's successful there, over the Grand Duke's opposition, he'll win the passive support of almost all the neutrals. Obviously, we have to stop them—preferably between 00729a and Oceanus itself."

00729a was the jump point most distant from the planet, and therefore the most suitable for military operations. Castellar admitted the logic of Keira's conclusions, and considered being angry that he had not been consulted. But then, the Navy's assessments were more important. He looked around the table, and saw the other majores coming to the same conclusion. Desolin Hamm'tt was busy with her keyboard, head down, probably trying to hide a grin.

"Your Grace," Keira said, and she looked up quickly. Castellar was suddenly struck by the fact that she and Lovell-Andriës were the only Domi nobles present. The Duke of Castille had sent a representative, Amarix Esty, Count of Chanoine Plains on Aragon, but that was not at all the same thing. "You intend to coordinate your own ship?"

"Yes, your Majesty, if that's agreeable to your plans." The Duke's voice was velvet, but there was steel beneath.

"Of course. I assume you'll do the same, Rohan?" St. George nodded. "Yes, Majesty."

"Hell-Lord, I understand that you're Circus-Master, not coordinator on *Makepeace*?"

"No, your Majesty," Castellar answered. "My wife is coordinator."

"Then I trust you'll have no objections to the Elector acting as coordinator for all the schooners?"

"No, Majesty, I've no objections." Castellar nodded to Lovell-Andriës, and got a broad grin in return.

"My Lord Esty, you will coordinate *Whistling Battle* for the Navy," Keira was saying, and Castellar brought his attention back to the plans in front of him. Lovell-Andriës would need someone to coordinate his corvette, if he was going to run the schooners—or had that already been settled? Yes, Castellar thought. One of the Somewhere majores, the lord of the satellite Somewhere Else, would handle that for the Elector. That made a decent fleet, Castellar decided. One cruiser, *Siva*; four corvettes, one of which was Navy; a couple of heavily armed Navy clippers; and the seven schooner Circuses—that should be enough. It was unlikely that Edouard would have any better.

Chapter 31

Twenty-eight minutes out of the final jump at OC173, sensors shrieked an unmistakable warning. Keira heard the noise through the deckplates and sat up straight in his bunk, clawing for the lights even before the intercom chimed alert. The marrow-freezing tones were quickly followed by FitzMary's voice.

"Coordinator to all hands. Enemy in sight."

Before she could repeat the message, Keira was out of bed and dressing, only half listening to the reports being relayed on the cabin speakers, and then through the single earpiece Doran handed him. As he rose up the main gravity shaft to the control deck, FitzMary's voice continued to sound in his ear: "No details on fleet make-up yet. They're too far off. Admiral estimates 2.03 standard to contact. Start preliminary security shut-down."

At the top of the gravity shaft, Keira caught the padded handhold and pulled himself out of the lifting field onto the control room deck. The last members of the control room crew were at his heels, pushing past him to take up their stations, the first pilot still closing the zipper of his coveralls. His hair was wet and the coveralls were beginning to show damp patches: he had been caught in the showers.

Keira took his place in the second command column, a virtual duplicate of the Admiral's station, but placed well to the rear of the control room, away from the main consoles. The banks of indicators were flashing from orange to green as various departments went to battle stations, and the inships channel was beginning to fill with voices. He set aside the temporary earpiece, took down the headset from its hook above the heavily padded chair, and punched the quick-tune button until the separate speakers were fully defined. At the same time, he adjusted the channel of transmission so that he spoke directly only to FitzMary and the Admiral. He was not involved in the moment-to-moment handling of the ship; like all majores, his role was purely tactical, translating the movement of individual ships and of fleets into patterns that could be interpreted by Talent, and mastered by the appropriate movement of his own fleet.

"Status report," FitzMary ordered, and lights flickered again as the ship's various departments—engineering, control and secondary control, the defensive gun batteries, and the offensive drone control—reported readiness. Keira, after once glance to make sure that the lights remained green, ignored them and concentrated on the plotting tank.

One of the junior pilots, assigned for battle to the main sensor bank, reported a change of course, her voice faint on the secondary channels. FitzMary announced it instantly. "Admiral, Majesty, they're turning toward us. The revised contact estimate is 1.54 hours and lessening. Make it 1.34."

Keira muttered an abstracted acknowledgement, and continued to study the plotting tank, a miniature version of the massive tank six decks below in his suite. It glittered with tiny lights, red and blue for the opposing fleets, green and yellow for the natural phenomena around them. The red lights of Edouard's fleet were as yet undifferentiated, all the same flat shade, but the blue lights ranged from the deep indigo that represented *Siva* to the cloud-blue pinpoints of the tenders. The schooners, when they were released, would show up as almost white. *Siva* was currently at the midpoint of the battle line, but that would change as PenMorgan shifted his forces to meet the advancing fleet.

The red lights shifted, some going darker, others growing pale as the flagship's computers analyzed the sensor readings. Just like a simulation, Keira thought—he could not make the picture become real. The drone pilots would be having the same problem, locked into tiny compartments identical to a gaming room. The drones themselves were little more than a battery of high-powered, hair-triggered blastcannons mounted on an equally powerful engine, and equipped with heavy plating and light screens. They were too dangerous to risk with live crew; the remote controls made them feasible, the tanks giving the operators an illusion of direct piloting.

"We identify three frigates and a brace of corvettes," FitzMary said, breaking into his thought. "Plus some smaller ships. They might be transports, or they might be caravels. Sensors can't make them out."

"I see them," PenMorgan said grimly.

Keira said, "Coordinator, give me a picture of the intercept point."

"Majesty."

The projection in the plotting tank swam again, and the red and blue dots disappeared. Only the others, the yellow dots that were suns and planets and asteroids, and the green dots and lines that marked the jumps and grav-lines, remained. Keira studied them, frowning. Oceanus was a bad place to fight. With space already honeycombed with jump points and complicated by the triple suns, the schooners were going to wreak havoc. He looked for the standard starmarks, the tangled asteroids that looked dangerous but could actually be approached quite closely in safety, and the multiple jump points out near the system's edge. Space was weak there, and the schooners loved to lurk in its shadows, where spatial distortion interfered with the sensors. The fleet would have to steer well clear of that area.

The existing jump points would be keys to the battle, he decided finally, regardless of what the schooners did. There were four within easy reach of the intercept point, not counting OC99, where Edouard's fleet had emerged. It was going to be too easy for the loser to escape. Then he smiled. It was possible that he would be glad of that before the day was over.

The rebel fleet was spreading out into an old-fashioned formation, the shallow crescent that had defeated the Federation during the Alexandrine wars. But Edouard—or whoever was his military coordinator—was making changes in the standard pattern taught at Sparta. The heavier ships—the tank still showed them to be frigates, no cruisers in evidence—were on the ends, supported by the corvettes. The smaller ships formed the body of the crescent. The left flank was heavier than the right, two frigates and a corvette, while the right was held by a single frigate and a pair of corvettes. The schooners would probably hold the center, making it even more difficult to break the line. Keira squinted at the tank, but the image was already beginning to fuzz as Edouard's foxers took effect. It would be impossible to tell the tenders from clippers until the schooners were released.

If he followed standard tactics, PenMorgan had two choices: to match Edouard's formation and try to fight ship-to-ship actions, or to try to punch through the line and attack in force when the enemy fleet was in disorder. Either tactic had its disadvantages, but the fact that the Imperial fleet was slightly superior in firepower seemed to indicate they should fight ship-to-ship. In any case, that was PenMorgan's decision, unless Keira saw some change in the patterns that prompted Talent to override the Admiral.

"Majesty," PenMorgan said. "The fleet will take a modified arrow formation, with the tenders at the point and the clipper reinforcing them. *Siva* and the frigates will hold the right, *Whistling Battle* and the corvettes the left. If that meets with your approval."

The question was almost a formality. The emperor did not override his Admiral's orders without good reason. Nevertheless, Keira leaned forward to feed the new information to the plotting tank, then moved both fleets forward to the projected intercept point before replying.

"It looks good, Admiral. Carry on."

"Yes, Majesty," PenMorgan answered. "Coordinator, execute."

Almost at once, FitzMary began reciting a string of orders, and Keira returned the plotting tank to its former state. The display showed *Siva* cutting across the rear of the formation, while the tenders drifted toward the center, to be flanked by the clippers. The Navy frigate *Whistling Battle* was moving to anchor the left wing, supported by the Lovell-Andriës corvette, *Balance of Power*, and Hamm'tt's smaller corvette, *Apollyon*. Against Edouard's lighter right, they should be sufficient. *Siva*, backed by two majore corvettes, anchored the right wing and should be able to roll right over Edouard's twin frigates. OC99 was now to the right of the battleground PenMorgan had chosen, the heaviest ships positioned so that the imperial line controlled that major jump point. But there were still three points, farther off and out of the plane of the battle, that Edouard's ships could reach if the battle went against him. Keira frowned, wondering if he had been right to approve PenMorgan's decision immediately. Experimentally, he adjusted the plotting tank, pulling the ships back to a formation that would break Edouard's line, but even before the lights representing his own ships finished rearranging themselves he could see that the pattern would not work.

"Transmission from *Far Moon*, Admiral, Majesty," FitzMary announced. "They've identified at least one of the following caravels as a merchant guildship."

Policy toward those ships was a matter of Convention, and thus the emperor's responsibility. Keira touched the switch that adjusted the images in the plotting tank and saw a cluster of small ships, now shown in flickering red and white, hanging back from the main line of ships. Those would be the troop ships, and as such, there was little chance they'd try to take part in the fighting. "Don't fire on the merchant ships unless they attack first," he said. "Do you agree, Admiral?"

"Yes, Majesty," PenMorgan said.

"Fleet orders," Fitzmary announced, her voice changing, growing hollow, as the multiple ships' channels opened. "Fleet orders. From the Admiral. Do not fire on Guild ships unless you are attacked. Repeat, do not fire on Guild ships unless you are attacked."

Over the acknowledgements of the individual ships' coordinators, PenMorgan said, "What's the contact estimate?"

"0.4, sir," a new voice answered.

"Captain Telem, I suggest we seal ship," the Admiral said.

"Very good, Admiral. Stand by to seal ship, Mr. Brisen."

"All green, Captain."

"Seal."

Keira leaned back against the heavy cushions, flinched anyway as the airtight door snapped shut across the opening into the column. Instantly, he felt the power plant beneath his feet vibrate gently, and the life-support system whined up to full power. A fuzzy holo appeared on the armsteel of the door, picturing the control room in front of him. Experimentally, he swung the column back and forth, and the holo matched the movement with only a fraction of hesitation. He sighed, and turned his attention back to the plotting tank set beside his couch. He knew the importance of the control columns—each armsteel cylinder, duplicating the controls of the main bridge station, was essentially a miniature spaceship, an armored lifeboat capable of protecting its occupant against anything short of a direct hit—but he could not feel comfortable, sealed into that restricted space.

"Light the screens," Telem ordered.

"Screens up."

"Power the drones, captain?" a new voice asked.

"Go ahead."

These orders were repeated along the line; Keira could hear them faintly, beneath the orders repeated through *Siva*. He drew a deep breath and tightened his hands on the arms of his chair to keep them from shaking, not knowing whether he was afraid or excited.

The same mix of emotions was in FitzMary's voice, beneath the professional silkiness. "The Overlord has dropped his schooners. Drones, too."

"Fire our drones," PenMorgan snapped, and *Siva* staggered with the launch. The plotting tank swam with two clouds of pale sparks, red and blue already beginning to mix: the schooners were in contact with the enemy.

"Watch the jump," a voice exclaimed, freakishly clear in Keira's headset: not someone from *Siva*, he realized instantly, but a pilot or coordinator on one of the clippers. A schooner had opened a new jump point—it glowed green in the tank, fading even as he found it—and the clipper had nearly been drawn in before the mormal laws of space reasserted themselves. *Siva* shuddered, and lights flared along the upper row of repeater screens: the cruiser was coming under the fire of the first of Edouard's frigates.

"Status?" PenMorgan demanded.

"Shaken but green." That was FitzMary. "Minor damage, all controlled."

Keira stared into his plotting tank, trying to shut out both the confused noise of orders and the fuzzy picture projected in front of him. The two lines of lights moved ponderously toward each other, already tangled in the center, where the pale lights of schooners and clippers moved through a globe extending above and below the plane of battle. Fresh green splotches bloomed and faded as the schooners flashed in and out of Drive, creating new jump points; others appeared farther along the wings as some of the schooners slipped away from the center and moved to harass the larger ships.

Siva staggered again, throwing Keira against the security webbing. Lights flashed red across the repeater screens, and he could hear, beneath the confused noise of the crew, the rasp of a depressurization alarm.

"Damage report," PenMorgan snapped.

"Breach aft of rib six," Brisen, the first officer, announced. "Starboard, under—the ribs are holding."

"We've tracked it to the lead frigate," Telem cut in.

Keira slipped his hands under the earphones of the headset, cutting off the voices. In the plotting tank, the lights moved slowly forward, each fractional shift bringing the ships closer to a configuration that was suddenly Talent-clear. When all the ships stood in that relation to each other—and the pattern was inevitable, latent in current positions—

Edouard's line was vulnerable to the proper move. Time seemed to slow as Keira stared at the tank, daring the lights to shift again and prove him wrong. As the ships slid on toward the moment, time became another dimension, briefly as predictable as the other three. He took his hands away from his ears, adjusted the tank so that the key point of intersection stood starkly clear.

"Admiral, *Battle Joined* will attack—there."

He could hear the Talent in his own voice, could hear it echoed from *Apollyon* as Hamm'tt cried, "Yes!" The other captains heard it, too. *Battle Joined* was already sliding toward its new position as FitzMary began to repeat the order. The frigate slid into place. On the opposite wing, *Apollyon* and *Whistling Battle* moved to support the unexpected attack, and Edouard's fleet shattered.

"That's it!" a voice shrieked. Keira thought he recognized *Dantean*'s coordinator. Where there had been seven red lights and a handful of schooners, there were only three lights moving, all heading at speed for the nearest jump point. His own ships were already moving out in pursuit.

"Majesty," a new voice broke in. "I have damage reports."

Keira forced his attention away from the tank. "Go ahead."

The pattern of blue lights had shifted, some dimming almost to nothing, but he did not remember hearing the distress calls.

"We've lost contact with *Whistling Battle*," the voice began, and Keira cut her off.

"Who is this?"

"Oh." The voice sounded vaguely surprised. "Maslin min-Renault, Admiral's flag."

FitzMary would still be busy relaying the Admiral's orders, Keira realized. The flag lieutenant was the logical person to handle the damage reports. "Go on."

"Contact's been lost with *Whistling Battle*," Maslin said, "but she still shows on the screens. We think the bridge took a direct hit. *Gabriel* and *Wild Hunter* have detached to investigate and pick up survivors. We've lost several schooners, Majesty, and *Makepeace*."

Keira nodded again. Castellar was gone, then, and his crew—but there was still a chance that the columns might have functioned properly as escape pods.

"*Balance of Power* reports damage to her maneuvering jets, but nothing she can't handle," Maslin went on calmly. "She's pursuing. *Siva*'s hulled, but the air loss is confined to the middle decks. *Far Moon*'s hulled, too, but not badly."

"What about the enemy?" Keira asked.

"*Delineation* and *Valiere* both show a lot of damage, but projections give them a better-than-even chance to make the jump. We'll overhaul *Objectivity*, though. She's lost an engine, it looks like. *Ruby's Love*—that's one of the Guild caravels, Majesty—is pretty badly shot up, but reports she's still spaceworthy." Maslin added hastily, "Admiral's apology for damaging her against your orders, but she tried to fight."

"Admiral's discretion," Keira said. "The corvettes?"

"Surrendered, Majesty."

"My congratulations to the Admiral."

"Thank you, Majesty." There was a burst of static, then the distorted noises of off-mike conversation. Maslin said, "Beg pardon, Majesty, but I'm needed elsewhere."

"Go ahead," Keira said, but the connection was already broken. His muscles were twitching a little from the released tension of the past hour, and he leaned hard against the oil cushions. The command column was still sealed, and would remain so until they stood down from battle stations. If this were a Federal ship, he thought, I could get up and walk around, look over people's shoulders and generally make a nuisance of myself. I wouldn't be stuck here, waiting.

He scanned his readouts again, seeing how the lights representing the damaged ships pulsed irregularly. There would be dead on those ships, both his men and Edouard's. Not many would be injured: a space battle either killed outright or left one alive and unhurt. But there would be the dead. Keira tried to think of the people he had come to know over the past week, but could remember ships better than faces. The battle had been an elegant game, and he still felt that pleasure. Owen Castellar, Hell-Lord, was probably dead, he told himself, fitting the face, the man he had drawn into his fight, to the fact of death. Not simulations-death, either, but the physical reality. . . . He could not make it real.

There was a burst of chatter in his speakers, one voice cutting above the rest: "*Objectivity*'s gone!"

Now there were only Edouard's two frigates left to deal with, *Delineation*, the flagship, and *Valiere*. Keira watched the chase in the plotting tank, eyes moving from the lights that crawled toward the jump point to the constantly changing numbers that gave relative speeds, course headings, and overhaul times. Even before the computer concluded it, Keira knew that Edouard would escape. First *Valiere*, then *Delineation* moved onto the jump point and disappeared. There was a savage growl of disappointment.

"*Battle Joined* requests permission to pursue," that corvette's captain said eagerly.

PenMorgan answered, "Denied. You're needed here."

"Begging the Admiral's pardon, we can take them."

"You're only a corvette, Yakob—"

"And they're damaged . . . sir."

"Denied," the Admiral said again. "Help *Balance of Power* round up *Objectivity*."

"Acknowledged," *Battle Joined*'s captain sighed.

Voices continued to echo over the comunit, but Keira heard them only dimly. It would be a while before they unsealed the ship, and he closed his eyes to shut out the holo in front of him, deceptive in its promise of open space, of freedom. Half of him was triumphant, filled with pleasure in the intricacies of space and ships and Talent that had given him victory. The other half tried to match victory with cost and failed. Oh, damn, he thought, I wish I had something useful to do. . . . But I wouldn't have missed this for all the worlds.

Chapter 32

Edouard crossed the emergency bridge, clumsy in space armor, to stand behind the navigator's station. The compartment was a shambles, three crucial panels shorted out completely, less important machines still sparking, though there was no fire in the soft vacuum. At least most of the crew had been able to seal their suits, or had been protected by the crash columns. But the damage, the losses . . . Hastily, he tore his thoughts from that, and touched his microphone.

"Where are we?"

The navigator turned helmeted head to him, face only a shadow beneath the heavy plastis. He tapped the side of the helmet to indicate a malfunction. Edouard swore silently and leaned forward so that the helmets touched. In this position the magnetic boots' grip on the floorplates felt distinctly precarious. They had lost gravity when the main engines failed, just after exiting the jump.

"We jumped blind," the navigator said defensively. "And we've lost the main locator. But it looks like we're at VLD 34—off Vinland, my Lord, on the Federal side of the system."

"What about *Valiere?*"

"Lost her when we jumped." The navigator couldn't shrug in the constricting armor, but Edouard saw the abortive movement of his arms. "I expect we were thrown farther. More of her power went to open up the jump, we were coat-tailing—but I couldn't even begin to make a guess. Not with everything down."

"Right. Well, get us a good fix. And if you spot *Valiere*, let me know immediately." Edouard sighed. He had expected that when he ordered the escape jump, but it still hurt. Now—his thoughts were broken by a tapping noise that seemed centered on his left shoulder. He turned to find *Delineation*'s first officer at his side.

"Sir, I'm informing you I've taken command."

"Captain Romaine?"

"Dead, sir. The captain's column took the worst of that shot to the bridge." Her voice was thick with tears.

"So. Byrger, let's hear the damage." Edouard focused all his thoughts on the present, though every nerve screamed for just a second's release, a moment in which to break down and weep.

Byrger said, "We're hulled in about six places. The only place we've still got an atmosphere is on the crew deck, and the air's pretty foul there. Navigation's lost the primaries, sensor suite is gone, we've only four-percent maneuverability, and engineering say they can only give us quarter power until they re-rig the converters. We've got five confirmed dead, and a couple more dubious until they can get more air into sick bay to take their armor off." Her voice steadied as she spoke.

"Right." Edouard concentrated for a moment. "How bad is it on the crew deck?"

"The intership seals are holding, and there's a good officer there to enforce air discipline. But it's going stale fast."

"So. Get some hand pumps in there, and men in armor to work them."

Byrger nodded. "Yes, my Lord. And I'll have the medic move the critical cases there as soon as possible."

"Exactly. Then get the hull repaired." He didn't

have to add that the other, vital repairs would be impossible while the crew remained in bulky space armor.

Byrger nodded and lurched off, lack of gravity and the stiff armor making her look less than human.

Edouard hesitated for a moment, watching the numbers and letters stutter across the navigator's screen. They were too close to Vinland for comfort, and there was a Navy base there that could probably scramble at least one caravel. Under normal circumstances, that wouldn't matter, but with *Delineation* so badly damaged, even a schooner would finish her off. If only they hadn't been separated from *Valiere....* *Oh, God, what have I done?*

"My Lord Edouard," a voice crackled in his earphone. "Lord Edouard, you are needed in damage control."

Edouard glanced down at the locator on his gauntlet—damage control had no fixed station, but went where they were needed, their position signaled by comunit—but the machine was dead. He looked at the navigator's wrist, but that machine was dead also.

"Where are you?" he asked. "My locator's gone."

"Sorry, my Lord, it's the main transmitter. Deck four, portside, rib nine."

"On my way." Edouard, feeling as though he were swimming through molasses, struggled through the round hatchway to the dropshaft. The blue pillar of the transport field was out, but he hardly needed it. He pushed himself down the ladder, keeping his magnetic bootplates well away from the passing decks. On the crew deck, the shaft was sealed, and he had to go halfway around the ship's waist to reach an unobstructed maintenance crawlway.

By the breach, a petty officer clung ape-like to a twisted edge of metal, looking out into open space.

The stars glinted off his armor, and Edouard could see Vinland's sun, a brilliant point half occluded by the petty officer's helmet. The tear in the hull was only as wide as two men, but it ran from just below the deck above to a point halfway down the next level. The floorplates were curled back and melted wiring dripped from the edges of the wound. A single crossrib spanned the gap at one end, the dull metal melted a little, narrowing where the enemy fire had struck longest. Edouard winced. If the ribs went— *Delineation* would break up under Drive without them.

"Thank you, my Lord," the petty officer said.

Edouard nodded. "What do we do?"

The petty officer—his armor read Ferenzi—swept his gaze across the waiting group. "Patch it, my Lord," he said simply. "Jyotis, you've got the other patch? Good. Now, we've got to drag it into place and hardweld it in. It'll take two patches, I think, so we'll have to tune the support fields very carefully so we don't blow the whole unit. You, Marty, snake that end across to me, and Laure, you take the other corner. My Lord, grab the bottom."

They did as they were told, first securing themselves by line to the ship, just in case the magnetic boots broke loose. Edouard walked up the inside of the hull—a simple job, but disorienting when he saw the rest of the crew, two men adjusting the welder for use in no-air, a third technician-minore calibrating support units, facing along two different axes. The patches themselves were of meshtex, not too difficult to carry and spread, capable of carrying a forcefield that would hold against hard vacuum. When the first patch was adjusted to Ferenzi's satisfaction, the welders clambered up the hull and secured it. Then the two who had positioned the upper corner came down again and passed the second patch to Edouard and the technician. They held it, making sure the overlap was adequate, while Ferenzi, floating freefall, hooked the two patches together. The welding was repeated, and they all dodged back behind a heavy bulkhead while the technician-minore Jyotis tested the field. The two units were aligned properly. The patches glowed, and Ferenzi said, "They'll do."

Edouard nodded, his breath loud in his ears. He switched to the command channel and said, "Byrger. How's it going?"

There was a pause before the first officer answered. "Not bad. We've got the worst holes patched. If you could return to control, my Lord?"

"I'm on my way," Edouard answered. He closed his eyes tightly, wishing he could rub them. Next . . . would his crew let him decide what to do, or would Byrger exercise captain's rights and insist that they surrender? I would hardly blame her if she did. I lost—how many ships? *Objectivity*, *Hand-to-Hand*, *Ares*—and *Ares* was destroyed—*Ruby's Love*, the schooners. . . . God forgive me.

He shook himself, and retraced his path to the control room. They had managed to bleed in an atmosphere, and unarmored technician-minores were fighting with the damaged consoles. Edouard unsealed his helmet and took a deep breath. The air smelled of burned wiring and less identifiable things, but it felt good to be out from under the confining weight. He reached for the clasps that sealed the chestplate, and Byrger said, "Don't."

"Why not?"

She looked bleakly at him. She had taken off her helmet and gauntlets, but still wore the rest of her armor. "We're picking up transmissions from Vinland, my Lord. They're dispatching ships."

Edouard removed his own gauntlets and ran his hands through his hair. "What's the time to intercept?"

"About three hours, maybe more if they proceed with caution."

"They should," Edouard mused. "We out-gun them, and Keira couldn't have gotten a good look at our damage. . . ." He realized he was thinking aloud and broke off abruptly. It took a great deal of effort to think objectively, to marshal his thoughts into any sort of order. He thought longingly of his cabin, of the privacy of just five minutes alone, to pray for all the wrongs he'd done and the men he'd killed, to beg Michael's forgiveness if he had broken honor. . . .

Stop, he told himself, brake and return. He was off Vinland with a damaged ship, with nowhere to go but out of the Imperium. He listed the nearest worlds, skipping over the Imperial bases. Davinsworld was Federal; it didn't have a drydock. Alexandria was also Federal, and the jump was too long. Dixie: that world didn't like outsiders, but it was close, and neither Federal nor Imperial. It was the best choice, if the hull would stand Drive, and Byrger didn't want to surrender.

"I've an idea," he said, "but first I'm honor bound to remind you that you could surrender, Captain Byrger. The emperor won't take any action against you for following your liege lord."

The woman drew breath sharply. "My Lord, I'm honor bound to stay with you."

"The rest of the crew?"

"They'd better—no, I owe them a choice, too." Byrger's voice softened on the last words. "Let's hear your plan, my Lord."

"Exile—self-imposed, but exile." Edouard smiled bitterly. "You may wish to reconsider. We'll take *Delineation* to Dixie. Once we're past jump Charlie, no one can touch us, and I'm sure the Dixie land-bosses will be glad to get another ship for their fleet, no matter how badly we're shot up."

He faltered under Byrger's level gaze, but the first officer said only, "I daresay I could find work there."

In the end, Byrger repeated the plan to the ship's company, and offered anyone who wanted to chance Keira's justice the opportunity to take the undamaged shuttle and wait for the pursuing caravel. Seven crewmembers, all of whom had lovers and family back in the Imperium, went aboard, taking the dead with them. Edouard took the shots the doctor offered, and managed to stay awake long enough to take the helm for the last jump. Power built in the engines, the technician-minores dividing their attention between the engines themselves and the strain-gauges in the hull. The numbers adjusted themselves, and then they were in the jump. Nontime swirled about them, interminable, and they were out again. Reports flooded in: there was some new damage, but most of the repairs had held. Charlie, the outermost planet of the Dixie system, loomed on the screens, and already local ships swarmed to investigate them. Beyond them, Edouard could see the bulk of the striped gas giant Beachball. Dixie was hidden, but he could picture it, the sluggish rivers and good farming land he had always heard about. God, Father of us all, Donna in the stars, Michael, I haven't deserved this mercy. Please, protect my sister. Let it be that my honor isn't completely gone. Protect my father and my sisters. . . . In the middle of his prayer, his mind went blank, and he was suddenly, deeply, asleep.

Chapter 33

The cabin was dim and cool, and in the darkness the bulkheads seemed an infinity away. Keira lay in a cocoon of sheets and blankets, his face toward the door so that he could watch the play of colors on the status board above the computer screen. The ship vibrated faintly to the beat of the power plants, but he hardly felt it. It did not matter that in the end they had all guessed wrong, he and Hamm'tt and St. George and Lovell-Andriës, that they were chasing *Valiere* while Edouard and *Delineation* made good their escape to Dixie.

Three hours had passed since PenMorgan and his captains had agreed that they no longer had need of majores, emperor and lords alike. Keira, grateful, had left them at the grisly task of collecting bodies—Castellar, to his intense relief, had been picked up alive, though he would need months in the regeneration ward before he would be fully well—and deciding who would be sent to Oceanus and who could be kept on board. The hull had been patched already; he had threaded his way through the mess of confused and confusing repairs to the sanctuary of the cabin, and now he couldn't sleep. He sat up, untangling himself from the sheets, and passed a hand across the plate that controlled the lights. The cabin shrank to normal size again.

It was his Talent, he knew. His mind had an overstretched feeling to it that warned of headaches and a sluggish Talent tomorrow. Still, it was awake and restless, and seeing farther than he could ever consciously see. He closed his eyes and waited, while great splotches of color swelled and shifted behind his eyelids. Then the vision came clear.

The futures stretched as he had seen them on Citadel, the hundred thousand interwoven paths leading from now to the inevitable end of the Imperium. The alternatives fanned away from him, branching to infinity at first. With time, the paths narrowed, rejoined, meshed, until there were only two choices, two ways of dying. He had known since Citadel that it would come to this, though the knowledge was a taste of ashes. Either way, the Federation triumphed, brought her wayward children back under her rule, but there was a way to spare his people the humiliation of losing everything their ancestors had lived and died to win. He followed that line back from its end, from the sacrifice of the last emperor to the rise of the commoners, who became more and more like the citizens of the Federation. He passed a point at which the borders became irrelevant. He traced the apathy of the nobility, decreasing only a little as he came closer to his own day. Then he was back in the moment, with all the lines radiating from this ship in pursuit of a de Terranin frigate.

He allowed the vision to fade. As he did so, he felt the prickle of a memory, as though some sound or smell had evoked an overwhelming image of the past. He resisted the impulse to snatch at it, knowing that to do so would only send that memory fleeing to his subconscious again. Instead, he stretched and twisted as prescribed by the Order, working out the unnatural tensions. He would have to set the Imperium on the path that would lead to its peaceful absorption—too many people besides the nobility would die if he allowed the war to happen, and he could not choose their deaths. How to do it? He would need . . . what? Information, first, on the Federation and its corporations, and then on his own commoners' organizations, and especially on those guilds with ties to the Federation. And then the memory hit him.

It was not his own memory, he knew that even as he lived it again. He sat on the terrace of Satan's House, with the sun at his back and the wind from the fans cutting sharply across the pavings. Denisov-Graham, a younger, less certain man than his descendant, sat in his shadow, head cocked to one side.

"What shall I bet?" he said again, an odd smile on his lips. "I suppose . . . yes, that's it. If your family becomes the Imperial Domus, we—my family—will arrange free trade with the Imperium."

"Free trade betweeen the Imperium and the Federation." Keira whispered the phrase aloud, savoring each syllable. That was the key, the only and perfect solution. His children could not be trusted to work for the union of Federation and Imperium for altruistic reasons—even had he not known that intuitively the probabilities he had Read would have been more than enough to convince him. But the glaring certainty, the thing that had made the Renaults what they were, was that his children would be willing to throw everything into a game. A simple answer, he thought, at least in theory. Denisov-Graham must be made to wager again. We'll get the trading rights—the advantages are so great I won't be allowed to refuse them—so I'll have to change the stakes. The form of the joint government, whether ours or theirs, will be the nominal prize; and the object . . . ? Of course: whether Terra or Avalon will be the center of the new state. Yes, my kin will work for that, and a great deal harder than they would to save the commoners trouble. But I must—I will have that bet.

He turned the plan over in his mind, looking for flaws. He could see none. Admittedly, there were rough spots, places where he would have to refine his technique because he could not afford even the slightest error, but the idea was sound. Suddenly, he was terribly impatient with the long process of pursuit and trial, the judgments and announcing who was a traitor, who would die and who would be exiled. He wanted to be back on Avalon, where he could, by a single action, set a new future. He stilled that longing with an almost physical effort. Nothing unless you settle your claim, he told himself firmly, even though he knew this victory was inevitable, indeed, had already happened. The foundation had to be laid before he could build.

The light blinking orange beside his bed woke the ambassador at last. Wincing, Denisov-Graham worked his arm free of the covers and groped for the intercom button through the flashing shadows. The lights, triggered as well, came up slowly.

"Yes?"

"It's over." Rubenstein sounded excited, more so than he'd ever heard before. The ambassador suppressed a moan and dragged himself up onto one elbow.

"What's over?"

"The war."

The war? Ah. "Dispatches? Official ones?"

"Yes, sir. From Keira. Three communiques—or so I hear—one for us, one for the Eger, and one for the news."

"I'll be right there." Denisov-Graham switched off the intercom and in the same motion turned the lights up all the way. He reached into the high-backed cabinet that held his clothes and pulled on the first thing that came to hand, not bothering to shave or shower.

In the screening room, Rubenstein was pacing nervously, a mug of coffee in one hand. She turned as the door swung open.

"Sir, you're here."

Denisov-Graham sighed at the implied reproach, but decided it was safer not to answer it. "What details do we have?"

Rubenstein stopped abruptly and turned to a portable console that stood in one corner of the room. There were tapes stacked beside it, black with the silver of the imperial seal.

"I got copies of the News dispatch as well, but I couldn't manage the Eger announcement. We'll get a digest tomorrow, of course, but. . . ."

Denisov-Graham nodded in sympathy. The digests were never as useful as the actual tapes. "Go on."

"The ambassadorial tape is pretty short, just a review of the battles and a statement of Keira's intent." She stopped and looked up from the notepad that lay beside the tapes. "Do you want any more details?"

"Yes."

"All right." She flipped pages, running her finger across the page until she found the facts she wanted, and then continued, "Keira intercepted Edouard's fleet off Oceanus—that was predicted, you remember?—and defeated it pretty soundly. However, both Edouard and Alesia, who were on separate ships, were able to make a wild jump and escape the battle area. Apparently, the imperial fleet chose to pursue Alesia." She looked up from her notes again. "I'm not sure if there was a real choice involved. It sounds to me as though they miscalculated which ship was heading where. Anyway. *Valiere*, Alesia's ship, was pretty badly damaged in the fighting, and they ended up rescu-

ing it rather than making a capture. That was off
Mist, by the way. Edouard apparently made it out
one of the Vinland jumps, and repaired his ship
enough to make it out of the Imperium. The communique says he's reached Dixie, but they don't
make it clear whether that's a prediction or a fact.
Keira is returning with his prisoners to Oceanus.
He'll hold the trials there."

"Trials?" Denisov-Graham echoed.

Rubenstein flipped the notebook shut and slammed
a tape into the console. As she adjusted the multiple controls, she said, "Yes, for treason. Against
Alesia and any other majores who were captured,
and probably against Nuriel de la Mar as well, if
he can prove complicity."

"Of course, how stupid of me." Denisov-Graham
shook his head. "I'm just not awake yet, Kedma."

"I'll play the official communique to the foreign
ambassadors after you've seen this," she said.

The room lights dimmed, but Denisov-Graham
could see the undersecretary clearly. The Mist system filled the lower third of the projection, sun
and planets and the wild satellite that cut through
the system at an angle. MT472 was a green glow in
the center of the holo. Faint stars speckled the
projected darkness. The scene was designed for
kiosk stages, and Denisov-Graham had to pull his
chair closer to appreciate the details.

"This part is all reconstructed, a conjecture,"
Rubenstein said quietly. "*Valiere* should—there she
is."

A corvette, recognizably damaged, missing the
hair-fine projections of sensors and screen projectors, a gaping hole visible in the engine casing,
emerged from the fuzz of the jump. A blue-white
glow appeared briefly in the oversized engine
nozzles. The light reflected as well through the
breach in the casing, but almost immediately took
on a sickly yellow tinge and winked out.

"Main engine failure," Rubenstein murmured. She was wearing the operator's headphones now, so that she could listen to the Herald's commentary. "And then they lost maneuvering, too."

In the projection, lights flashed, tiny jets of flame along the hull. A few fired perfectly, but most flickered and died. One, obviously malfunctioning, flared, then kept on firing, throwing out a tongue of flame nearly as long as the ship's width. It pushed the corvette steadily toward the plane of the Mist system, then exploded. Denisov-Graham blinked, dazzled. When his sight cleared, he could see the ruined slag that had been the engine cup, surrounded by darkened and twisted hull plates. At one point, he thought he could see the shimmering line of the main rib. A few remaining lights along the main hull flickered and died, to be replaced by the sickly green glow of the "last chance" lights.

"How many dead?" the ambassador asked.

Rubenstein reached across the console for her notebook, momentarily shadowing the holo. She flipped through the pages, then answered, "Eight or ten, the News said, wounded and killed, but they didn't give an exact count. That's nearly half the crew right there."

"Probably mostly engineers and gunners," Denisov-Graham mumbled.

"They drifted for about an hour," Rubenstein said, one hand on the earphone. "They've speeded up the projection considerably. When Keira showed up, *Valiere* was pretty deep into the gravity well of the sun."

The model corvette slid off sideways, falling down the invisible contours of space toward the sun. There was something pathetically graceful about the slow descent, a sort of serene acceptance of natural laws that Denisov-Graham knew was belied by the frantic activity within the hull. He could imagine only too clearly the frenzied efforts to make repairs on the ruined engines, to patch the hull, to create some sort of atmosphere for the wounded, the crew knowing all the while that the repairs would not be completed before the unshielded corvette came into the zone of killing heat and radiation. Or did they try? Denisov-Graham wondered suddenly. Would the Imperial minores recognize defeat and sit back to make their peace with their respective gods? He put the question to the undersecretary and saw, through the shadowy edges of the projection, her shrug.

"I really don't know. It depends on the terms of their allegiance, on their own temperaments. If they see the future as unalterable, I don't think they would try. If they see them as plastic—and I think more do—they'd probably try anyway." She listened to the commentary for a moment. "There's nothing here about it— Ah, here's Keira."

"The cavalry arrives," Denisov-Graham murmured irrepressibly.

More ships emerged from the green fuzz—first a corvette, then the great bulk of a cruiser, and finally, a clipper. *Valiere*'s drift had slowed so much that the ship appeared motionless; its movement could be detected only when it slowly eclipsed a ghostly star. The other ships swung ponderously into line of battle, the maneuvering jets flickering along the hulls. Denisov-Graham could almost sense their alignment with the lines of gravity, conserving power for their possible battle.

"Alesia surrendered under Convention," Rubenstein said. "Primarily to save her people. The captains debated a couple of ideas, then decided to take *Valiere* in tow. She was already right on the edge of the radiation zone."

The emperor's ships converged on *Valiere*, or rather, two of the three did. The clipper hung back, and Denisov-Graham looked up inquiringly.

Rubenstein said, "It was agreed that *Far Moon* didn't have the power to be of any help."

The ambassador nodded—it made sense—and turned his attention back to the projection. Cruiser and corvette moved into position on either side of the crippled ship. After a moment, a faint greyish haze showed around each one: their shields were up against the steadily increasing radiation from Mist's sun. The force fields expanded slowly, met, and merged. There was a brief sparkling along the line of meeting as the engineers strove to match the frequencies precisely. Then they had it, and all three ships hung safe within a single field. That would take up a lot of power, Denisov-Graham thought, but with a cruiser's enginers to draw on they should still have enough left to set the tow. Even as he thought that, pale lines of light lanced out from the projectors in the ships' bellies, and played futilely along *Valiere*'s battered sides before finding the uncharged anchor plates. The color of the light deepened, first by almost imperceptible stages, then more quickly, until the three ships were connected by pencil-thick bars of energy. The engine lights, until now pinpoints of white in the depths of the cups, intensified and spread until they seemed to cover the entire stern of the ships, their brilliance obscuring the shadowy control machinery that surrounded them. Perfectly in tandem, linked by tow beams and enclosed together in a single screen, the ships began their slow ascent.

"They pulled *Valiere* free, then transferred what was left of her crew to *Siva*," Rubenstein said. Denisov-Graham had to make a conscious effort to see the scene before him as a holo again, rather than the reality it mocked. "The Navy base on Mist was ordered to recover *Valiere*. The rest of the tape is just a commoners' analysis and the bookmakers' report."

"In an official dispatch?" Denisov-Graham asked, his tone more amused than surprised.

Rubenstein shrugged. "Official odds, to compare with your bookie's?" She switched off the projector, the ships dissolving into momentary static before the blackness, but did not put on the room lights. Instead, she slipped another tape into the machine and said, "This is the official announcement to the ambassadors."

"Go ahead."

A new scene came to life on the projector's stage, a creamy smear of color without form. Rubenstein, almost completely hidden by it, frowned and adjusted her controls. A figure came into view in the center of the holo, but the details of his surroundings remained unclear. Keira's projection faced the machine operator, and Rubenstein quickly rotated the image.

"Ambassadors," Keira said. He wore coronet and formal coat, but somehow looked more dashing than regal. "You will know by now that the pretender Edouard, late Overlord of Verii Mir, has been defeated in open battle and has fled the Imperium. Should he seek asylum in your territories, we must demand that he be returned to face our justice."

"He's on Dixie, last report," Rubenstein murmured.

Keira's image continued, "Those majores who fought openly against us will be tried for treason at the ducal court on Oceanus, at the request of the Grand Duke de la Mar. Those minores who, under Convention, followed their lords, will not be punished—though they will swear their loyalty to us—but those minores in the Navy's service who so forgot their duty as to fight for the pretender will be deprived of their rank."

"I assume that means officers only?" Denisov-Graham asked quickly, and Rubenstein nodded.

They had missed a few words of the emperor's speech, and the ambassador made a face.

"—on all ambassadors to inform their governments of our decisions, so that no false accusations may be brought against us to the detriment of relations between the Imperium and your worlds. The emperor has spoken." Abruptly, the picture disappeared.

Rubenstein flicked on the lights, then began the tedious work of shutting down the projector.

"So," Denisov-Graham said. "That's how things stand."

"It seems to me that he handled things very neatly," Rubenstein observed.

"Mmm." Denisov-Graham nodded. "And I'll say as much in my report, of course. But the real test will be how he handles these trials. If—"

"Ioan, do you really think he'll have any trouble?" Rubenstein interrupted.

The ambassador looked up, startled, then smiled. "I suppose not. I don't know quite what I'm worried about—hubris, maybe."

"You'll notice the Imperium doesn't have that concept," Rubenstein said.

"I know." Denisov-Graham reached for the printer on its rolling stand. Drawing it close, he snapped it on and keyed the preliminary courtesies into the tape. "But I do."

Alesia paced the length of the cabin-cell and back, counting her steps. Four, five, a hand outstretched to touch the stiff padding of the bulkhead, then back again. Her thoughts were as restless as her body. How could they have lost? The Readings were not deceitful, not like the Terran oracles that lied and cheated to gain their ends. A Reader saw truths, not a single truth, saw possibilities rather than certainties, and then chose among them. She had seen the necessity of the war, seen that without it Keira would destroy the Imperium. She had seen ways in which they could win, and she had seen many possible defeats, but not this one. How could the necessity be so strong, and still mean that we must lose? she asked silently. Talent and training gave the answer: the war was necessary for Kiera, not for Edouard.

The thought was enough to stop her in her tracks. Her Talent had betrayed her, made her serve Keira rather than her brother, and trapped her here in the bowels of *Siva*, where the world seemed made of double and triple meanings. . . . It was not to be endured.

However. She forced herself to remain calm. This was not the way to fight despair and fear. Slowly, she lowered herself to the soft tiles of the deck. She sat on her knees, willing herself to accept each separate sensation: the way the tiles gave fractionally beneath the tops of her feet, the weight of her buttocks against her calves, the look of her hands as they rested passive on her thighs. Her back was stiff, her skull perfectly balanced at the top of her spine. Tension retreated, held at bay by the Reader's training that her stance invoked. This was the Pedestal, the base on which a Reading was built. Her Talent was present, more apparent now that her worries were pushed aside. It brooded in the corner of her mind, waiting. She took a deep breath, then another, and began the invocation to St. Michael.

The prayers ordered her thoughts, triggered the Reader's calm that allowed her to look dispassionately at the events of the past months, and at her own Readings and choices. There were things she now knew about Keira that would have changed her decisions, other factors she had not seen—could not have seen—but the necessity still remained. Without this test, Keira would have destroyed the Imperium, as he still could if he were not continually challenged. That, she saw, was the weakness of his line.

And there would be no more great challenges. The Federation was too strong, and too closely allied to the Imperium to provide any test. The Council was, and always would be, too much an unknown quantity to be lightly challenged. The nobility were not willing to take the risks of rebellion when no tangible gain was possible. Keira would soon be bored, and he would have to plunge the Imperium into civil war. She saw those possibilities ahead of her, all leading to the end of the Imperium, an amorphous fact, without details, without adjectives, somewhere at the end of the chain of possibilities. If Edouard could return—but he could not: breaking Convention would lead to even more destructive civil war. She could not rule. Her priesthood prevented that, even if her own inclination had led her to seek power. Nuriel? Keira would defeat him, and the Duke de la Mar would help him destroy her own son.

She shifted the focus of her thoughts from the long chain of futures to the immediate present. Her first approach had proved sterile. Her answer must lie elsewhere in her art. She would be tried soon, as soon as they reached Oceanus, and it was only at her trial that she could make a last, legal move. It must be within Convention, yet leave Edouard free to return and claim the throne. It must also be a grand enough gesture to inspire her allies again, to prove that her Talent was ultimately greater than the Renault genes.

There was nothing. Her mind remained empty. It was over, then. She saw no answers, not with her rational mind, not with Talent. She bowed her head. Aii, Edouard, what have we done?

Chapter 34

The Oceanan throne was very slightly dusty. It had not been used for some time, Keira guessed. Of course, the Grand Duke had been ill for years, and even when she made an appearance in the Oceanan Assembly of the Majores, she could not leave her gravchair. Nuriel, despite his ambitions, would not dare use that throne while his mother lived. Keira seated himself deliberately, resting his hands on the ornate seashells that capped the throne's arms, and waited for de la Mar to bring her chair into position on the steps of the low dais. From his elevated vantage point, he could see out the narrow windows that ran the length of the hall, just below the ceiling, could see the massive structure of the landing table, now crowded with his warships, rising from the purple waters of the Inner Bay.

"My Lords," de la Mar began, her reedy voice heavily amplified. She was wrapped in a satin gown that seemed several sizes too large for her shrunken frame. "You are summoned here on a matter of some urgency. His Majesty has defeated a traitor who attempted to deprive him of his rightful throne."

She paused, and there was reluctant, loyal muttering, led by Doran and the Guards. "His Majesty has chosen not to subject the majores captured in battle to the discomforts of the journey to Avalon, and has decreed that they shall be tried here. The accused are—" she glanced at a portable viewer that lay half-concealed in her lap "—Gregor Burian, Altus-Lord; Sister of the Order Alesia de Terranin; Commodore Frear Valin min-Renault, Captains Zakarij, Isenham, and Melan-Lera, all min-Renault. His Majesty also declares that Nuriel, Overlord of Oceanus, conspired with Edouard to seize this planet and hold it against its rightful ruler." In spite of her rigid control, her voice broke slightly on those words. She recovered herself quickly, and went on. "The prisoners will come forward."

The order was merely a formality. The prisoners already stood on the crimson stone of the pleading bar, Nuriel a little apart from the rest.

"You have heard the accusation, my Lords," Keira began. He had not spoken in this hall before, and it took him a moment to grasp the acoustics. "What say you to the charge? Sister Alesia?"

The woman smiled, hands clasped in front of her, almost hidden by the wide sleeves of her gown. She had been provided, through the Order House, with formal robes; the other prisoners had not fared so well. "Your Majesty, I was my brother's Reader and coordinator, and I would do that again gladly."

"Your Majesty." That was Burian, the Altus-Lord. "I think the sister has spoken for all of us. We served the Overlord, and admit it freely."

"And you, Lord Nuriel?" Keira asked. This was the test. If Nuriel admitted his guilt, it would all be over, and he would have won.

The Oceanan Overlord had been staring at a stone beneath his feet, his formal coat of stiff brocade dwarfing him. He raised his head slowly, jeweled face haunted. Then, as Keira watched, the worried expression changed subtly and he looked the emperor in the eye. "Yes, your Majesty, I planned to support Edouard."

Thank you, Nuriel, Keira thought. You may think you're giving me trouble, but you've played into my hands. "My Lords, all the accused have admitted complicity. What is your verdict?"

The Oceanan majores had no choice. They bent over their consoles, and then the speaker came forward with a slip of computer paper that he handed, bowing, to de la Mar.

"Your Majesty," she said. "The verdict is unanimous. They are found guilty."

"Thank you, my Lords." Keira rose to his feet, willing all eyes to him. "It is the emperor's prerogative, as the injured party, to pronounce sentence. Therefore, you of the Navy are cast from my service, without pension or privilege. Gregor Burian, your heir is of age; I declare your place forfeit to him."

Burian winced, but said nothing.

"Sister Alesia," Keira went on, "I offer you a choice. You may remain a recluse in one of your Order's houses—you may have your choice, subject to the approval of the Order, except for the houses on Verii Mir and Altus. Or you may join your brother in exile."

Alesia's eyes widened. Clearly she had not conceived of that possibility. "I will join Edouard."

"So be it." Keira pitched his voice to draw every eye. "And you, Nuriel de la Mar. You have admitted that you would have sided with the pretender, but were not able to do so. Because of this, I see no reason to punish you by exile or death—intent is not crime in and of itself. However, your loyalty and honor have both been called into question. I give you over into your mother's control, to be ruled by her until your own child is old enough to take up your duties as Overlord. You will swear to this, on your word as the Duke's heir and on the honor of a majore."

After a long moment, Nuriel whispered, "Very well."

"Come forward."

Nuriel knelt on the top step of the dais, moving

as though the heavy coat dragged him down. Keira
looked down into the Overlord's pale eyes. Oaths
of allegiance could be broken, had been broken
before, but even if Nuriel chose to throw Convention to the winds and raise a second rebellion, this
condition, the deprivation of status, would prevent
any of the other majores from following him. And
the Grand Duke de la Mar supported the sentence
completely.

"Your Majesty," Nuriel said. He sighed deeply.
"I, Nuriel de la Mar, Overlord of Oceanus, pledge
that I accept the sentence passed on me by Keira
emperor. I swear this on my honor, as majore and
system's heir."

Keira nodded. That was the most binding oath
any majore could swear, without loopholes of Convention or questions of the delicate balance between person and position. Indeed, by swearing,
Nuriel had lost all individual status, existing only
as his mother's heir, legally bound by her will. No
other noble would follow him now.

"I accept your oath." He looked up, found the
Heralds with their recording devices standing at
the back of the hall. "Heralds, you will publish our
verdict. The emperor has spoken."

The snow was falling on Peter's Port as it had
been for days. Desolin stared through it, no longer
fascinated by the swirling patterns. She had been
on Verii Mir for three days now, sent by Keira to
secure Matto de Terranin's full allegiance and to
accept from him the Chancellor's regalia. That grant
would be confirmed later, of course, in the same
ceremony that bound the two Domi in marriage,
but the Chancellor's power had been hers from the
moment Keira had left her in command of the
smaller part of his fleet, to take over the ships
captured from Edouard and to make sure of Verii
Mir. The power was nothing new—she was a Grand

Duke, and ruled four planets—but the odd sense of responsibility, a loyalty not to her people, an abstract mass of inferiors, but to an individual who was her equal, was strangely pleasant. It was Convention speaking there, she told herself, Talent recognizing necessity, and refused to explore the feeling further.

A movement in the snow outside caught her attention, and she stood restlessly, walking forward to lean against the narrow window. In the street below, a massive plow moved slowly forward, packing the snow for the hovercars that travelled between the Guest Tower, where she stayed, and the ducal palace. The Tower was heavily fortified—it had been built by emperors used to recalcitrant subjects—and her own soldier-minores held its key points. Nevertheless, she was glad of the corvette that sat, guns ready, on the Peter's Port field, and gladder still of the Navy frigate that swung in orbit above the city. Peter's Port was sullen-quiet, minores and commons alike stunned by their favorite's defeat. De Terranin was even quieter, choking on unspoken anger.

Desolin sighed, turning away from the window. De Terranin was due at the Guest Tower in less than a local hour, to hand over the Chancellor's regalia—he had been scheduled to do so three hours earlier, but his steward had called with insincerely profuse apologies, explaining that the Duke wished to view the tape of his daughter's trial. Desolin, who had viewed the tape the night before, as it was transmitted, had agreed, privately wishing him the joy of it. Now she wished she had insisted on the original time. Alesia's sentence, and her choice, mild though it might be by Conventional standards, would only anger the Grand Duke further. Still, he would have been angered by her refusal to accept his excuses.

"Your Grace." A soldier-minore appeared in the

doorway, blastrifle at his shoulder. "The Duke de Terranin approaches."

"Thank you," Desolin said. "Have you secured the Outer Garden?"

"Yes, your Grace. Everything's in order."

"Then I'll go down."

At the lock that opened onto the chill, formal garden, she waited while the leader of her household troops inspected the escort a final time, and accepted her coronet and a newly made fur-lined coat from the attentive serbot. Glancing into its mirror, she was not displeased by what she saw. The full trousers hid her braces completely, and the wide collar of the coat framed her face in white fur, making her skin look even darker.

"Everything's ready, your Grace," the escort leader said, and she turned away from the machine.

"Let's go, then."

The garden itself was unnaturally green, kept clear of snow by an elaborate heating system beneath the turf. The same machines fed and nurtured the exotic grasses, some of which were scattered with forced gaudy blooms, their bright hues incongruous against the snow-topped grey of the garden walls. Despite all that effort, however, the air above knee level was still cold, and she was glad of her heavy coat. Snow was falling less heavily here, deflected by the design of the Tower and the surrounding buildings. A few flakes struck her face and were caught on the fur of her coat. The rest melted as they reached the ground, leaving shallow puddles in the path.

De Terranin was waiting for her at the far end of the Garden, in the shadow of the massive arch that was the formal entrance from the road, flanked by his own minores. The grey stone, patched with snow where the wind had driven flakes into crevices in the carving, seemed far more suited to this world than the glowing greens of the garden.

Desolin halted her own troops opposite him, and tilted her head slightly in acknowledgement of his presence. "Your Grace," she said. Her voice seemed thinned by cold and the snow-dulled light. For a moment, she thought she imagined de Terranin's sneer.

"Your Grace," he answered. "I have come at the emperor's request, conveyed by you."

"I thank your Grace," Desolin said. "The emperor and I acknowledge, and respect, your willingness to comply."

"It is Convention," de Terranin said.

Desolin nodded gravely. Keira had told her, in the confusion as the fleets separated, that he would be willing to come to an understanding with de Terranin, if the Duke showed any interest in such. He had left to her both the decision to make the offer and the details. However, de Terranin had made clear his enmity. "So be it," she said quietly. "The regalia, your Grace?"

De Terranin gestured to one of the waiting minores, and the man came forward, bowing. He held a flat box in both hands. With something of a flourish, he lifted the lid, displaying the chain and staff of the Chancellor's office. Desolin nodded to the escort captain, who took the case, closing the lid over the gleaming jewels.

"Thank you, your Grace," Desolin said again. "I am to inform you that I will be leaving Verii Mir within the next two days, but the Lord of Somewhere Else will remain in the Guest Tower, as liaison between yourself and the emperor."

"Of course," de Terranin said.

Desolin carefully repressed her smile. Both knew that Dasan would remain to keep an eye on the de Terranins, and to command the naval force that effectively dominated Verii Mir and Altus, but neither would admit to that knowledge. "Excellent, your Grace," she said. "Then I will take my leave."

In the privacy of her own rooms at the top of the

Tower, Desolin set aside the heavy coat and stared at the flat case that held the Chancellor's regalia. The minores had left it with her, as if it were already hers, and in a sense, she thought, it was. Keira had promised it to her, and had already allowed her to assume a Chancellor's functions. There was no reason she could not also take up the symbols of her office. Now, alone and unobserved, she could put on the chain and take up the staff, making the office in some sense the result of her own labor, not the emperor's gift.

She touched the latch gently, but did not press it open. Keira had trusted her not to do that. He knew, as well as any majore, the temptation to assert self and Domus. And she, in turn, trusted him to keep his promises in full. More than that, she did acknowledge that the Chancellorship was his gift, and would do so publicly. She stood, and touched the button that would summon a serbot of the Imperial Household. When it appeared, she ordered it to open the strongbox in its belly, and set the regalia inside. Armsteel doors closed over it, protecting it not only from theft, but from herself. Keira would understand the gesture, would appreciate the offering.

The Cathedral had been less crowded for the coronation, Denisov-Graham was quite certain of that. The floor was jammed with nobles, majores to the front, the minores scrambling for the better places in the back seats despite the attempts of the Heralds to seat them according to their rank. The galleries were packed with commoners, members of the various commons' councils, and representatives of the major guilds, as well as multiple camera crews. Part of the ambassadors' gallery had been sacrificed, temporarily partitioned off, to make room for some of the Guild leaders.

"It's a madhouse," Sakima said, from her place
at Denisov-Graham's shoulder.

Rubenstein answered, "The nobility don't dare
not be seen here. Besides, this is something completely unprecedented."

Denisov-Graham nodded, and smiled to the
Delrwa ambassador as she took her place, escorted
by younger females in the elaborately embroidered
vests that were the main ceremonial wear of their
people. The ambassador returned the greeting with
her customary poise, but the escort seemed ill at
ease, their double-thumbed hands indicating amusement and embarrassment at witnessing such a delicate event as a wedding. Denisov-Graham had
forgotten just how odd human ways seemed to the
Delrwa.

The other independent ambassadors arrived on
Imrea's heels, and finally Njru made his entrance,
light glinting from scales polished to simulate
youthful brightness. Denisov-Graham counted the
ambassadors, trying not to be too obvious: everyone was there, and none too soon. In the nave
below, the influx of people had slowed, and the
Heralds were making a last effort to put the minores
in order. Then they vanished, to take up their
stations by the main doors. The senior Herald
stepped forward, and at the same moment, the
Cardinal-Archbishop appeared at the altar, flanked
by resplendent attendants.

Emperor and Grand Duke entered together, as
was the imperial custom, their households following, two by two. Behind them came the witnesses,
Lovell-Andriës and a woman in St. Katherine's
colors for the majores, Doran and a Saharan land-
minore for the minores. Then came the honor guard,
led jointly by a Guard officer and the captain of
Hamm'tt's household troops.

The procession halted at the altar rail, and a
flourish of trumpets enjoined silence. Denisov-

Graham reached into the pocket of his jacket and brought out a miniature set of distance glasses. Heedless of protocol, he focused them on the figures before the altar, adjusting the lenses with an expert hand. At this distance, he could pick out the details of the blood-dark embroidery at the hem and sleeves of Keira's cream-colored coat. The emperor was smiling slightly, his feelings unreadable. Hamm'tt looked more stern, very aware of the solemnity of the occasion.

"So much for romance," the ambassador muttered, and put away his glasses.

Sakima had heard. "It's a question of policy," she said. "A marriage of state. At least imperial law accepts degrees of relationships outside of such marriages."

Denisov-Graham nodded reluctantly, a little annoyed with himself for having admitted to a childish wish for a storybook wedding between royal lovers. *At least the two seemed to have come to some sort of understanding,* he thought, *and I suppose that's all that matters.*

The ceremony moved on, through the ritual challenge to the signing of the marriage contract, to the exchange of rings that were a visible symbol of the contract. The Cardinal-Archbishop pronounced the blessing.

Keira turned away from the rail, and Denisov-Graham waited for the procession to form again, leading back to the Palace complex and the festival that was waiting. But instead, the emperor paused at the transept and held out a hand to Hamm'tt. At the same moment, an acolyte came forward, carrying a cushion on which rested a heavy-linked chain of office. Denisov-Graham scrambled for his glasses again, adjusted them until the jewelled collar was poised, trembling slightly, in the lenses. It was the official collar of the Chancellor, tangible symbol of the second most powerful office in the Imperium.

"They're making the reasons pretty blatant, aren't they?" he whispered to Rubenstein.

"I suppose they have to," Rubenstein whispered back.

On the floor below, Keira lifted the chain from its cushion, holding it in the path of the sunlight that streamed in through the cleared walls behind the altar. It sent flashes of light through the entire Cathedral.

"Desolin Hamm'tt, Grand Duke, ruler under me of Sahara, El Nath, St. Katherine." The emperor's voice was almost too light for the sonority of the names. "I, Keira, emperor, here create you our Chancellor, our right hand, our speaker in the Eger, according to Convention."

He lifted the chain even higher and laid it gently across her shoulders. Then he nodded to her, his smile broadening just a little. Hamm'tt smiled back, and bowed her head for a moment. Denisov-Graham, still watching through the distance glasses, started slightly. He and Rubenstein had both been wrong to think there was no feeling between those two, though it was certainly nothing romantic. Instead, the gesture had spoken of respect, of an acceptance, on both sides, of their own and each other's positions. Perhaps there was more, apparent to someone who truly understood Convention, he thought, and saw Sakima wipe away a tear.

The Guard leader struck the base of his ceremonial spear against the floor, and the sharp sound brought all eyes to him. "The Emperor and the Chancellor!" he shouted, and the acclamation was echoed instantly.

Keira inclined his head slightly, acknowledging the cheers, and that set off a fresh wave of shouting. The trumpets that signalled the end of the ceremony could barely be heard against it, but the Heralds caught their cue and swung open the main doors. A wave of sound rolled in from outside: the commoners, allowed into the Palace confines for the first time since the coronation, were cheering wildly.

Chapter 35

Denisov-Graham stood with the emperor on the topmost balcony of Rising Sun, the pleasure palace, if such a thing could be said to exist on barren Hellmouth, built three hundred years before by another Renault. Half the court was still on Avalon, where Desolin Hamm'tt was acting as regent while Keira consolidated his claim to Hellmouth. Denisov-Graham was flattered to have been invited to join the emperor, and equally uneasy. Rising Sun was sunk deep into the rock of Orleans Province's largest single mountain, only one tower protruding from the jumble of cliffs and rockfalls. The air already felt like the draft from a furnace, though the sun had not yet risen. The heating rocks smelled like metal, and some other acrid, alien thing. The emperor leaned out into the hot eddies of wind. Below him stretched the slope that hid the rest of the palace, a plain of rock like all the other faces of the mountain except for the converters and hidden solar cells that were occasionally visible in the heaps of rock. Denisov-Graham could pick out a few of these—there a solar cell, there the entrace to a lightshaft, there a vapor trap—but he knew these were only decoys, though functional ones, and that the vital components were too well hidden for him to find without sophisticated equipment. That was only too typical of the Imperium, to build even their palaces as fortresses.

The emperor stirred, the voluminous desert robes

rustling. They were made of rock-silk, an insulator designed to keep human beings relatively cool in Hellmouth's abominable climate, but Denisov-Graham could feel sweat creeping on his back beneath the robes and thin shirt. What must this place have been like in the old days, he wondered, not for the first time. Hell itself, I imagine, could have been no worse. Transportees, criminals of varying degrees of guilt, all thrown into the mines and factories, some of them allowed to leave the planet when their term was up, most condemned to remain in the cities for life. And they built the most intricate of the Imperial societies, on which Alexander I was able to base his empire. The Olde Federation could never have intended such a thing.

"There," the emperor said softly, and pointed. The horizon glowed yellow, like the color of white-hot steel; the rest of the sky was burnished copper to the zenith. A single point shone momentarily brighter, and then the sun leaped free. Light poured across the plain, the Dusty Sea that lapped at the base of Rising Sun, chasing shadows before it. Denisov-Graham could think only of a tidal bore, the light running like the free water Hellmouth had never known. The wave of light struck the base of the mountain, broke, and shot upwards. Denisov-Graham flung up a hand to shield his eyes. The emperor laughed. They stood so a moment longer, Keira's face turned to the Mars-pink sky. No, not Mars-colored, Denisov-Graham told himself, trying to bring things back to an understandable level; this was more metallic than Mars' thin air, harder and brighter both. The emperor slipped desert goggles over his eyes and turned back to the Terran.

"If you'll come around to the other side, you can see Satansburg," Keira said. Denisov-Graham, moving carefully because the sun-dazzle still filled his eyes with green clouds, followed the other man to the far side of the tower. Here, mountains broke the line of the horizon, lifting dark and sullen in the new light. The ambassador, having landed at Satansburg's spaceport the day before, knew that the range was really sharp and majestic, towering higher than seemed possible. At this distance, however, the Devil's Range looked puny, insignificant. Light glinted, very faintly, from the spaceport at its base, and Denisov-Graham could just make out the trail of a shuttle as it rose toward the orbital docking station that served the entire planet.

"We'll go below," Keira said. "I'm glad you were able to see a sunrise here. Perhaps you'll join me for a nightcap?"

Because of the climate, it never took Denisov-Graham very long to reaccustom himself to the nocturnal habits of the Hellmouthers. With a sun as fierce as their primary one and three close, bright moons, the population tended to sleep during the planet's day and do their work at night. "Yes, your Majesty, thank you."

The emperor's quarters were austere, the furnishings old-fashioned glass and gleaming metal, a few foam-cube chairs providing spots of color. Keira dismissed his Guard escort at the door but remained standing there, fingers poised over a control panel.

"Sound or picture for the security?"

Denisov-Graham considered. "Picture, I think. If that's agreeable to your Majesty."

"I prefer it," Keira said, and touched keys. He considered a moment, then touched a second key sequence. Light flared in one wall, and it seemed to dissolve, opening onto a harsh view of the Reefs. The slabs of rock, fissures filled with crystals like gleaming teeth, lifted from the grey-brown sands of the Dusty Sea. Denisov-Graham caught his breath, unable to stop himself from reaching into the hologram, touching the smooth wall for reassurance. He had known it was an illusion, but the compulsion to make sure was overwhelming.

"I understand you've received word from Terra," Keira said, turning away from the controls.

Denisov-Graham had long ago stopped wondering about the emperor's sources. "Yes, Majesty, I did. I had my sister go through the family records, as I promised I would."

"And the bet?"

"Was recorded, or the stakes were." Denisov-Graham looked him full in the face, struggling to hide the indecent triumph he felt. "We agreed to arrange free trade with the Federation."

"So." Keira hissed the word. "You were to win, no matter what."

Denisov-Graham bowed slightly. "As your Majesty pleases."

"The Imperium cannot commit itself to free trade now," the emperor said. "Our commoners would suffer."

"I doubt all of them would feel that way," Denisov-Graham pointed out. "Trade with the Federation has been much sought after—Federal goods are still very popular. I'm not sure you could turn down the offer."

"And if the Federal worlds trade directly with my worlds, we're one step closer to the union of Federation and Imperium, with Terra at the head of that union," the emperor said. "Let's not mince words, for once. If the two states are to be brought together—and this will do it—I'd rather see them ruled from Avalon."

"You don't know Terra very well," Denisov-Graham murmured.

"On the contrary, I recognize her virtues," Keira said. "But Avalon is comprehensible—is ours."

"Do you refuse to accept the rights?" Denisov-Graham asked.

Keira shook his head. "No—as you say, I cannot.

But I do oppose Terra." He smiled. "I'll offer another bet, that we—my Domus—can stop you."

"There's nothing left to bet," Denisov-Graham protested. "If the merger's inevitable, what else could the Federation ask?"

"The form of government. If we win, the neostate is an empire. If you win, a—representative democracy, or whatever you call your Federation."

Denisov-Graham considered the offer. He knew he should not accept it, any more than he should have revealed the stakes of the original bet in private. That should have been sprung on the Eger, where Keira would have been forced to accept it, and thank him for it. But . . . the whole thing was too tempting. He would win, though it might take generations before Terra regained her hold on the human-settled stars, and only his remote descendants would see the results and know the victory. "All right," he said slowly. "I accept."

"Excellent," Keira murmured. "Excellent."

There was something in his voice that made Denisov-Graham look up sharply. Keira's face, momentarily unguarded, showed enormous relief. What have I done? the ambassador asked himself warily. Where's the trap? But he could see no way for the Imperium to emerge victorious. If Federation and Imperium traded freely, the major Federal corporations would be able to cement their present loose ties to the Imperial consortia. The commoners would gain an economic power that would eventually supersede the political power they had surrendered. Deprived of their function, majores and minores alike would die out. Eventual merger was inevitable once the trade connections were made, and the bet, the question of the nominal form of government, meant nothing. It was a matter of name only. Surely Keira saw that.

He looked again at the emperor, and their eyes met. Keira's eyes were very tired, and filled with a longing to be understood and the certainty that he would not be. Denisov-Graham, remembering the other Renaults, the long and dangerous history, their flawed strength, realized suddenly what the wager really meant. He had been witness to a trust. He had become the keeper of a family's honor.

"You've won," he said simply. "No matter what, you win."

"You hardly lose," Keira pointed out, but the lines that bracketed his mouth eased a little, belying the bitterness of his words.

"You've made certain that the gamesmasters will be good rulers," Denisov-Graham went on, speaking not to Keira's words but to the man he had glimpsed behind the mask. "They'll play the game, and ultimately you'll win." He could picture the chaos that would result if the Renault emperors chose to destroy the Imperium through war, rather than steering it to the easiest death. "They'll do what's right."

Keira shook his head. "The Imperium was lost long before I was born, and nobody noticed. The game is ended, forever. All I've done is made it a clean death."

Denisov-Graham bowed his head. There was nothing he could say to deny the emperor's words.

"But the ending," Keira went on, and for the first time pain and anger and the terrible aching loss were naked in his voice. "How we come to that ending. It matters. Oh, God, say it matters."

The ambassador rose from his chair, knelt beside the emperor. Very carefully, not wanting to be presumptuous or patronizing, he touched the other man's wrist. Keira looked at him as if for the first time, the very stillness of his face a mute appeal.

"Yes," Denisov-Graham said. "It matters."

Epilogue

The image of the last emperor stood in the Eger chamber, in the center of the holostage. The remnants of the nobility gathered to hear his abdication and their own deposition. They were old, most of them, and those that were not were impatient with the ceremony. The young ones had given up their nobility long ago, all but the empty titles. The old ones clutched at the knowledge of what had been, but they, too, recognized that they were not what their ancestors had been, and welcomed an end to the pretense. They were grateful, however, that it was done within Convention.

In the projection room on Terra, the last emperor waited in the circle of the cameras, blinded by the lights that ringed him in. He was a slender, spare man, whose hair still held a hint of the Renault copper beneath the brown. He held himself very erect to compensate for the braces that stiffened his twisted legs. They were well-hidden beneath the archaic, floor-length gown, but he knew they were there. They were the price he paid for his Talent. The imperial crown, elegant lines upswept to hold the single steel-white jewel, was strangely light against his skull. From the day of the coronation until this instant, it had been a dead weight, unbearably heavy. Now that he was about to give it away, it seemed to be made of quicksilver, liquid and light and treacherous.

He spoke the words that had been planned for

him three hundred years before, and slowly lifted his hands to the circlet. His eyes searched the circle of light, vainly trying to see the faces that waited behind it. They were Imperial and Federal alike, but when he had first seen them, these new Counsellors that would rule his kingdom, he had been unable to tell citizen from commoner. The memory gave him strength, reminded him that his act was not betrayal, but necessary consummation. He removed the crown and placed it carefully on the velvet stand that waited within the lighted circle. No one else would wear it; it would be a symbol of a not-ignoble past that would, thankfully, never come again. They had described it to him in those words, expecting him to agree, and he had done so, hiding the pain born of his Talent. He had been bred to rule, with that constellation of Talents, and had known because of this that there was no reason to cling to power any longer, when he was nothing more than a symbol without meaning. It still hurt, an ache bone-deep like the pain in his legs, and he felt his eyes fill with tears. There's no shame in it, he thought fiercely, let the people see. He stared defiantly into the cameras.

Mercifully, the lights faded then, but crowds came from behind the green clouds that blocked his sight, asking questions in a multitude of accents. He ignored them all, searching the unfamiliar faces that surrounded him, past the block of Counsellors, until at last he found the last of the other family, the last Denisov-Graham, standing a little apart from the others. He was a Navy man, unlike his ancestor, face coarsened by the weathers of a hundred planets. The emperor fixed his eyes on him, willing him to turn, to acknowledge the game.

You know what I've done, and why, he thought. You understand what you've won—that you've won.

Denisov-Graham looked up under the pressure of that intense gaze, and the emperor almost wept again. The captain's face was polite, but blank, showing no hint that he understood what had happened.

No, the emperor thought, it can't be. We haven't played this game for all these years to find out we never had an enemy.

Then Denisov-Graham's face changed, and he nodded gravely, acknowledging the victory.

Afterword

THOUGHTS ON THE FUTURE
OF CONFLICT
by
C.J. Cherryh

The question of any war depends initially on
politics, which is to say the relations—or lack of
relations—between two or more sets of individuals.
If within a single large set, it has the characteristics and motivations of civil war; if between two
sets, it has the nature of general war. This has
been a human view of war since the first alterca-
tions on the banks of the Nile and Tigris on Earth.

No island culture survives without a good deal
of luck: beset with storms, prey to local famine
and internal dissent, most go the way of many a
one before them. Likewise planetary cultures are
foredoomed to shortage and upsets of internal
dynamics, if they meet no externally originating
disaster such as dustclouds and large meteor
impacts—which can take out not just one species,
but most. So the Earth's future would not be as-
sured were its inhabitants to forswear conflict
tomorrow. The only viable solution for island or
planetary survival is getting to the ocean—or to
space—and broadening chances of survival beyond
the vicissitudes of one fragile unit.

We can suppose in questions of future conflict,

as we suppose we will survive, that humanity will have taken this option and extended human settlements into space. Otherwise we can suppose that shortages will have driven us to increasing unrest and to wider and wider conflict on our finite planet—and we need not discuss much about a future.

But let us take the course of common sense and say that we do get a viable gene pool and a viable self-replicating technology off the planet, which is the reasonable goal of any species that wants to survive beyond its embryonic, planetbound phase and discover the universe it lives in.

Achieving this technological escape velocity says something about us as a species: namely, that we have acquired the command of energies that can lift more than one rocket off the planet—and that we have declined to use that energy to blow the species out of existence before we could do so. There are probably other cultural approaches to handling such power and doubtless other cultural mechanisms for controlling its use, but spacefaring cultures do not get to space without at least achieving the physical potential to blow themselves to perdition. We can assume that any species which has survived to get into space has not gotten there by levitation or enchantment, but by applying much the same discoveries as we have, in probably much the same sequence; and has done so, whether by luck or wisdom, without ruining the planet or killing themselves before they could get off it.

This does predict a certain commonality of experience among spacefaring species, at least among those of oxygen and carbon sort. It indicates a certain level of self-control, if not of good will toward all other species and types.

So, what kind of conflict is most likely in the future?

First, intraspecies conflict. It is possible to get

into space on the basis of an arms race. And particularly on a local, intra-solar system basis, unresolved political questions are possible—although the vast scale of a solar system is enough to take territorial pressures off a species whose territoriality scales have been historically restricted to planetary sizes. One of the most likely scenarios within the human species is rebellion against an authority which has lost its immediacy and its mandate due to the very months-across size of the territory to be governed. The politics of colonies and founding powers in the 1700's are an excellent example of this phenomenon. Another type of conflict is the dynastic struggle: the longer a political figure stays in power, the greater the likelihood that instability will follow the demise of that leader. And there is the war of fragmentation, in which a plurality of segments seek the dissolution of a government which has lost its mandate. Least likely within a developing solar system is the intergovernmental conflict which on Earth is generally the heritage of old empires: the dynamics which propose to the fragments of the Roman Empire that they ought to be reunited willy-nilly, or to fragments of certain other terrestrial empires that they have enough in common to justify a reunification, are not easily duplicated in the wide vacuum of space. Such explosions require confinement and proximity, and extraterrestrial real estate travels in annual orbits which render boundaries a difficult proposition. The dynamics which produced empire-conquerers are not yet foreseeable in the early colonization of space: it may happen, but the complex situations which lead to an Alexander or a Thutmose or a Genghis Khan do not arise out of new civilizations—at least within humankind.

At least within humankind.

At least within the first century or so. It is likely that early conflicts among humanity will be localized, much as tribal conflicts in the Earth's early years were local; and that any would-be Caesars may lose themselves on even a systemic scale, insignificant to the majority of humanity in the solar system. Not unnoticed: we have modern communications to thank for that. But at distances that need months and years to send an attack across the solar system and which take minutes and hours for messages regarding such intentions to cross the same interval . . . it would seem very difficult to sustain a fever-pitch of hostility in what must be a year-long voyage with messages flying back and forth at the speed of light. War might be cancelled on the larger scale, at least sublight, simply due to fatigue of the participants and the wide separation of potential combatants.

Faster-than-light war would generate even stranger problems, particularly if ships can go FTL but no one finds a convenient way to get messages across interstellar space at an even greater rate.

For instance, neither radio nor radar are of any practical use to a ship at the high end of sub-C travel: i.e., above half the speed of light. First, there is the matter of scattering, which diminishes efficiency as range increases: system-wide radar doesn't work. Second, there is the time factor. Since radar consists of an impulse sent out and bounced back to a receiver, the time it takes to get an image has to be doubled: and if a ship at 1/2 Light tries to use radar, the ship will reach the object just as the radar warning arrives at its dish to tell it the object is there. This certainly creates unique difficulties in navigation, not to mention the difficulties of streaking into another solar system to find an enemy and engage in a spacefaring dogfight.

There are other difficulties, such as trying to radio ahead to friendly ships, while arriving on a continually diminishing wavefront of timelag: the incoming ship is continually chewing down the roundtrip timelag for an answer and conversations are bizarre at best—unless someone invents hyperspace radio to go along with FTL ships and solves some of the problem.

The difference between an insystem conflict and an interstellar one is a concept to boggle terrestrially-habituated minds, but as an example, consider that even an insystem ship far more sophisticated than any we could presently build may take a year to get, say, across a 93 million-mile interval such as that between us and the Sun. And a ship traveling at one Light would cross that same distance in 8 minutes ... about the time it would take the cook on that first ship to microwave a frozen dinner for that ship's first lunch.

On the one hand, space war between early, non-FTL ships might be an incredibly slow process of hunt and realign and replot the course and re-replot, and time the burns and scheme and plan ... much beyond *any* difficulties of stalking another ship in the days of sail and wood.

And on the other, space war could be so quick only computers could handle the difficulties. At 93 million miles in 8 minutes, a *planet* becomes an unavoidable navigational hazard—not because of its gravity slope, but because a ship going that fast does not turn very readily. Or at all. Eight minutes is a very short time in which to do complicated interception calculations, and far too little time to veer and get response from the ship. As for a course reversal, that enormous velocity would have to be totally dissipated to get even *zero* progress in the unwanted direction; and that is a fuel-expensive proposition, even if there were time. Stopping mass takes energy, and diverting it from its inertial course takes energy; and the upshot of it all is that any maneuver at those speeds takes a great deal more fuel than one could spend cavalierly, even granting an economy and a fuel system as far above our present global economy as we are above that of ancient Egypt.

And weapons: if that lightspeed warship had one good-sized rock in tow and let fly at a planet, it is very likely that that planet would suffer climatic change and the calamitous extinction of most of its ecostructure. Such may have happened to Earth around the time of the dinosaurs—as, we trust, the result of cosmic accident and not a passing starship disposing of debris. Tossing one good rock at C will take care of almost anything it hits. *Hitting* a stationary object at C would be equally hazardous for a ship, and solar systems probably tend to be cluttered—so the general dirtiness of star systems may serve as a natural screen against this sort of strafing.

But a ship that lost track of what it or its enemies or its allies had launched could destroy itself in collision: spaceborne ammunition would not go away without a timer-destruct. And the relics of a previous battle could be hazardous for shipping for a very long time to come.

All this considers the difficulty of operating warships between two relatively near stars.

The difficulties of maintaining a war in a larger volume of space, even a dozen or so stars, multiply out of hand, particularly since the geometries of the conflict are not on a plane surface, but are borderless areas suspended in three dimensions and separated by a fourth—*time* for travel and difficulty of communication. The closest analogy would be that of trying to organize fish in, say, the Indian Ocean—In murky water, which might well symbolize the difficulties of dust and other debris which might play havoc with transport and communications at long range.

And there is also and necessarily the consideration that there may be sharks which might be attracted by the conflict.

* * *

There are several kinds of aliens readily conceivable. First, species who have territorial urges much like our own, which might be subdivided into species who understand negotiation and those who never developed the concept, those who recognize boundaries and those who never developed the concept, and those who had it once and no longer have it in this third-dimensional space. There might be humanoid types—we are, after all, the best and most viable design for a carbon-oxy planet of our size and type; and while coloration and tegument might vary, bipedal upright structure is very handy for tool-using generalists. (Standing on two feet frees the hands for invention, and having the nose downturned makes it a gravity-flow device, but the amount of hair we have is probably a minor accident of genetics and climate, and not overall of quite as great significance as upright posture and thumbs.)

However, whales are not fish and do not behave quite like fish—despite similar environment and their similar external structure. What is inside an alien skeletal frame may be different; the brain organization may be different; and considering the possible complications of culture even on a single planet, it is very likely that the culture overlaid on a very different brain may make for very different values and very different ways of doing business. Not all humanoid species may understand trade, or war, or negotiation, or borders, or individuality, or family, or governments, or any other concept humans take for universals; nor may we expect to understand theirs.

And that leaves aside biologies of completely exotic and non-terrestrial worlds, whose psychologies have to be left to the imagination, and with whom humanity may have less in common than it does with the starfish.

It is quite possible at any time that an alien of completely bizarre behavior might come straying through human boundaries, and it would probably be wise to let anything that behaves peculiarly from our point of view meander through untroubled, since negotiation may be one of the concepts it does not share—along with territory.

It is equally possible that humanity could encounter benevolent and wise aliens; or find the occasional xenophobic species which got into space by destroying everything that opposed it from the very start of its world, achieved some sort of ethos or social mechanics to avoid self-annihilation, and made it to space to the grief of all its neighbors. There is no guarantee for the behavior of other species, since the only ones we have observed on this planet have been interlocked in layered eco-structures of predator and prey; and given the complexity of the ones we know, we may surmise that space itself is an ecosystem of sorts, in which neighboring species will have to work out certain behaviors which assure their mutual survival. The ritual of conflict and negotiation is a mechanism we have carefully worked out within our own species, knowing its limits in many instances well enough to use it as a calculated solution, even to the fine points of *proposing* conflict without actually carrying it out, which is the mechanism of much of terrestrial politics from the tribe to the superstate.

On the one hand there are characteristics of living in free space which will tend to isolate and separate humankind into pockets; and others which may be uniting factors, such as the first contact with an alien mind, which may convince us we alone are sane. Conflict among ourselves there is bound to be, in some degree in some instances, and it is probably unwise to disturb the neighbo with it. Some of them might be offended, and others might find it an attraction to a degree we would not wish.

There will be neighbors. And they will have neighbors . . . if they observe boundaries at all. The inventiveness we use in devising a flexible politics which can deal with all sorts of mentalities and species-histories may be the ultimate test of species survival long after we have gotten off this planet and taken to space as our natural ocean.

Perhaps among interstellar species, as on our own planet, we occupy the niche of the Great Average: neither the fastest nor the strongest, and probably, on the interstellar scale, not the smartest; but primate-like, curious, only moderately territorial, moderately aggressive, and very flexible in our patterns, which may yet be the qualification that admits us to the class of longterm galactic survivors, even among the favored and fortunate species who make it to the stars. ★

Coming soon by Melissa Scott:
FIVE-TWELFTHS OF HEAVEN

Balthasar's voice sounded through her earpiece. "You have control, Silence."

All around them, the keelsong changed. It deepened, and at the same time gained a whole new range of sound. The dome of the hull quivered, then quietly faded to translucence. The stars shone through.

The yoke moved smoothly under Silence's hand. She smiled, allowing herself a brief moment to savor the experience of flying a new ship, then turned her attention to her course. She took a deep breath and sought her voidmarks.

Almost immediately, the Carter's Road took shadowy form before her: first the curve of the great wheel's rim, the fire-edged ghost of the spoke, then the entire shape of the cart-wheel, turning lazily against a purpled starfield splotched with the gaudy coronae of uncountable suns. Silence marked her course with a practiced eye: over the top, onto the rim and then down it, moving with its spin, then out through the white-hot hub. *Sun-Treader* seemed to float on a river of fire, beneath a sky of fiery cloud.

From FIVE-TWELFTHS OF HEAVEN
Coming in 1985 from Baen Books